TWO WHO LIVE ON

MN BENNET

Hardback ISBN: 978-1-967397-05-1
Paperback ISBN: 979-8-9872532-7-4
Ebook ISBN: 979-8-9872532-6-7

Edited by Charlie Knight (CKnightWrites.com)
Paperback cover art by Miblart (miblart.com)
Hardback cover art by GraphicSoul (https://www.graphicsoulart.com)
Formatting by Mayonaka Designs (mayonakadesigns.com)

www.mnbennet.com/

To everyone who gave Dorian and his world a chance, from the angsty teenagers to the ever-cheerful Enchanter Evergreen. I hope you enjoy following his journey as much as I enjoyed creating it.

READERS BE ADVISED

Thank you so much for returning to read *Two Who Live On*! I'm delighted to share more of Dorian's journey and the wonderful world of witches living in a complex magic industry. There's so much swoon factor in book two which I hope readers will enjoy. That said, there are elements I'd like to make readers aware of before diving into the second semester. For those interested, I've included a list of content warnings on the following page.

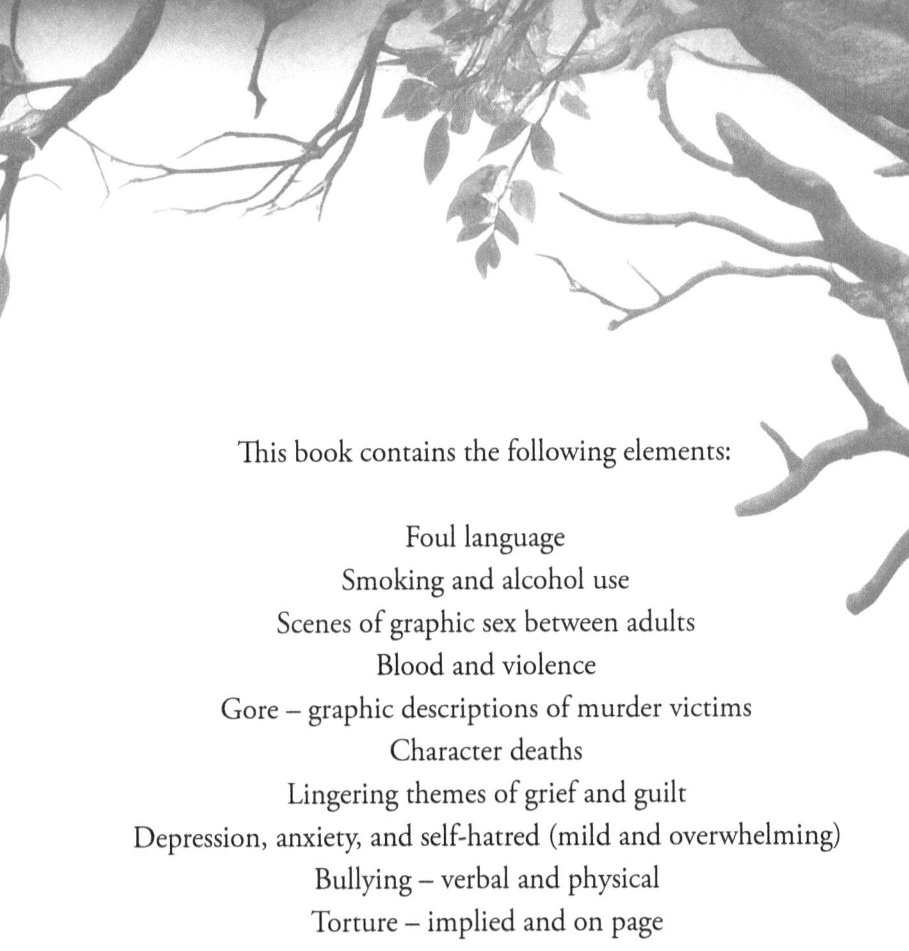

This book contains the following elements:

Foul language
Smoking and alcohol use
Scenes of graphic sex between adults
Blood and violence
Gore – graphic descriptions of murder victims
Character deaths
Lingering themes of grief and guilt
Depression, anxiety, and self-hatred (mild and overwhelming)
Bullying – verbal and physical
Torture – implied and on page

I believe in HEA and HFN in all my works, something I strive to bring no matter how long winding the journey is. I'm grateful for you to see the next chapter in Dorian's journey; however, if any of these elements seem like too much, please consider waiting. Dorian and his homeroom coven will be here if and when you're ready to return to Gemini Academy.

There is a codex in the back of the book
explaining the magic and world in a bit more
detail for anyone who is interested.

WARD
REJUVENATION
PSYCHIC
PRIMAL
HEX
ENCHANTMENT
AUGMENTATION
BESTIAL
COSMIC
ALTERATION
ENTROPY
ARCANE
TELEKINESIS
SENSORY
BANISHMENT
LEVITATION

CHAPTER ONE

MILO'S perfect date looped along his surface thoughts the entire time we strolled through the art district of the Lower West Side. His memories flashed in crisp stills like he'd photographed our past. There I was, twenty years old, hidden beneath an umbrella so my pasty pale skin didn't burn under the beach's harsh summer sun, which was nothing like the overcast gray winter sky we found ourselves walking under right now.

I cringed at how I'd glared at both him and Finn the entire time the pair played along the shore, splashing each other with waves through their telekinesis and wrestling over a volleyball. Finn's smile filled more snippets of Milo's mind than usual.

Though nothing particularly special had happened that day, this date bloomed in his mind, making it difficult for me to focus on the streets of the art district. I'd spent so much time tethered to Milo's thoughts lately. Still, this date… Why was it special compared to the date he dragged me on now? We were just three goofy acolytes, unknown by the world, unburdened by the responsibility of the magic industry.

My heart hitched. Perhaps that was what made it so significant to Milo. Back then, we could go anywhere, do anything, and no one noticed. It was much harder to hide from his adoring audience these days. Plus, the beach wasn't nearly as crowded as the sidewalks we strolled along on our current date. It bustled with people either enjoying their weekend or annoyed to be working. Thankfully, the one-way street had no parking, which afforded minimum traffic. Then again, the minds of each passerby buzzed louder than the hum of any revving engines.

Skimming Milo's thoughts made everyone else more bearable. Truthfully, I would have preferred staying home and doing absolutely nothing. Maybe reading. Probably watching television instead. Maybe practicing my magics. Probably quelling my telepathy because my neighbors were insufferable. Maybe planning a lesson. Probably catching up on grading because I'd already added a mountain since the second semester started. I sighed at how many things I should have been doing opposed to enduring a busy art district.

Right now, though, I was less concerned about that and more worried about the anxious surface thoughts Milo had snuffed out.

"What's wrong?" I tilted my head, stepping slightly in front of him.

"What? Nothing." Sunglasses hid his eyes, and he tugged the cap he wore downward like the bill somehow gave him total anonymity in his trademark suit and tie. "Absolutely nothing."

I tsked. "Liar."

Despite Milo reminiscing perfect dates Finn, him, and I had once upon a time while also fixating on the perfect day date he wanted right now since it was only the two of us, his thoughts continued turning into static. I'd linked to his mind on all our outings—from guild events to grocery shopping—because no matter where we went, the spotlight found him. Milo struggled to find outings we could enjoy publicly, exploring the sensations of a new relationship without navigating his publicity. It didn't help matters that I preferred our relationship remain private because his stardom came with a very big spotlight—hence him freaking out over a good date so I wouldn't freak out, which made me freak out about him freaking out.

Fuck. I've been around teens too long.

Music funneled from the various stores we walked past. People were noisy, both internally and externally. Their fucking chatter never ceased, and it helped to fixate on the rhythmic melodies since Milo's mind continued drumming in and out.

Earlier, he'd been teeming with day date thoughts, yet now, everything remained blank. Everything he'd researched on the exhibits became obscured, even his memories of the sunny beachside date fizzled in and out. Which could only mean Milo's thoughts had drifted into a vision. Sure, I'd merged my telepathy with a single void vision that I'd nearly fucked up last semester, but since then, our psychic branches hadn't intermingled. His clairvoyance remained unseen by me. So if he were weaving between a perfect date that had been and visions, he was probably foretelling a thousand paranoid possibilities of ruining the perfect date that could be.

"You know, I'm okay just staying home." I forced an uneasy smile. "Honestly, it's easier between my branch and your whole Enchanter Evergreen thing."

Milo made a sour face. He hated when I called him by his industry title. Well, more likely the formality in my tone. Milo's head swam into what he wanted, visions he needed, and concerns he'd gone about this day wrong. My face heated.

I'd said the wrong thing. Of course, he already knew I preferred lounging at home, but he wanted to find new things for us to try and enjoy together. I understood his craving to live in the world that he fought so hard to protect; it made sense he wanted to experience the balance and normalcy he brought to the city. Yet, ever the asshole, I had to say the rude thing, nitpicking his ideas since I liked my isolated routine. A habit I hated because it distanced me from so much happiness. There were parts of our past relationship I'd never get another chance at, yet the point of exploring this was to find our way to a new type of happiness.

That's what I should say.

"Overall, this is a really fun day," I finally said, mustering the most hollow enthusiasm.

"*It's literally the worst. I'm screwing up this entire date and it hasn't even started.*" Milo smiled, big and goofy but lacking charm as anxiety poured out of him along with thoughts he failed to hide. "*Dorian's already annoyed, wishing he were home. Just wait until he—"*

Milo's eyes widened, and song lyrics filled the air of his thoughts. Despite being caught off guard, he recovered rather quickly.

"I like the exhibits you found." It was true. Two things I enjoyed: art and no audience. These little Sunday setups were actually the perfect outing. "Why don't we just check one out, then head to the restaurant?"

I wasn't hungry, yet Milo kept directing us further from our original destination and toward—

Erratic thoughts burst in rapid, incoherent succession. A stampede of terrified thoughts lapped like a tidal wave from all the people on this street. I grabbed my head, barring my mind against the invasive internal screeches that sent psychic fractures further along my skull with each passing second. Bracing me, Milo held my shoulders with a faulty grin.

"Guess you figured out the date is off, huh?" Milo blinked, silencing the static of a vision and the tremble of his surface thoughts.

"Did you plan on this?" I thought, connecting our minds. It required more magic and consideration to link our thoughts but had the added benefit of dulling others. All my channeled energy kept our minds synced together, making Milo a literal life raft keeping me afloat from the streaming fear. Maintaining a steady flux on someone I trusted helped when the volume in my head amped up to the max. Better to dwell in Milo's mind than crumble in the barrage of chaos.

Milo sighed. *"I'd planned on it being dealt with by others."*

"What's going on?"

"Damn acolytes not following my directions is what's going on." Milo squared my shoulders, rubbing the tension away until my body stopped shaking. Even without explaining, he knew the contact helped conjure a stronger link between us. Once established, he released me.

"Is this a warlock?"

"No. Just an overgrown fiend or two. Maybe three." Milo kissed my cheek and flew away. *"Doesn't matter. Enchanter Evergreen is on the case."*

"That's not the explanation you think it is," I snapped.

People stared at my outburst, completely unaware of the incident a few blocks away. With Enchanter Evergreen here, they wouldn't have to concern themselves. I glared, shrugging off their faint surface thoughts.

My breath hitched, but I refused to stand idle. If Milo knew about this, prepared for it, worried about the outcome so much so he'd planned our date nearby… It could be serious. Deadly.

Tightening my core, I levitated above the street. After a steadying breath, I channeled telekinesis and chased Milo. It wasn't easy. Following him was out of the question; he'd flown away so quickly, I'd lost him after the first block, but the further I went, the louder a cacophony of terrified thoughts boomed.

Black tentacles whipped across the pavement, rattling the ground and lapping at any lingering magical energy. I froze midair, hesitating because of the horrified minds nearby. This fiend was enormous. Its sludgy blobby body swelled, covering the street and reaching well above the single-story buildings. Heat radiated off the fiend, mixing with the frigid chill of winter to create a humid steam. Tar splattered with each strike of its hungry tendrils, scalding the cars and buildings.

I shook away the bewildered dread of bystanders and channeled my banishment root, eliminating a few chunks cast aside from the fiend.

An unnecessary action since Milo quickly swung a fist, channeling a precise telekinetic flow, wrangling all the tentacles whipping about chaotically, and tangling them into each other. All the while, he used his other arm, carefully shifting people too slow or stunned to flee out of the way from smaller fiends barreling onto the street.

Once they'd all seen that the amazing Enchanter Evergreen had arrived on the scene, their relief and belief bubbled above their panic. Milo furiously eradicated the smaller fiends, punching pulses of banishment which rippled through the air and slapped goopy tar until it erupted into glowing white wisps.

Those glimmering lights bounced together, seeking to regather and become destructive again. I ground my teeth, unable to discern if that aggravation came from Milo or me. I banished a handful of wisps, irritated by each person gawking at Enchanter Evergreen's work instead of fleeing so they didn't get in his way. He was pissed too but mostly at some acolyte.

"She had one job today. An opportunity that would properly cement her position. Instead, here I am ruining one of my few well-crafted **carefree** *days off."*

Milo cleared away each of the lesser fiends and their wispy fragments, then focused on the behemoth of a fiend growing with each toxic breath. Despite all the energy it enveloped, its thoughts remained disorganized. A dangerous fiend in size and might but still quite far from transcending into a sentient demon.

Yet Milo's mind flooded with terror at the idea an actual demon would emerge.

Why? So few demons surfaced in cities, and this behemoth was still far from self-awareness and the level of devastation a demon could cause.

My throat tightened at the bloody images Milo and I both kept buried in the past, horrors neither wanted to unbox. That was why his mind went to the worst first. Finn.

Milo wasn't worried about a vision he'd had of a fiend ascending but remembering the genuine terror that came when encountering one. I swallowed hard, struggling to compose my reaction to his thoughts while he worked faster and harder to demolish this demonic creature, unfazed by his own panic attack.

Milo flew forward, pummeling the body and breaking off tar limbs with precise use of his combined root magics. The fury inside him intensified, but he turned to his audience, instinctively smiling for their benefit.

Milo had worked hard to come up with an outing for us to enjoy this weekend. Each of his well laid plans faded with every blow he struck onto the fiend.

Our walkabout in this nook of the city.

Our shopping spree which I was okay losing out on.

Our lunch at a restaurant where he was absolutely certain no one would recognize him—that was never true.

He was always recognized, but we'd gone on a few dates unbothered. Mostly just curious onlookers who'd never worked up the nerve to ask for his autograph and assumed I was a random client. I preferred the discretion. It was difficult enough sorting through my feelings for Milo; I didn't need everyone else in my head evaluating my relationship with the great Enchanter Evergreen, too.

I hovered in the air. Tar erupted into nothingness. A shimmer of white wispy orbs mixed with a screeching smog holding the last uttering roars of a dying fiend. Sweat trickled down my brow, evaporating as I channeled my sensory root.

The moisture from my body caused a spasm in my calves from the swift dehydration, but I pressed on, searching further with my banishment at the ready. Two root magics purely tailored for seeking out and eliminating any demonic presence, yet there was nothing to find or remove.

In an instant, Milo had arrived and cleared the entire scene. I'd say our date was still very much intact. Well, once his adoring fans had their fill.

My muscles were tense from channeling all four root magics, so I quelled sensory and banishment immediately. Carefully, I severed my use of levitation and telekinesis, lightly landing onto the cleared street. The asphalt made my feet ache through the thin soles of my shoes. Or perhaps I ached from too much casting. It didn't matter.

This helped me improve. I wasn't a guild enchanter by any means, but I had an enchanter license, and I wanted to put it and my magics to use. Especially since my rusty magics nearly cost me and my students our lives last semester.

Milo smiled at the crowd, his audience, and eyed me out of the corner of his bright blue eyes. "*This is going to be awhile.*"

"*I can wait.*" I reached for my smokes and propped up against a lamp-post.

"*These fiends funneled from elsewhere, so once I've secured things here, I've got to handle that.*" Milo grimaced for a fraction of a second, which only a single small child caught. "Hey there." Milo knelt, making eye contact with them, and beamed. "You okay?"

The kid nodded, smiling back.

I stuffed my pack of smokes back into my pocket. This was why he'd wanted to avoid intervening. Enchanter Evergreen didn't have quick and easy jobs. Eliminating threats. Securing an area. Showing off in front of citizens. Rinse, repeat, and answer the call to the next clairvoyant vision.

I sighed. Between my classes and his never-ending guild work, time alone was challenging. Milo's surface thoughts shifted between addressing his adoring audience to searching for wherever the demonic energy originated.

No point sticking around, given his mind had locked onto another case. The whole reason for a day date was because Milo's nights had gotten longer since ending the surge of warlock factions. Now we couldn't enjoy a simple Sunday afternoon. Well, he couldn't. I was going to spend it feeling this clammy and anxious no matter what. Now, I had the pleasure of doing that at home alone.

Locking myself away from everyone else used to be a reprieve from the world. But as I went home without Milo, it was just isolating.

Gratitude from several dozen minds beamed brighter than the sunlight cutting through the cloudy sky. Each person exuded elation for their Enchanter Evergreen. That was the difficulty of walking beside Milo, or in this instance, standing on the sidelines. None of this felt like my story. Perhaps an involuntary drawback to telepathy or teaching or both. I spent so much time wrapped in other people's worlds, it had become impossible to discern what I wanted in my own.

CHAPTER TWO

ONCE I walked through the front door, I had two demanding orange tabby cats to contend with. Charlie meowed, pleading for the serious pets he needed because it'd been a whole four hours since he'd seen me, and Carlie meowed, whiny and wispy over the audacity of me leaving her with pâté. The bowl remained full in protest. She'd sooner starve than eat pâté, yet the dry bowls—hers and Charlie's—had been devoured all the way to the shiny silver bottoms.

"It's not my fault, fat cat." I retrieved a can from the cupboard, closely examining the label since they looked so similar with pâté secretly scribbled under the logo and flavor choice. "It was an accident."

I scraped her bowl clean, rinsed and cleaned it, then gave her a meal she desperately hopped onto the counter for, too impatient to wait. After I'd tended to the cats, I made myself a screwdriver and plopped onto the couch to watch television. Not quite the mimosas Milo had in mind, but I hated the fucking bubbles anyway. The sugary tang helped mask the acidic bite from my heavy-handed pour of vodka. The booze dulled my senses, the television muddled my mind, and each kept noisy neighbors out of my dreary head.

A few drinks and hours later, I'd drifted into a dazed delirium. This would be a restless night. I tossed and turned on the couch, Charlie nestled in my neck, swatting me with his tail every time I repositioned.

Milo's presence stirred nearby. He'd invited himself right the hell in, which I'd told him I hated. I couldn't help being reclusive and distant; it was ingrained in my every breath. But he'd ignored my complaints, which I secretly appreciated. It was wonderful having him come here because it cut right through the noise.

"Shush," Milo whispered, stroking bangs out of my face.

Had I said something? No—Charlie's chirp was what Milo shushed. I was too groggy to open my eyes for certainty.

Milo's arms gripped me and pulled me up off the couch. Faded cologne hit with each nasally breath. I rocked my head, turning Milo's chest into a pillow. His hand cradled my back and cupped his other under the back of my knees. In a few breaths I was on my bed, blanket slung over my head before my fluttering eyes adjusted. I wanted to wake. The night had been restless enough. If I resisted a bit more, I'd find myself up and alive, eager to finish the date we'd missed.

The mattress shifted; the blanket tugged. Warm hands slid under my shirt, pulling it off, and Milo rested with his head on my shoulder. The skin-to-skin contact was a dose of total silence, and the world vanished. Wrapping my arm around him, I hugged Milo tightly and fell into his thoughts as his dreams stole him from this world.

Soon, I faded into my own subconscious, thanks to the soft white noise. On dreamless nights when nearby neighbors attempted to keep me from falling into a blissful slumber, Milo's joy outshined their meddling minds.

This wasn't a dreamless night, though.

The past seeped in, melting away Milo's presence like an oil painting hit with turpentine. His thoughts rippled away.

Flames from failures illuminated the dark sky of the street I'd found myself catapulted onto. My legs wobbled—not mine, but those belonging to my younger self who gasped for breath due to exhaustion. Tall buildings burned brightly with fiery demonic magic too powerful for someone as weak as I'd been then to banish. Even now, reflecting on my younger self in the prime of his enchanter career at twenty-two, I doubted I possessed the skills to handle such ferocity.

Debris littered the busy road along with broken vehicles and corpses. Those left alive internally begged for help or faded in and out of consciousness, their thoughts making each breath challenging. Some were coherent enough to call for help; they screamed and begged for a rescue I couldn't offer—not then or now. This was a horror no amount of closure could have prepared me for.

I recoiled within this awful memory, screaming in my mind for it to end, change, hold some subtle message. It didn't. All it offered was a carbon-copied memory I'd endured too many times.

My body was mostly numb at this point having overexerted my magic tenfold, so that even the loudest thoughts buzzed in as whispers until I focused everything on Finn. It did no good.

Half a block away, Finn stood tall, taking tired breaths, face caked in dried blood and a shaky smile he refused to surrender. *"Contain the situation. I've got this."*

If I'd listened to his words, a few of the civilians crying out for help might've lived. Some of the lesser fiends roaming might've been extinguished. Instead, I raced down the street, wincing from the pain in my body, ignoring it all so I could reach Finn.

Back then, I was willing to let the city burn for a chance to rescue him. I would've let the entire world drown in blood to pull him to safety.

A black portal opened behind Finn. This dark magic would transport him far out of reach. I'd seen the ending for this story a thousand times over, relived this guilt in my waking hours with almost as much clarity as now, yet the agony inside my younger self pushed him ahead, desperate but just out of reach, and it always struck a nerve as freshly as the first time I'd experienced it. I stumbled forward, falling to my knees, crawling. Deep cuts and blood loss blurred the world around, but I continued worthlessly dragging myself toward Finn.

A secret part of me hoped for Finn's intervention. I'd had a few dreams of our past since the warlock incursion at the academy, but none where he spoke to me so vividly, so vibrantly. I waited for Finn to break the mold as he'd done so many times a few months back. I wanted him to give me anything. A fleeting word off-script. A warning of something new. A chance to change this awful moment.

Mostly, I wanted to apologize.

"I'll be okay, Dorian. You'll see," Finn thought as he had every single time I relived this nightmare memory.

Nothing had changed. Not a damn thing.

My eyes watered as a sapphire scaled arm reached from within the black hole, long talons cast shadows along Finn's body. The demonic palm had a mouth of its own, filled with jagged teeth. The crooked smile glistened under the light of nearby flames. In a swift motion, the teeth snatched Finn by the jugular. Blood gushed down his neck, and his face went white, hollow, and pained. Still, even as he was enveloped by the portal, his smile never wavered.

"Give him back!" I screamed, my voice hoarse and as broken as the rest of my body that collapsed onto the ground.

The road beneath me vanished.

My heart surged momentarily, startled at a plunge into endless darkness. I scrambled, waking mid fall and terrified I'd crash out of my bed and into an infinity of desperate flailing. Memories always hit based on whatever whim my subconscious wished to process. Whether the fiend from yesterday sent a reminder or some hidden piece of me regretted moving forward, I didn't care to discover.

Milo's arm wrapped around my torso, hand squeezing my chest until my heart slowed and my frantic mind collected the dim morning in my bedroom. My skin was sticky with sweat and Milo's chest clung to my back, but he remained close, running his hand along the hairs on my stomach and hugging me tighter.

Accepting my feelings for Milo didn't magically wash away the guilt I held for Finn in those last moments. It didn't erase the twelve years I'd lived adrift, unwilling to embrace happiness. But these memories no longer carved out my insides when they struck. Not like they used to. I had Milo here; even half-dazed and lost in a dream, his mind reached out and filled that emptiness in mine with his joy.

He'd spent many nights here since I'd accepted what we had, have, and could still have as a pair.

"Wanna talk about it?" Milo nuzzled the back of my ear. His dream-lost thoughts boomed.

"Just demons. Nightmares. Something I'd rather forget."

"Demons are the worst." He kissed my neck, sending positive, light, and humorous images. They trailed down my spine until the worst of the memory washed away.

Our minds and magics had synced so seamlessly again, picking up from our youth and elevating to a degree I barely comprehended. Even sleeping in a bit, Milo knew how to predict my day in the best way.

I scoffed. Knowing Milo, even without skimming his groggy morning thoughts, he'd known a dream would hit me soon. One I wasn't ready for and prepared accordingly. Hell, it was Milo. I'd given his clairvoyance too much credit. Sometimes, he'd know when I struggled just by the stiffness in my muscles, lull in my voice, or change in my breathing. He was annoyingly perfect that way, and yet I still questioned what to make of us.

"I have to get ready for work." I kissed him, soft and light as I spun around and slipped off the bed. "I'll see you this evening."

"Doubtful. Got that Cerberus thing tonight, remember? Gonna be a long day, evening, long something—and not the long something I like." Milo kept his eyes firmly closed, refusing to let the outside world take what remnants of his trickling dreams remained. How I wished that beautiful, playful dream had invaded my slumber, but I wasn't so blessed it seemed.

"I can stop by, keep you company." I grabbed clothes to slip on after a shower.

"It's a silly ceremony. No networking worth your time. Trust me, I got a good sense on stuff."

Milo had been ranked the number one Chicago enchanter, something he was less enthusiastic about each year. He didn't make a big deal about it because he'd held that ranking every year since the Night of the Fiend Massacre. Not that there weren't others constantly rotating among the top ten enchanters and closing the gap between themselves and Enchanter Ever-green, but then something would happen, and his popularity would surge again. Most recently, it had to do with his role in thwarting the warlocks that threatened my homeroom coven and the army of fiends that would've eviscerated countless people.

"Thought it was an award?" I paused, rooting through his hidden insecurities for this event.

"What? No. The award was whenever ago. This is like the guilds way of showcasing it happened. It's completely unnecessary, and it'll be a real drag for you." Milo rolled over, tucking his head under a pillow, like that'd quell his thoughts. "I'll just see you tomorrow after."

Milo had dragged me to a few Cerberus events over the holiday, but since the start of the second semester, he'd eased up, likely due to my reluctance. I continued exploring our relationship, what it was, what it could be like, but that was much simpler in privacy. Prying eyes followed the great Enchanter Evergreen everywhere, and when I'd accompany him or even show up to an event on my own, Milo was often the height of conversation—both aloud and in thought. I didn't fit into the industry when I worked in it, and it had become apparent that I belonged even less now.

I wanted to support him because his surface thoughts cycled with excitement for the event, yet he kept quiet and pushed them away whenever I'd brought it up. Half of me believed it was because he knew today, this week, truly—okay, the next few months—would be grueling considering the testing we had in store for the kids. The other half of me screamed I'd embarrassed Milo so much, he questioned why we'd ever found our way back together. Clearly someone so undevoted to his career wouldn't make for the right happily ever after as he'd so incorrectly predicted a million times over.

I sighed, releasing that paranoid part of myself into the ether, but lingered at the doorway while Milo slept. He'd buried himself beneath the blanket, drifting further from his dream state slumber—one of the few times when he didn't carry the world on his shoulders—and toward muddled concerns over demons. I shuddered. They were fiery and destructive images like the night…the night we lost Finn. But so many of Milo's thoughts burst into staticky blobs. This might've been tied to some potential he'd prevented when banishing the fiends yesterday, or maybe Milo dwelled on the horrors of our past as much as I did.

I channeled my root magics before getting ready for my shower, so I could prepare myself to quickly fly to work. The distance was still fatiguing, and if I didn't prepare my levitation and telekinesis while getting ready, I found it challenging to maintain flight over several miles. My stomach burned as the muscles tightened. Admittedly, I liked how so much constant casting had gotten rid of the bit of flab on my belly. I wasn't rocking a six pack like Milo, but all my muscles had toned from constant use of my root magics.

Since everything last semester, I wanted to ensure my four root magics were as sharp—*no sharper*—as when I worked in the industry. I traced my fingertips along the scar across my neck while the shower heated up.

CHAPTER THREE

CHANELLE sauntered down the hallways long before anyone else had arrived, her magenta heels clicked with each swift step, echoing in the near-empty building.

Frustration festered in her head, but her cheeks tightened as she smiled because she was incapable of holding onto rage. It clogged the happiness she found for everything in life, and knowing how fleeting it all was, she refused to give energy to things that didn't utterly delight her—a sentiment I never understood. Yet she forced smiles and positive thoughts until they became her reality.

So, an email sent far too late for her to handle, threatening to steal the joy from her successful academy launch simply wasn't allowed. Not when she'd dedicated most of her vacation, weekends, and late nights ensuring everything went perfectly.

I puffed on a cigarette in the parking lot, leaned against one of the brick pillars lining the entryway to the campus, and drifted alongside her telepathically as my smoky exhale wafted.

Since my near-death experience, my telepathy had magnified tenfold. Even without summoning a manifestation, I could easily link onto another person's mind, unweave their inner thoughts, and follow for a short radius like a ghost trailing alongside them. Something that used to take much more applied effort, I now slipped into this enhanced state as naturally and unknowingly as breathing. Ironically, though, I hadn't been able to summon an actual manifestation since the attack on the academy. No deep dives into any minds or memories like I'd done with Caleb, Kenzo, and Tara. It was frustrating losing that skill while gaining another, but I had too much on my mind—quite literally, other people's minds included—to make it much of a priority. When life slowed down, I'd figure it out.

I'd need to gain more control over this shift in my telepathy especially before mentioning it the next time I renewed my enchanter license. I took a sharp inhale and grumbled. This improvement would likely increase the yearly cost for my license, or they'd tax the hell out of me because while having great magic didn't cost a thing, the right to freely cast it was expensive.

It wasn't something I had to consider for months, though. The only thing I needed to focus on now was Chanelle's current location so I could dodge whatever early morning meeting she'd scheduled for staff.

Not that I planned on avoiding Chanelle forever, but until she eased the brakes on her academy position, it was the easiest way to keep tabs on her so I didn't get dragged into an extra workload. I hated it. I often got my best work done for classes by arriving early and spending some time alone in a quiet classroom undisturbed by the bustle of the building with only faint thoughts trickling in. She knew that and used my productivity to her advantage.

"*Dammit, Dorian.*" She reached my darkened room and huffed. "*I know you're here.*"

"Not today, Miss Hotshot." I took another drag off my cigarette while she trailed down the hall and further from my over-the-shoulder view. I didn't require a reminder on the tech we were presenting to the students, its importance to ranking our first years, or how it tied into new security measures.

"Good morning, Mr. Frost." Gael waved a spiked hand from across the parking lot.

```
Name: Gael Martinez
Branch: Augmentation (Spikes)
```

I'd kept their stats close at hand all year, and soon, I'd have to update them based on the new and improved ranking system the academy wanted to roll out. I chuckled to myself, which invited a smile from Gael, but in truth, it was Gemini's old ranking system that they'd brushed off and tweaked and poured way too much funding into without a second thought that almost brought a smile to my face.

Gemini—like too many academies—cut the old ranking system because it was a strong determining factor on incoming enrollment, and they all wanted to increase their roster influx due to the state's new rollout on increasing licensed witch proficiency to eighty percent. Of course, now academies were worried about impressing guilds for extra funding and sponsorship, so they'd created this new and improved system.

Except it wasn't. That was how education worked for the most part—someone disliked a system already in place and removed it without something new, or someone had a half-assed idea that sounded great in theory, but they impatiently tossed it out to the world and expected teachers to figure it out through trial and error. *It's not as if these errors affect the kids or anything.*

Gael's sharklike teeth beamed brightly as he flaunted his new hairdo. The first day of February was official, and he'd dyed his black roots a deep red to commemorate the upcoming holiday. His long, gelled spiky hair, emulating Enchanter Evergreen's style, was dyed a light pink with frosted white tips. Admittedly, I rather enjoyed Gael's festive looks. New spikes continued blossoming as his augmentation increased, so the occasional rips were to be expected. But without the blazer, his overly wrinkled short-sleeved dress shirts were highly noticeable. It was irksome that he wasted so much time on his hair and not nearly enough on his overall presentation or his studies.

Dropping my cigarette, I squished the ember beneath my shoe along with the invasive thought—I certainly didn't concern myself with Gael's somewhat aloof behavior. Oh no, that honor belonged to the student walking alongside him.

Gael had spent more time with Kenzo since the end of the first semester, training to improve his abilities and academics. I was grateful Kenzo had taken an interest in Gael's success, but his tactics involved early mornings and late-night study sessions. Hence why they were always the first to arrive on campus.

"Better be doing something useful today." Gray static coursed along Kenzo's temples, surging across his forehead, and running through his short, jet-black hair. It added a shimmer.

"I'd say today's going to be pretty eventful." I grinned, which only intensified Kenzo's frown.

"Dammit." He ground his teeth and stormed ahead inside.

```
Name: Kenzo Ito
Branch: Hex (Disruption)
```

Of all my homeroom students, Kenzo took the warlock incursion on campus the most seriously. He'd added to his already rigorous training routine, and with the added benefit of his fledgling permit, he spent all his time working on perfecting his disruption. We'd even turned it into a little game. Well, I'd turned it into a game, deluding myself into believing this was some type of bonding exercise for us, but his constantly irritated thoughts about me made it clear this was strictly a way for him to improve.

To hex another person's magic, Kenzo either had to directly strike the user or the magic itself when cast in the atmosphere. However, psychic magic such as mine proved harder to pinpoint. He needed precision when obscuring his thoughts from my magic. Nine out of ten times, he floundered at blocking his thoughts. If it were any other student, I'd let them think it was seven out of ten, but Kenzo would take a considerate curve to his success as a slight, so here we were practicing at every opportunity when our paths crossed.

"Hurry up, porcupine!" Kenzo growled.

Gael rushed past me, tightening the straps of his book bag as he trotted beside Kenzo. I followed them, casually making my way to my classroom while they turned off and headed toward the library.

I sat alone in my room, unboxing the biggest academy investment I'd seen thus far. Partly because it helped bring back the ranking system and partly because Chanelle pitched it as a way to streamline our security in new and improved ways. I sighed. Our administrators had ordered these specific to each of the students' branch magics but hadn't bothered with much else, which meant I had the ever so enjoyable headache of dealing with errors while syncing them to my homeroom coven's specific channeling frequencies.

These overpriced hunks of junk our administration team called state-of-the-art devices got rather temperamental if not calibrated just right. They'd crash and require a time-consuming reboot. Thankfully, I had a lot of data on my classes' particular frequencies for casting and spent what remained of my morning setting them up.

The bell rang, and I stood in the hallway, awaiting my homeroom coven's arrival. Students flooded into the building, and Gael boldly cut through the crowd, walking beside Tara.

"It's gonna be the event of the year," Gael said loudly. He continued riding the wave of success my homeroom coven had before winter break and flaunted his honorary Cerberus emblem on full display, pinned above a colorful pocket square on his academy jacket.

```
Name: Gael Rios-Vega
Branch: Bestial (Familiar)
```

"Is it, though?" Tara raised a questioning eyebrow, resisting a desire to comment the contrary.

They'd become an inseparable duo—well, trio, with King Clucks plodding between the two as they walked into the room—since the warlock incursion. Their friendship had blossomed somewhere before but had continued increasing this semester.

"I just wish we could go." Gael held his phone close to his face like it had a secret invitation. The bright light of the screen illuminated his bronze complexion.

I had no idea what event he wanted to go to, but considering he was one of Milo's biggest fanboys, I guessed it had something to do with that so-called tiny celebration for Enchanter Evergreen. The fact Milo continued downplaying his own accolades, worried it'd scare me away, left an unsavory taste in my mouth because I had no way to convince him I was here to stay. Especially given my longstanding history of pushing him away.

"Well, the Whitlock's are officially off everyone's RSVP list," Tara said. "So if you're subtly fishing for an invitation, I can't help."

"No. Sorry, I'm making this all about me." Gael ran his fingers through his fauxhawk while his rooster clucked. "And it really sucks everyone's still icing you out like that."

It didn't suck, though. Tara kept it to herself, like so much, but her mind fluttered with excitement just above that somber ocean she carried with her every time she thought about how free she'd become since falling from social graces, thanks to the scandal her father weathered from a distance, one that took him on business outside Chicago.

```
Name: Tara Whitlock
Branch: Ward (Sealing)
Branch: Cosmic (Shadows)
Branch: Arcane (Intangibility)
```

It didn't change the fact we still had a lot of work to do when it came to her branch magics and the restrictions she suffered from her casting overlap, but I'd focused much of my time reading materials to pass along to her. There was so much guesswork to it since every case reacted differently depending on the individual's branches and temperament.

My students funneled into the classroom and took their seats. Ignoring their casual conversation, I channeled my telekinesis. My muscles still ached from the long flight, but I was determined to spend every waking opportunity, big or small, honing my roots.

Caleb's vibrant green eyes widened as I telekinetically moved small boxes to each of their desks. His persistent determination had rubbed off on me, and I found myself equally driven to enhance my root magics.

"You all can go ahead and open them," I said.

"You got us gifts, Mr. Frosty?" Gael asked, batting his lashes and twisting his lips into a minxy grin. "Aren't you the sweetest?"

I rolled my eyes.

Each of them opened their box, unveiling the stylish gold bracelets fitted with the best technology and magic had to offer when it came to monitoring and improving magical practice.

"This is…" Caleb's jaw dropped.

Gael squealed so loudly it startled everyone, even his rooster. Despite the outburst, everyone's thoughts surged as they examined the sleek screen that lit up bright blue from a simple touch.

"Whoa. A Cast-8-Watch."   *"So pretty."*

"These haven't even been released yet."

"And the academy's just giving them to us?"

"What are they playing at?"

"Of course you didn't get one. How's it supposed to fit on your chicken legs?"

"BAWK!"

"Thank you so much, Mr. Frost."   *"It's so bulky and gaudy."*

"The color is kind of bland." Katherine scrunched her face, raising her glasses to the bridge of her nose. *"And I just bought the newer model. Maybe the academy will let me switch them out."*

```
Name: Katherine Harris
Branch: Enchantment (Spell Craft)
```

Her light brown fingertips brushed along the smooth surface while she mused over the device. Everyone had strong opinions about the Cast-8-Watch's the academy had provided, but Caleb's thoughts torpedoed above them all.

"I was looking at the used model seven but they're still like 1,200 bucks. No way could Gramps swing that." Caleb gulped, tapping the screen of his watch and studying every facet of its functions with curious delight. *"Even if I was able to save up without bills, I'd never be able to afford one of these. It's got so many extra features even the most advanced Cast-7's couldn't handle processing. SO COOL!"*

I'd spent so much time fixated on saving his life, unraveling the mystery, that now his thoughts often rose above everyone else's when he was nearby. The incident hadn't deterred him for a second when it came to his goals of becoming an industry professional working as a top-ranked enchanter at a guild. In fact, it pushed him to work harder on enhancing his root magics.

```
Name: Caleb Huxley
Branch: N/A
```

I attributed that mostly to his determination and partially to the fact he was never aware how close to death he'd really been. Whatever the world would've looked like without him in it, Milo clearly believed it'd be darker. It didn't matter whether I had insight on how much he'd truly improve the world or not, I wanted to make certain he learned everything possible before graduating.

"These are not gifts. They're state-of-the-art tools, and it's Gemini Academy's intention to streamline your training in and out of classes." I grabbed a manual and instructed them to do the same since each of them had started tapping buttons without so much as glancing at the how-to setup steps. Granted, they all had this naturally annoying affinity for tech I still struggled to wrap my brain around.

"I knew there was a fucking catch."

I ground my teeth, tuning out Kenzo's suspicions because they weren't far off. Nothing about the industry came free, and this investment was no different than any other. Katherine's eyes locked onto mine as I explained the purpose of the Cast-8-Watch they were each assigned, from how it was synced to their specific channeling frequency for casting, to how it'd record their progress and growth in all four root magics and their branch magics.

Those fledgling permits they'd all obtained allowed them more practice in and outside the academy, but now we'd track every second of progress or lack thereof.

"Branch magics." Tara dropped her head slightly, hiding behind her long blonde hair.

"These devices will allow the academy to record your improvements so we can properly rank students and see who among you will participate in the Spring Showcase. It's not as important to place your first year, but for second year students, it can be make or break when it comes to internships. Consider this your one practice run. If you don't place this year, you don't get to practice, so take this time you have to train seriously. Any and every opportunity."

Except it was make or break in some cases. These kids needed every edge they could get to stand out by the time they reached their second year where they'd compete for internships against every witch at every academy across the state. Each young witch held the same dreams they all held, and as much as I wanted to guarantee their hard work would pay off, life had a tendency of proving me wrong.

"Place?" Caleb asked with a shaky voice.

"Only the top 160 first-year students will be considered. We don't have the time or resources to present an event for every single first year." Well, we did, but administration wouldn't consider committing that much when the Spring Showcase for the first-year students didn't bring in a quarter of the revenue the second-year showcase did.

"There are 600 first-year students. Without considering the variables on how we're ranked, those numbers give me a .0016 percent chance of placing." Caleb scribbled numbers and variables, all of which floated about his surface thoughts like an insufferable mathematical jigsaw puzzle. *"Depending on the specifics for evaluating, that could increase my likelihood or massively decrease my chances."*

I silenced his mental ramblings because the stats and figures hurt my head. "This is about more than the Spring Showcase, though. These will also help specify exactly which areas of magic you need the most assistance with."

There was a lot of truth to that. While I wasn't a fan of these devices or the fact my twelve homeroom coven students held tech in their hands that, when added together, cost more than twice my yearly salary, I did like this would provide in-depth data on their magical output, where they struggled, and help isolate and pinpoint ways for improvement.

"Can we backtrack to what you mean by ranking us?" Katherine raised a hand, asking her question before I'd even responded to the gesture. "I thought the purpose of academies opening their doors was to move away from those outdated practices. Hence why the entrance exam was tossed because it's archaic and does little to truly evaluate all forms of magic or success in this very diverse industry."

She made a lot of valid points, but they were directed toward licensing in general, which wasn't the purpose of these rankings or Gemini's reasoning for implementing them.

Kenzo huffed. ***"Shut up, know-it-all."***

My breath hitched, fighting the piercing strike of aggression.

"You bring up some great points, Katherine." I cleared my throat, ignoring the profanities leaping from Kenzo's thoughts and the mutterings under his breath. "But these rankings are important to the guilds who wish to sponsor interns. They often won't commit to such intensive training and fieldwork experience without having some assurances on skill sets prior to signing you."

"So you're telling me if there was a guild looking for an intern with an enchantment magic like mine, they might pass because of my ranking?"

"Possibly. Some guilds and enchanters won't consider any applicants below a particular ranking," I said, almost immediately regretting my choice of words as fear funneled from students. I squeezed the bridge of my nose, burying the burst of thoughts before they reached me. "It's also possible some won't consider rankings at all," I said, attempting to calm their minds. "Many guilds are looking to highlight unique magics they currently don't have. There's no set rule on how the industry works. It's all very subjective."

"*Subjective?*" Katherine crossed her arms and pouted. "That's a terrible system."

Agreed, but the industry wasn't changing anytime soon. All I could do was prepare them to navigate the one we had.

"Obviously, they have to have some type of evaluation in place." Kenzo glared. "Otherwise, guilds wouldn't know our capabilities, and they'd hire any idiot loser off the street just because they wanted it."

Kenzo's gaze shifted to Caleb, who shrank in his seat. While aggressively rude for no reason other than to assert his dominance in the room, he wasn't incorrect.

"*Ranking us based on our branch magics… How much of that score will be based on our branch alone? Will I have the same evaluation? Will they omit that score because I don't have a branch, or am I just going to lose the points?*" Caleb continued sinking further into his seat, dwelling on questions to things I still didn't have answers for.

I paused. A whirlpool of doubt circled Caleb, filled with thousands of words wailing how he'd never be good enough, picked the wrong path, wasn't special or chosen or meant for anything great because he was just another average branchless dud. I cracked my neck, quelling my telepathy before he dragged me into the depths of his worry, when suddenly, he shot up in his seat.

"*If I'm already starting in the negative because I'm branchless, then that just means I'll have to make sure I score above everyone else in every other area.*" Caleb straightened his posture and raised a hand.

"Yes?" I said, resisting smiling back at Caleb as his determination swelled and a smile filled his face.

"What other areas will our rankings be based on?" he asked, reaching for his notebook and prepared to take a thousand notes to bury the doubts and voices and memories that said he'd never be good enough for the guild industry.

"Everything from academics to personality," I said. "It's something we'll focus on as the semester progresses."

"Please, they've been evaluating us since we stepped

through the front doors."

I ignored Kenzo again, but again, he wasn't wrong. The kid rarely was. "For today, let's just make sure you've all got your Cast-8-Watch synced up and working."

These rankings wouldn't affect chances of obtaining a license or internship—that was an academy guarantee. But poor rankings would limit their options, preventing certain pathways, and I wanted them to walk away from Gemini with every possible opportunity, not just the basic academy guarantee.

"*Guilds expect the best of the best, and I'll show them I am the best!*" Caleb hyper-fixated on the directions, reading each step closely while jotting notes in preparation for his many what-if thoughts bouncing about. "*If Enchanter Evergreen can master the rankings, I'll just have to do even better.*"

Not that the ranking systems for guilds were identical to Gemini Academy's, but they were cut from the same cloth. Guilds had more functionality with their system whereas academies had more fluidity. Ranking witches under close scrutiny by evaluating their every movement was something these kids would never escape if they pursued professional casting. Milo's continued high ranking as a guild witch wasn't anywhere near Caleb's situation, yet he clung to the comparison.

My homeroom coven read over their manuals and set up their Cast-8-Watch while I walked around the room, assisting those who needed it. Gael's spikey knee clinked against his desk as the words jumbled. I paused a few desks away, next to Tara, who struggled with the frequency settings. Gael took a breath and steadied his shaky knee as he reread the words until he'd tackled the setup independently. He preferred not to draw attention to his dyslexia, and I did my best to respect his choices.

"*It's like the academy found the perfect way to track how shitty I am.*"

I pointed to notes I'd added in the margins based on what Tara and I understood about her casting. There was still so much to unravel, and I hoped it helped in even the smallest way.

"Thanks." Tara turned in her desk, facing away from me.

I sighed. Clearly, I was still mostly unhelpful.

"I don't need a fucking babysitter." Static popped on Kenzo's watch as he attempted disrupting the tracking software. It figured he'd be the first to realize the connection to the academy's added security measure.

"Having trouble linking your hex?" I shook my head, feigning concern. "I warned admin you might not be able to cast without breaking it. It's unfortunate your precision is still floundering."

"What?" Kenzo's pale face burned bright red. "That's not why I'm—"

"HA!" Gael and King Clucks chuckled in unison.

The way the rooster's chest puffed when imitating his human partner's laughter was such a bizarre sight, but it worked to settle Kenzo, who gave up messing with the device out of sheer spite and simply synced it to his magical frequency.

I spent the rest of homeroom helping them each lightly cast their roots so their watches would register their channeling flows without destroying my classroom.

CHAPTER FOUR

AFTER a full day of instruction, continuously casting small doses of magic, dodging every adult who wanted conversation—except for Chanelle, who bitterly ignored me as punishment for this morning—and flying home, all I wanted to do was pass out on the couch. Charlie had curled himself up into a perfect little orange ball of fluff. If I picked him up, he'd beg for attention, so I chose the lesser of two evils and sat on the chair opposite the couch. I didn't want to sleep anyway. A nap would keep me up all night. I wanted to rest without movement or thinking or casting.

"Meow." Carlie trotted into the living room, her call whiny and seeking sympathy for her equally exhausting day.

Ah, yes. How dare I consider relaxation when she only had dry food in a bowl and could quite literally starve to death. She rolled on the carpet, flashing her fluffy white gut because that was somehow supposed to show how vulnerable and underfed she was.

"I'm coming." I walked into the kitchen.

Charlie perked up and raced behind me, weaving between my legs. I reached for cans while Carlie whined at my sluggish pace. Paper rustled, and Charlie chirped. I turned, and there he was, biting into a torn notebook page tucked beneath the fridge.

"What are you doing, cat?" I grabbed it from his mouth.

**Had time between jobs so figured I'd feed the kitties! Think
they're warming up to me.
— Milo**

I eyed Carlie. She'd quieted and started licking her paws like this page didn't have her claw marks all over it. How many other times had Milo dropped by to feed the cats only for his note to conveniently end up batted under some hidden nook of the house?

"Thank you, Charlie." I picked up my adorable tabby, who was in no way warming up to Milo because he was all mine, and glared at Carlie. "You're crafty. Too crafty."

I was half convinced she was more than a pet but some poor witch's familiar who'd stuck around here because of how comfortable I'd made her lifestyle. Carlie slapped her bowl and scurried out of the kitchen to the back of the house. Well, not that comfortable a lifestyle.

I hugged Charlie tight and plopped onto the couch, petting him despite my sore arms. He purred and nuzzled my chin before kneading my shirt. Repositioning myself so I didn't disturb Charlie, I stretched for the controller and turned on the television. I was too tired to read and sitting in silence just filled my head with the thoughts of my neighbors.

My phone buzzed as I flipped channels. Charlie purred louder like somehow that'd convince me the vibration in my pocket came from him and there was no need to stop petting him. I checked the alert, which was just a notification about a special report involving Enchanter Evergreen doing another news piece. I'd spent so much time Googling him, somehow my phone auto-set alerts based on my interests. Or Milo fucked with my phone. In either case, I didn't know how to turn off the notifications.

I flipped to the news station where Milo's face filled the television screen. The camera reeled back, displaying the crowd of guests lined at the entryway to Cerberus Guild. Not quite the tiny ceremony he alluded to this morning or every time I'd inquired.

"Quite the turnout Cerberus has brought to celebrate," the reporter said.

"A bit preemptive, I'd say." Milo fussed with his hair, shyly scratching the back of his head, yet grinned. This was his best "I'm-so-humbled Enchanter Evergreen" expression, which he rarely broke out. It wasn't preemptive, it was overdue, and obviously Cerberus agreed given the party Milo kept downplaying.

"Early nominations are out," the reporter said. "You're finally on the list for the Global Ranking's Ceremony, a feat few enchanters ever make and something many think you should've been considered for a lot sooner."

I sat up, annoying Charlie who leapt off me and walked out of the living room, leaving orange hairs across my dark shirt. Milo made this guild event out to be no biggie!

I scoffed, completely tuning out the reporter as B-roll footage played during her brief explanation to the importance of the Global Rankings. The Global Ranking's Ceremony was a yearly event acknowledging the most elite enchanters based on missions, accomplishments, and a thousand other thinly veiled selective factors that all boiled down to who-knew-who and how well they played the game. As if that in itself wasn't annoying enough, they painted the ceremony like it actually acknowledged witches across the globe when the worldwide rankings were only based on U.S. enchanters. Still, for a list that considered millions but only selected a few hundred, this was a triumphant accomplishment.

"While I'm so honored to be considered, I feel like Cerberus is making a much bigger deal out of this than necessary," Milo said. Correction, Enchanter Evergreen said, because he always picked his words so precisely.

But people in the city loved his accolades—even his showboating from time to time—so who was the audience he kept coy for? I doubted the panelist for the Global Rankings cared.

"This year's most eligible enchanters will be announced soon, and with that fancy new ranking, I'd wager a lot of viewers are curious if you'll be on that list again."

Milo blushed. "There are so many other more eligible and amazing enchanters in the city. Honestly, I hope they're considered before anyone from the Chicago Casting magazine calls me."

"More eligible?" The reporter had a tartness in her voice, a lull like she'd caught him in wordplay, which she had because Milo and I hadn't announced our relationship publicly.

It was a lot—letting him in, accepting I deserved happiness again—and I'd reluctantly expressed my fears of too many outside voices evaluating our relationship. I wanted us to work, but I knew what an emotionless prick I could be and didn't want to shove Milo away for my own convenience.

Milo paused on her leading question. His anxiety swelled while he considered his response, worried his hesitation might feed into a result he didn't want. I pressed my temples. Milo didn't worry about that. He was on the other side of the city, well out of range to even my best telepathic pulls. I was anxious. I was worried. I dreaded what he'd say next because I couldn't decide if him suddenly announcing our relationship was a move I wanted or if I'd be more upset if he continued with the ruse. A ruse I'd pressured him into.

My stomach sank with indecision. I was a fucking moron.

"Does that mean you've got someone special?" the reporter followed up. "Rumor has it sparks may've possibly rekindled between you and Enchanter Campbell since she took the guild master role?"

"I don't think workplace romances are for me," Milo said. "Besides, she's far too enchanting for someone like myself. Have you met the woman? She's a force unlike any other, piecing together the fallout those warlocks caused. Honestly, she should be attending the Global Ranking's Ceremony."

"Does this mean you'll be supporting her bid for taking over as the executive guild master?"

The reporter prattled on, complimenting Milo. Somehow, I found myself pacing between the living room and kitchen, cleaning things I had no desire to tend to. I should have just turned off the news. Or maybe I should have checked in on Milo. It wasn't like he'd reply to a message mid interview, but I could send something supportive for his *small* event.

"There's also been talk about you and Hellrazer working more together lately despite the fact Kraken Guild has taken a solitary approach since the fallout with Whitlock Industries. Any chance there are some rekindled embers to that romance?"

"You should know The Inevitable Future would never let a bit of business strife stand in the way of ensuring a brighter future for everyone."

That'd been a concern of Milo's since the fallout of Whitlock Industries. Sure, Tobias Whitlock remained strong, but he was reclusive since his implications on illegal contracts and government sanctioned human experiments. Every guild in Chicago clamored for independence, which meant those collaborative joint missions Enchanter Evergreen often relied on for the best outcomes became more difficult to acquire.

"Does that bright future involve you with the brightest flame this city has?"

I clenched my fist so tightly, I wove telekinesis and knocked an empty glass off the table. Thank God for carpets and for being too winded to accidentally fling it against a wall. I took a deep breath, composing myself. Milo and the obnoxious bad boy wannabe Hellrazer didn't bother me. I wasn't concerned about Milo straying, and I knew about his relationships when we weren't together. He had charisma, he had needs, and he shouldn't have had to isolate himself simply because that was what I'd done. So, no, I didn't worry about his mountain of exes or how well he maintained platonic relationships with them or the flickers of memories he carried for each of them. They were a part of his life, like everyone he'd worked with, befriended, rescued, and so forth.

What made my hands clammy and throat dry was how the two exes that damn reporter mentioned both fit so neatly into Enchanter Evergreen's world. The Inevitable Future might regret that I was no prize and incapable of openly accepting his profession or our relationship.

"Enchanter Ortiz is quite phenomenal, but unfortunately, his flame burns bright for another. Or will. Or could. Or should." Milo laughed off her prodding questions, adding in some jokes and doing what the public loved so deeply about him: he talked candidly, like there were no cameras with thousands of eyes on him, but instead, he sat in a closed room chatting with his best friend.

Screw this. I went to my bedroom, rummaging through every cheap suit I owned. I was halfway out of my clothes and tossing on a button-up before it dawned on me what I was doing.

I was going to Enchanter Evergreen's little celebration because I wanted Milo to know I supported his world, his role in it, and every accomplishment he'd earned.

Chapter Five

I STOOD outside Cerberus Guild, teeth chattering from the frigid cold and the nerves of rushing across town. They'd closed off entry to the general public on account of the party inside. Even my best 'storming in like I belonged here' approach wouldn't get me in tonight. Plus, I honestly only felt comfortable barging in when actually infuriated, which was usually because the suave Enchanter Evergreen had withheld something vital from me. This was also something he'd withheld, but I struggled to piece together whether it was to protect my feelings or his.

They'd practically rolled out the red carpet for this not-so-tiny event. Only this carpet was gold, which seemed like the perfect flourish on Enchanter Campbell's design; her subtle jab of having everyone in attendance walk over Tobias Whitlock, given his branch magic of abjuration created golden shields. Maybe I was reading too deeply into it—like everything in my life. But it wasn't my initial thought, more a collective musing that crossed many of the guests' minds as they stood in line for the event.

Lighting a smoke, I savored the inhale as my telepathy waned. Thanks to the actual obsessed fans lined against the steel crowd control fence, I didn't look too creepy casually observing from across the street by the L train exit. What was clearly preferential to photographers had evolved into a curious free for all as folks clamored to meet some of the best enchanters in Chicago.

Small Cerberus event, my ass.

I took another drag and followed the envious thoughts to a more discreet side entrance. A line of guests not flashy enough for the front door was let inside after having their tickets scrutinized. Fuck. I could always fly to the roof, but it was probably locked or had security of its own. The parking garage was out since the valet was in and out of there.

"You could always ask me very nicely." Chanelle walked over wearing a powder blue silk dress. The vibrant pastel complimented her brown complexion. It perfectly fit her shapely frame, and suddenly, I felt even more awkward swimming in this wrinkled tux.

"Ask what?" I snuffed out my cigarette.

"To join me inside." Chanelle looped her arm through mine and yanked me toward the side door entrance. "You're far too shabby to be my date; however, since Kyle's working, I guess you'll do."

Images of provocative nights she'd had with her husband at parties like this flashed in a haze of tantalizing titillation. Her perfume mixed with the memories of sweet sweat and musk, and I broke my arm loose to escape her reminiscing.

"How'd you even land a ticket to this event?"

"The perk of being the academy liaison is I get to kiss what little free time I have away as well as a few asses. Gotta make sure Gemini is ever so grateful for the new tech."

Chanelle's confidence radiated off whispered thoughts—her choices, her presence, and the reminder that she could captivate any room, even a room full of professional enchanters. Those intangible fragments filled my footing with courage as I trailed next to her.

She'd always walked through life confidently, but her pride had grown since the attack on the academy, taking on the teacher lead for Gemini Academy's improved security measures. It meant more innovation from the staff and required a liaison with the guilds closely affiliated with our campus. Chanelle loved the position, the added responsibility—as if her days and nights weren't already consumed by tutoring sessions, coaching, or whatever absurdity the academy threw our way.

"Doesn't look like you're too upset about all the ass-kissing you're going to have to do tonight."

"What can I say?" She pursed her lips. "I find a way to enjoy any position."

"A position you gladly took," I huffed, ignoring her innuendo. "And you were the one pushing for those expensive Cast-8-Watches."

"Better me at the helm than some annoying asshat. Plus, the tech seemed like a win."

And it was. That tech streamlined every aspect of our data for improving magical proficiency, with the added perk of registering every person entering the academy. Unfortunately, they couldn't splurge for staff. Instead, we got upgrades to our badges for comings and goings.

I cracked my neck, quelling thoughts, but Chanelle's had coiled around my magic so easily. It was annoying.

Chanelle was unabashedly proud of her open relationship and the many facets she explored with and without her husband. The pieces of themselves they'd learned over a decade of love lingered in each breath she took. I was already confused enough about my relationship; I didn't need to spend the night locked in memories of Chanelle's very adventurous marriage. There were more than a few questions I had about her relationship, but after that colorful snippet, I didn't want answers. Chanelle was as free with her words as her thoughts. It was quite liberating to observe yet irritating to endure. Perhaps that was what drew Milo toward her for friendship. Then again, he managed to make friends with anyone, anywhere, anytime. Still, for the boldly confident Enchanter Evergreen—he selected all his words rather carefully, unlike Chanelle, who spouted them right as they bubbled in her mind.

"I've always wondered how you two worked, but after what you keep on the surface, I think I get the idea." I strolled beside her, getting closer to the line. "Don't expect me to play wingman for your night out."

"Please, Dorian. You're far too dull. Now, your ex on-again, off-again were-you-ever-a-thing again—he's a cutie. Even without his enchanter title or those fancy rankings, I think we'd each reel in quite the catch for the evening."

I furrowed my brow.

"Kidding." Chanelle ushered me into the line. "You're here for him, right? Milo. Just guessing. Don't need to be psychic to figure out the vibes there. He hasn't mentioned you once since you were released from the hospital. And you haven't mentioned him either, but then, you're not one for divulging. I thought maybe there was something going on. Now there's all this talk on who's on Evergreen's arm, who will, who should be, who could be. My guess is the grumpy little telepath wants to shoot his shot. I'm all for making dreams come true. Just ask anyone who's ever been lucky enough to have me grant theirs."

Chanelle smiled. Her bright white teeth filled her face as her dimples sank in deep. She had a pretty accurate assessment considering how little she knew. Whatever friendship Milo and Chanelle had developed, he'd respected my desire for privacy, which said a lot considering how candid he could be and how often she pried secrets out of people. That was what this all came down to, what brought me here. A desire for something different. I just hadn't figured that part out yet.

"It'll cost you, though."

"Seriously?" We moved closer ahead.

"With the Spring Showcase coming up, it's going to get pretty cutthroat with everyone doing their damnedest to ensure their students qualify. I've got a million things on my to-do list, but I don't want my homeroom coven to suffer as a result, so if you want into the event of the season, I want your assistance with one of my projects."

"This isn't the event of the season." It was barely the event of the month. Yes, they'd pulled out all the stops to honor the esteemed Enchanter Evergreen, but they'd have more celebrations leading up to the actual Global Ranking's Ceremony, which was months away. Maybe that was why he didn't hype this. Maybe he knew there were plenty of others soon to come.

"Tick tock, agree to assist or face the lock." Chanelle pointed to the attendant at the entry we stepped closer toward. "*Then you'll get no cock.*"

"I hate you more than words can express." I released a breathy sigh.

"I thought it was rather whimsical." Chanelle continued rhyming crude words in her mind. "Everyone's a critic."

"What do you want?"

"I'm running the Wisp Prevention Program," Chanelle said, prattling on about the volunteer program like I didn't already understand every detail.

As far as favors went, this was something I'd gladly sacrifice a few evenings for, considering it'd allow me more time to help the students who'd signed up with their magics and hopefully improve their scores before the Spring Showcase rankings were issued.

"Consider me at your service."

"Oh, please lead with that when you see Milo tonight."

I rolled my eyes as Chanelle flashed her embroidered ticket that the attendant cross-checked with an enchantment before allowing us to pass. The hallway leading to the event was well-lit, with doors blocked off and people trickling through on their way inside. My stomach dropped once we walked into the ballroom. I'd attended dozens of these events at Cerberus, among other guilds in the city, but they rarely brought out their best when hosting academy staff or meet and greets for potential student interns. Everyone was dressed so finely, even Chanelle barely looked the part. I tugged at my loose tie, hoping to cover the stain on my wrinkled dress shirt. I should've grabbed a blazer. Bought one before coming. What was I thinking?

"Good luck, lover boy." Chanelle winked. "If you don't manage to pry Evergreen from his adoring audience, you can circle back and find me."

"You're leaving me already?" A tremble nearly creaked from my throat. These types of parties were aggravating, but they didn't make me anxious. Not like this. Why was I here?

"Aw. You miss me already. But there are some lovely enchanters I need to felicitate." Chanelle rubbed my shoulder, her confidence in conversation lingered in my thoughts, and I leapt at it to compose myself. Perhaps her way to assist me or pass along some flirty pursuit she intended on ditching me for. Either way, I held onto that confidence while exploring the ballroom.

The lighting stung my eyes; between the sparkling glasses and shimmering outfits, there wasn't relief in any direction. Making my way through the crowd, it didn't take long to find Milo. He stood next to Enchanter Campbell at the edge of the ballroom floor, facing away from me. This place was so vast, swimming with countless thoughts, and a part of me was desperate to throw myself into someone's mind to escape my own apprehension.

"I can't believe Cerberus threw together this premature celebration when they should be prioritizing resources toward the growing demonic energy striking the city."

I shook away the guest's annoyance for Enchanter Evergreen. Well, secondhand annoyance that was actually disgust for lavish events, a sentiment I understood. Still, they were a day late on the news since Milo had already dealt with the surge in demonic energy during our not-so-successful art district date. He'd eradicated all traces of that horde.

Others in attendance fawned over Milo, making me realize no matter how anxious I was to be here, I needed to be here in my own head—not theirs. I inched closer to Milo and Campbell, eyeing the dancefloor no one used. Guests casually walked across it, but no one joined in while the band played a mellow instrumental tune. Still, many minds were eager for when the event would kick off.

I cleared my throat, hesitating when Milo turned. This was probably a mistake. His bright blue eyes noticed a cater waiter's tray tilting ever so as he weaved past a guest who'd flung their arm while gesturing. He caught the tray, smiled, and grabbed a champagne flute to hand to Enchanter Campbell.

"I suppose I have you to thank for the lovely rumors about our rekindled love story." Milo's half expression from his turned face didn't carry an ounce of concern or annoyance, but I'd always seen deeper than what he revealed to the world. *"Not exactly the detour I want to take for her success or my happiness, but it's an easy enough roadblock. Maybe. Just have to steer this in the right direction, which I wish would present itself."*

"It's your own fault for having a winning personality." Enchanter Campbell sipped her glass of champagne. "If it costs you a few casual one nights, oh well."

"Ouch." Milo chuckled. "Is that really all you think I do these days?"

"I haven't seen someone serious on your arm in almost three years,"

Enchanter Campbell said. "You tell me, Mr. Annoyingly Dashing."

I grabbed a champagne flute off a passing tray and gulped in unison with Enchanter Campbell, struggling to work up the nerve to interrupt their conversation. This was a bad idea. I shouldn't be here. Shouldn't be crashing Milo's event because of some impulsive feeling. This was his night and should stay that way. If anything, I should leave, talk to him tomorrow and explain in a proper adult way how I wanted to invest in a more public and committed relationship. My face burned.

"I've had serious relationships since you," Milo said. "More serious, in fact."

"Of course. Look, just go with it. The board thinks I'm too rigid," Enchanter Campbell said. "Me."

"Impossible." Milo didn't even attempt to hide his sass.

"Shut up," Campbell continued. "Overthrowing a capitalist pig who uses his wealth to monopolize guilds and run illegal operations isn't enough to demonstrate leadership qualities. Apparently, I need to do all that with a pretty smile, an iron fist, and a dainty hand accompanied by someone more charming."

Enchanter Campbell referenced Tara's father, Tobias Whitlock. Between the news and Milo's occasional surface thoughts, I knew there was a real power struggle between his hold over many guilds while he fought off allegations, maintaining his stock holdings, authority, and ruthlessness.

"I can think of a hundred more charming men that'd look fantastic on your absolutely unrigid appearance," Milo said.

"Save the sarcasm. Had you left the whole operation to me instead of putting your narcissistic face all over, I might've swayed the board members into making me the permanent guild master. Instead, some are on the fence, believing you'd make a better fit."

"Yuck." Milo grabbed his own champagne flute and washed away the repulsed thought of him taking on a real leadership role. "I'd run Cerberus into the ground if someone gave me actual authority."

"That's what I said. Your off-the-books charitable cases already exceed your department's funding." She raised a hand to cut him off. "And save the

PR speech; your fan-fuck board members already said it all."

"I'm sorry."

I balled my fists. Milo was seriously debating her proposal, weighing pros and cons like it was a possible investment.

"It won't be so bad. After all, we weren't terrible together," Enchanter Campbell said. "And nothing's going to happen. Maybe a few lunches, a work dinner when the cameras are rolling. You're always better in front of an audience."

Anxiety consumed Milo. I waded through the slosh rolling off him and brushed past guests who walked between us. He searched for ways to decline Enchanter Campbell's proposition without offending or affecting potential futures. I couldn't glean what he saw, but he picked apart his next words very carefully as if one faulty phrase would topple over what he'd worked so hard for.

"How's Dorian going to handle this?"

I froze. All he cared about above any potential future was if accepting or rejecting this singular moment would affect me. If he declined, would I think he took things too seriously? If he accepted, would I be jilted? If he shared this with me like an anecdote, would I get angry? If he withheld it, would I be bitter?

Milo cared too much, and my crippling self-worth forced him to consider our relationship with more attention because he worried I didn't care for it enough to stay.

I did care. He wouldn't need to find the right words or reason. I didn't want to play games or consider anyone's future but ours.

The music sped up, and Enchanter Campbell extended a hand to invite him onto the dancefloor. "Well? Your thoughts?"

"I wish you the best of luck, Enchanter Campbell." I stepped forward, burying all my doubts. "Sounds like you've been dealt an incredibly unfair hand."

"Dorian." His smile wavered into a boyish grin, the same anxiously excited teen I'd met what felt like a lifetime ago. Shock filled his expression at my arrival. The witch who'd seen a million potential possibilities could still stand slack-jawed and stunned by possibilities he'd never dreamed of considering. His eyes watered joyfully as he allowed himself the briefest opportunity to question this outcome, curiously awaiting the words on my lips.

"You'll have to find someone else almost as charming because Enchanter Evergreen already has a date."

Milo was as concerned by what might follow as I was simply showing up, but his doubts didn't guide my steps toward him. His hope did. I wanted to cement those feelings, prove I could be a part of his world.

I grabbed Milo by the jacket and kissed him in front of everyone in the ballroom.

"Well, damn."   *"What's he wearing?"*

"Who's that with Enchanter Evergreen?"

"Go, Dorian. About time."   *"He's so…"*   *"Frumpy."*

"Isn't he that teacher that nearly let his students die?"

"Guess, if incompetent is your type."

"Suppose I'll find a different dance partner."

Silencing all their words, I synced to Milo's mind. He pressed his forehead against mine, grabbing me by the back of the waist and pulling me in closer. *"Are you sure you're ready for this, Dorian?"*

"I told you, I want to be with you and see what our future has in store." I gripped his biceps as he directed us out onto the dancefloor, which admittedly was the literal last place on the entire planet I wanted to be backed onto.

"It'll put you in a much different spotlight, and we both know how much you loathe the attention."

"For you…anything."

Chapter Six

WHAT had I done? Of course I couldn't make a grand gesture at the end of the party. No, I had to sit through the entirety of this ceremony and all the speakers, applauding Enchanter Evergreen before and after his speech, answering questions from curious guests, and navigating my way around others with far more intrusive thoughts than they vocalized.

Somehow, I survived the event, and when Milo dragged me out through the back doors, I gladly ran with him.

"I can't believe you did that." Milo kissed my neck, backstepping and guiding my every step. "I mean, I can. I saw it once, tucked within a dozen different outcomes to steps you were definitely going to take when we officially announced we were dating. You slapping a kiss on me in front of the entire Cerberus Guild was not a potential future I entertained, though."

"Don't tell me I've gone and ruined the happiest ever that ever aftered." I yanked his tie to slow his eager hands from working their way under my tucked shirt.

Milo quirked an eyebrow, stumped by my lightheartedness, and honestly, so was I. But embracing him and this decision, boldly declaring my love for Milo, Enchanter Evergreen, The Inevitable Future, in front of everyone had propelled me higher than any magic I possessed.

"I'd say we're still very on track," he said.

The slightest touch of his fingertips against my waist sent a flash of images. Everything he envisioned us doing right here and now. His surface thoughts painted his desires. In a matter of seconds, his channeled telekinesis would have me pinned against this wall. Milo would end up on his knees before I knew what to say.

My breath hitched, equally exhilarated and nervous. Countless images looped from our previous encounters. Every time he'd run his hand delicately along my back, when he'd wrapped his thighs around my hips—all these stirring memories carried our lust as Milo debated which sensation he sought to elicit. My back hit the wall, and I shivered. A primal vibration eager for what came next. But in my peripheral, the neon exit sign tempered my cravings.

"Not here." Two simple words that proved almost as challenging to say as it was to contain myself before slipping into a very public display of affection.

"I can guarantee no one will walk in." Milo licked his lips. "Most likely."

"Milo." I cupped my hand under his chin, keeping him from kneeling.

"Fine," he sighed. "Did you drive here?"

"Took the L."

"Perfect." Milo's minxy grin filled his face, and he snatched my arm, dragging me down the hallway.

Next thing I knew, he'd whisked me outside, and we were flying through the night sky faster than I could move on my best day. Milo didn't even need his arms for guidance, using the slightest twist of his ankles to take us back to my place. Pressed against him, my body warmed in anticipation, ignoring the frigid wind that whipped across my face.

It all blurred once we landed. Somehow, I unlocked the front door with Milo's hand down my pants. The keys had fallen somewhere. Didn't matter. Milo's lips were on my neck, kissing me, nibbling, while he walked me faster into the bedroom. The moment we stepped through the doorway, I lost my shirt and fell back onto the bed with my pants pulled to my knees while Milo unbuttoned his shirt. His tongue slid along my stomach as his fingers tugged at my waistband. There was an explosive urge to please me, gratify my every—

"Fuck me," Milo said, lifting his head.

He stood tall at the end of the bed, eyelashes fluttering ever so subtly.

"Didn't realize you were feeling that excited, but I'll gladly oblige." I sat forward, smirking and unfastening his pants.

"Huh? What? No." Milo sucked his teeth with an apologetic grimace. Every yearning desire he'd bombarded me with since my public announcement of our relationship poofed into thin air. "It's not the end of the world, just the end of someone else's."

I frowned, catching snippets of his trailing mind drifting toward puzzle pieced scenarios wrapped into some vision he'd just had. Whatever it was, he worried that without his immediate action, it'd cost someone something awful—a few someone's based on how his thoughts rifled through the core of his mind.

"Would I be the absolute worst if—"

"Yes, yes you would." I slipped to the edge of the bed and tugged on the loops of his pants, pulling him closer. "But that's why I love you."

I raised my head to meet his gaze. His eyes stared down, bright and glazed as he bit back a thousand immediate surface thoughts. It wasn't the first time I'd said I loved him. It wouldn't be the last time. But I struggled with the words so much. However, every time I spoke them aloud to Milo, they came a bit easier, and I loved that he made me feel that way. Yanking his tie, I pulled him closer for a soft kiss.

"Not to rush your valiant efforts, but if you hurry up, I might reward your heroics."

"Yes, sir," Milo growled.

And then he was out of my bedroom as quickly as he'd thrown me into it. I laid back and sighed. Tracing my fingers along the fabric of my boxers, I considered the probability of his return. Since he'd started spending more nights at my place, there weren't actually many when he'd stayed through the night. Always a new vision. An altered objective. A life in some type of need. Hell, once he bailed to literally rescue a kitten stuck in a tree. And sure, the little fella would go on to become some young witch's familiar, and the potential of good they'd do together was apparently great, but like…someone else could've done that.

That was the thing about Milo, though. He never wanted to gamble someone's future on a maybe if he had certainty on his side.

After sliding my boxers down and relieving a bit of my anticlimactic expectations for the evening, I dozed off. It was a restless slumber between the cycling thoughts of nearby minds and the constant buzz of my phone. Since the internal and external noises made lying in silence an impossibility, I dragged myself out of bed before the sun rose. I wobbled in the bathroom half-awake with a cigarette dangling from my dry lips.

The brightness of the phone stung, and the screen held a startling display. My jaw fell, and I dropped the cigarette into the toilet. The ember hissed, snuffed out. I skimmed through the 40+ notifications displayed on my phone. And there was a lot more flooding the app.

My pulse thrummed in my ear. My face was hot, and I panicked. The comments were mostly about Enchanter Evergreen, but it hadn't taken long for people to tag me, @AnnoyedObserver, in them.

Scrolling through the DMs made my skin crawl. Some of the half-displayed questions were as bold and intrusive as the thoughts I'd glimpsed at Milo's ceremony last night. I couldn't believe how many people had found me online considering I used a pseudonym across all platforms and rarely engaged with others. It was mostly curious musing or boredom when I hopped online. But damn, did they all care, and their opinions were strong.

> Alyce Lynn ✦ COMMS OPEN ♠
> @MagicPenGirl
>
> Not sure who Enchanter Evergreen's locking lips with buuuuut I am here for ALL the cuteness! Check out my WIP!!! 😍 🤩 🫣

She'd sketched a rather favorable animated version of Milo and I at the Cerberus event last night—though I could've lived without the artistic license to draw my leg bent and kicked back like some sixteen-year-old girl having her first kiss. Scrolling through the comments, most were curious eye emojis, compliments on Alyce's piece, or a jumbled scrambling of letters stringed together to convey exacerbated glee. I huffed.

It didn't take long to find the tags and added images of me. From my staff photos to candid yearbook pictures all the way to the occasional selfie I'd taken. Ugh. One person had even delightfully taken the time to highlight and draw attention to each and every flaw I possessed. My weak jawline. Eyes too close together. Stringy hair. Wrinkles. Yellow teeth. Crooked tooth. A thousand other assumptions. I exited the screen, unable and unwilling to glimpse any of the hundreds of other comments and threads and apps.

Fuck all this. I deleted every single app connecting me to the outside world from my phone. Social media. Gone. Local news. Gone. Weather—I already knew it would suck. Gone. I didn't know how Milo managed these hellscapes with ease, but I wouldn't be the hot topic of the day. Or if I was, I wasn't going to stick around for it.

Geez. If this was how people who didn't know me reacted, how was everyone at the academy going to act? The questions. The thoughts they would blurt out. Worse, the thoughts they wouldn't ask. All of it was so overwhelming I hovered over the sick app for work. It'd be so easy to take a day…

Nope. This would pass. Like anything, I just had to ignore it.

After showering away the exhaustion and frustration, I dried off and covered the bags under my eyes with eyeshadow. The broken blood vessels were so vibrant that I would've loved the look if my eyes weren't so wide and twitchy. I crinkled my forehead and finished my morning routine before flying to work.

A part of me wanted to text Milo, see what he was doing or how he was handling the barrage, but another part just wanted to get to work. Considering the lack of sleep, I should've driven—well, maybe taken the L—but Enchanter Evergreen wouldn't stop training from one restless night, and neither should I. Besides, the icy wind helped shock me awake.

The best part of flying high came from the strain it put on my telepathy.

Channeling my levitation and telekinesis root magics in tandem coupled with moving too fast to linger on passing minds. I soared with the rising sun at my back well above the highest buildings. A white sparkle flickered ahead. A small growing cluster of wisps tearing their way into our reality, and left unattended, they'd form into fiends. I maneuvered an arm, directing it to banish the wisps, but kept the other fixed on flight. The wisps burst into a glimmer of dust and I flew on.

"Info was right. He takes this route."

I twisted my body so I could scan for the voice without sending myself spiraling in a completely different trajectory. Not something I usually worried about when flying but damn was I tired. Flying to a destination wasn't an uncommon practice for those licensed, but I'd picked this route for three reasons: a quick way to work, enough wisps to practice my banishment and sensory without becoming overwhelmed, and fewer people. A small blip of a person grew as they flew closer, camera in hand, and thoughts all fixated on *"Enchanter Evergreen's new boyfriend."*

Scowling, I spun away before he could snap a shot of what he considered quite possibly the scariest expression and then nosedived until I reached the crowded city block. I whipped above people, slowing my descent until I reached the platform of a stopping train. I shoved my way into the car interior, cramming myself between people and grabbed a handrail. This wouldn't get me to work, but I could switch at the station or attempt a second flight without the press. The bustle of thoughts hitting me in waves made my skull pound. Thankfully, it appeared no one on the car knew or cared who I was.

Christ. What the hell had I gotten myself into?

When I arrived at Gemini Academy, my phone buzzed in my pocket. I ignored the vibration against my thigh. I rushed through the crowd of incoming students, well behind my preferred schedule, but the flurry of curious minds didn't make it easy to navigate the blurring hallway.

"There he is!" Peterson thought, standing at my door with a clipboard pressed against his chest. His eager mind was so loud it made my homeroom coven's surface thoughts faint by comparison. I rolled my eyes. Half of my students had arrived before I did and waited in the hallway next to Peterson.

He'd come with favors to request dancing along the surface of his mind yet couldn't be bothered to open the door for my students.

"You're late." Kenzo glared.

"I'm not late," I said, unlocking the door for my students. I simply wasn't early, so by comparison, I was late for me, but not actually late.

"Whatever." Kenzo stuffed his hands in his pockets and walked in after the others shuffled inside. ***"Better not make it a habit. Punctuality is the only thing he's got going for him."***

Ouch. Ignoring Kenzo, I reached for my thermos of coffee. I needed the caffeine and something to avoid responding to Peterson's incoming question. And of course, I'd forgotten to grab my coffee.

"Good morning, Mr. Frost." Peterson etched his way into the doorframe like he was ready to bodycheck me if I brushed past him. "I was hoping to have a word with you."

"I'm running a bit behind. Maybe later."

"It'll only take a moment, and I don't need a response this minute. I want you to think it over. Well, actually, I was hoping you could run it up the ole flagpole—not that flagpole." Peterson chuckled loudly, practically ready to nudge me to join in. He truly thought I'd enjoy the innuendo since, in his mind, we bantered quite frequently. We didn't. I simply overlooked or ignored his comments because he bored me to death. "Maybe you can get back to me when—"

"No." I kept my influxes indifferent and my frown more bland than irritated.

Peterson stared with bewilderment. "I haven't even asked."

"You were wondering if I could ask Enchanter Evergreen to come as a guest speaker for your homeroom."

"Of course, telepath. You're truly gifted, Mr. Frost. I bet you pick up on every little thought."

"Fewer than you think."

"Fascinating. Must be so fun getting that insight. About my request. Look, I just think it's something he'd be interested—"

"No."

"You haven't even let me ask." Peterson's face turned red, and his thoughts slipped in and out of half-formed profanities he quickly hummed away, paranoid it'd hurt his chances of convincing me to do something I had zero intent of doing. "I've got a proposal with different lessons Enchanter Evergreen could come by and discuss."

Peterson flipped through his clipboard, handing me things Milo would never do. Whenever we coaxed guild enchanters into coming to campus, we often did so in alignment to particular standards and professional practices they could offer. The great Enchanter Evergreen didn't do that. He improvised at every opportunity he had. Perhaps it was because he spent so much time rehearsing for potential visions to futures he attempted to keep on track.

"This all looks detailed." I clutched the papers Peterson handed me, keeping my gaze locked onto his, and he was so intent on nodding in agreement, he didn't register I hadn't looked at the forms. "You know who would love to see this? The administrator in charge of coordinating schedules with guest speakers who visit."

Although, admin had found a way to pawn that role onto Chanelle since she'd taken on her new liaison position. She might attempt to reach out to Milo with the paperwork. He'd say no in either case, but I wouldn't pretend to pass on Peterson's request.

"Here." I handed back the papers.

"Hold onto them. Maybe pass them along." Peterson smiled.

He knew as well as I did that this would make for a quicker and better possibility of having Enchanter Evergreen drop by. After all, when an academy inquired, they reached out to the guild itself, and they passed on the request to their enchanters when it suited whatever schedule they worked with. It was a tedious process, which was why I'd never personally relied on guest speakers unless they were new in the industry and clamoring for attention to build their names and brand. It was hard enough wrangling quality enchanters for internships.

But this wasn't about Peterson's students. If it were, I might've considered it. Nope. This was a way he planned on making himself look better.

"I've given you my answer. Twice, in fact." I dropped the papers Peterson refused to take back.

"*Oh, but he was fine bringing Enchanter Evergreen here for an absurd ceremony to show off his fucking homeroom coven.*" Peterson grumbled, kneeling to pick up his scattered forms. I ground my teeth and stifled a snarl. "*Being a shit teacher and letting warlocks in really—*"

I stepped into my classroom, quieting Peterson's pettiness, jealousy, frustration. It was the last thing I wanted in my head. The agenda in store for my homeroom coven was what I needed to prioritize. It involved something very close to home for what many of my students dealt with before winter break. My magic and my mind needed to remain sharp and ready to handle the emotions they'd face. The fallout, shock, fear, and hopefully perseveration.

More of my students filtered inside, each of them staring at my agitated expression and staying awkwardly silent like I somehow didn't realize what they had on their minds. Even their consideration was tiresome.

"*Maybe he'll bring Enchanter Evergreen for lessons.*"

"*Did they meet at my dad's gala?*"   "*I wonder…*"

"*His emotions have been cheerier. Well, cheery for him.*"

"*Tengo mil preguntas.*"   "*Did he…*"

"*If this turns into a fucking gab fest on his pathetic love life, I'll vomit.*"

"*He wasn't popular, but Mr. Frost was a professional enchanter, and he did work with Enchanter Evergreen during his time at Cerberus Guild. Maybe their paths crossed again because of the warlock incursion. It's clear Enchanter Evergreen was doing his best to protect our homeroom coven from something sinister. Even with so much veiled by that hex magic, he must've known the connection Theodore had to Tara and Kenny—from there, he connected to Mr. Frost and found a way to save our class. He's so amazing. I hope Mr. Frost brings him…*"

I glared at Caleb because I was too tired to quell my telepathy. His eyes widened, and his thoughts simmered momentarily before shifting to ramblings about whether I could still hear his thoughts and theories on how instantaneous thoughts were so he couldn't know if and when they'd formed, which transitioned into mutterings about how precise my telepathy was or wasn't, which he jotted into his notebook. It was irksome, but less so than his fanboying over Milo.

Gael strutted into the classroom, his rooster perched on his shoulder. Balling his fist, he raised it for a bump, and I cringed at the thoughts he was about to speak without a second of filtered hesitation.

"Look at you getting it, Mr. Frosty!" Gael blinked with a hint of innocent curiosity that almost hid his minxy grin. "Bet you clapped them ch—"

"Finish that sentence, thought, or even musing, and I'll fail you."

"*With that attitude, he's clearly not clapping anything.*" Gael pouted then scrunched his face when his rooster pecked his forehead until his mind swam with apologies.

Okay, King Clucks wasn't the worst familiar out there.

I walked to the front of the classroom as my students found their seats. Leaning against my desk, I crossed my arms, furrowed my brow, and gave them my most menacing expression until half of them straightened their posture out of sheer dread.

"I realize the news is out and some of you might have questions." I glanced around, my gaze meeting curious eyes, annoyed eyes, and bored eyes. "Don't ask them. Don't think them. The only thing any of you should be thinking about is your training because your rankings are at stake."

"*Don't think it. Don't think it. Don't think it.*"

"Cluck!"

Gael flinched, and the rest of the class laughed, their thoughts finally simmering and centered on the lesson at hand.

"Today, we're going to be working on banishing fiends."

Apprehension bubbled throughout the classroom.

"Is this real fiend training or that same bullshit you pulled on the first day?" Kenzo had a leg propped on his desk and his arms crossed, frowning.

"No bullshit," I said, frowning back at Kenzo who merely huffed in response.

Caleb bit back a gasp, by far the only one in the class shocked that I, his surly yet proper teacher, swore. It was perplexing to be on such a high pedestal in his mind where I lacked personality and was framed solely by his preconceived expectations. Both Gael's snickered, drawing my attention, and Katherine rolled her eyes so hard her thoughts smashed everyone's mild opinions. "*Maturity much?*"

Clearing my throat, I resumed the conversation.

"Every other first-year student proved they could banish fiends in the field to receive their fledgling permits. I'd say about half of you actually managed to banish a single fiend during the attack last semester."

I paused, giving those who needed a second to collect their thoughts, compose their nerves, and breathe out the bits of fear dwelling in them the time to do it. But I was unwilling to show sympathy. While they were cheered on for their successes, they'd be expected to meet the same goals as everyone else this semester.

"Everyone is waiting to see if you all lucked out last semester, or if you each have what it takes to be a professional enchanter." I waved a hand, whipping the door open. "Now tell me, are you ready to prove you belong here? Prove you belong in the Spring Showcase?"

CHAPTER SEVEN

WE'D RETURNED to the auxiliary gym many times since the warlock incursion; however, this was the first time I stood by the open arena that linked different terrains for training and recalled my near death so viscerally. My chest tightened. Images of my bloody pale body filled my head, and I wheezed in unison with my dying memory. Wet, red hands pressed to my exposed neck, funneling magic not meant to save a life. I ran my fingertips over my cheeks, making certain the teardrops of the memory weren't actually running down my face.

Carter stood beside me, trembling. This was his memory, too, his terror surfacing.

Name: Carter Howe
Branch: Rejuvenation (Vitality)

This memory haunted him, so much so he fixated on improving his branch this semester, fueled by a drive never to let anyone fall to harm, but Carter's root fundamentals floundered in the process. Among those who hadn't banished any fiends, he was at the top; I wanted to change that.

The idea of combat frightened Carter in a way it hadn't before the warlock's arrival. This could be a case where he was on the wrong pathway and the reality of the industry was too much for him. But I believed this was my fault, like throwing a toddler into a crashing river filled with alligators and wondering why they feared swimming. I wanted Carter's bravado to return. Of course, I'd immediately deflate it like I would with any student, but first, I needed to build him back up for success.

Jennifer stepped close to Carter. "We got this."

Her black hair covered her eyes but not the soft smile she gave him, something she rarely displayed with anyone else at the academy. She adjusted one of her spiked bracelets and kicked her steel-toe boots against the dirt.

```
Name: Jennifer Jung
Branch: Psychic (Empathic)
```

We weren't the same by a mile or a hundred, but I understood her style and perhaps a small inkling of her connection to Carter, since using her magic to soothe his nerves while the pair had saved my life.

"What?" Jennifer grimaced when she caught me eyeing her. "*Save the butterflies for someone who gives a shit.*"

And with that, all my sympathy vanished.

"Since you both look ready, you can start us off." I furrowed my brow and glared at Carter and Jennifer. "The objective's simple. Banish the fiends before they devour the wisps and attempt to ascend."

A few students tensed, hiding their trembles. I wouldn't be releasing enough wisps for any fiend to reach the level of power needed to create an actual demon. It was impossible to do with the academy systems in place, anyway. Still, they didn't know that, so when I pointed for Carter and Jennifer to go to the starting line leading to the rock terrain, they hesitated.

"*This must be part of the academy making preparations for the potential demon threats,*" Caleb thought, beaming his theories loudly. "*They're always ahead of things, and given the recent surge Enchanter Evergreen's been handling, it makes sense his boyfriend would...*"

Christ. Seriously, Caleb? I fought a scowl as he practically paraded toward Carter and Jennifer.

Why was everyone freaking out about demons? Chicago hadn't had an actual demon scare in over a decade.

I froze, and my mind reeled back to that threat, that devastation they caused. I took a breath, listening to the unsteady beat of my pulse in my eardrum, desperate for it to replace the buzzing thoughts of students. After a few shaky breaths, I reminded myself that Enchanter Evergreen, along with so many other enchanters, would never allow that kind of carnage again.

I composed myself, inadvertently glaring at Caleb. Considering he was such a fanboy of Milo's, he should have paid more attention to the news. Milo already handled the fiend outbreak. It ruined our date, which in all honesty wasn't the worst outcome.

"This'll be awesome. We've totally got this," Caleb said, leading his coven mates ahead. *"I've handled real fiends and real warlocks. Time to remind everyone why I'm a real threat when it comes to the ranking challenge."*

"Actually, you're not going first," I said, burying a twinge of guilt for shattering the excitement booming from him. This kid always got to me—his belief, his curiosity, his hope for everyone. But this wasn't last semester. His life wasn't at risk, his future wasn't in question. I frowned. "I'm changing up your teams."

Caleb sighed as he returned to our group, and Carter and Jennifer sulked their way toward the starting line.

Each of my students had adapted well to their particular group the first semester, more so when their lives were at stake; however, part of the ranking system was determined by a witch's ability to collaborate with any coven combination. If I wanted them to be the best of the best, if they sought to eventually partner with witches in any guild for any possible job, they had to learn how to seamlessly work with all the members of their homeroom.

This was one of the biggest challenges I had at Gemini. My telepathy should've made it the easiest of lessons, but my instructor knew then how reliant I'd become on Finn and Milo's minds and magics. Like all the things in my life, it was a lesson that involved a lot of falling headfirst. I'd prepare these kids, even if they nosedived this semester.

"Jamius, Yaritza, go join your team for today's practice."

"We're going first?" Jamius squeaked, turtling his neck into his blazer with his shoulders raised high.

"That's what he said!" Yaritza squealed, delighted and attempting to drag Jamius along. "Come on! We got this!"

Jamius puffed his cheeks, producing three copies that pushed him ahead to join his eager teammate.

```
Name: Jamius Watson
Branch: Alteration (Duplication)
```

I'd paired those two with Jennifer and Carter because they'd encountered fiends, yet neither used their banishment that day, relying instead on their skilled branch magic control and leaving the fundamentals to Tara.

"I'm gonna obliterate those fiends with explosions!" Yaritza twirled in the air, levitating above everyone and releasing flaming pebbles.

```
Name: Yaritza Vargas
Branch: Cosmic (Star Shower)
```

They cascaded across the arena, forcing her classmates to weave around them. A pebble struck Gael's sandal.

"*Caliente.*" He swatted the strap around his spikes.

Kenzo rolled his eyes, observing as Gael made the fire worse. I channeled telekinesis around the edges of the flames, preparing to lift the magic entirely. Gray static circled the flames nullifying the magic, including mine, until all that remained was a tiny, cooled pebble melted onto his sandal.

"Thanks." Gael's sharklike teeth filled his happy face.

"Whatever." Kenzo huffed.

I groaned because while Kenzo had handled that problem with a quick disruption, I didn't focus my attention where it should've been. Another flaming pebble had hit one of Jamius' copies square in the head, knocking him onto the ground.

"I'm on it," a second Jamius copy on the left shouted, rushing to resuscitate his fallen ally.

"No, I'm the one trained in first aid." The third copy shoved the second and began examining the faint welt on the fallen copy's forehead. The struck copy sat up, rubbing his head. The third copy grabbed the injured copy's shoulders and shook him furiously. "Don't die on me. You've got such a long life ahead of you. Easily twenty to thirty more minutes. Think about your family. Think about your friends. Think about your future, man."

"Shut up." The fallen copy smacked the not-so-helpful duplicate.

And they began rolling on the ground in an argument that washed away any anxiety my homeroom coven had from the barrage of miniature comets and created a kerfuffle of laughter. So irritating.

Jamius' copies were a lot more outgoing than him, hiding his insecurities because in a matter of moments, they'd cease to exist, and he'd be the only one left to endure whatever embarrassment he felt from their extroverted presence. A tradeoff to get out of his shell that never seemed to work since the original refused to make the same efforts his copies did. To a degree, I understood that struggle, considering my psychic manifestations. Frustrating duplicates who believed they knew best but in reality, they didn't have to live with the consequences of their thoughts, actions, or impulses.

Speaking of impulses… Yaritza faked concern, barely hiding her smile behind her knuckles covering her face. "Oops. Guess I'm too flashy for some of y'all."

"If you're participating in this training, it'll be without your branch."

"What?" Yaritza descended to the ground, stunned. "But how am I—"

"You need to show me you can handle a fiend without the razzle, dazzle, and explosives."

"*It's not razzle dazzle.*" Yaritza crossed her arms. "*It's majestic fireworks of fame and glory.*"

"This ought to be good." Layla nudged Melanie in the ribs. "Looks like Mr. Frost picked a team of duds so we could learn from their screw ups."

"At least Yaritza did something against the fiends. Jamius just played decoy the entire time." Melanie snickered. "And Carter and Jennifer just…"

I glared at her, and Melanie gulped, lowering her head and hiding behind her red curls.

"She only managed to be that efficient because she was teamed with Tara, who's awesome," Layla continued, ignoring my gaze. "If she'd gotten stuck with asshat over there"—Layla nodded at Kenzo—"he would've killed her for her annoying nonsense."

"Maybe you two should talk less about your classmates," I said. "If I recall, your only involvement with fiends was running for your lives."

"Yeah, but that one was super huge," Layla snapped.

"That's what she said!" Gael shouted.

"Cluck." The damn rooster fluttered.

Layla rolled her eyes, hairs prickly across her face in frustration before shifting her eyes back to me. "You barely banished it."

"I was half dead. What's your excuse?"

Layla snarled, and hairs on her face sprouted further, but she shook away the shift and remained in her tiny human form.

```
Name: Layla Smythe
Branch: Bestial (Therianthropy)
```

"*That's why I didn't change up our coven setups,*" Caleb thought, reaching for his notebook. "*We already had a solid base for each other's magics. Plus, Kenny definitely wasn't about to work with anyone else, and Tara needed Gael's support. Still not sure why she holds back so much with her branches. We've been working on the overlap for weeks. Hopefully she'll share a bit today.*"

Caleb glanced at the team I'd assembled to go first, jotting notes and theorizing their compatibility based on hunches he had for my choice in partnering them together.

I had chosen this team specifically because of their lack of fiend involvement. Jennifer had the best sensory in the group but had yet to encounter a fiend; Carter possessed the strongest banishment yet fixated on his vitality since my incident; Jamius and Yaritza each needed to prove their root magics were more than add-ons to their powerful branch magics. But his thoughts created a valid point.

"Actually, Melanie, why don't you change places with Yaritza?" I waved a hand calling Yaritza over. "You'll have to wait a bit."

"Oh, man. I so wanted to show off. Everyone always remembers the opening act." Yaritza skipped back to her classmates with a pep in her step and a smile on her face. "*Thank God. I was so not ready to make a total idiot out of myself going first without using my branch.*"

"I got this." Melanie flicked her zippo.

"You're also required to prioritize your roots today."

Melanie stuffed the lighter back into her pocket.

```
Name: Melanie Dawson
Branch: Primal (Fire)
```

"That doesn't mean you're not allowed to use your branches, but branch magic doesn't remove demonic energy," I explained. "Remember, only your sensory root can track it, and only your banishment root can expel it entirely. I'd like to see each of you locate at least one fiend and banish it today. How you four choose to go about that is entirely up to you."

The first team took their places, eyeing the timer and nervous they'd fail the objective. I escorted the rest of my students to the proctoring room. My phone buzzed, but I ignored it. Whatever app I'd missed this morning, notifying me what a terrible match I was for the great Enchanter Evergreen, would have to wait. I had to prioritize my students' lesson.

In the corner of my eye, Caleb used enchanted weighted blocks to practice his root magics. Four sides of the cube were covered in sigils meant to absorb root magic casting while the final two sides radiated false demonic energy.

These etchings allowed Caleb to pinpoint the blocks with sensory while hitting it with subtle blasts of banishment. He kept them afloat using telekinesis, juggling them overhead. In this small way, he continuously practiced three of his four roots in tandem. Sweat drenched his forehead, and his legs quaked. Impressive. Upon a closer look, his feet remained flat but a full inch above the floor. He maintained constant levitation, too. This was a reminder of a conversation we'd need to have about the ranking system for the Spring Showcase—one he'd struggle to take part in given he lacked a branch.

But Caleb continued training his roots, not allowing his lack of a branch deter him, so I'd make sure to help him open as many doors as possible. Even those that remained firmly sealed in favor of flashy branches like this Spring Showcase. For now, I sat on that uncomfortable conversation and focused on the four students facing fiends for the first time.

Carter and Jennifer stayed close together while Jamius led the group, surrounded by a dozen copies. That'd end badly. I'd come to realize his roots struggled enough as is, but the more duplicates he created, the more his fundamentals waned.

I opened the upper vents, releasing wisps around the forest terrain, which would force their team to move quickly. Four small fiends scurried between the thicket of trees, clawing at each other. They fought over the small amount of glowing white orbs. A fiend lunged high, snapping its jaws around a wisp. The energy popped between its yellow fangs, and the fiend's tarlike back shuddered as it slicked its thirst for magic. It wasn't satiated long, sniffing out more wisps to feed its hunger.

With the team more hesitant than anticipated, I opened another vent with the push of a button and dropped wisps around the four of them. Jamius whisked them away with telekinesis, aware this would lead the fiends I'd unleashed upon them. I'd gone with four fiends, only intending to release another if someone in their group managed to eliminate two. At this group's rate, I wouldn't have to worry about that.

Carter sucked in a tense breath and banished three wisps circling one of Jamius' copies.

"Hey," the copy said. "I had that."

"No." A second copy nudged the first. "I did."

"Teamwork, guys," Jamius said.

It was easy to tell the difference between the original and his copies. Sure, they were completely identical, from their deep brown complexion to their short tight twists with the same three slightly longer strands that hung down as bangs along the left side of their faces. Each of them used all the same gestures while wearing their oversized academy jacket with the sleeves rolled up. Their goofy expressions of shock or confusion were on point too, but the copies smirked, whereas when Jamius smiled, it was genuine and framed his face. And he rarely smiled when others were looking.

If that weren't enough of an indication, I'd learned something from when Caleb used a spell version of Jamius' branch magic—copies lacked depth in thought. Sure, they had surface thoughts, and some of Jamius' copies had a wide range of interests well beyond what popped up in his thoughts. But that was all they possessed. There were no deep inner workings to their minds I could delve into if I wanted. Jamius had a well of insecurities surrounding the core of his thoughts, one he worked to fill with thoughts collected by copies he retained and wished to explore someday.

The first fiend darted out of the forest terrain, lapping up the trail of glowing wisps with its elongated tongue. Each tiny wisp it devoured increased the fiends speed and heightened its senses. It didn't take long to sniff out the four trembling witch appetizers.

"I've got this." Melanie flicked her zippo, creating a small flame and allowing it to swell between her palms. Once it'd grown large enough to shield her body, she propelled it forward. Melanie's control was outstanding; the massive blaze weaved between all the Jamius' and struck the fiend.

Tar splattered and burned, but the fiery assault simmered. The fiend gnawed on the flames, and its broken off burnt flesh, quickly regenerating itself and growing larger. Melanie's branch was effectively useless in this situation since she had to funnel her magic into the fire to control it. The flames themselves were deadly to the fiend, but the magic inside fed it. Unlike a primal witch who conjured flames, the magic to control them was much easier for the fiend to digest.

Melanie quelled her control, petrified and unable to decide her next move. Watching the fiend devour her magic rattled her. She'd grown paranoid that if her banishment was off by even a fraction, the fiend would devour that magic too. But it was one of the few lessons she'd paid full attention to in class—she knew better, yet everything she'd learned about root fundamentals went out the window.

My phone buzzed again. Frustrated, I silenced it without looking.

The reason root magics were effective against demonic energy was because demons couldn't feed off it. She knew this. I could see it bubbling beneath her terror as she looked to her teammates for assistance. As expected, the group hadn't gone in with a strategy and now scrambled to eliminate the fiend by waiting for someone else to handle it.

Jamius sent his copies headfirst, buying the group time.

"Charge!" the copy leader shouted.

The fiend lunged, and the copy's head burst into watery nothingness. *Ugh.* This was painful to watch. Jennifer fixated on Carter's trepidation, swirling in self-doubt cast by him. Instead of using his powerful banishment root, Carter channeled his vitality so Jamius and Melanie could cast again. This was a major problem.

The other three fiends were working their way closer to my students, and I'd hoped this exercise would remind Carter what he had to rely on—his strongest root.

Jennifer had encouraged him so much when my life was on the line, yet now she'd lost that composure.

This was my fault, coddling these two in particular once we'd returned from winter break. I let them lie in their feelings just a bit longer, believing it was best. They didn't need a cheerleader telling them they'd do better next time—at least not one like myself who lacked the rah-rah enthusiasm. They needed a stern prick who'd push them on the right path.

Linking my mind to theirs, I called out. "*You're both being too reliant on your branches.*"

"Mr. Frost?" Carter asked, eyeing his surroundings.

The students in the proctoring room stared, confused and uncertain what was going on with Carter.

"He's fucking lost it. They all have."

Quelling Kenzo's mind and the strategy he'd started weaving together for them, I returned to Jennifer and Carter.

"*I said branches weren't off the board, but you each have powerful control over your roots. Utilize that.*"

"*I suck with my roots,*" Jennifer thought. "*The only one I'm half decent with is—*"

She clapped her hands together, casting sensory around them, and pinpointed the incoming fiends.

"Jamius," Jennifer pointed to the few remaining wisps, "throw them this way."

Jamius scrunched his face as his final copy splattered into watery goop between the fiend's jaw. It used its sticky tongue to lap at the magic soaking into the ground. Ignoring his nerves, Jamius swept the wisps further out, scattering them. It was invigorating and gave him the confidence to banish a few as well. That rejuvenating boost came from Carter's vitality.

"Wait," Jennifer said, a plan in play.

Another fiend leapt from the trees into the rock terrain, chasing the remaining wisps that bobbed about. Carter pieced together Jennifer's plan and cast banishment toward the first fiend that'd arrived. It'd grown strong off Melanie's flame control and Jamius' copies. Despite all his precision in the root magic, only bits of tar shattered to nothingness. Taking a deep breath, Carter unraveled the tether of vitality he'd linked to his teammates and channeled everything into his banishment.

I smiled. It was sloppy, but he'd destroyed the fiend, leaving only a handful of white wisps. Jamius and Melanie handled them.

"Wait," Jennifer said again, prepared for the last two fiends to arrive.

Fighting over the remnants of the first fallen fiend, the pair was distracted, and Jennifer explained her plan to her coven mates. It was far from perfect—messy as fuck, in fact—but the four of them managed to group together, and each of them banished a fiend.

After they'd finished, I called them up to the proctoring room. I wanted to congratulate them all, convey how impressed I was, but their kinder classmates had that covered with cheery compliments.

"You went into this all wrong but managed to pull together a half decent strategy in the end. That was very impressive." I eyed them as they lined up by the door. "Which of you would like to explain areas for improvement? I have quite a few in mind."

Carter stood taller than the rest of his team, more slender and lacking the confident pose I'd grown used to. His blond bangs were damp with sweat, and his tight smile didn't hide the anxiety he avoided dwelling on in close proximity to me. Gripping the back of his neck with a shaky hand, partly from nerves but mostly from how much magic he'd exerted, Carter led the discussion on areas of improvement. That in itself was proof of growth—he'd not only learned mid-task how to alter where he'd gone wrong and fix it, but he'd acknowledged it.

After each of them reflected, I checked my watch.

"Let's take a break and resume this in the afternoon class. It's almost time for first block."

"They get the whole day to prepare?" Melanie pouted. "Figures."

"Really such a shame." Yaritza flipped her hair, walking past Melanie. "I'm jealous. Would've loved to show off my magics this morning, especially considering my stars don't burn out."

Melanie ground her teeth.

"Time's short," I said, "but if you're that eager, I'm sure I can whip up a solo round for you."

"NO." Yaritza grinned, her cheeks twitching from the forced enthusiasm. "I can wait. Working on my patience and all. Sort of becoming my best virtue, out of so many others. I really just, you know, um, know how much this lesson is about teamwork, and I want to have teamwork. Solo is so selfish. And I'm not shellfish; I'm a star. Get it?"

"Rambles, you're in my way." Kenzo shooed Yaritza who blocked the door.

I shook my head at her flimsy excuse and allowed her and the other students to wander out of the proctoring room, making use of what time we had left to their own desires. Reaching for my phone, I paused.

Caleb's concerns over the ranking system spiked. Whether as a way to avoid checking the barrage of the notifications on my phone, reminding me of all the ways I didn't fit into Enchanter Evergreen's world, or guilt for how difficult it'd be for Caleb moving forward, I went to have a discussion neither of us wanted. Explaining this would burst all the enthusiasm he'd carried in his growth since arriving at Gemini Academy.

"I know you were curious, perhaps even a little concerned, about the Spring Showcase." I stepped outside the proctoring room, joining Caleb who lingered close to the door, jotting notes.

"Not concerned." Caleb stopped writing and twisted his wrist, staring at his Cast-8-Watch. "I just want to make sure I'm practicing the right things."

"There's no wrong practice, it's all going to help prepare you for licensing and graduation, but those are far off goals, and you want to prioritize this goal. I understand." I cleared my throat. "I'd planned on covering this in the afternoon, but since you're curious, I can give you a bit of a heads up."

Caleb brimmed with anticipation, and it'd all be deflated the second he learned no amount of training would help because the ranking system was practically set up to ensure his failure.

"The rankings will fall into six separate categories," I explained, and as the words spilled out, Caleb's mind raced to write them in the most logical way he'd comprehend.

Collaboration 10%	**Physical Endurance 20%**
Academics 10%	**Root Proficiency 20%**
Aptitude 10%	**Branch Proficiency 30%**

"Wait. If branches are thirty percent, does that mean…" Caleb bit his lip.

"It means you're already starting off with a major deduction." It was something I'd tried to fight when administration presented their ranking system for the Spring Showcase. Prospective guilds wanted to observe our students' branch magics, which was logical, but no case I presented offered a better alternative.

They'd refused grading him with a different category breakdown because that'd make things too complicated, and soon, every kid would want their own special grading system. They'd rejected my proposal to have his root proficiency calculated times two in place of his missing branch proficiency; it'd still ensure a ten percent deduction even if he managed a full twenty percent on his root proficiency. They rejected any alternative I concocted because, again, it simply wasn't fair to others.

I didn't even suggest giving him the points outright, but Peterson had offhandedly brought it up as if that was my next option. *"Next thing, you'll just want to give him full credit because it's unfair he doesn't have a branch."* Peterson's words were grating in my thoughts. *"But tell me, how is that fair to students born with difficult branches they actually have to master?"*

There was nothing I could do to change the circumstances facing Caleb in this ranking system. It was designed against him, and now, he had full clarity of that.

Caleb's mind swirled with doubt, casting tidal waves which would consume his spirit in an instant. I fought for the right words, any words of encouragement, but truthfully, nothing I had to say would lift him from that ocean of despair. He needed time to absorb the shock, and then we could talk.

"If I'm already out thirty percent, then that means I need one hundred percent in every other category. No. One-hundred and ten percent in every category." Caleb looked up at me. "Does extra credit count?"

"Not particularly, but everything you do in and outside of the academy is evaluated by your Cast-8-Watch, so it can't hurt."

Caleb beamed. Unlike Tara, unlike me, unlike any person I'd ever met, he swam against the current of his own self-doubt, defying the sea of sorrow the moment he was plunged into the depths. Determination burned inside his thoughts until all the sadness evaporated.

"You're pretty optimistic."

"I'm not optimistic; I'm determined. Maybe arrogant, slightly, but there's a difference. I hope. I realize the hand I've been dealt, and I understand no one's going to change the system on my account. But I know I'm capable of succeeding despite it. If they want to start me in the negative because I lack a branch, fine. I'll succeed inside the system, and when I do, maybe I'll change it so other branchless witches don't have to scrape by so hard. You know?"

I nodded, soaking in Caleb's confidence that radiated throughout the auxiliary gym in a hue of violet pride. Blinking away the colors, I eyed Jennifer. This array of colors was something she spotted with ease thanks to her empathy, but I rarely glimpsed the colorful spectrum of emotions unless I'd unraveled my telepathy all the way, like when releasing a manifestation.

Caleb walked away determined, and I ran my fingertips along the scar on my throat. Since that attack, my psychic branch had grown intensely. Perhaps it came before that. I spent so many years repressing my telepathy, it was hard to know how much of my branch I kept boxed away just to make it through the day.

Of all the students I'd helped over the years, delving deep within Caleb's mind to guide him away from death, delving into Kenzo's and Tara's too, unlocked something inside me. Since then, my telepathy amplified faster than I could keep up.

After having a discussion I'd dreaded, I felt a bit lighter, which had nothing to do with my haphazard delivery and entirely to do with Caleb's way of handling it. And if he could handle the academy of his dreams literally conspiring against his success to showcase others, I could handle a few offhanded comments about my relationship with Enchanter Evergreen.

I sighed. Whichever app I'd forgotten, I would read through the notifications and delete.

I pulled out my phone and smirked. I hadn't been the subject of more online chatter. Or, likely I had, but no missed apps, which was a win in my book.

Nope, the bombardment came from text messages. I rolled my eyes scrolling through a few casual "hellos" from folks I hadn't talked to in years— or ever—but then found a flurry of unread messages from Milo.

My heart thumped faster, and my cheeks warmed. Even before reading through the texts, I felt his concern synced to each inhale I took. He must've been nearby for work. The passion and care thrumming through the air was soothing, though, completely vanishing the annoying start to the day that work had practically washed away already.

Milo: I know today's been a lot. A LOTTA LOT.

> Sorry I didn't warn you about the reporter this morning.

> If it makes you feel better, they were never gonna run the picture.

> Not to worry. You're a press dodging master. I could use some tips!

There was a slight time difference between this flurry and the next batch of unread texts Milo hurled.

> I should've said something I know. But didn't see the possibility till mid job.

He was out late, probably most of the night. Maybe he'd gone home, but more likely, Milo had gone back to the guild and fallen asleep at the office, finishing paperwork or making sense of one of many other visions too early to sort.

> Milo: Not an excuse but it'll pass soon. The hype. Not your feelings about today.

> Those you can have however long you want.

I scrolled through all of Milo's self-conscious texts, emojis, gifs, and still saw floating bubbles by the time I'd reached the end. I quickly typed back, upset he'd been consumed by panic this morning. It was pleasantly strange, this thump in my heart, the idea he'd spent all day concerned about my feelings, but all I wanted in this second was to alleviate his nerves.

> Me: It's all good. I'm good. Fine. Really. Honestly, don't worry.

And I was. I hadn't kept track of the thoughts glomming onto me out of curiosity or the one's eager to pry for info since arriving at the auxiliary gym. Work was a wonderful distraction. I contemplated adding an emoji, something kind and smiley. Something that'd make my comment resonate. My phone buzzed. Too late.

> Milo: That's a lot of reassurance. You sure?

He followed his comment with a questioning gif. Something to show his humor and lightly address his concern. I bit back a chuckle.

> Me: I am. If you say it'll blow over soon, I believe you.

I added a kissy emoji. Gross. Removed. A heart? Tacky. Maybe a black one. No. Love eyes? Worse. I sucked my teeth, taking a deep breath and pushed all the outside voices rattling in the back of my mind like static noise. These damn teenagers were in my head and Milo didn't make it any easier liking these coded text conversations that were impossibly difficult to decipher.

The perk to work was it helped distract me from how openly dating the great Enchanter Evergreen had put my life under a microscope, and if he said it'd pass soon, I believed him. I trusted him even when I didn't believe him.

Damn clairvoyants, always playing some angle. Especially this one, determined to make the brightest future possible he could for everyone involved in his life. A future I was eager to get to as I wasted time sending silly texts back and forth like instruction didn't matter, work didn't exist, and the past was washed away. It was a calming few minutes.

CHAPTER EIGHT

MILO was right. It'd been a week, and the intrigue had fizzled out. Sure, people still stared, their surface thoughts teeming when they saw me walking down the hall, but overall, the excitement had faded. It helped Milo didn't indulge the press but remained candid during interviews. And sure, I'd chosen media blackout—which also massively helped—but it was important for work purposes to stay on top of current events, so I had to keep up on the news. I couldn't help it if I was a part of the events. Still, fuck all things social media related. Enchanter Evergreen could navigate that storm on his own.

With lunch wrapping up, I made my way outside for a quick smoke before my afternoon classes. I took a deep inhale, allowing the nicotine to ease my stress, which settled the tension of my magic as I sat in my car. The minds in the academy fizzled for a few puffs before bouncing back to start bubbling thoughts. Then something struck out at my telepathy—a seizing chokehold between me and the mind. I dropped my cigarette, gasping and coughing when this tether yanked at my chest, reeling my heart into an unsteady thrum.

I stomped the cigarette out, barely snuffing the ember that burned a tiny hole into my driver's seat floor mat. Fuck. Pressing a hand to my chest, I forced breaths that didn't help. Still, joy reeled me toward it. I blinked away my spotted vision of the parking lot until all that remained was Milo. What was happening?

I was completely and fully engulfed by everything rattling around his head, minus the redacted visions streaming between his musings. This made no sense. Yes, my magic had grown, and syncing to Milo intensified much like our relationship, but he was on the other side of the city. My telepathic range on its best day might reach a mile if I truly put in the effort, further if I broke off a manifestation. But I hadn't conjured a manifestation. Had I? No. All the same, despite the incredible distance, I could feel Milo's emotions, hear his thoughts, and see Milo's office alongside the staff parking lot like a dual screen.

Closing my eyes tightly, I let Milo's office envelop me as I processed this. Somehow, I'd linked to his mind, completely silencing the thousands of thoughts bustling between us. I hovered beside him, intangible and invisible, and glued to his thoughts by my psychic magic. Milo sat in his chair, hands gripped against the leather, staring at a newspaper slapped atop his desk.

VAMPIRE STRIKES A SECOND TIME!

"Definitely not a vampire." Milo smirked. "It's never a vampire."

"I don't care if it's a goddamn warlock with a kink. Word of a demon in the city isn't what anyone wants right now." Enchanter Campbell jabbed a finger against the article, crinkling the page.

"When would someone want a demon in the city? Asking for research purposes."

"I want you to get rid of the demon."

"Which one?"

Enchanter Campbell's jaw clenched, a familiar sight for Milo because it was the only giveaway when something stunned her. Despite his aloof commentary, she didn't feed into it, and after a single blink of Milo's eyes, Enchanter Campbell had shifted her expression to something neutral.

"I see you're aware of the demon or potentially others," she said. "When were you planning on sharing this information?"

"Nothing potential about it. There's some moving about," Milo said. "I planned on bringing it up when I had a plan. Honestly, I'm surprised you care."

"Why wouldn't I care?"

"Because they've all been warlocks. Well, except the latest, which explains the sudden interest." Images of blood and missing limbs flashed so instantaneously, I barely comprehended the horrors seen in photos he'd collected from the Chicago PD investigation.

I gagged at the sight, drawn back to the parking lot. The connection hadn't waned, merely my nerves shaking the telepathy into something staticky. My chest heated. Why hadn't Milo mentioned demons? Sure, he didn't talk about work or visions, but all things considered—a true demon threat was something he should've brought up. I dug my nails into the leather of my seat, trembling to keep this link between us because I needed to know.

"It has nothing to do with the latest victim being a witch. Warlock deaths alone makes this situation a priority to me," Enchanter Campbell said, her voice loud in Milo's ears and helping draw me back to his office.

"You almost sound like you care."

"Don't test me, Milo. We're on the precipice of change. Guilds aren't collaborating, licenses have never been this easy to gain or lose, and our warlock population has finally settled since arresting that doctor and Theodore Whitlock. If those labeled as warlocks start dying left and right, and we don't put a stop to it, what's to stop them from illegally casting again?"

"Fines. Prison. Bad reputations?" Milo asked sarcastically, though it concerned him too—the dangers unchecked demons could cause, the federal oversight if this investigation wasn't closed soon, and most of all, the lives ended.

"We rely heavily on rehabilitated warlocks to remain such. That happens best when guilds have a strong presence and offer security to all their citizens."

I scoffed, almost drawn away. She spoke like it was actual rehabilitation. They'd been labeled a warlock, penalized for it, and in most cases, would never be referred to as a witch again. This was their life now and forever. What guilds and governments *actually* relied on was the fear that punishments outweighed the desire for illegal activities.

"I'm on it. No need to worry yourself about another guild swooping in," Milo said. "I'll be following up on a lead soon. Just looking for the right team to assemble."

"I'll have one for you by the end of the day."

"No, you won't." Milo propped his legs on the desk. "I'm not letting your stress over a position cost someone a limb or life. Or both in the cases so far. There's a lot I can't fix about this situation, and I empathize with the pain any death these demons cause. That said, I'm not concerned about you saving face with the board."

He was, though. It circled his thoughts, ensuring the path he chose didn't harm Enchanter Campbell. There was a faith he had in her leadership I didn't grasp. Perhaps it made more sense wrapped into the visions guarded by his magic or the memories he held for her. That didn't stop him from challenging her gaze with a wicked smirk. Just like me, she read his motives poorly. Whenever I thought he'd pivot left, he'd zigzag right. If I believed he had a plan in store, it'd be an improvised agenda.

Milo's mind was a hive of endless directions, the bees in his head all working toward the collective good he wanted for everyone. It unraveled in different layers that I often didn't see from him when we were together outside of work. Somewhere tucked away, he had a switch he knew to flip once off the clock. Even if he never truly clocked out, Milo kept his sanity by creating those barriers.

He'd accomplished what I'd never achieved, a separation between work and home, an understanding that while the world sometimes weighed down on him, he had to take a breath to enjoy the simple things. Everything out of his control would still be there, and if it shattered, he'd gladly sweep it up and put it back together.

The academy bell chimed. *Shit.*

I blinked away the link to Milo, rushing out of my car and through the hallways leading to my classroom.

I'd reached my door, where a few students stood outside waiting for history class right as the late bell rang. Gael coughed, gagging absurdly loud when he caught a whiff of the smoke wafting off my long-sleeved black shirt.

To add injury on top of annoyance, the damn rooster joined in, clucking and coughing in an ear-bleeding pitch that was tenfold worse than any of his morning crows.

I wanted to return to Milo, figure out what he had planned, learn of the dangers these demons posed to the city, but I had to prioritize work.

"*They're so dramatic.*" Tara held her stack of books high, covering the faint smile she struggled to share around others and watching Gael and his familiar pretend to choke to death on secondhand smoke. Every time I saw Tara, she had more reading material from books detailing magical overlaps to insight highlighting things about the world she didn't have experience with, all the way to fun fiction meant to offer a brief distraction.

I enjoyed when her thoughts reached far above the depths of her ocean of sorrow. It wasn't something she'd escape soon, maybe not ever, but I was glad she'd found ways to come up for air every now and then.

"*What's with Mr. Frost's face?*" Tara raised her eyebrows. "You okay?"

I frowned, covering up whatever contorted version of a smile my face tried making. "Just realizing only one of you did the reading for today's lesson."

Glaring at them, I unlocked the door so my class could enter.

"Bawk." King Clucks' red comb jiggled as he nodded at Tara.

"*Snitch.*" Gael strutted into the room.

"Cl-cluck."

I set up my laptop and projected our lesson for the day. What a fucking ironic twist of fate.

DEMONIC ENERGY & DANGERS TO ASCENSION

Maybe that was why my mind linked to Milo's. I'd been focused on the history unit of demonology all week, and now Milo's case had… No. My magic didn't have this type of range.

"Last class, we were discussing the importance of separating guilds and government. Can anyone remind me why it's important to keep these two separated?" I asked in my casual recap tone like I'd suddenly forgotten the information. Of course, today, I actually had gone completely blank on the lesson plan.

A room full of hands rose, and I contemplated calling on someone from Chanelle's homeroom coven, along with a few other teachers. Last semester, I was so fixated on the void vision, I'd barely forged connections with my homeroom students, let alone any of the other students in my History classes. I couldn't keep allowing myself to flounder that way, even if Milo's mind whispered from afar, encouraging me to reach out…

"*Is he **fucking** blind?*" Jamie snapped the fingers of his raised hand, drawing my attention.

He was a student in Chanelle's homeroom, one who screamed a furious strategy above others in this classroom. Despite the rage, he remained decisive and brutal in the most unpalatable sense for the sake of cutting someone he didn't know down through some arbitrary social politics he'd conceived.

```
Name: Jamie Novak
Branch: Arcane (Whirlpool)
```

I buried his practiced speech on recapping the lesson and tying it into a jab directed toward Tara. He was worse than Kenzo in that respect because Kenzo's fury was directed as an aversion to his internal strife and suffering. As misguided as he was, he was young and willing to learn from it—he just needed a better teacher. Jamie, however, was fueled by calculated rage that bordered the creases of the classroom, ready to devastate anyone in his wake for the sheer thrill of the takedown. It was methodic, coated in spikes.

I squinted hard at Jamie, ignoring his rehearsed speech and well-timed cuts, and pushing his bubbling thoughts down to a low simmer. He ground his teeth and I frowned, letting my gaze pass him entirely.

"*I had **my** hand up **first**.*" Jamie lacked consistent fury; his anger remained erratic, wedged into his feelings, almost like he forced it. A fabrication for the show. But it wasn't. These came from his inner surface thoughts so quickly he couldn't rehearse them. There was something about his mind that was fractured, spiteful, and hateful. All the same, he was a fucking headache.

I couldn't shield Tara or any of my students from every offhanded comment, but I could choose to ignore him and offer him no voice in this classroom. At least until I figured out where his hate stemmed. The Novaks were a powerful family, one likely affected by the rumblings and changes within guilds due to Whitlock Industries. Perhaps that was the source of Jamie's envy which coiled around him like a serpent of snark and wit and venom, ready to strike.

"Tara." I pointed.

She'd rarely contributed to class discussion despite having more knowledge and understanding of the industry than most of the staff here. There was an insecurity in raising awareness of her presence in front of an audience, something I believed she wished to work on since she'd raised her hand for the first time this semester. Okay, maybe that was my hope.

"*Of course he called on **her***." Jamie tsked.

"We talked about Sacramento v. Sirens and how before guilds were standard, demonic energy often led to fiends ascending," Tara said, her eyes glancing toward Jamie's sporadic clicks. "Their city was overrun, which bled into other parts of the state and resulted in the military responding." Tara paused. Jamie's eyes burrowed fervently, and his surface thoughts became pricklier and more profane. "And yes, the National Guard removed all the unwanted demonic presence but also left two-thirds of California under government guidance. Practicing permits were further restricted, casual casting misdemeanors were met with heavier penalties, and only those enlisted were deemed an adequate source of trained witches to handle these disruptions."

"I'm sorry, but"—Jamie raised a hand, interrupting—"I thought you asked for a recap, not a repeat of the last lesson."

"Jamie, please don't interrupt others."

"Sorry, Mr. Frost." Jamie frowned, but it didn't hide the smug glimmer of satisfaction in his eyes or thoughts. "Just feels like Tara doesn't understand simple instructions."

Tara clammed up, lowering her head and hiding behind her long blonde strands as a few students giggled at her expense.

"It's ironic you decided to contribute to this lesson of all lessons." Jamie locked his gaze on Tara. "You know, since the Whitlock's love mixing guild and government so long as there's a profit to be made."

Jamie's smile filled his whole face, and his trickling thoughts wandered about as he wondered which would be the deadliest and how many cutting comments he could contribute before being interrupted. Composing myself, I buried his envious hate and made sure he added nothing else.

"That's enough, Jamie." I cleared my throat, yet that alone didn't deter the questionable entertainment. Students were engrossed with his follow-up. Fine. I cracked my neck and silenced their surface thoughts. "Please continue with your recap, Tara." I glared at each snickering kid that remained hopeful to fit into whatever fucking bandwagon Jamie offered. "There are giddy individuals here that could use a repeat of our previous lesson. Perhaps even a repeat of the entire course since *many* in here haven't demonstrated a basic grasp on the history of magic, let alone guild industry standards of comprehension."

All the side chatter settled as thoughts shifted to quiet paranoia.

"That's really all I had to say." Tara adjusted her Cast-8-Watch, the very one monitoring how little she'd improved or used her three branch magics. *"Can't even fucking talk right. Can't do anything right."*

I shook away her ocean, turning my attention from the magics she struggled with. The same magics she didn't realize how much improvement she'd made in. Small, gradual growth so subtle it appeared nonexistent. But I'd delved deep into the recesses of her mind and knew all too well where she'd begun. I'd watched her and failed to help her first semester. Tara had improved, and I hoped to push that further second semester.

"Still struggling with your branches? Shocker," Jamie whispered, which did little given the acoustics of the room, my well-trained ears after years of teaching, and, of course, the fact kids were terrible at truly whispering.

I furrowed my brow, having had enough of Jamie's antics and liberal use of making my classroom his staging area to bully Tara.

"Well, they're a hell of a lot more complex than your dishwasher magic," Gael said, whooshing loudly to imitate the rush of water.

The class laughed at his well-timed joke, and Jamie sneered. King Clucks puffed his feathery chest, glaring back at the angry blond. I snapped my fingers to draw everyone's attention back to the lesson.

"Guilds are important because they allow counties, cities, and states all the freedom to enforce and defend themselves without national oversight. This also creates more avenues for licensing. Guilds help professionals establish careers outside of the industry by reinforcing independent licensing programs."

"Like what you do, Mr. Frosty," Gael chimed in, truly proud of his contribution.

"Correct." My response gave him enough satisfaction to leave out whatever offhanded comments bounced about his head. There were too many vague references and unfunny jokes to understand the mutterings of his mind. I continued, "If guilds and government didn't remain separate, then most licensed witches would be forced to follow and serve a military pathway under government rule if they wished to practice their magics. It is by no means a perfect system, but industry witches have a freedom in the jobs they take and perform, whereas those enlisted only retain a license at the government's discretion."

After the brief lecture, I walked around the classroom, grouping students for the reading, and then went to my desk. No one appeared in need of immediate assistance or redirection. Usually, I'd use this time to catch up on grading before moving around the room to check in on their progress, but my mind wandered. So I channeled my telepathy, wanting to reach out for Milo. Nothing.

I took a deep breath, quelling my roots entirely and sending every ounce of magic toward my telepathy. A cacophony of clustered thoughts invaded the link of my exposed branch that grabbed every internal conversation. I ground my teeth, quickly silencing the academy. Whatever part of my magic honed in and pinpointed Milo across the city had vanished. More pieces of my branch I hadn't fully mastered.

Unfortunately, that was an issue for another day. Right now, all I wanted to know about was this demon Enchanter Evergreen planned to track.

I reached out again, hopeful or desperate.

CHAPTER NINE

WORK was oddly silent, with my telepathy all but muted. It hadn't extended at my command, yet occasionally, it'd stretch far and thin like putty tugged too much, ready to break or collapse. Milo's mind buzzed like a staticky microphone off and on through the day, fading away before the words made concrete sense. Exhaustion weighed heavier thanks to the erratic change in my magic. Usually, a pinpointed precise connection to a single mind alleviated the bombardment of several dozen voices.

Milo ignored my texts even after I'd arrived home. Another insufferable thing I had to endure. He playfully avoided conversation in favor of work because he was unaware my telepathy had reached beyond its capabilities, eavesdropping. Between his entertained dodging and the subtle tug linking our minds, an intense headache drummed along my skull. I could call him out, bluntly explain I knew exactly what he was doing while I lay face down on the couch, my head buried in pillows.

But this was momentous. No, that made it sound positive. This was awful and needed a delicate, carefully phrased conversation in person. Also, I wasn't entirely sure what Enchanter Evergreen was doing. What Milo was doing. All I knew for certain was he had a demon case Enchanter Campbell quite literally slapped onto his desk.

Once I settled, nearly falling asleep, the link between us amplified and sent my mind hovering alongside Milo as a silent specter while he flew across the city. I couldn't make much sense of what he was doing, glimpsing flashes of his travels throughout the day as he ran through a mental checklist of places he'd gone, ensuring he hadn't forgotten something. Perhaps he was handling smaller cases or searching for leads; it was impossible to know since I couldn't filter out where my thoughts began or his ended.

This was why manifestations were a necessity when delving so deeply into someone's thoughts. They allowed me a powerful connection but a psychic valve I could close. This wasn't delving deep, though. Every time I glimpsed at Milo's actions, I was nothing more than a phantom hovering over his shoulder, catching snippets of his surface thoughts, glancing the colors of emotion radiating when powerful, and observing the silent hum of his visions when he sorted potential possibilities. Actually, this was very reminiscent of how my telepathy acted during my near-death last semester when it locked onto Caleb, Tara, and Kenzo during their battle against the warlocks.

Resisting or severing the tether linking our minds didn't work. The continuous loop made it impossible to create something tangible, like a manifestation, to serve as a psychic block or assistant. Unable to discern anything but the call to Milo's thoughts, I obeyed, melting into his mind until each breath we took synchronized.

Milo enveloped me.

Milo secured a basket he'd bought in the passenger seat of his Mercedes like he was fastening a toddler in its car seat. Okay—perhaps an exaggeration since he'd probably put it in the backseat on that account, but he checked the buckle three times over, shifting the bottle of wine so the neck sat snuggly under the belt strap. The contents inside the basket were impossible to read, given he'd covered them in frilly gift tissue papers, yet they filled him with glee. All he wanted now was to wrap up his evening and finally visit me.

I clutched a couch cushion, fumbling for the phone in my pocket, curious if he'd responded to any of my messages. It was easier following him, waiting for this job to reveal itself, and for him to arrive on his own afterward.

Milo hopped in the neon orange sports car. A true eyesore that only made him that much more noticeable, but he rarely took the time to enjoy the simple ride in his baby because as fast as this car went, Enchanter Evergreen flew faster and was less confined by traffic flow. Personally, as Milo zipped down roads, weaving between drivers and cutting corners to race against every yellow light he crossed, I considered his confidence in his flight speed a bit boastful. It hadn't taken long for him to reach the heart of downtown, where the best bars and clubs didn't care it was a Monday. People crowded along the sidewalks, and Milo nabbed a parking space a block away from his destination.

Chicago PD followed their thin leads for the latest victim. Everything seemed random and senseless, as none of those targeted had any similar connections. That was what drew Milo to this place, one he hoped would lead to something more concrete or a vision.

Gwendolyn's Guns & Gals flashed in bright neon lights.

Fuck. Of all the businesses he could've gone to for answers. I ground my teeth, an action that loosened our link when Milo entered through scrutinous security.

Gwendolyn's Guns & Gals was a burlesque club founded in 1926. It was owned and operated by Gwendolyn Gardner, who ran a burlesque show by night and operated the biggest front for distributing illegal enchantments in the history of Chicago. She didn't have actual guns, merely an augmentation to her biceps that made leveling a building as easy as one of her girls discreetly waving a fan.

The business left an unsavory taste in my mouth whenever I crossed by it, given how the operation preyed on anyone desperate enough to seek a magical solution they couldn't otherwise obtain.

"How can you hate this place?" Finn asked, his voice pulling me into a memory, a dream.

He'd always loved the way the business went back and forth with authorities for decades until finally cementing its historical landmark status and very carefully navigating their illegal activities.

I fought the blissful dream, the beauty of his voice steering me to a favorable memory, and maintained my link to Milo, who strolled into the club, eyeing the seductive performers on stage and patrons eagerly enthralled either by the magic cast or the dancer behind feathers.

Approaching the VIP bar, Milo stepped past the security, not so much as a wave of approval or hesitation on his part. One muscular man with a light tan stepped between Milo and the bar. He folded his arms across his broad chest, scowling at Milo and towering over him as well.

"Gavin, ease up, and let my favorite little enchanter through." Alone at the small, private bar sat Cassidy Gardner, the current owner.

Milo winked, inciting a snarled response from Gavin, who refused to move aside. Sipping her drink, Cassidy waved a delicate hand, casting a powerful yet precise collection of telekinetic bursts which knocked Gavin out of Milo's path and kept the man from hitting anything in the club or falling to the floor, simply locked in a turret of continuous strikes until his calmed, broken temperament pleased Cassidy.

"Looking dapper as ever, Enchanter Evergreen." Cassidy wore a forest green dress, tight-waisted and poofy at her hips. Her emerald heel clinked against the metal leg of her barstool.

She acted as one of the unofficial undercity warlocks. Unofficial because she was properly educated, licensed, and never convicted for any casting irregularities. It was amazing how the right legal team could throw out a landfill worth of illegal activity, and guild witches like Milo knew when and how to sit on the right intel.

"And you get lovelier each time I see you." Milo kissed her rosy cheek, eyeing a golden bracelet on Cassidy's wrist, one which held his gaze every time he visited.

A trinket compared to the other jewels she flaunted this evening, but a gift Milo had given her long before he was ever Enchanter Evergreen or The Inevitable Future.

Cassidy had attended Gemini back when we were students. Back then, Milo and Cassidy were pale comparisons of the boldness they each embodied now. I'd never given Cassidy a chance considering her family background and the legalized warlock profiteering that occasionally skirted her surface thoughts in class. I harbored no guilt for judging her connections or savviness to thrive in an exploitive business; however, Milo had always considered the Gardners a lesser evil and one he'd gladly indulge.

Milo tolerated this club because all crime couldn't be stopped. It was a part of human nature he understood. Either by impulse or necessity, there'd always be some layer of skirting the rules. And Milo didn't think every rule should exist since many were implemented to oppress those with strong magics and weak resources. A sentiment I understood. After all, most of the enchantments sold under the table were to folks trying to survive, but there were definitely some used to commit heinous atrocities both local and global. Granted, the same could be said for enchantments legally purchased and handed out to the wrong hands with the right license. All arguments for another time. What I wanted to argue about was him walking right into a den of witches and warlocks who all knew him.

"Given the warlock fiasco a few months back, I thought perhaps you'd have sought my council sooner." Cassidy grabbed her martini glass off the counter.

"I knew you weren't involved." Milo's eyes fluttered playfully—not lost in visions—which was nice to see even from a distance.

"Don't have to be involved to have a close ear to the ground." Cassidy sipped her drink, leaving the faintest red on the rim. "I could've helped you find that hack of a doctor, if people insist on calling her one, and that spoiled rich boy summoning demons because of daddy issues."

Theodore Whitlock and his associates were still echoes of conversation months after their failed warlock incursion.

"He was summoning fiends," Milo said. A simple correction that resonated along the tether connecting us.

"Whatever, it's all the same demonic garbage I don't want in my business."

There was a huge difference most didn't grasp between fiends and demons. The sentience. The power. The magic.

Finn's death cemented that difference in both of us. It clung to Milo's thoughts, forefront and threatening to expose emotions he never showed publicly. Vulnerability, sensitivity, weakness—each held its right time for public observation, but working a case wasn't one of those times. The anguished final expression on Finn's stilled face faintly rose in Milo's mind. A murky haze filtered through the morgue where Finn lay, and I couldn't be certain if it was Milo burying the memory himself or me severing my magic entirely so I wouldn't have to ever see that expression again. One I refused to cement in my thoughts.

Flashes of blood splatter, broken body parts, and a woman's face vacant of life rattled in Milo's head, pushing away his past and any threatening guilt, allowing him to remember what brought him here this evening. His most recent case. His most recent failure. But motivation to keep his demeanor from shifting as he pursued closure for this lost life.

"Maybe I avoided you because I didn't want to cause you any trouble." Milo grinned, grabbing a martini from the bartender, who quickly made themselves scarce from earshot. "Little ole me, stopping in here, asking the right questions to the wrong people. It could've caused waves, and you know I only enjoy the ripples I control."

"Please." Cassidy fiddled with her bracelet, unsnagging it from a diamond-encrusted watch. "A few fiend-fucked warlocks wouldn't have intimidated me, and you know better."

"I know a woman of your caliber would never let a few warlocks or fiends rattle you," Milo said. "But I'm here in search of something far bigger than either of those."

"Here about that demon thing, I assume. Tragic." Cassidy's eyes remained locked on the stage as a new performer sauntered out. "You can speak to whomever you wish. Patrons, performers, Gavin. Though they already answered questions for the detectives."

"I'm sure you enjoyed those leading questions on the case." Milo had read the police reports and gleaned enough from those investigating that they were more interested in a welcome invitation to snoop behind closed doors of Gwendolyn's Guns & Gals than search small leads on one of Cassidy's employees, warlock or not.

"No one's interested in that girl's death, myself included. I barely knew her, no one here did, so if you're hoping for one of the six degrees of separation visions, doubt you'll find much." Cassidy's expression shifted from aloof amusement to vacant indifference. "Truthfully, she lacked in every way on and off stage and wasn't much better at serving drinks or making conversation. The one saving grace she had was her magic."

"A magic which appealed to the demon who devoured Melody Mauve."

"Oh, you memorized her name."

"Memorized a lot more than that." Milo had read her file, learned her fate, found connections or lack of to any family, and learned she possessed a powerful arcane branch.

Milo held back all the potential possibilities that'd crossed his path when researching this latest victim. All the visions he'd stored in his massive vault of a person he'd never met and now never would. A simple life with nothing grand or glorious, so it went untended in his ever-growing list. No immediate danger should've lied ahead for her. But demonic interference was a difficult thing for Enchanter Evergreen to predict. None of that mattered. He clung to the seven visions he'd had of Melody Mauve, tucking them away in his mind, even though they were snuffed out since she'd died, and now simply took up space in his head. He held onto them out of guilt.

"She wasn't involved in any extracurriculars, which is why I paid her no attention."

"Then why'd you hire her?"

"Gavin has a soft spot for small-town girls with big-city dreams." Cassidy nodded to the man posted at the end of the bar, fully alert and glaring at Milo. "Plus, as I said, she had a wonderful magic that would've sold high. Figured, a few months of waiting tables and she'd realize the benefit of selling her branch."

I ground my teeth, nearly rousing and severing my link again. The Gardner Family enchantment schemes. Cassidy would find those with powerful and unique magics and assign them to work alongside a witch who possessed an enchantment branch, so the branch could be written through spell craft copies or bottled in potion crafts, then distributed. I'd skimmed enough off her surface thoughts when we were students to understand the inner workings of her family business. Not that my findings were considered admissible at Gemini or a court of law.

"I need to find out where Melody was when she was abducted. I already know where she wasn't." Not at work, home, friends, or her local haunts.

"Why does it matter where she was? You can't exactly read the memories of the scene." Cassidy's comment skirted a reminder of Finn, which fueled my magic. Everything in the living room shook, and Milo's thoughts became faint echoes.

"Not why I'm looking for it," Milo said with a smile, unphased by Cassidy's comment or better at hiding it in his mind than I was. Each of the victims had been unaccounted for, the same as Melody, and if he knew where she was, he'd know the demon's hunting grounds. "But hey, if you can't figure out where one of your girls, with a magic you never had a chance to taste, snuck off to, I understand. Guess there are still hidden nooks in Chicago Cassidy Gardner is unaware of, or maybe new ones."

"Goading me because that works wonders."

"Simply suggesting you might be out of touch." Milo eyed the empty box office above the bar. "Sure, you're seen here, but you're still a mile away from everyone else in this club."

"Christ, you're annoying. Look, I'll ask around, but do yourself a favor, Enchanter Evergreen. Don't stress yourself out over this girl or a handful of nobodies." Her expression shifted, stone cold, eyes tightened, matching the cutthroat demeanor of her grandmother's portrait proudly displayed on the bar wall behind her. "If any of these 'victims' mattered, they wouldn't be dead. They'd have popped up on the great Enchanter Evergreen's radar that much sooner. You should honestly leave the sweeping up of corpses to less impressive guild witches."

Milo's stomach sank. Something few people called out, but something commonly acknowledged was that The Inevitable Future worked to make the world brighter one life at a time, so if you didn't make the cut, you didn't matter. Milo worried too many others saw it that way too. In truth, every lost life represented a failure, one he'd never found a way to prevent.

"Ask around, Cassidy." Milo's smile vanished, and his face soured into something stern. "Unless you've finally reached the end of your usefulness."

"I'll find out where she was." Cassidy tugged Milo's tie, adjusting and tightening it too much. "Here's some free advice for you, though—don't fuck with demons. They don't stay in big cities long. Let them enjoy their visit and move on."

"They don't stay long because enchanters like me banish them back to the Hell plains they crawled out of." Milo leaned in close to Cassidy's ear. "Now, if you don't mind, I have a late-night date."

"You could do better."

"So could he." Milo strolled out of the club, dwelling on how he hadn't contacted me because he prioritized the case, which didn't get him far.

Taking in a deep breath of cold air, Milo contemplated going home instead of surprising me, worried I'd be more annoyed than entertained. Part of him wanted to put off stopping by until the weekend. No. I clawed my way up from the couch and grabbed my phone, texting him.

Short. Simple. Eager. Something to say I had to see him. Now. Somehow, I needed to explain how my telepathy swelled, explain how I'd tracked his case alongside him, invaded his thoughts from halfway across the city.

Milo's blood rushed, and his face heated, giddy and already compartmentalizing his career and his desires because he believed tonight would be blissful. Unfortunately, I'd have to burst that bubble when he showed.

Explaining my damn telepathy problems was going to ruin everything between us.

CHAPTER TEN

MILO arrived at my place, and I opened the door before he knocked, ready to discuss what I'd unintentionally overheard from the office all the way to the burlesque club. With a smirk on his face, a bottle of wine in one hand, and a basket of goodies in the other, he stepped inside, maintaining deceptively aloof surface thoughts. Dammit. He'd come prepared to dodge any conversation.

"Sorry I haven't been around, despite our coupling being the talk of the town. Well, city. State really. There are a few international sites that adore me. You too, now. It'll pass." Milo grinned. "It's the honeymoon curiosity phase. Who are they as a couple? Where are they as a couple? What are they, a couple?" He playfully raised his eyebrows. "Yet, I've been so busy with work and endless paperwork, we haven't really coupled. Hopefully, tonight can change that."

He was already playing defense with his words and thoughts, avoiding the giant demonic elephant in the room.

"Paperwork?" I asked.

"Ugh. Blegh. Yuck." Milo's mind glossed over infinite fine prints, countless signatures, and necessary notaries seared into his memories, which wasn't an avoidance tactic. He really despised all the legal paperwork and contracts involved in guild work. "It's endless forms. I swear the most dangerous thing an enchanter suffers from dying of these days is carpal tunnel syndrome."

"Your poor wrists." I snatched the basket from his hands, glaring.

"Don't worry. They're still able to handle any late-night tasks you may desire." Milo winked, clicking his tongue at the same time.

Insufferable.

This was the basket he'd safely secured before his trip to Gwendolyn's Guns & Gals. And it wasn't some random gift basket he'd picked up, but one he'd specifically filled with my favorite things. From soft cheeses at Lee's Deli on the North Side, to the toast points at Paula's on the South Side, all the way to the pork buns in Chinatown, along with a half dozen other goodies I loved but never made the time to go out of my way and grab. Even the cheap wine easily stocked at any store was a favorite. It wasn't too sweet, not bitter at all, and certainly didn't try too hard. I aspired to be that wine most days.

My breath hitched at the idea he'd flown across the city putting this together. Was this his best attempt at a distraction from a conversation he wanted to avoid? A conversation he may or may not be aware of considering his clairvoyance? What an ass.

"Thanks." I eyed him, then walked the basket into the kitchen, setting it on the countertop. "You didn't have to."

"I know, but I wanted to surprise you."

Speaking of surprises, I accidentally found out you're tracking demons. Care to explain? I shook my head. Probably not the best way to start the conversation. This wasn't an attack. It was concern. What he was doing was dangerous. Deadly. And whether I had a role in the industry or not, I didn't want Milo shutting me out of these conversations especially depending on the tier of demons involved. They were all hellishly horrendous after ascending past the fiend state, but some…some were abysmal.

"So"—I reached for a wine opener, struggling for the right words—"demons attacking the South Side?"

"You can't believe anything they print these days. It's all so sensationalized."

He wasn't wrong; however, I'd looked up every article during classes, and not one mentioned the South Side. That was a thought I'd gleaned from his conversation with Enchanter Campbell.

Milo stepped behind me, twirling his finger. The cork wriggled. I'd fallen so far behind him when I walked away from life as a professional enchanter. Even my daily regime to catch up, and avoid ever being put in a situation where my life or my students' lives were at risk again, paled in comparison to his talents. The lightest touch of telekinesis sifted between the tight space of glass and cork. The bottle trembled in my hand, but that came from my tension, not his. Milo's breath tickled my ear, and his carefree thoughts shifted to far more provocative ideas he had in store for later. After a glass or two, Milo planned to pin—

POP.

The cork flew off, frozen midair, thanks in no part to my magic. Milo grabbed two glasses from the cabinet, waving the cork into the trash can. I poured the wine into the glasses. Red glugged out of the bottle, splashing as I filled one glass to the brim.

"Thirsty." Milo wiggled his eyebrows, casting a suggestive innuendo for the word.

"Very." I gulped half the drink. Tart sweetness danced on my tongue while I formed an elegant way to share my new discovery.

"Never understood why you loved this brand so much." Milo sniffed his glass before taking a dainty sip. Whether it came from the fancy bottles his guild provided or a more refined palette, we shared a very different taste in alcohol.

"About that vampire attack."

"It wasn't a vampire. Told you, the press will run with anything."

"Save the speech. I sort of, definitely, overheard you today. It wasn't intentional, but I linked to your mind while you were at work. Also, saw you at Gwendolyn's. Cassidy seems well, considering her occupation."

Welp. Guess I dived right in. I finished my drink and poured another.

"You spied on me at work?" His brow furrowed.

I wasn't looking at him, only the glug of the wine, but his emotions cast a crimson haze.

"No. I said unintentional. I just… It's my telepathy. It's been enhancing."

"Evolving." Milo grinned, revealing the giddy thoughts in an aura of gold he'd masked with an expression of shock.

"You're not mad?"

"Why would I be?" There was delight in his blue eyes until they fluttered. His long lashes batted while he delved into his own world of infinite possibilities. "I use my branch on you all the time. Sometimes intentionally."

"Damn clairvoyants." I half smiled but mostly glowered. Cheery expressions were difficult; grouchy was my default face.

"I don't see any way this could go wrong. You're more than welcome to observe me whenever you want. And if you give me a heads up," he slid his hand into his slacks, just the fingertips, exposing the cut in his muscular definition and flashing a shaved happy trail, "I can give you a show."

"No. I didn't mean to link to you. It was an accident."

"I don't mind. You're often in my head. Magically or just in thought." Milo's grin faltered into a soft smile from his youth. The kind of shy expression he held when we were teens, and he was too embarrassed to share his feelings. Even internally, he used to bury his surface thoughts in panic and disarray.

"I'll try to work on it."

"Don't. I'm okay with it. My branch syncs up to your life all the time. I've had a million lives cross my clairvoyance, and yet I've had your life play by a million times on its own." Milo set his glass down next to mine, running his fingertips over mine. "I get that sensation—the uncontrolled, fluttery one, and I'm okay with it. Besides, I don't know if you realize this, but you can be a bit obsessive."

"I'm not obsessive." I wasn't.

"Oh, you definitely are. It's your most toxic trait. That and your need to completely shut down and cut everyone and everything off so you don't become obsessive." Milo puckered his lips and blew a kiss. The light telekinetic burst tapped my cheek with a smooch from his lip balm. An aggravating gesture to tease me. "Personally, I find your two modes endearing. I just can't have you obsessing and interfering."

"I won't. I wasn't going to."

"Okay, then sync your magic with me any day of the week. I promise all the meetings aren't boring snooze fests. And some of the jobs are pretty cool, too."

"Wait. Is this one of your clairvoyant reverse psychology moves?" I squeezed his hand, rooting out the truth no matter what he'd say next.

"Huh?" Milo feigned confusion as his surface thoughts tiptoed toward song lyrics.

I frowned. "You know exactly what I'm talking about."

"Perplexed is all that comes to mind." Milo winked. "*That and how hawt you look in those skinny jeans. Trying something new? I'm loving the look. Love it even more when I—*"

"When you tell me not to do something because you know that's exactly what I'll do," I blurted, flustered. My neck warmed. "Because I get concerned, and sometimes when I can't do something, I realize I can do something, and you feed into that…subtly. Which, of course, makes me have to take action and fix things."

"Wow. Way to make me sound manipulative."

"The point stands." I crossed my arms. "Are you telling me not to get involved seriously or suggestively?"

"If I were being suggestive, telling would ruin it. And if I were being serious, you wouldn't believe me anyway." Milo stepped toward me, closing our distance. His chest practically touched mine, and he raised a single arm up. Playfully, he tapped my forehead. "You've got too many thoughts in there, and you're always anxiously sorting them. I understand why me tracking demons makes you nervous. It's not anything like what happened…before."

He shifted his gaze, and his mind spiraled into intangible nonsense like he feared the wrong word, wrong thought would burst what he believed I'd worked so hard to improve on. I hadn't worked hard on anything. Every step of progress came from his patience and love and trust.

"It won't be like with Finn?" I asked, thinking of the other person I owed every fraction of my growth to.

Milo's eyes widened. Finn's name no longer burned my throat when I mentioned him, my body didn't feel like it'd shatter into a thousand pieces at his mere memory, and I stopped having the urge to fling myself from a cliff when I remembered how much I'd fucked things up in my youth.

"It won't. What happened then was awful, devastating, but I know more now than I ever did then. This isn't the first time I've dealt with demons trying to migrate into a bigger city." Milo rubbed his hands up and down my biceps, comforting with a hint of desire. "Occasionally, demons forget the strength of guilds and think they can get lost in a crowd."

He had a point. Cities held an allure for demons and all forms of demonic energy, given the massive surplus of magic in them. Wisps weren't sentient, so they moved purely like magnets, and fiends were base creatures fueled by hunger. But demons knew to stick to rural areas with less guild and government oversight, someplace they could remain unseen. All the same, it didn't make them any less dangerous, and whether experienced or not, I worried Milo was overhyping the strength and skill of Enchanter Evergreen.

"As much as I like you being all supportive," I said. "And only mildly manipulative—"

"Hey!"

"While having your blessing to delve into your mind whenever is great, the biggest problem is I'm not sure how to turn it off when it happens." I chose each word carefully. "Which makes functioning difficult."

"So you're saying I constantly turn you on? Or turn your magic on. Interesting." Milo didn't muse over his words half as thoughtfully, blurting whatever popped into his head. "No, I get it. Sporting a psychic boner for your boyfriend at work would be challenging."

"That's not what I said."

"I know what you said. I'm in your thoughts because you're in my head."

"Just saying sorry in advance for any eavesdropping. I'll try my best to quell my telepathy. It's just been erratic lately."

"How many times do I have to say it? Don't quell anything." Milo leaned close, his lips soft and sweet against mine. "*I like having you in my head. When I feel you here, I know it's because you care. The fact your branch is growing, improving, and seeking me out above everyone in the city—I want to believe it's because maybe we have something real."*

I pulled my lips back and pressed my forehead against his. *"It is real. Everything I feel for you is beyond my limited vocabulary."*

If I had a lifetime to explain it, I'd never find the right words. But I wanted that lifetime to search for them. That lifetime to spend with Milo.

Milo tilted his still-pressed head until the twinkle in his sparkling blue eyes met mine. "If you're that worried about it, focusing on being here and there and everywhere, why not make a manifestation?"

"That just feels weird, intentionally creating a manifestation to follow you around all day." Plus, I still hadn't been able to summon one.

Not that my apparently obsessive magic stretching across the city to stalk him wasn't strange enough. At least, I didn't do it intentionally. Maybe subconsciously. Letting Milo back into my life, into my heart, being completely unaware of where or what he was doing, and the idea of losing him like I'd—no, we'd—lost Finn made it clear there was no maybe in my subconscious. My branch had grown and used the development to shield me from scars that'd never quite healed.

"I don't mind you inside me." Milo stifled a giggle. "In fact, I quite enjoy it."

"Oh, shut up." I pushed him back.

"Mmmm." Milo growled. *"Yes, sir."*

I rolled my eyes. His surface thoughts danced in a hundred suggestive scenarios and some brazen imagery on his mood for the evening. Milo often stirred in more dominant desires, but when his submissive cravings struck, he made a point to make it blatantly obvious what he wanted.

Ignoring his desires, I took his suggestion and amplified my telepathy. The kitchen transformed into a haze of colorful emotions, all permeating off Milo. His emotions wafted around like lingering perfumes, displaying his physical, carnal desires from the seductive pinks to the aroused reds. It was the violet haze radiating at his core that showed the coupled intimacy he craved above it all. Violet waves exuding desires for a simple touch, cuddling, hand-holding, romance. But, as much as Milo yearned for each of these now and always, his immediate intimacy shifted toward sex. With my telepathy at its peak, I summoned a manifestation to link to Milo, something to watch over him quietly, one I could recollect when time permitted.

Nothing. Nothing. Nothing.

There wasn't a single fiber of my consciousness I could scrape off and conjure. I stood, blinking away the confusion.

"There's something wrong with my manifestation." It'd been a few months since I last used them during the void vision investigation, but I'd gone years without summoning them and never felt this stunted when performing.

"Dorian, I don't think I've ever seen you struggle to get it up before." Milo coyly stepped forward, grabbing my hand. I grumbled but continued channeling. "Jokes aside, channel my frequency, and maybe it'll help your manifestation latch on."

Still, nothing.

"It'll be fine. I'll figure it out." I'd coped without conjuring them before, like when my branch first developed, and I'd bounce between so many minds, it became a monsoon of desires, thoughts, and memories. I had survived it then. Randomly springing into Enchanter Evergreen's head while working or simply at home couldn't be much worse than surviving my teen years lost in folks minds, navigating a way through mine.

"Question." Milo released his hand. "Are you in my head now?"

"*Well, there's the telepathic link.*" I hadn't severed it, but it didn't help reel a manifestation forward. I was always in his head when he was this close, he knew that, but he meant something deeper. Was I merely glimpsing his thoughts and desires, making sense of them in my own head, or was I simultaneously over his shoulder observing him while he stared at me lustfully? It was the former.

"No, I mean, whose sensations are you feeling right this second." Milo brushed his fingertips along my forearm, tickling the hairs. "Did you feel my hand or your skin when I touched you?"

"I don't know." Oh, I knew.

"How about this?" He leaned in, nibbling my ear.

"Just feel your tongue along my neck."

"So, no taste of sweet skin or the scent of your shampoo?"

"No, why?"

Despite publicly declaring our relationship, we hadn't had much alone time since. We hadn't had much before. Balancing schedules was a headache, one we could ignore for a minute. Given the ferocity of Milo's hungry thoughts, we'd ignore the outside world for a few hours.

"Curiosity, I suppose." Milo unzipped my jeans, slipping his hand in and grabbing hold of my cock. "Wondering how we can test the limits of our melded minds."

Milo dropped to his knees. My face heated, and I took in a deep breath as he wrapped his lips around my tip and went all the way to the base in one swift twist of his head. "*It's fascinating, is all. Like if you could feel yourself getting and giving h—*"

"*Stop overthinking that and think about...*" I growled, primal and synced exactly to the mood Milo desired.

He wrapped his hands over my hips and steadied my stance while keeping me pinned to the counter. I grabbed his hair, tightly squeezing until my knuckles turned white. Milo gagged, struggling yet satisfied.

Clenching my jaw, I fought back a grunt as I enveloped his throat until I couldn't take it any longer. I pulled him away and panted, so the fulfilled excitement eased ever so.

Waving a hand, I guided him to his feet with instruction and telekinesis. Staring at each other silently for seconds I never wanted to end, I finally broke the pause, adjusting my pants enough to walk, and grabbing Milo by the loops of his dress slacks.

In that tiny lull, there was no sound. No thoughts. No voices. Only Milo's feelings and my instinct. Pulling him closer by his slacks, I kissed him, moving my hands behind his thighs and lifting him into my bedroom. Between the passion blurring everything and the swift pull of telekinesis, we were wrapped together naked on the bed in a moment.

Milo rolled over, and I licked the space between his shoulder blades, eliciting a delightful shudder, before telekinetically reaching for the lube in my nightstand. Milo positioned himself on all fours, and I grabbed his hips, aligning him, gently instructing him to rise a little more and arch a bit deeper.

Slowly, I eased myself inside him, taking gentle yet forceful strokes, holding his hips in place. Milo bit his lower lip, and mine quivered at the sensation. I continued, hastening my thrusts, and arching his back, pushing his chest and head deeper into the mattress as I entered further. His slick sweat became intoxicating, wrapped in the musk of his cologne. Each second alluring and every panted breath enticing.

Keeping one hand at his waist, I slowly trailed my other from Milo's lower back, up his spine, and settled with a firm grip on his shoulder. He tensed, and I stopped. Resisting every desire to pump faster and harder and more aggressively into a willing Milo, I relented.

His appetites in thought often superseded his physical adaptability to receiving since he rarely did. Still, those passions mixed within my mind making it difficult to stop when every fiber wanted more, but I knew his body needed a moment longer to adjust.

"I'm fine." Milo arched, leaning upward and pressing his back against my chest.

Sweat held us together like glue.

I released his shoulder, cupping his jaw forcefully and kissing him. The calm seduction between our lips allowed him to loosen and relax with me inside him. We hadn't been intimate in the busy week, yet it'd been well over a month since Milo hungered for a submissive position.

The last time he'd wanted a more passive position, he was still on top, sexually speaking, but physically I'd taken the assertive role. That was what this desire was, an overwhelming need to be satisfied and controlled.

That said, I took care to be gentle because Milo often overestimated what he wanted versus what he could handle. I'd topped Milo enough to know his threshold of pain and pleasure mixing into satisfaction.

Kissing his nape, I guided him back down, pushing him deep into the mattress, and clung to him as I lay on top.

I wrapped my arms under Milo's, running my hands through his blond hair as my fingers interlocked. His biceps squeezed against mine, and anticipation and nervousness spiraled in equal measure.

Lightly running my teeth along his neck, I kissed him each time I slowly thrust.

Steadying my hold and pace, I continued speeding up, encouraged by Milo's muffled moans and relaxed muscles. He whimpered, convulsing and close to cumming beneath me, so close it made me throb more, electrified by his intense pleasure.

"Wait." I grazed my teeth against his neck, wanting nothing more than to finish at the same time.

I pounded him harder, swept away by the euphoric delight he took in each stroke of my cock burying into him, the grunts of authority that sent his mind whirling, and the feel of my skin slapping against his. My entire body warmed, feeling Milo's every sensation—the pleasure I brought him, the intoxication he gave me—and I grunted, taking light, twitchy thrusts as we came together.

Chapter Eleven

I STOOD in the hallway, sipping coffee and more exhausted than usual. When Milo spent the night, I typically slept better, but we didn't exactly sleep. Not a fucking wink because of, well, all the fucking. The pent-up stamina between the two of us, combined with the anticipation of finding a minute together, was wonderful and came with screwing late into the night; however, the roar of students parading through the hallways bright and early was the fallout for choosing sex over sleep. How Milo managed to spring up at dawn and rush to his office with a smile on his face, I had no idea.

The minds of students and staff drummed inside my head, exasperating my sleep-deprivation headache. Whether from my confession to Milo or his willingness to invite my strange telepathic tether, the synced link hadn't hit yet. Maybe my magic was too tired, or more likely, I didn't know a thing about my evolving branch, and it'd strike a chord when it damn well pleased and not based on my guessing games.

Katherine and Caleb walked toward the classroom. Katherine had her grimoire out, scribbling notes to a spell she planned on tweaking. Caleb balanced the weighted blocks above his head, the only student in the hallway training his four root magics first thing in the morning. The only one possibly training his magics at all times.

"Quick question." I stopped the pair before they entered the classroom. "Do you like using those support tools?"

"Yeah," Caleb said. "I know they're kind of kiddish, but I've made some tweaks to the weight limit, so that's been helping."

He wasn't wrong. Few witches used these tools; the academy didn't even provide them because, while useful, they were considered most effective during elementary years. It was fascinating he'd increased the weight limit.

"Do you mind?" I reached out telekinetically, grabbing hold of one of the small, cubed weights. The sigil immediately recognized the hint of two telekinetic holds and dimly glowed.

"Sure." Caleb released his telekinesis from the one I had.

The weighted block nearly fell from my grasp. I furrowed my brow, ignoring the sharp tug on my muscles. This wasn't a slight modified increase to the weight limit.

"What'd you put in this tiny cube, an anvil?" I was only half joking. Though it would easily fit in the palm of my hand, it felt closer to carrying both my cats. Not a tremendous weight, but enough to make a small continuous effort applied all day exhausting.

"Oh, that was me." Katherine beamed. "Took a spell I had, altered the sigils on Caleb's weighted blocks, and bam. An easy three-step process."

Interesting. A three-step process that involved a half dozen prerequisites, each based on Katherine's capabilities and understanding of enchantments.

"Could you modify these to respond to any magic?" I continued keeping the heavy cube afloat and passed it back to Caleb, who circulated it with the others he used for practicing.

His Cast-8-Watch beeped, passing through another marker of registered magical practice. Confidence brimmed alongside anxiety as he dwelled on whether this would be enough to impact his ranking for the Spring Showcase.

"Definitely. What'd you have in mind?" Katherine's smile filled her face, eagerly awaiting an opportunity to tinker with more magics.

I eyed Tara and Gael, who walked into homeroom.

"Just a little project that might help someone. We can talk about it after class, Katherine."

Milo's mind returned, calling out as I taught. The duality of standing in my classroom, fully present, while another part remained connected to Milo, hovering in his thoughts, proved difficult to navigate. Though, I'd found a trick by latching onto nearby minds. None of my homeroom coven students were in this particular history class, so I latched onto a student from Chanelle's homeroom.

```
Name: Harrison Heywood
Branch: Enchantment (Potion Craft)
```

He buzzed with recipes and ingredients that blended into his two passions in life—a love for cooking and for crafting. Potion crafting usually involved making tonics, elixirs, and remedies of all kinds, but how beneficial they were solely depended on the witch creating them. It was similar to Katherine's spell craft branch, except Harrison used potions instead of pages.

"Today, we're going to discuss demon classifications and the tonics—er, types—which present themselves when a demon fully ascends."

Harrison's bubbling thoughts caused more confusion than clarity as I taught the history behind demonic incursions.

Considering the explosive spells teeming along his surface thoughts, I was grateful he had to keep his cauldron at home. The fanny pack strapped to his waist—such an ironic throwback—had enough dangerous concoctions to create a Yaritza-level firework show.

I bounced from Harrison's mind to another, hopeful the students would keep me firmly planted here while I pushed Milo's actions to the back burner of my mind, a technique I hadn't used since my branch first developed. Like with cooking—or at least I assumed from how those who cooked described it—I was able to move it out of the way, but I couldn't ignore it either.

If I didn't tend to the constant flux of Milo's mind when the chord struck and the tether linked us, I'd end up with the pot overflowing. Or, in this case, Milo's thoughts bombarding me so much I'd pass out like I'd nearly done when he took the demon case.

I ground my teeth. Maybe I was mixing metaphors. Whatever. I missed being able to summon a manifestation, something to create a buffer for all this psychic energy. Despite my blossoming telepathy growing rampant and more invasive, I couldn't steady my mind enough to summon a manifestation.

Honestly, this trick for latching onto nearby minds would probably work best on familiar ones. Another reminder I barely knew the hundred and twenty-six students on my rosters.

Milo read files on all the enchanters and acolytes at Cerberus Guild, annoyed he was limited to his own guild's magics since there were a few witches at Kraken and Vixen that'd make this investigation smoother. He had no clarity on the type of demons he'd encounter and wanted certainty.

Enchanter Campbell stepped into his office. "Have you made a decision, or do I need to put together my own team?"

"Unnecessary." Milo placed two files at the edge of his desk, separating them from the large stack. "I'd like to work with these two acolytes."

"You'll want another enchanter," Campbell said, grabbing the files and reading them over.

"Trust me, I really won't."

I wrinkled my brow, pausing during instruction. Milo really only wanted two acolytes for a demon investigation? Reckless. Dangerous.

"*Is he okay?*" A thought that bubbled on the few minds still paying attention to my lecture. I continued while more fixated on the discussion in Milo's office and his plans.

"After reviewing their files, both are incredibly skilled, hyper-focused, and more than capable of handling this investigation alongside me." Milo strummed his fingers on his desk, drawing me back in and painting a scene of his office through the vibrations.

"Weren't you the one complaining an acolyte dropped the ball on a case you'd handed them on a platter?"

Our day date, which was true since he'd ended up dealing with the fiends himself. The dominos fell in an unexpected direction. He had hoped for something fun and light that Sunday, knowing his upcoming Global Ranking's Ceremony might've put me in a mood or questionable state. Though, considering how it resolved itself, he didn't seem upset. I'd gone to show support and openly address our relationship, the absolute smallest of possible variables. He wondered if he was losing his touch at predictions or if he didn't know me as well as he believed.

"The point stands. This'll be a complex case, and based on the victims, I'd prefer talented and low-profile witches."

"Acolyte Novak is hardly low profile."

A Novak? Surprising someone from that family would work at a Whitlock-owned guild, not that there were many other reputable ones to choose from in the state, but given the spite Jamie held for Tara purely based on her name, I could only imagine what resentment this Acolyte Novak held.

"You want this done quickly or correctly?" Milo stood up and straightened his jacket.

"Both."

"Then those acolytes are our best bet." Milo strutted toward his door.

"Where are you going?"

"Got a lead to follow up. Doing my part to be efficient."

Enchanter Campbell gagged at Milo's minxy wink.

Jamie walked faster, attempting to cut Tara off at the doorway to the classroom.

"Ba-ba-ba!" King Clucks furiously flapped his wings, sidestepping between the pair, his clawed feet click-clacked against the floor. His comb jiggled as he tilted his head and pecked the air, forcing Jamie to backstep.

Jamie continued being a thorn in my side, taking any and every opportunity to bully Tara through any tactics possible.

It took all I had to muster even a modicum of enthusiasm for this class as I buried a dozen different thoughts and the waning thread of Milo's mind.

"Today, we're going to discuss demon classifications and the types which present themselves when a fiend fully ascends." I talked on autopilot, regurgitating information I'd already said verbatim for the most part to three earlier classes.

Lessons often started the same way, but when my mind was more my own, I'd steer discussion toward student interests and heighten conversation in areas that needed more elaboration to increase their understanding while also keeping lectures from wandering too far off-topic. This wasn't one of those days.

"A fully ascended demon is considered a high-tier threat as it feeds on more and more magic to sustain its demonic energy. The most important role guilds play is disrupting and banishing demonic energy before a fiend gathers and absorbs enough magic to transcend into a fully sentient demon. We've discussed how cities have become overrun in the past—"

"We should be talking about how it's happening again," Jamie interjected because of course he fucking did.

"Meaning?" I fought the snarl building in my throat as I attempted to allow a bit of civil discussion since nothing bubbling in his head seemed like it'd lead to a carefully crafted insult toward Tara.

"Just that Chicago's currently crawling with demons. Next thing you know—"

"We're not crawling with demons," Gael blurted.

"Many high-tier demons have attacked the city. Sort of reminds me of that Sacramento v. Sirens lesson we had," Jamie said, thoughts bordering on the student who'd referenced that lecture: Tara. "They said Sacramento was so infested, it was more demon than witch by the time the military acted, which begs the question, how will—"

"It's not the same," Gael said, once again cutting Jamie off with a smile on his face which only increased the more Jamie sneered in response. "They didn't have Enchanter Evergreen."

"Ba-bawk!"

"*I know he's trying to change the conversation to guilds so he can talk shit about the Whitlocks."*

"Cl-cl-cluck."

"Yeah, Tara says she doesn't give a fuck about that, but I'm not going to let Jamie worm his way into any kind of conversation that gives him a voice against her. I'll fuck him up."

My face flushed. Gael never vocalized it. Hell, most of his thoughts were so random and vulgar, it was difficult finding these deep, caring gems.

King Clucks crowed.

"We might have an Enchanter Evergreen"—Jamie's eyes flitted past Tara, past Gael, and landed on me—"but even he couldn't handle a devil."

I quirked an eyebrow. "Excuse me?"

"Oh, hell no. He's not trying to talk shit about my boy, Evergreen. Mr. Frosty better step up for his man before I—"

I squashed Gael's thoughts.

"I simply mean, the demons which practically consumed Sacramento did so at the behest of a devil." Jamie had a menacing expression, his eyes locked onto me in some effort to taunt or goad me, yet his thoughts remained hollow. "Or so they say. Who really knows, right?"

"Devils aren't real," Gael exclaimed. "They're a total superstition. Some demons just look human-y depending on their classification, which you'd know if you did the reading."

He folded his arms, proudly boasting and leaving out the part where he had, in fact, not done the reading but relied on Tara and King Clucks to fill him in on the previous lessons. I rolled my eyes, quelling his ego.

Admittedly, Gael's timely interjection helped shake away Jamie's haunting attitude and helped me realize his thoughts weren't empty, but rather my telepathy continued fizzling out in bizarre intervals.

"Devils are real," I said. "Possession happens. Demons have been known to take hold of a witch's body."

"Some people say really strong demons take everything you were and scoop it out." Jamie leaned his desk, using telekinesis to tilt it closer to Tara's. "They wear your face, a devil in disguise, without all the baggage of a broken mortal coil."

"But that's a much rarer instance." I waved a hand, slamming Jamie's desk back in place and rattling him in the same manner he intended to rattle Tara. "So uncommon, in fact, it's not something covered in our curriculum. Those of you who wish to learn more about devils are welcome to take my Advanced Demonology course in your third year, but for the time being, let's cover the basics of demon classifications."

With that, I kept the conversation from students to a minimum and did my best to cover the content I had planned for the day.

Once we returned to homeroom, I brought my students to the auxiliary gym, joining Chanelle's class for practice. She had them all focused on training their root magics, the same as what I'd planned, but not in the fun make-a-game-out-of-it way.

"Here I figured you were avoiding me," Chanelle thought.

"And why oh why would I be avoiding you?"

Chanelle's eyes widened, momentarily startled I'd linked to her mind so seamlessly, something I'd never done before. An easy thing for me, even with my branch acting wonky. The only thing really affected was glimpsing Milo randomly and my inability to summon manifestations.

"Calling in my favor. I need you to cover the Volunteer Program." Chanelle quickly recovered and rambled off a very long checklist of dos and don'ts for supervision.

"A bit short notice." I glared.

"Please, as if you've got better things to do." Chanelle eyed me up and down, judgment in what she considered grungy. *"We both know Enchanter Evergreen's busy, so no late-night rendezvous."*

"Must you?"

"I must."

Their friendship was still irksome. Sometimes, the way Milo and Chanelle boxed thoughts of their conversations away when I was around, it felt like they were conspiring when together. They probably were. Ways to make grumpy anti-social Dorian Frost more outgoing and emotionally involved. I shuddered. Now, that was a scary thought.

Ignoring Chanelle, Milo, and all my thoughts, I addressed my homeroom.

"All right, let's get working on some compatibility activities." Minds bubbled, and before a single person uttered a word, I cut them off. "Yes, I know it's not a huge percentile in the ranking system components, but it's still a factor. And a very important one every guild witch requires. Mastering compatibility can make or break a mission. It's more than simply understanding how to work as a team or how a teammate's magic works. Compatibility is a skill that allows witches to channel each other's frequencies and strengthen one another."

Given all the showboating that went into guilds, especially now that they'd all cut ties on working together, it was a skill these kids didn't believe they needed. Maybe not with the present response of the media, but it was an important skill and one I'd engrain into their heads whether it helped their odds at the Spring Showcase or not. It'd help them survive this industry, which was all I cared about.

The fact Milo continued scouring for helpful and compatible magics throughout Cerberus Guild for his current case was proof of that.

"I'd also like to note that Mrs. Whitehurst runs a volunteer program that is an opportunity to help in other ranking percentiles. It's a wonderful way to improve your casting proficiency and increase your compatibility."

"We know that, Mr. Frosty," Gael said alongside his rooster's cluck.

"Yeah," Katherine said. "You told us about the program last semester, same speech, except you added it'd help us impress the panel for our fledgling permits."

"And look good for internships." Gael rolled his eyes. "*Not that any are knocking on my door.*"

"Bawk!"

"*Yeah, I know it's a third-year thingy. Just saying they could scout early. We're badass.*"

Right. I'd forgotten. I was so wrapped in the void vision last semester, a lot of my lessons and discussions were sort of on auto-pilot. Turned out many of my students had signed up for Chanelle's program at some point. Few made the time to attend regularly, yet it was impressive they'd taken it upon themselves.

"I actually love helping out," Gael said.

"You spend the entire time flirting," Tara said.

"I can't help it if all the second- and third-year hotties can't get enough of me and my cock."

"Cl-cluck!"

"On that unfortunate note, can we begin?" I cleared my throat and gave them instructions on the lesson for the day.

As everyone went off to practice, Katherine smiled, making her way toward me. She carried the weighted blocks I'd inquired about.

"Next time, offer me a real challenge. It was fun scraping the root magics away. I just wish you'd have let me make them more accessible. They only register three types of branch magic, and I could've easily—"

"They only need to handle three types." I eyed Tara, who worked alongside a resentful Kenzo and enthusiastic Caleb, awaiting Katherine's arrival. "Thank you, Katherine."

I let them all finish their practice before sending them off to their next class and pulling Tara aside.

"You've been improving at using your branches together."

"I've got three branches and can use exactly one move." Tara shrugged. *"Wouldn't call that improvement."*

I feigned a weak smile—less chipper, but at least I'd resisted a natural frown—and reached into my satchel for a set of four weighted blocks.

"Hopefully, this isn't presumptuous, but I've been thinking about ways to enhance your growth in your branch magics."

The irony of discussing ways to help her control her branches while my own continued evolving, leaving me no control or understanding of the new aspects.

"You don't need to use these. Not if you don't want to. And if it feels like I'm overstepping, let me know." I held the blocks in one hand, all four stacked in my palm, while I traced the altered enchantment I had engraved for Tara. "Lots of witches use support items, for training, for really whatever reason they need to access their branch. Or, in your case, branches. I didn't want to advertise offering these to you, especially if you didn't want to use them or found them unhelpful. But they are helpful. I think. Probably."

"Just fucking say it already." Tara's cheeks burned bright red. "Sorry."

"For what?" My expression didn't shift.

"He didn't hear? Good." Tara smiled. "Nothing. Just thinking—over-thinking, probably."

"You and me both." I handed Tara the blocks. Honestly, if I reacted to every single thing someone thought about me, I'd never function most days. Whether my squirmy wordiness came from genuine anxiety or Tara, I pushed past it. "They're accessories usually specified for practicing root magics, but witches have them augmented all the time to specify particular branch casting or use different support tools more suited to their casting."

The blocks hovered above Tara's fingertips, delicately twirling. I'd given her the lowest weighted ones because her telekinesis wasn't something I wanted her to focus on with these items, unlike Caleb, who'd amplified the max weight. Still, she wiggled her fingertips like she was running them through her blonde locks as opposed to juggling the four support tools.

"I know you have the sphere which allows you to conjure all three branches simultaneously as a defensive support measure. I also know you've been working on ways to optimize and transition that into an offensive attack."

"Which is going awful according to Gael constantly professing the best offense is a good defense among other sports analogies." Tara rolled her eyes, briefly lost in her time spent with the most audacious person she knew. "Yep. One tiny step at a time."

At this point, she had to know I'd heard that commentary. And while there was a lot of baggage to unpack in her taste in friendships, I was happy the self-appointed captain of cocks was helping her train.

"These weights are designed to handle any and all impact from root magics; however, a simple alteration of the enchantment, and now they're capable of handling your branches."

"How'd you have these specified to my branches?"

"You're not the first person to use sealing, intangibility, or shadows—probably the first person to use them all together, but there are apparently easy-to-follow blueprints online." I left out the part where I'd offered Katherine extra credit for a class she already had an A in to alter the sigils. She liked testing her own enchantment magic, and it was a lot quicker than filing for an official supplemental tool to support a student's needs. Basically, I was assisting two students with one casting project.

I explained how the enchanted blocks would assist Tara. Sigils covered all six sides of the cubes, allowing them to properly absorb, contain, and reflect Tara's three branch magics. Due to her branch overlap, it was impossible for Tara to cast one of her branches independently. Three powerful branches that unfortunately didn't collaborate well with each other aside from a sphere Caleb had hypothesized last semester.

It'd be difficult pinpointing two of her branches onto the weighted blocks while exercising one in a different direction, but it wouldn't be impossible. If anyone could master this technique, Tara could. Her proficiency with her root magics rivaled most second- and third-year students. With these support tools, she could alternate channeling sealing or unsealing techniques, intangibility, and shadows interchangeably.

"Although it's easy to theorize, you're the one who has to put it into practice."

Shadows coiled around the blocks covering a golden glow of her sealing magic that pinged along the sigils. Tara took a step toward the auxiliary gym door, running her fingers intangibly through the metallic bar. Simply amazing. In a few seconds, she'd already shifted the precision of two branches onto the items. The blocks collapsed onto the ground, all the channeled magic in the air quelled. Tara knelt to pick them up, stuffing them into her book bag.

"Definitely something to work on," she said. *Later.*

"Of course."

CHAPTER TWELVE

I STOOD outside the academy bus heading for the South Side, wishing I had time for a cigarette. Instead of slipping away for a few minutes, I wiggled the pen for my clipboard with a roster between my index and middle finger. It didn't help settle the cravings. Thankfully, Chanelle had already arranged for the bus and the driver since she figured I'd forget to fill out the forms. I had. It wasn't my volunteer program, and I had a lot on my plate. Also, I was pretty lazy.

Students arrived, gave me their names and filed onto the bus. A lot of the second- and third-year students were kids I'd taught. A few of my former third-year homeroom coven students averted their gaze. We hadn't spoken really at all this year since they were thrown to the industry wolves without a lifejacket, and I spent the bulk of last semester prioritizing the void vision. They probably all assumed I didn't care about them or their struggles.

Chester paused before getting on, wry smile and humming a pleasant country song in his head, a technique he'd learned after a few years as my student.

"Hey, Mr. Frost," he said with a strong southern drawl. "I was wondering if you'd had a chance to reconsider that internship recommendation."

I blinked at him, tilting my head and staring at the growing line of students.

"It's like Kraken Guild is great and all, and I thought it'd be everything I wanted." He sighed, singing louder in his head. "It's just I didn't realize how truly compatible with certain enchanters at Cerberus Guild I'd be. I thought—"

"No," I said, having already told him no the last time he stopped by my classroom to 'just say hello' and conveniently switched the topic to how 'perhaps maybe by chance I could possibly' put in a good word for him to Enchanter Evergreen since he believed his magic would be more compatible with Enchanter Zion's at Cerberus. Zion had an amazing alteration branch and was quite skillful, but he wasn't the best instructor, which was why after studying countless student interns he had who'd flounder and fail, I refused to send any of mine.

"Just maybe try listening and hear out my reasoning on why this would probably definitely be a good—"

"No." I glared. "Get on the bus, Chester. You're holding up the line and boring me."

"*Well, fuck you, too, you angry raccoon-eyed jackass.*" Chester stormed onto the bus.

I huffed, biting back a chuckle. A few of my current homeroom coven students arrived together. Tara, Caleb, Katherine, Gael, and Kenzo. Though, Kenzo kept distancing himself until a smiley Gael nudged him back in line, carefully given his spikes.

Caleb stood close to Katherine, floating weighted blocks as they discussed something surprisingly not from her grimoire but a textbook from one of their classes. Caleb had taken our conversation to heart, but it didn't weigh him down. He knew the odds were stacked against him, yet he'd planned to do everything in his power and outside of it to increase his chances at success, including over-studying for a test. It all started by getting into the Spring Showcase, which he believed every extracurricular and successful academic score would improve. They would, but it was unlikely they'd outweigh the most important factor—his branchless status.

"Where's Gael and K…the rooster?" I asked, noticing them missing from my otherwise full roster.

"He said he had a side hustle to handle." Caleb shrugged, filing in line behind Tara.

"Code for something perverted." Katherine giggled.

"His moms are making him work at the restaurant after school." Tara stepped onto the bus, the weighted blocks in her hands and a small smile on her face. "*King Clucks ordered a bunch of stuff online, or so Gael swears, but I bet…*"

"Good." Kenzo brushed past Caleb to get on the bus before him. "He's fucking annoying."

I ground my teeth, possibly channeling Caleb's frustration, but also— Kenzo had a knack for inciting irritation.

Gael giggled, letting Caleb and Katherine go ahead, and looked at Kenzo. "Are you still pissy because of what King Clucks said about—"

"No," Kenzo snapped at Gael. "I don't care about a damn thing that chicken sandwich says."

I snorted, quickly covering it with a cough, uncertain which elicited more humor. The idea of King Clucks mocking Kenzo or Kenzo calling him a chicken sandwich or, most likely, the fact that neither Gael, Caleb, or Katherine could hide their laughter, and that joy easily synced to me.

After collecting myself and getting all the students on the bus, we drove to the South Side. On the bus sat six annoyed third-year students who'd rather attend whatever party buzzed in their heads. Instead, they'd been roped into assistant chaperoning this program once a week. Twelve second-year students and twenty-two first-year students each boomed eagerly. Most were thrilled when they discovered the Wisp Prevention Program could greatly affect their ranking in the Spring Showcase, something first- and second-year students wanted to make a solid impression on.

Chanelle was worse than Milo with words. She didn't lie—it could potentially help them make the cut, but only in the most basic sense of training their magics which registered on their Cast-8-Watches; however, when selling the program, she didn't lead with that factor. Truthfully, this might confine their training depending on the areas they needed to prioritize. Speaking of confined casting, I grabbed the long-winded speech of dos and don'ts Chanelle had prepared for the outing.

"A friendly reminder." I stood, jostling a bit from the rocking bus. "While this volunteering program allows each of you to train your magics and finetune your expertise, it is not an excuse to cast carelessly and damage property. Your fledgling permit grants you clearance to cast but doesn't exempt you from fines."

Immediate sighs, followed by "*again?*" bustling in minds. Apparently, this was a staple discussion of rules they'd heard over and over again. Good, then it wouldn't hurt if I summarized the three pages of directions because fuck if I was going to read the entire script.

The bus reached our stop, and the students shuffled out. I assigned the third-year students groups to monitor and stuck with my own homeroom kids. It might have been cruel or lazy, but Milo's thoughts tugged at me, and having familiar minds close would keep me from linking to him and losing focus.

"There are a lot of wisps here," Tara said, hesitant to train with the weighted blocks when she needed to prioritize her roots for removing the threats.

All cast magic populated the atmosphere with trace amounts of residual energy. It was this energy that drew demons to shatter the veil separating our realities and led to wisps breaking through and feeding off any magic they could find.

"It's difficult for citizens here to afford to hire guilds to clean up demonic energy problems," I explained, leaving out a few of the unpleasant aspects. "Removing them requires skill in banishment and a license."

Things people here didn't have. Skill perhaps, but risking fines by casting illegally came at a high price. Literally, fines, penalties—worse if it was a repeated offense. Since guilds typically didn't get involved unless actual fiends appeared, wisps became a nuisance. Those who couldn't afford guild intervention either suffered constant demonic disruptions or had to wait for the city to get involved, which caused higher property taxes for securing the space. By securing, it meant the city outsourced to guilds who overpriced their public service, and in turn, the city gouged residents unfortunate enough to be too poor to hire help or practice legally.

It was a fucked system.

And while Enchanter Evergreen did his fair share of community outreach programs, there was a certain balancing act he maintained to appear objective and remain in high demand to the elites who funded his freebie cases. No one was allowed to do anything charitable without considering every single political, social, and financial angle. Why was he in my head? I cracked my neck, quelling his distant thoughts and remaining here and attentive.

Tara had only recently joined the Wisp Prevention Program due to Gael and King Clucks' constant pestering, and now they'd abandoned her. Tara tucked her support tools away and instantly banished a small cluster hovering at a streetlamp.

I joined in her efforts to clear the glowing wisps.

"It's really a shame, these poor people," Jamie said, strolling close to Tara.

"I assigned you to Chester's group," I said.

"Sorry, I'd just feel more comfortable with a proper instructor. I'd hate to make a mistake under the guidance of peers." Jamie feigned a weak smile and eyed Tara. "*Besides,* **my** *chaperone clearly* **sucks**. *Must be the* **shitty instruction** *he's gotten over the years.*"

I scowled.

"Sorry. My mind isn't my own sometimes." Jamie blushed, actually faking embarrassment.

"Uh-huh. Let's go." I led them down the street.

Jamie kept close, which I'd say I preferred because I didn't trust him, but his thoughts bubbled with nefarious comments.

"This place really is flooded with demonic energy." Jamie banished a cluster of wisps outside a convenience store, warily eyeing those standing at the entrance smoking. "Probably wouldn't be so bad if people didn't cast illegally so much. But—"

"Not everyone can afford a casting club to train in," Caleb interjected, preventing Jamie from segueing the topic to how this was all the Whitlock's fault. A speech Jamie had perfectly planned. Caleb didn't know that but held disdain for Jamie all the same. The cutting comments he'd made about Caleb, Tara, Katherine, Gael, Kenzo, and other students lingered in Caleb's surface thoughts. He refused to let this kid put the blame on the people of the South Side. This was his neighborhood.

"That's all well and good, but casting clubs really are for a select group." Jamie eyed Caleb. "The problem is, they don't have the decency of cleaning up their own messes. That affects all of us, you know? I just worry about demons being unleashed."

I shuddered at Jamie's comment, reminded of Milo's case, my mind aching to reach out to his.

"Root magics are incredibly difficult to master." Caleb banished six wisps before Jamie could channel his magic.

"You're right. Thankfully, you had the motivation to master your root magics because, well, you know." Jamie smiled, and Caleb fought back a frown at yet another reminder that his roots weren't enough for this industry. "I just think if they're going to poorly cast their branches and can't learn to sense and banish demonic energy, maybe they could complain less about handouts from us."

"From you, you mean." Kenzo glared, burying the way it stung when Jamie directed his cutting comments at Caleb. It tugged at his past, reminding him of all the time he'd spent with Caleb, how they played in these neighborhoods for years, and he wasn't about to let someone like Jamie talk down about his home, even if he hated the emotions this place brought up when standing so close to Caleb. He was, as always, a perplexing student. "You talk too much. It's annoying. I've lived in the South Side my entire life, and not once have I heard someone complain about the scraps academies offer because they need a write-off. More often, it's the disingenuous bullshit people spout when helping."

"I'm sorry, what's your name a—"

"Frost," Kenzo cut Jamie off, bored by every word Jamie said. "I'm scouting ahead unless you have some teacherly bullshit nonsense you call wisdom to add."

Rolling my eyes, I waved him off. Kenzo, for once, was the least of my angry worries.

"Can I also scout ahead?" Caleb was antsy, eyeing me and his Cast-8-Watch. "Um, to help clear the neighborhood?"

"Of course." I sent him ahead.

"I've actually got an amazing combination spell." Katherine held up her grimoire. "It might not be ready today or ever but would massively improve demonic regression, which, as you know—"

"Go." I held up a hand, unable to comprehend half the words buzzing in Katherine's surface thoughts. "Have fun helping."

"*YES!*" Katherine soared away.

I clenched my jaw, biting back her bursting excitement.

"Well, looks like it's just us." Jamie stepped closer to Tara.

Dammit. Jamie didn't ease the tension in my tight jaw.

"Don't forget me." Gael brushed between Tara and Jamie, careful not to hit either with his spikes, yet those along his shoulder next to Jamie bulged, jutting out, forcing Jamie to backstep. "Oops. Sorry. Some of us aren't as amazingly skilled with their branches as you."

Gael's sharklike teeth beamed, genuine and sincere, but his thoughts held a few profane Spanish words which I recognized. This might be the first time I'd seen Gael angry, faking a smile for the sake of choosing joy over anger but refusing to let his kindness allow someone he considered a friend to be bullied.

It was sweet and depressing.

I should be doing more in this moment. Instead, I put out a few fires and kept a watchful eye on Jamie's carefully worded bullying, unable to act without actual evidence of wrongdoing, which would still be questioned.

I sent my students around, tracking wisps clustering between alleyways and in the crevices of bridges while monitoring them. It was relatively easy to keep up with the casual casting of Tara and Gael. She held back her roots, perhaps lost in thought, and Gael favored teamwork over showboating. In the distance, Kenzo and Caleb proved harder to keep up with. Each competitively sought out wisps. I floated away from Tara and Gael, noticing Jamie had left for an easier quarry, and I tracked Kenzo and Caleb. They shouted their count unnecessarily as their Cast-8-Watch tracked proper banishments while monitoring the frequencies of their other used roots or branch magics.

Aggression from each of them drew me down the street. Caleb and Kenzo competed purely against each other, desperately proving they were the best in the class. Not our homeroom coven, but the first-year class. Since holding his weight during the warlock incursion, Caleb's faith in his roots had blossomed tenfold. I was grateful he didn't hesitate anymore. He'd tasted real combat, strategized, and succeeded. More than anything, he'd survived. However, I worried once the reality of the industry proved hard work didn't always pay off, his plummet would be devastating.

"Twenty-two, twenty-three, twenty-four." Caleb struck wisp after wisp, conserving his other roots and running from one block to the next, sweat drenching his academy uniform.

The Cast-8-Watch easily tracked their numbers of banishments, magic allotted, and percentile of success, along with ratios of magic utilized versus wasted in casting. Truly state-of-the-art tech. But Caleb knew that. When shouting his numbers, he'd hoped to unnerve Kenzo because he'd also kept a mental track of how many his former friend had banished. For the first time since Kenzo came to Gemini Academy, I think this was the closest he'd come to second place. The pair banished nearly all the wisps in a six-block radius—skirting the edges on where we were allowed to volunteer—and were neck and neck on numbers.

Four wisps bounced along the pavement, inching toward the street corner where I'd instructed them not to pass. Caleb, having conserved his other roots up until this point, sprang off the ground and flew next to Kenzo, ready to banish the wisps and win this little match of theirs. I rolled my eyes. *Children.* Katherine lingered in my peripheral. Was that her thought seeping in or mine?

"Not bad, branchless blunder." Kenzo smirked, and gray static popped around his fingertips and coursed subtly along Caleb's torso.

Caleb winced, clutching his abdomen, and plummeted toward the pavement. I quickly shifted my telekinesis and caught him before the crash.

Kenzo banished the last of the wisps. "Ha, I won. Unsurprising."

"You cheated." Caleb knelt on the pavement after I lightly released him.

"I didn't cheat. You simply lack any skill sets, branchless. That's your problem. You expect everyone to play at your level, your capability. The rest of us shouldn't have to limit our greatness simply because you don't have any."

Caleb slammed a fist against the pavement, cracking the ground.

"Oh, a tantrum. How mature," Kenzo gloated.

"Stop." I hovered closer.

"I know it won't happen"—Kenzo scoffed at Caleb—"but I hope you manage to weasel your way into the Spring Showcase."

Caleb scowled.

"That way, I can personally show you why you don't belong here. You do one thing right and think your dreams m—"

"That's enough, Kenzo," I snapped.

My mind was too broken or stilted or selfishly fixated on my own problems; I couldn't offer anything here.

"Whatever." He stuffed his hands in his pockets and strolled away, skipping with levitation to continue practicing his own casting. "There's no demonic energy here anyway."

"Are you okay?" I knelt next to Caleb.

His eyes watered, staring at the cracked pavement, which he'd broken in anger and had no way of fixing. But that wasn't why he teared up. I held my breath, hoping it'd wane my telepathy. Caleb believed last semester mattered. Believed it had built a bridge between him and Kenzo. More than anything, he wanted to relive so much before it disappeared. Distantly, Kenzo's voice echoed the same, wanting to acknowledge Caleb, wanting to bury his rage, but he couldn't. He moved forward, unwilling to sacrifice his goals for someone else.

Using telekinesis, I pulled the cracked concrete closer together. I couldn't fix it. Not fully. It wasn't a real fix. I wasn't certain even a witch with perfected telekinesis could undo that damage. This took either a patch job or specialized magic. Little things like this couldn't be repaired with root magics, and I certainly didn't possess a branch that'd benefit healing the sidewalk.

Caleb stared at the crack, guilty and upset. Not only had he failed to keep up with Kenzo yet again, but he lacked the ability to repair what he'd broken. This broken pavement represented the tiny fractures inside Caleb, threatening to burst and collapse if he continued to fail. Threatening to continue further fracturing his broken friendship.

"Caleb, I think—"

"I'm going to find Katherine. She has my…" He swallowed hard, eyes welling up. "She's got my notes. I need those."

"Of course."

"*Weak. Useless. Pathetic.*" Caleb hovered ahead, faltering because the constant practice with the weighted blocks ached his muscles.

At the edge of the block, Kenzo lingered.

"Don't give up like that. You've got more to—" Gray static pulsed through Kenzo's entire body, internally and externally. It did nothing to silence his thoughts, but I quelled them myself. He'd improved the effectiveness of his branch so precisely. Simply amazing.

There was so much broken between Kenzo and Caleb that I didn't know where to begin. I was the worst person to fix these two—if they needed fixing. Milo would know. Chanelle too. Bet she didn't endure this pain and struggle when dragging students out for this outreach program.

I sat alone, fixing the pavement while my students continued doing their best to improve their branches, roots, assistance, and every broken flaw I'd overlooked.

Did I really care? I couldn't decide, fixated on the link developing between Milo and me. Dreams, hopes, and desires sprang forward. I doubted my intent. Was it mine?

CHAPTER THIRTEEN

*"**I CAN** only hope Cassidy's intel is useful. The attacks have remained sparse and mostly limited given the targets, yet I doubt active demons will be content taking scraps much longer."*

And the pot on the back burner of my mind began to overflow. Milo's thoughts circulated so triumphantly that I put all my attention on him, remaining on autopilot once I got home. He wouldn't visit me tonight; I didn't bother checking the buzz of my phone as he sent a phony text about being stuck in the office.

"Shit," he mumbled as he drove toward Cassidy's club. *"If you're linked, you know the paperwork was an autocorrect by my damn phone. I'm working a case."* Satisfied by his correction, he smirked. *"If he's not linked, he'll never know."*

For someone who knew my telepathy better than most, he still missed catching some of those thoughts that spun through his head. I chuckled. It was a really difficult thing to avoid a thought, even when someone was aware they were thinking it. Pesky thoughts slipped by so swiftly.

Milo walked up to Gwendolyn's Guns & Gals and found himself immediately blocked at the entrance by Gavin, the tall, muscular guard who still wore the same scowl the last time Milo crossed his path. Milo skirted around

Gavin, only to have a broad arm slung in his way.

"As someone who very much vibes off angry energy—I have a type, I know—gotta say, you're sending me mixed signals here." Milo grinned, unable to recall Gavin's name, and knew full well neither his charm nor sass worked.

"Cassidy doesn't want you here."

"Really? Is that why she called me with the intel I inquired about?" Milo hadn't outed her or their association. He'd seen enough potential and cemented futures of Cassidy with Gavin at her side to understand they held no secrets when it came to her business or who she did business with. However, he couldn't say the same for her guard. Something about him was difficult to read here, yet it didn't concern Milo.

"She'd prefer discretion." Gavin pointed to the alleyway leading to a side door entrance. "Your last unwelcome visit left some guests feeling uncomfortable."

"Hmm." Milo exaggerated a shudder. "I've been accused of many things, but causing discomfort. My PR team's gonna have a field day with that accusation."

Gavin led Milo to the alleyway. Whether because of how frivolously Milo treated the situation as the pavement turned into gravel in the seedy alleyway or the fact I couldn't hear a single thought from Gavin, I was left paranoid and unnerved. I couldn't hear anyone else's thoughts when attached to Milo this way.

The sun faded the further they walked toward the entrance at the back of the club. This felt very much like a trap, yet Enchanter Evergreen, with tenfold more experience than me in the industry, didn't treat it as such. Maybe I was overworked or too close to him and worrying for nothing. Still, I amplified by telepathy, casting a link.

"Milo, be cautious. This feels like a setup. Like a really, really obvious setup." Nothing. Either it didn't work, or he didn't acknowledge my link. I'd consider it the latter since his thoughts vanished into visions I couldn't read or hear or make sense of.

"Have to say, I've made my way to many backdoors and never been so unaware of what to expect." Milo winked, turning the corner with Gavin at his side. "Usually, there's more foreplay."

Gavin, the burly powerhouse, shoved Milo ahead toward a crowd. "You talk too much. Make light too much. It's disgusting."

"Rough and not the foreplay I expected." Milo kept his gaze on every person he faced but listened closely to the shift of Gavin's feet against the gravel. In a matter of seconds, Milo had assessed each person and gathered a headcount of twenty people. Despite his close proximity and channeling his branch, he couldn't see a single potential thing in any of their futures. He couldn't even ascertain if he'd already glimpsed their possibilities before. Something shielded every single aspect of his clairvoyance.

"Wondering why it's so quiet?" Gavin asked with this smug, arrogant tone that infuriated me.

"Probably because no one's talking," Milo countered, still observing silence.

My heart raced, and I leapt toward the door, ready to fly downtown and help Milo, but the link fuzzed, obscuring everything. Dropping to my knees, I reached out. I squeezed the doorknob, focusing.

Silence.

Not a single thought in the air.

Absolutely nothing—even nearby minds.

My heart thumped so hard, my throat ached.

"Ah. Enchantments with hexes to block psychic magics," Milo said with a big smile.

I rolled my eyes up, resisting tears as I remained linked to his mind, ready to help. Not that I could. How could I fight twenty likely warlocks?

"Psychic branch—sure," Gavin said, his voice fueling me with fury as I stood still, maintaining the link. "Specifically, all these sigils are designed to block clairvoyance, so you're utterly useless, Inevitable Failure."

Sheer force helped me through the door, into the sky, and heading toward Milo.

"Theodore proved you're nothing without your branch, so each of us has an enchantment blocking your visions."

"Specifically, clairvoyance. Nice touch," Milo said, growing agitated by the continued support for the warlock incursion he believed he'd squashed.

Theodore Whitlock's supporters had created fanatics clamoring for the liberation of magic for all, which continued sprouting far and wide across the world in little pockets, but it dawned on Milo that the wicked warlock Whitlock still had a faint rallying call even behind bars. I ground my teeth, recalling how the doctor carved up witches, bound fiends inside their minds, and slaughtered branchless witches to perfect her experiments in liberating magic for all, something these warlocks surrounding Milo clearly didn't care about. It didn't bother Milo either. He maintained perfectly calm when recalling the damage warlocks did to the city months ago; he compartmentalized it, still studying those surrounding him now.

He acknowledged it, understood the cause and reasoning, and fixated on ways to steer something extreme to something successful. He'd focused much of his time snuffing out followers and possibilities which might lead to an onslaught that'd cause a city-wide rebellion. Remaining delicate because there were folks who needed to raise awareness about the injustices of licensing. Still, he regretted not taking a more thorough approach. Had he, there might be a chance he caught sight of these individuals who'd set this trap in the back alley.

Wind splashed my face as I flew in the air while struggling to maintain the link. How would he have known this possibility when they'd designed enchantments specifically to block his branch?

"You're awfully calm, Enchanter Evergreen." Gavin approached, channeling fire in his fists.

"Just wondering how closely you lot examined those sigils." Milo eyed each of them, studying their movements, the release in some magics, and delving into countless scenarios of assumption. "They aren't specific to my frequency, which will be your downfall."

He boasted, knowing full well he didn't have the time or energy to override the sigils. Sure, if Milo focused, pushed his psychic energy ahead, he could overpower the weak hexes and reveal whatever intricate details necessary on their futures, this trap, and the reasoning behind the attack.

There wasn't time for that, however, and in an instant, Milo leapt forward, grabbing two attackers by the throat and dropping them to the ground.

He channeled enough telekinesis to stun them into submission before lunging for his next target.

The only purpose behind his comment was meant to invoke hesitation, which worked. He'd struck three others with telekinetic bursts before a single person raised a magical counterstrike.

Enchanter Evergreen didn't need his branch for this battle.

The dual-screen vision shook my flight. Each breath was tight, painful, merged by the thinned air and confining alleyway battlefield where Milo fought.

I was too worried about his safety to focus, which meant the only way I could safely reach him was by quelling my telepathy entirely. But the second I turned it off, if I even could, I'd have no idea how he was.

My teeth chattered, watching flames, toxic smoke, ice, and bullets all aimed at Milo. My levitation faltered, frightened, sending me propelling downward faster since my telekinesis continued at full strength. I plummeted like a rocket.

Milo eliminated each one, telekinetically shifting ice to catch the bullets, propelling the toxic smoke into flames that he'd guessed was flammable. Not guessed. Predicted, based on experience.

He soared with levitation and telekinesis at heights none of his attackers matched. Predicting when they would cast, strike, or parry, Milo struck each foe down one by one.

A telekinetic punch rendering them unconscious; a low swoop of his leg to drop them to the ground; shifting their body right as they cast magic and causing chaos onto another one. It had nothing to do with his clairvoyance.

I panted, channeling his strength, my own exhausted body waning. Crashing into a nearby rooftop, I skidded across the shingles, wincing. I needed to help. I punched the roof, cracking a stone shingle.

It wasn't nearly as effective or powerful or precise as the telekinesis Enchanter Evergreen unleashed. I couldn't do anything to help. Every step I took, every attempt to use my roots drained my telepathy and hid the scene of Milo's battle unfolding before my eyes.

He weaved between each of his attackers, dodging branch magics, countering blows, striking opponents, and thinning his enemies faster than I could take a fifteen-minute flight downtown. Hell, I hadn't even escaped my neighborhood before he'd dropped half of those in the back alley.

"How'd you… We planned… You couldn't see…" Gavin stumbled on the gravel, the last one standing, his flames fizzling out as I started to stand again.

"I've fought thousands of battles, seen millions." Milo grabbed Gavin and dragged him toward the steel door. "Each was a learning experience and held a mistake I won't make again. This one too, in fact, has its own learning process."

"AH!" Gavin shouted.

"Point is, there's not a damn thing that can shock me."

The burst of the door off its hinges created a rattling cacophony in my skull, cascading down the columns of my spine. It made it difficult to stand, to breathe, to cast, or quell.

I needed silence. True and absolute. For just a few seconds.

Enchanter Evergreen slammed Gavin against Cassidy's bar, leaving the unconscious man there for all to see. Everyone froze, stunned by his actions, so much so the music came to a halt.

"Explain yourself." Cassidy rose, ignoring everyone and glaring at Milo.

"Seems you're sharing loyalty." Milo ripped the enchantment off Gavin's chest, handing it to Cassidy. "Hopefully, these don't hit the market soon. I'd hate to see it cut into your business."

She studied it closely, examining the intricacies that likely differed from those she'd created for purchase. Each enchantment branch had a signature, honestly too subtle for me to register, and right now, my heart pounded for Milo, wishing he'd leave this place before his luck ran out. He stood there, waiting for Cassidy to finish her short analysis.

"They're quite intricate, almost sophisticated." Cassidy eyed the half-conscious Gavin. "Shame, really."

"Why's that?" Milo's nonchalance made me shiver.

"I would've loved to meet the individual with this branch. It's artful. Yet, I'll be busy snuffing them out."

"Careful." Milo grabbed Cassidy's wrist, gleaning unknown futures, but filled with blood that made each step I took to lift myself off this rooftop unbearable. "I'd hate to see you make a choice we'd both regret."

"So sweet, The Inevitable Future always looking for the best outcome when the world's shit." Cassidy broke her grip free, snapping her fingers simultaneously. "Please, escort Gavin to my office."

Two employees grabbed Gavin and pulled him off the bar, which Milo didn't object to. In fact, with the enchantment removed, he studied all the outcomes Gavin McCoy might face in this situation. Nothing gave him pleasure, silent as the potential pathways were to me, but he prioritized the future of far more and didn't see anything worth interjecting over. Gavin's fate was his own—an unfortunate one he'd have to live with; Milo's words would have little effect on it, so he didn't bother.

My heart pinched, synced to his own. Even a man he knew so little about, despised in the moment, it pained him. Milo wanted to care because that was his responsibility to focus on every potential future, even those he couldn't predict, hopeful for the best. Still, he swallowed that guilt and used the event to easily assuage Cassidy to pass along her information.

"Despite the pleasantries, I'd prefer you leave." Cassidy slid an envelope across the bar. Turning her head away, she ran her fingers through her hair, paying Milo no attention. "I will say, your profile's way too big to walk through the front doors."

"That much I caught." Milo smirked, half tempted to kiss her cheek or hug her for nostalgia and because he'd longed for a future where they each dropped business and simply enjoyed the company of the other. It was a future neither believed possible. "Thank you."

Milo exited confident the demonic threat hadn't blocked too much of his branch, despite his lack of focus. Demons held too much immunity to branch magics. Still, he'd called it right. Smaller industry witches would work best at resolving this problem before it escalated.

My phone buzzed. Lingering on the rooftop, I answered.

"Hello?" The gruff rasp of my voice echoed either from a glitch or the fact my mind was still linked to Milo, who was on the other end of the call.

"Thought we had an arrangement. I couldn't take two steps into that alley without seeing potential futures of you barging into Cassidy's club."

"You were in danger."

"I'm always in danger. You know this." Milo took a heavy breath. It hit the phone harshly, and he straightened his tie on the other end, his composure shifting. In this brief conversation, he had a sterner expression than when faced with actual combat. "You said you wouldn't interfere or involve yourself, remember?"

"That was before you were surrounded by twenty warlocks."

"Half were warlocks at best, though a few others are certainly on the path to becoming them if they don't change their ways."

We sat in silence, his thoughts wandering around, avoiding topics and skirting past things he knew he shouldn't say—shouldn't think. He didn't want to scold me. The idea of me throwing myself into a fight, ill-prepared, altering fates or plans, or leaving him unguarded because he feared any outcome that would bring me there. Then, he dwelled on the battle he had thrown me in last semester. His hands wrapped along my bloody throat, his world falling apart, my death imminent, and he had only himself to blame. Milo would never allow a future like that to come so close again.

"I won't do that again. Get myself involved." I picked myself up, brushed dirt from my pants, and walked across the cracked rooftop. "I'm sorry I worried you."

"I'm sorry I worried you, too."

"I should probably apologize to the owner of this house."

"How bad is it?"

"Not terrible. I'll exchange insurance info and watch my casting liability premium skyrocket."

"Just go home, Dorian."

"They have specialists for this," I groaned. Witches whose sole purpose was to track magical infractions. The damage done was mild, so if I stayed, it'd be a couple questions, a few forms, and a simple fee; however, casting, damaging property, then bolting—that was something that could get my license suspended.

"Text me the address, and I'll have an acolyte file a Cerberus incident report. It's easy peasy, and since you caused that damage chasing me, the guild is sort of liable. Trust me, the accountants will love the write-off."

"Liar."

"I'll be working late. Please, get some rest." Milo hung up. "*I love you.*"

"*Love you, too.*" I hopped off the roof, lightly descending, and went home.

Chapter Fourteen

TAKING Milo's advice, I returned home and passed out. My telepathy soared while I wandered through a dreamless night. Perhaps no memories haunted me because the present frightened me enough. Perhaps my mind simply couldn't sort past regrets and maintain such a powerful tether. Not that an answer mattered. I hovered beside Enchanter Evergreen as he strutted into La Maison de l'Infini, flashing an invitation Cassidy had been kind enough to acquire for him. Something about this secret club would help him solve the demon case and stop the murders.

It was stunning how he waltzed inside without raising a single quizzical response. Sure, he'd gotten enchantments laced with glamours to alter his appearance, but La Maison de l'Infini had hundreds of sigils, glyphs, and wards to hide its location and monitor all their clientele. Inside, those enchantments lined the high-arched ceiling and marble floors. Then again, in a place where everyone hid who they were so they could be who they wanted, it wasn't too shocking his glamoured appearance passed the check-in, especially since the support items Cerberus Guild provided were top-tier crafted.

The sigils in the diamond stud earrings he wore were quite discreet, despite nothing about his current glamoured look being inconspicuous. Pretty certain they called this peacocking.

Flashy to draw attention, yet Milo believed in a place like this, doing everything he could to stand out would ensure he went unnoticed. He'd changed the color of his eyes to a bright purple, which might explain why no one questioned his glamour enchantment. It seemed more than a few guests altered their aesthetic to stand out; either that or they possessed an augmentation branch. Milo had traded in his spiky blond trademark look for gelled-back black hair, closer to my length than his. Though his complexion hadn't changed from his usual tan, he'd gained a small face tattoo of two hearts.

The appearance was something he didn't mind for blending, but the outfit irritated him. The polo shirt was itchy compared to his soft dress shirts, and the raised collar tickled his ears. And the jeans. While I very much appreciated the view of his assets, he hated the feel of denim.

As expected, La Maison de l'Infini had a lot of illegal activities to offer, enough for him to spot in a few quick glances and shut down the club if he so desired. Milo eyed the upper floor lined with portals and a sign.

Le Port Sans Fin

Some portals had rippling watery blues, others made of fiery red mist, and a few made of sheen forest green. Each cosmic doorway was linked to a different lounge in a different city somewhere across the world. This place was international, and Milo had merely gained entry to the Chicago Lounge. Each glowing portal had a bouncer positioned and another necessary invitation to cross through.

Ignoring the warp portals that led to nearby lounges offering the same delights for the right price, Milo walked through the casino section, making note of every table, bar, and guest as he perused. Milo didn't want to shut the place down. It'd simply open somewhere new in the city after a few weeks or months, and he had no interest in exploring the other guarded locations. He wanted to focus on this singular hotspot that'd become a hunting ground for a dangerous demon.

With the number of victims so low, Milo figured the demon might be traveling through the portals, killing in different cities across the world while maintaining a low profile. He ground his teeth, annoyed La Maison de l'Infini had such lax protections against demonic energy. When someone met his gaze, he instinctively forced his tense frown into a chipper grin. It didn't matter if the demon hunted in other areas. It came to Chicago's port to kill, and he'd find it here.

Besides, he lacked the jurisdiction necessary to investigate through the portals, which would require more permits and too much time. Time that'd leave more bodies. Bodies Milo didn't want to carry guilt for, so he pressed ahead, exploring the fighting pits.

The crowd cheered. Gambling of all kinds occurred at La Maison de l'Infini, but nothing reeled in an audience quite as much as their fighting pit. Powerful and flashy magics were used to eviscerate opponents. A blood sport everyone at the cages delighted in, and something Milo suspected helped lure the demon. Based on Melody's branch and the state of her corpse, he suspected the woman partook in these events. She had many older healed-over injuries that showed a history of combat, much like several of the other victims.

In the ring, a woman levitated above a man twice her size, grabbing his shoulders and flipping behind him. When her foot made contact, she channeled telekinesis which threw him into the chain-linked fence. Milo was pleased Acolyte Novak had arrived and entered the competition per his instructions. She looked nothing like her brother, Jamie. Either they didn't favor any features, or she used a glamour enchantment, too. Though where she hid it, I couldn't tell.

She had short black hair, barely reaching the nape of her neck, and wore no visible jewelry, unlike Milo, who'd flaunted enough to make him worth pickpocketing—something he suspected would make his task of glimpsing futures a bit simpler since some folks would stroll right up to him, seeking an easy mark. Acolyte Novak wore a black tank and tight matching sweats. Her arms were covered by sleeve tattoos, which Milo noticed had changed from the ones in her file pictures. He'd have preferred she used a glamour that covered them instead of altering them. And there it was. She had a tattooed enchantment tucked somewhere in one of her arm sleeves, making no one the wiser she'd changed her appearance.

The man who Novak had thrown against the chain-link fence turned, roaring at her. The arena rumbled, and his echoed voice carried terrible screeches that ripped the flooring apart. Milo winced at the piercing sound, which clearly packed a powerful punch if the audience members were affected. Novak used her telekinesis and levitation to easily evade the echoed strikes.

"Didn't pick you to show off, Lena." Milo tsked, crossing his arms. *"Well, not your roots, anyway."*

Lena dragged out the fight, toying with her opponent. It didn't matter how much time witches and warlocks spent fighting in pits like these for entertainment—an industry witch always held the finest training to maintain their stamina and casting endurance. Clearly aggravated, the man belted out an outrageous sound burst. The entire arena vibrated, rattling the fence and breaking wards in place to nullify the fighters' magics from spilling into the crowd. In that instance, Lena twirled round and round in the air, unleashing bubbles from her palms and silencing the attack. Each tiny bubble popped when hitting a vibration and dulling the shrieking roar.

```
Name: Lena Novak
Branch: Arcane (Bubble Burst)
```

There it was. The powerful arcane branch Milo wanted the acolyte to flaunt in the fight. Every victim had possessed an arcane branch or no regis-tered branch at all. It was possible some of the victims were branchless, but considering demons sought powerful quarry to whet their appetites, Milo suspected the unlicensed victims simply never disclosed their branch with the state, likely avoiding any tax penalties an arcane branch would incur. Arcane branches were among the most coveted branches due to the fact they usually acted as a unique merger of two or more different branches creating something mysterious.

A flurry of bubbles popped in quick succession, clearing a path for Lena, who easily soared at the man she fought. Much like her brother, Jamie, her arcane branch mixed with the primal water element. Unlike Jamie's whirl-pool, which used water and warp portal traveling, her bubble burst magic seemed to distort or destroy magic the bubbled water encountered.

Lena closed the distance between herself and her opponent, swinging a fist, unafraid of his much more muscular arm barreling to counter her. Each of them swelled with telekinesis channeled into their knuckles. When they collided, bubbles released from Lena's wrist, eating away at the telekinetic burst both had created, yet a few popped along the man's arms. A caustic strike, which made him wince, and his muscles waned. Unable to maintain his stance, Lena easily overpowered him and knocked him directly to the ground.

Clearly, her bubble burst affected more than magics. It seemed to weaken anything and everything it came into contact with, including her own root magics. A powerful yet dangerous branch. All Enchanter Evergreen focused on was if it'd be enough to entice a demon for the evening. He didn't expect much luck but kept a close eye on the crowd, glimpsing snippets of their potentials and immediately crossing them off his suspect list.

Demons possessed heightened resistance to magic which was what made me so uncomfortable with Milo taking this case. Any case involving demons. Their resistance made it nearly impossible for him to predict outcomes. However, he believed if he encountered one directly, his clairvoyance would have a better chance of interacting, deciphering.

After observing everyone he could, he stepped away, allowing the crowd to cheer on Lena for an encore. At the entrance, a young woman frantically made her way inside, adjusting her skirt and wobbling in the heels she had no coordination in. Milo regretted whoever picked out Acolyte Reed's undercover outfit because her frazzled expression and ungraceful strut drew more attention than the role he'd intended for her this evening.

Milo swaggered toward her, popping his collar and wrapping an arm around her shoulder. "Hey, darling. How about I get you a drink?"

Acolyte Reed reached into her purse. "If you don't get your arm off—"

"Go with it, Ellie. You're already late enough for this assignment." Milo stared into her hazel eyes, expression stern before shifting to something carefree and aloof. "Come on, sweetheart. One drink. On me."

"Okay," Ellie said, playing the part before lowering her voice. "I didn't mean to be late. My shift ran longer than expected, and traffic was hell, and then I needed to talk with Specialist Williams to get suited up, or in this case, suited down."

Milo released his arm when they reached the bar and ordered drinks. "Second time I've given you a case and you fell short."

"I'm sorry, Ench—" She bit her bottom lip, almost announcing to everyone who he was.

"Carl," Milo playfully dragged out each letter of the name and shook Ellie's hand.

I shook my head or perhaps simply rolled over in my sleep. It felt a lot like head shaking with the judgment I barreled at each of them. Milo should've picked enchanters, not acolytes. And this acolyte should've prioritized the case file he'd passed along to her earlier that day. I empathized with Ellie. She clearly had to work another job to get by financially since acolytes weren't paid for their guild work. Something that didn't affect Lena Novak, who'd arrived before Milo and inserted herself within La Maison de l'Infini, but for industry professionals like Ellie, who didn't come from a family with the financial resources to support her during the years of unpaid acolyte service, it was difficult.

Part of why the change in education wouldn't help shift the industry. Sure, academies had opened their doors to help aspiring students obtain licenses, but how many of those newly licensed students would have to give up their industry dreams because they couldn't afford years of unpaid labor? How many would have their license suspended because they couldn't maintain the cost of keeping it active without a steady income in a casting field?

I buried my resentment for a broken system and observed Milo and Ellie. They discreetly chatted—each occasionally blurted something random or obnoxious if eyes fell their way—and Milo informed Ellie to keep a close eye on those watching Lena.

"Your branch is perfect for subtly sussing out threats." Milo finished his drink and walked off.

Hours passed. Milo and Ellie worked throughout different parts of the club, him observing the crowd from a roulette table, where he continued blowing his money on bad guesses.

"All on red." He rubbed his palms together. "Feeling lucky this time."

He wasn't. But he didn't need to draw the ire of the owners by cleaning them out. Unlike state or federally-regulated gambling, Milo found it easier to loop his clairvoyance on the odds here. No publicly endorsed betting allowed for casting influence, which Milo had learned every time he bought a lottery ticket in his youth. Still, the enchantments lining La Maison de l'Infini were potent, and if he wasn't careful, they'd notice him using his branch to intentionally lose. He figured they were less likely to question someone going into an evening of debt than someone cleaning out the casino. It allowed him to fluctuate his clairvoyance on other guests between losses.

Having observed nearly every person here, Milo hadn't found one individual eyeing Lena during her fights that he couldn't easily read potential futures on. When the matches ended for the night, the crowd thinned some, but Milo stayed. As instructed, Lena went to the bar for a post-celebration round of drinks, keeping company with anyone willing to talk to her. None of them were more than human based on the easy predictions Milo managed. A lot of them were overly flirty, though, and Lena's strained smile suggested she bit back aggravated responses.

Finally, Milo's eyes locked onto a woman who cut through the chatty onlookers accompanying Lena, taking a seat beside the young acolyte. Not a single person objected to her interjecting. In fact, after a few words from her out of earshot and a delicate hand on each of their arms, everyone left. All that remained was Lena, still slick with sweat from her fights, and the woman in a white dress covered in gold and magenta flowers. Milo fixated on the woman talking to his acolyte, the energy around her vibrated, and he couldn't glean anything about her future. In fact, Lena's became murky when he glanced in her direction.

Nothing about this woman's appearance held demonic features. There was usually something obvious or even subtle that gave a demon away, aside from the black blood and eating people. It was part of why witches with certain augmentation or bestial branches had to carry waivers of identification. Gael's spikes didn't resemble any demon of public record, yet those possessing non-human features would fall under suspicion.

Although, this woman possessed nothing altering her appearance. No elongated ears, no tucked tail based on the skintight dress; since she wore her hair in a tight high bun, it was easy to note she lacked gills on her neck or horns on her head. Milo might've stated it definitely wasn't a vampire to his boss, Enchanter Campbell, but I couldn't think of a single known demon with entirely human features aside from vampires. Was it a devil inhabiting a human host? I trembled. No. Not possible. If one had surfaced, even Milo wouldn't sit so casually observing without a trace of fear in his mind or body.

"Wait, wait, wait." Ellie rushed toward Milo, no longer keeping a quiet distance. "I thought you said we were only supposed to observe, not engage."

In a matter of seconds, Lena had gotten up while the mystery woman paid the tab, and the pair walked together toward the exit.

"I did." Milo cracked his neck and followed with Ellie. "My guess is we're dealing with a succubus or siren. Each can compel with words or contact." He wasn't able to narrow it down since the woman had whispered kind nothings and delicately touched the others she sent away before doing the same to Lena and convincing her to leave. "They can also augment their appearance to be aesthetically pleasing to any audience."

Really? I didn't know that.

Milo and Ellie exited La Maison de l'Infini, and he held her back momentarily.

"Your only job here is to release the demonic casting she's done, lock her in place, and keep your eyes open for other threats."

"Understood."

"I'm serious," Milo said. "No banishment until I assess the situation."

"If we've got the demon, why can't we—"

"Because she's not hunting alone," Milo interjected.

His reasoning was fuzzy, like it came from something deep and guarded, but he'd seen this type of targeting and pattern before. A demon used to lure and capture prey for a bigger, scarier monster. He needed to ensure the demon puppeteering these killings was banished more than the deadly smaller threats.

Tossing off his earrings, Enchanter Evergreen took form, and he followed the demon leading Lena through back alleys.

CHAPTER FIFTEEN

MILO kept distant, tracking with his sensory root, which the demon couldn't obscure her presence from, while he had Ellie maintain distance on the rooftops. The danger with demons—aside from their insatiable appetites and need to constantly feed to keep a foothold in the human plain—was, like wisps and fiends, they could sense and sniff out all magic nearby. Unlike their lesser forms, they could ignore magical energy in the atmosphere, not snapping jaws at any and every whiff in the air, and they were quite keen at making note of magic directed toward them. As such, Milo kept his clairvoyance off her and his sensory subtle and soft.

When they'd reached a less populated part of the city, the plan was ready. Milo waited for Lena to spring to realization, which came down to Ellie's branch. I clamped my jaw so tightly it roused me into a groggy half-sleep state, nearly awakening. But I couldn't. I had to stay completely focused on Milo's mind, his plan, and the danger he threw himself in to protect the city.

He kept a close eye on each of the young acolytes' potentials during this mission. Whether because I slept, the evolution of my branch, or the closeness Milo and I had achieved, I saw his clairvoyance in action. My heart hitched, stunned by how our magics synced so seamlessly. The futures themselves still alluded me, cloaked and shielded, but I glimpsed Milo's branch as he utilized it.

A white map filled with thousands of colorful lines weaved alongside and through each other like an overlapping maze or roadmap or both. Each color, an infinite spectrum of shades and brightness, represented a different life, different future, different potential. Their crossed paths meant opportunity or fateful chance or things I couldn't comprehend. Some lines snapped off and ended shorter than others, but different paths for that same potential lifeline glowed with the possibility for a different outcome.

Milo fixated on the pale yellow, representing Ellie, perhaps. He was currently less concerned for that one's outcome, though still watchful on the ways it'd interwoven with an indigo line. A line he prioritized with each step he took. That was Lena's potential futures. It had to be. There were so many directions each of their lines went, Ellie and Lena. How Milo sorted them out among the tens of thousands also here at the moment while also glimpsing the futures and keeping ever present in the now, I had no clue.

His thoughts, his consciousness, seemed to trail alongside the potential paths where Ellie and Lena's futures intersected more than those where their fates divided. He'd picked each of them knowing full well they didn't know the other, not really, not truly. Two very different acolytes who hung in different circles and worked different cases. Still, Milo wanted to make sure he hadn't jumped the gun when requesting them for this case, make certain those interactions, whenever and however, would remain viable. It was hard for him to predict because the indigo lines became fainter the longer Lena spent with the demon woman on her arm. The demon's presence veiled all of Lena's potential either from demonic energy interference or because she'd cut Lena's futures off here and now.

"Now," Milo shouted, turning the corner.

The demon shifted, eyes glimmering with golden flecks under the moonlight. Light which a shadow loomed above as Ellie leapt from the building rooftop. She waved a hand, key in her grip, and Lena's eyes widened as a fog lifted.

"Acolyte Novak, fallback."

Obeying Enchanter Evergreen's order, her bubbles fizzled, popping in the air between her and the demon that'd compelled her. Ellie landed on the opposite side of the demon, which was now in an alleyway between two towering buildings and three guild witches.

"Lock her down, Acolyte Reed."

"On it." Ellie swung her arm. Moonlight shone against the large metal key used to support her branch magic. "Lock, lock, lock."

```
Name: Ellie Reed
Branch: Ward (Skeleton Key)
```

Bones cracked. Muscles stiffened. The demon paused. Acolyte Reed possessed a powerful warding magic that allowed her to seal things when directing her casting at them. From doors to body parts, there wasn't a thing she couldn't lock in place, which was exactly why Milo chose her. A branch that wouldn't intrigue the demon hunting for prey yet could contain it with ease.

"You think your pathetic branch can hold me?" The demon twitched, her aura glowing black and demonic energy devouring the magic trapping her in place. In an instant, she raised both her arms. Outstretched fingers grew long and far—slender talons elongated and deadly—ready to pierce Milo, Lena, and Ellie.

Milo slammed his palms together, banishing the talons aimed at him and Lena, while Ellie weaved around those targeting her—barely evading— which Milo believed she'd only pulled off by redirecting a lock on the attack to slow the pursuit.

"Fine. Demon doesn't want to stay in place. Plan B, then." Milo flew ahead. "Off with her head, Acolyte Reed."

"Unlock." Ellie sliced the air with her key.

A thin, red line trailed across the demon's neck. Her golden eyes sprang wide. She retracted her clawed hands but not fast enough to catch her head which toppled off her shoulders, hitting the ground.

"I know you wanted to contain it," Ellie said. "Sorry, Enchanter Evergreen."

"What're you talking about?" He approached the demon's body that fell to its knees, unable to maintain posture with no head to guide it.

"I didn't banish her, but I did—"

"How fucking dare you!" the demon screamed, almost as loudly as the shocked Ellie shouted.

Ellie's key flew out of her hand, and she fumbled to catch it, shakily aiming it at the still-talking head.

"You filthy trash witch! You think that disgusting branch will stop me! I'll rip your insides out!"

"Unless you have something nice to say"—Milo pressed his foot against the demon's lopped-off head—"shut your mouth."

"You seriously thought you'd killed the demon?" Lena rolled her eyes at Ellie. "Such a rookie."

"At least I didn't get mind controlled by the demon." Ellie made a face at Lena.

"I didn't." Lena held herself properly—stiff, in fact. Her expression was completely different from the wild fighter earlier this evening. "Obviously, I allowed myself to fall prey to the compulsion to lure the succubus out and assist in Enchanter Evergreen's case."

"Sure, you did," Ellie huffed.

"In other words, you disobeyed my direct orders when I sent you here because you had a hunch?" Milo smiled at Lena, genuinely proud of her despite his words meant to invoke hesitation. Lena's expression was apprehensive as her jaw dropped, lacking any words. Ellie snorted until Milo's gaze fell on her. Her posture straightened, and her grin disappeared.

Milo's smile didn't falter. He was sincerely honored by how the two held themselves on this mission. Though he knew the anxiety a well-timed smile with eyes not matching the joy could do to induce a bit of fear. Luck and skill had favored them tonight—all three of them—and he didn't want either of his acolytes to convince themselves their talent could let them drop their guard for a second. He was also impressed by Acolyte Novak confirming the demon was actually a succubus, something he'd suspected based on compulsion. Her taloned augmented fingers were another tell-tale sign. What he was most thrilled about in this moment was the converging paths of yellow and indigo and how many lit up with possibility when he stared at the acolytes.

"Now, succubus, do you have a name?" Milo pressed his foot against the demon's skull harder. "Or should I just continue calling you by your demonic type? Or do you prefer I simply address you as demon? I'd hate to be rude before banishing you."

"I thought you—"

Milo glared at Ellie, who immediately slapped a hand over her mouth, remembering not to give away their hand.

"You're hurting me!" the succubus cried, blubbering loudly as her head cracked under Milo's foot. "Please, stop!"

"You almost sound sincere." Milo added a telekinetic pulse, which created a crunch beneath his heel. "Did you learn to mimic that from one of your victims?"

The tears stopped, and the frightened headless succubus's expression turned sour. Her eyes carried hate, and the twinge in her expression held malice and resentment. This was an individual who wanted desperately to eviscerate the witch who had her head pinned to the ground. It was also an expression I'd become used to observing over the years. Teens who wanted to attack someone or something held only in check by morals or rules or confused hormones.

"Can't blame a girl for trying," the succubus sighed, releasing her rage in a single breath. Now, she stared at Milo, unamused by the situation and mostly bored. "Go ahead and banish me."

"You're ready to die just like that?" Milo quirked an eyebrow, continuing to keep his foot pushed firmly against the demon's head as he attempted to sync his clairvoyance to the succubus.

Banishment didn't destroy demonic energy; it merely pushed the energy out of our plain and back to the demon realms outside our own. However, the consciousness of the demon wasn't banished. It was obliterated. Destroyed. Dead and gone.

When demons broke into our reality, the collision would shatter their physical form until all that remained were wisps of demonic energy. Their consciousness then floated in the ether, awaiting wisps to gather, create fiends, for a single fiend to store enough magic, and for the demon consciousness to then possess a suitable host. It was bizarre this demon was so willing to cast aside her very existence.

"I'm ready for death. Anything to escape the nauseating smell of your unsavory magics."

The nonchalance left Milo perplexed. Demons did everything to maintain their life, which was why they feasted so continuously. Unlike witches who stored and channeled magical energy, demons oozed and leaked the magical energy of this dimension quickly, making it impossible for them to retain their life and form without constantly devouring magic.

Ignoring his concerns, Milo kept his branch fixed on his acolytes and a thousand other nearby lives but used the bulk of his magic in an attempt to weave around the succubus's potential future, hoping to glimpse allied demon threats.

"You spend a lot of time with clairvoyants?" he asked quite politely, even lifting his foot to stop squishing her cheeks.

"Not even sure what branch that'd be," she said.

"Fibber."

"What's going on?" Ellie asked.

"Demons have a natural immunity to branch magics," Lena explained. "However, that resistance can be superseded by a skilled enchanter."

"However, however," Milo said playfully. "The more a demon encounters a particular branch or the type of magic from that branch, the stronger their immunity to it becomes. It also makes it less effective for them to feed on."

In other words, this succubus might've had a big diet in arcane branches now like all the current victims, but perhaps in the past, she'd fed on lots of witches with a psychic branch similar to Milo's. It all came down to his specific frequency and the skill he had in channeling and overpowering the demon's natural resistance.

The succubus's body lunged forward. Lacking a good vantage point to see her target, the body missed Milo's chest as he leaned back. Lifting his leg, he kicked the air, pinning the demon's body to the wall and holding it in place with telekinesis. Redistributing the telekinesis into his arm, he kept the body bound and stomped his foot onto the demon's head. Harder. More force. More magic.

"Melody Mauve, Jonathan Graves, Tyson Beck, Angela Mayes…" Enchanter Evergreen said name after name, recounting victims that'd died since the demons arrived in Chicago. *Returned.* The word clung to his thoughts furiously. All the lives snuffed out. Whether bright, gloomy, or mundane, he'd never know now. I couldn't see the colors or broken threads clearly, but there were potential futures ripped away. He studied other threads, the ripples next to them, the alteration in pathways that'd taken root. "Who are you working with?"

Images flashed, muddling my connection. Milo's eyes fluttered, having established a link to the demon's energy, and he searched through her possibilities, seeking leads.

"Me," a deep voice called out, sending a slithering shudder down my spine.

A familiar voice. A haunting voice. A voice I'd never wanted to hear again.

Wisps illuminated the alley. Milo spun around, realizing another demon had arrived. He vanquished the succubus and now stood squarely between Acolyte Novak and Reed. Neither young witch had noticed his demonic energy or reacted to his physical presence. How could they? Enchanter Evergreen had been caught off guard by the sheer speed of this monstrosity. The white lights of wisps created a sheen sparkle among the sapphire scales covering the demon.

No. No. No.

This was a gorgon. There were countless gorgons. This was not the same one. It couldn't be. His eyes lingered on Milo, slowing his reaction time. Their gaze caused petrification, allowing them to slow the speed of anything their vision had sight of.

Gorgons were deadly. Dangerous. Even the best enchanters… No.

I took a deep breath because the fear consuming me began breaking the connection of my telepathy linked to Milo. This wasn't like then. This wasn't the same demon. Milo was more prepared, more powerful, than we were then.

"It's been a long time since our paths crossed, Enchanter Evergreen." The gorgon's eyes shimmered, and he took an inhale, sucking up all the wisps of the fallen succubus, feeding on her magical corpse. "Last time I saw you, you killed me."

I sprang forward in my bed, completely severing the magic connecting my mind to Milo's.

No. No. No.

This was the same demon…the same gorgon…that…that killed… Finn.

CHAPTER SIXTEEN

I CLUTCHED the blankets of my bed, searching for Milo's mind. A thousand nearby thoughts collided with my telepathy.

"Shut up!" I leapt off my bed, quelling the world around me.

Channeling my telepathy so distantly, so precisely, was like threading a needle from the opposite side of the room with a stack of needles surrounding it. Impossible. How'd my telepathy manage it so inherently when I didn't want it to? Why couldn't I control it?

How was this demon alive? Milo had killed it. I saw… I saw it. Dead. Broken. Banished. Not a fiber of its presence remained. Even the demon said… No. I struggled to breathe. Grabbing my chest, I stumbled forward. This wasn't happening. It couldn't. I wouldn't allow it.

Milo's thoughts pounded against my skull, rocking me to my knees. Flashes, too chaotic to gain a grasp. I clenched my jaw. Everything about this fight strained my vision. The acolytes had disappeared. No—they'd been thrown back by Milo. The gorgon continued slowing Milo's speed, but not his magic. Focusing everything on telekinesis and levitation, he soared and zipped around the demon, evading the gaze. He couldn't maintain that in the tight space of the alley.

I needed to… I had to…

My feet moved of their own accord, dragging me out of my bedroom and into the living room. I'd find him. Help him. This would never happen again.

I opened the front door and collapsed onto my front porch. No. I… wouldn't allow…

I followed Milo's frantic thoughts.

Enchanter Evergreen's thoughts screamed with fury and rage and hate. Three powerful emotions Milo had almost never felt. I lingered in the doorway, wanting to help, knowing I needed to make up for my failures before.

No. No. No. Not now. Not when Milo was presently in danger.

My younger self scanned the abandoned building searching for Finn's thoughts. Even unconscious, there should've been some trace of thought. I knew that much then but was unwilling to accept what had happened. I deluded myself into believing it was Milo's infuriated emotions that blocked Finn's thoughts, that it was my fright which kept me from controlling my telepathy enough to pinpoint Finn.

It wasn't. I knew how this story ended, and I hated every second of this nightmare memory.

I had to wake up. I had to find Milo. The Milo of now, not this hellish memory. *Dammit.*

My younger self took weak, shaky steps through a corridor. A lump grew in my throat. The creek of the floorboards didn't distract from the agonized roars of the demon. Each step brought me closer, helping me see flashes of Milo's fight then. The demon lay on the ground as Milo repeatedly punched him. His knuckles were bruised, bloody, and split with cuts. It didn't stop him. Didn't slow him. He continued attacking, banishing pieces of the gorgon and unleashing all his anger.

After what felt like an eternity of standing outside the room, my younger self finally entered. The gorgon's limbs had been broken off, banished, leaving a few stray wisps to bounce around the bare room, their light illuminating the thick coat of dust freshly splattered with tar and blood. The demon's blood. Milo's blood.

"Killing me changes nothing," the gorgon hissed.

"Changes a lot of fucking futures, you goddamn monster." Milo squeezed his hand closed, banishing the rest of the gorgon, shattering the demon into hundreds of wisps, which Milo quickly removed.

"I will not... I am... I..."

And with that, the demon's thoughts had ceased. With the body banished, I recalled believing that it made it easier to latch onto those dying thoughts. It didn't matter then; it didn't matter now. We had scoured that building for the faintest traces of demonic energy. The gorgon had died. And yet, he had somehow returned and was currently in the midst of ambushing Milo while I was stuck reliving the worst day of my life. I screamed internally as my younger self fretfully took in each slash across Milo's bloody clothes.

It was one of the few memories I had of him working in sweats. His hair was damp and curled—no product, no time. When Finn had vanished, he worked around the clock in pursuit of the demon that'd taken him. No time for his image or other cases or his behavior. It'd almost cost him his guild position.

My younger self approached, hesitant and holding onto a fiber of hope. I reached out to console Milo, but he slapped the hand away. He didn't want my comfort then. He didn't want the physical contact because he knew what it'd mean. Even in all his fury and rage and hate for the demon, he did well to hide the horrors in his mind. But in that brief second when his hand met mine, I'd seen the image he longed to hide.

In the next room, Finn lay lifeless. His body broken and contorted and missing parts. Blood splattered everywhere. His face anguished beyond any expression I had ever believed humanly possible. And his...

I had dropped to my knees, hyperventilating.

His eyes had been gouged out.

I sobbed on the floor. This nightmare was never-ending. That pain stirred inside me for years. I couldn't return to guild life after finding Finn's body. I couldn't do anything for so long.

I snapped my eyes open, refusing to relive that horror, that failure, again. I wouldn't let anything happen to Milo.

The dream-state memory clouded my head, and wind slapped my face. Where was I?

Outside. Even unconscious, I had felt the tug of Milo's thoughts, and they drew closer with each propelled movement of flight. How had I managed that? Sheer will. Force. Protection. It didn't matter. I'd reached the entrance of La Maison de l'Infini. Milo should only be a few blocks away. Channeling sensory, I searched for the gorgon. The demon wouldn't catch me off guard. I'd stop it no matter what.

I flew fast, tracking the swelling demonic energy. Turning down a street, I found Milo winded yet unharmed. His outfit was shredded in a few spots but there was no visible blood aside from a few light nicks and scratches. He'd grown so much since the last time he'd encountered the gorgon. Descending, I spotted the gorgon, arms gone, chest impaled or banished. I couldn't be certain. What I knew was Enchanter Evergreen had once again stopped this demon.

"Dorian." Milo's calm, tired expression shifted. Stunned eyes with a half-smile, almost hiding his sadness because without asking, he knew what'd brought me here. "We agreed—"

"That was before this…this bastard."

"Dorian." The gorgon chuckled; black tar spurted from his lips. "Dorian. Dorian. Dorian. That's a name I recall quite fondly. It was one of two names I remember a certain someone—can't recall the human's name—screaming out for."

My blood boiled. All the telepathy in my body quelled. The world fell silent. Everything except this demon's laughter.

"Dorian will find me. Milo will find me. They're, they're," he mockingly imitated Finn's voice, stopping only to laugh. "You didn't, though, did you? Shame, really. The Ubiquitous Present and The Inevitable Future. Terrible names for pathetic witches. That one took a few days but he shared all his secrets in the end. Love when they do that. Time spent cracking that witch's noggin open, though… Guess you boys really decided to drag your feet in the whole investigation. So much for three meant to be.”

“Shut your fucking mouth!” I channeled everything into my fist, stepping forward.

“Dorian, don’t.” Milo moved to stop me. “He’s goading you.”

I brushed past him and unleashed enough telekinesis to keep the gorgon pinned to the ground as banishment pulsed through my pores. He didn’t even have a chance to break into wisps; they crumpled and faded faster than I’d ever cast banishment before. Every piece of his essence was dead. I fucking killed him and obliterated every trace of his demonic energy.

“Thanks, Dorian.”

“Stay dead this time.”

“I told you to stop,” Milo snapped. “I had him. I had seen—”

“He killed Finn. Tortured him.” I shoved Milo. “I don’t care about your case. About those affected or any damn other demons involved. This one doesn’t get to come back. He doesn’t get to mock…to mock Finn.”

My eyes watered, and I could feel my rage and sorrow sweeping across the neighborhood like a tidal wave.

“He returned,” Milo said plainly. “He returned because some other demon made it happen. Some demon convincing other demons to join it. Why? I don’t know. How? I don’t know. Who? Guess I’ll have to wait for more bodies to drop and hope another lead falls in my lap.”

“I’m sorry, I just…” I bit my lip.

“You didn’t think. You reacted. The gorgon will come back, get resurrected in a way no one understands. We don’t know how. But hey, maybe we’ll get lucky. Ten more years. Twenty more. A hundred bodies. A few thousand. Maybe then someone will solve the case. But it won’t be here and now.”

I shivered. Milo’s eyes rolled up, tears brimming, but his lashes fluttered, and he delved into visions. The countless colorful threads snapped and pivoted as he followed every direction of so many potentials endlessly. Leaping further into his core, Milo studied the infinite screens storing his visions in his mind. All static fuzz for me, which was an improvement since they were blank the last time I’d seen them in his inner core. Perhaps our branches were syncing closer. Doubtful, since he felt a million miles away, not even acknowledging me in his mind's core as he studied visions with a dissatisfied expression.

All my unbridled rage fizzled out, the satisfaction that came from ending the gorgon was replaced by gnawing guilt. Guilt for not listening to Milo. Guilt for not thinking about other victims. Guilt for not caring.

"Go home, Dorian." Milo closed off his thoughts. "You've done enough."

We stood alone on the street.

"Milo, I'm sorry. I didn't—"

"You didn't care. Yeah, you already said that." He stormed off, searching for his acolytes and leaving me alone on the street with only the moon's light and flickering lampposts to keep the darkness at bay.

CHAPTER SEVENTEEN

I LAY in my bed, ignoring the buzz of my phone. Someone undoubtedly checking in on my absence or complaining that I'd called out last minute without leaving lesson plans. I didn't care. Couldn't. My mind spun in a million directions, each leading me to answers I hated.

I fucked everything up.

I failed at everything.

I was selfish. Worthless. Shortsighted.

My telepathy didn't latch onto Milo, either from the exhaustion of sitting in my bed awake well into the mid-morning or because my magic knew he'd only be thinking the same thing I already knew. I couldn't do anything right.

A part of me lingered on the satisfaction of ending that demon. Executing it for what had happened to Finn. For what could've happened to Milo. Vanquishing demons was good. Justified. If it'd been a warlock, would I have done the same? Would I have hesitated? Would I have cared if the law of the world was on my side or against my actions? I didn't know. I did know Enchanter Evergreen had likely returned to work, ready to solve a case from scratch and save as many lives as possible. He cared about everyone's futures. And me? Did I care about anyone or anything?

Charlie and Carlie clawed at my door. One desperate for affection, the other desperate for food. I was so worthless and selfish; I couldn't even care for my cats. I lay in bed, ignoring them and the rest of the world, desperate for an escape into isolation. They meowed. Faintly. Carlie's heavy feet trotted further away. Charlie cooed, his purr mixed with a meow for attention in full effect.

"Hey, hey, little buddy." Milo's voice echoed in the other room. "Daddy got you a new toy. Don't tell your dad, though. I know he has a fun limit."

He was here? My heart lurched into my throat. Why?

"Yes, yes, Madame of All Things Wonderful, I've got those treats I promised. Just don't leave any evidence."

Carlie's loud crunches made it evident she wouldn't leave a spec of the treats behind. Hopefully, Milo knew how to slip a few along to Charlie unnoticed because Carlie was especially selfish with treats. I slipped off my bed, pausing at the door. Charlie chirped. A chirp he only made when eating and getting pets. His special pitchy chirp. Milo knew to slip him snacks because Carlie hadn't hissed once, clearly distracted by her own meal. The cabinets clicked, and Milo rinsed their food bowls.

I returned to my bed and closed my eyes. He must've figured I'd gone to work. That was what brought him here. Maybe he'd had a vision about me starving my cats and was kind enough to care. *Care.* I'd repeated it a thousand times since I killed the gorgon and said I didn't care, so now the word held no meaning. I lacked an understanding of it. Care. Care. Care. Foul and strange as it rumbled in my thoughts and hung on the tip of my tongue.

Milo's feet thudded across the carpet down the hallway leading to my bedroom. I flung the blanket over my head like a foolish teenager expecting him to believe I'd left body-shaped pillows beneath my blanket.

"Wakey, wakey, eggs and no bakey." Milo ripped the blanket off the bed. "Sorry, they were out. But I got you some sweet sausage."

I kept my eyes firmly shut. Afraid to face him.

"That better not be a euphemism." The aroma of meaty maple filled my bedroom. I loved maple sausage.

"Damn, it would've been so great if it was."

I opened my eyes. Milo had a huge smile, Charlie in one hand and a bag of greasy fast food in the other.

"Told you he was warming up to me." Milo nuzzled Charlie, who immediately leapt off and ran away, cry meowing. It was a betrayal meow he'd give when either he or I prioritized someone over each other. Charlie was quite possessive, so usually, that meow was reserved for me and my betrayals of work, Milo, or literally saying hello to the vet.

"I'd say you still have a long way to go." Me too, given how I'd fucked up so much. I didn't say that part, though. Couldn't.

"Were you actually asleep or pretending?"

"Huh?"

"The glimpse I caught, I couldn't tell, but I knew you were here."

"And that I would fail to feed my cats?"

"You were awake." Milo sighed. "Please don't take away Charlie's new toys."

"Toys?" I frowned. "I thought you bought him one."

"He has so few."

"That's because he destroys them all. He's got to learn to make them last and value—"

"He's impulsive," Milo interjected, plopping onto my bed and setting the fast-food bag on the floor. "Aren't we all?"

I froze. Damn. He'd steered casual conversation about the cats directly into how much I'd fucked up his case. Ugh. Clairvoyants. Stalling for time, I levitated the bag onto the nightstand. Also, food—bagged or not—was easy prey for Carlie to steal.

"I'm…" I took a deep breath. "I…"

"Fifty-fifty, FYI." Milo scooted closer.

"Huh?"

"Fifty-fifty on you starting this conversation with I'm sorry or I love you. I've seen a lot of versions, so let's go off script and have me start." Milo pressed a hand on top of the blanket, delicately rubbing my thigh beneath.

"How many conversations do you actually have off script?" I fought back a little laugh because Milo really did plan everything in his life, even the things he didn't plan for.

"One in five. Okay. One in seven."

I stared, expression unshifting.

"All right, one-ish in ten." Milo smirked. "What can I say? I math badly."

"Uh-huh."

"I don't blame your actions. I sort of saw it, maybe. It's hard to get a clear picture when demons are involved."

"You should blame me. Every friend and family of the next victims should blame me. I am selfish."

"You're not. Selfish people don't acknowledge it, and when they do, it's usually for leverage. I know you too well to think you'd ever use self-loathing words to strike a chord for empathy. You do it because you can't sort your feelings into words, and the best way you can express yourself is to blame yourself."

"Christ, maybe you're a manifestation, and that's the whole reason I haven't been able to summon one."

Milo chuckled, running his fingers back and forth along my leg.

"I can't blame you, though. I did the same thing twelve years ago." Milo quivered; the joy in his eyes and thoughts vanished. "I've been carrying that failure for twelve years, and last night, I almost fixed it."

"What?"

"I didn't know or think this case involved the same demons. Didn't want to believe it, anyway. I'd encountered enough slinking around Chicago to give up hoping I'd fix my impulsiveness. But something about this case stirred potentials. They were—"

"Too hazy," I interjected. That much I already knew, but the rest remained new to me.

"Exactly. Demonic energy is the worst." Milo half-grinned, mostly to fight off a frown. "First time around, when I found that gorgon and saw... saw..."

It was Milo who struggled to say the name, so opposite of our dynamic. I'd always struggled to mention Finn in conversation over the years up until recently. Tears pooled in the corners of Milo's eyes.

"You saw Finn's body and acted."

"Yes. I attacked the gorgon, blaming him for every horrible thing Finn had endured." Milo's shoulders shuddered. "I wanted to hate him, make him culpable."

"He was."

"To an extent. In the last moments, I'd seen void visions, snippets revealing another. It didn't matter, though. I was so angry and wanted so badly to satiate it then that I banished the gorgon right then and there."

I tensed. His words were incomprehensible.

"Another demon? Then?"

"It makes sense. Gorgons can't open warp portals to new places. Still, the first time around, I acted in haste, desperate for vengeance, and when the connections linking the gorgon to another source faded, I pushed that regret and impulse away. I couldn't face it."

I wrapped my fingers around Milo's as they began trembling. Without words, without thoughts, I compiled all the rage and fear and sorrow and regret wrapped in the moment Milo held for when he'd banished the gorgon twelve years ago.

"I understand."

"Then you understand why I can't blame your actions last night. I can't expect you to act right, logical, long term, when I couldn't."

"But you are now."

"I am because I failed before. Failed so many lives killing a demon that turns out can't die. How many others have resurrected themselves? Is it a new ability from demons? Is it a branch at play? A higher-tier demon no one has encountered? I don't know. Probably never will, but I want to try."

"Milo, you can't carry the world—"

"It didn't bring Finn back. Didn't change his fate. My actions then didn't stop any real horrors from continuing in this world."

Milo held onto every life lost in the city, the state, the nation, and the world. Hating himself for every failed move he'd made when predicting outcomes. That single impulsive banishment weighed on him every single day he worked toward fixing the world, one he kept carefully tucked behind the white wall of strings that lay just past the wall of screens in his mind's core. It also acted as a driving force, motivating him to always thoroughly root through visions, searching each and every single one so he didn't accidentally screw up.

"What are you going to do now?"

Milo shrugged. "The best I can. And I want you to do the same."

I nodded.

"Focus on work, Dorian. Help your students be successful. Maybe I find a new lead; maybe I don't. Maybe the demon or demons stay or return or whatever; maybe they move on." He shrugged again. "I just don't want this to be our story. I don't want to hurt you or fail you or blame you."

"I don't think any of that." I scooted closer to Milo, unable to bear the distance between us any longer. "I'm sorry."

"Stop saying that." He kissed me softly, gentle and without tongue, but his mind spoke a thousand words, instantaneously explaining I never needed to apologize to him because he'd love me no matter what.

He moved further on the bed and lay down. I wrapped my arms around his waist, hugging him as our minds synced. For hours we laid together, silencing the entire world.

My nose rested against the back of his head while we remained in this embrace, simply enjoying the touch and company of one another.

As the sun faded, our appetites returned. Milo craved something other than the cold fast food sitting on the nightstand.

I slid my fingers delicately up his stomach, carefully unbuttoning his shirt.

Milo rolled over, nuzzling his face into my neck and kissing me. Quickly, he lifted my shirt over my head and then positioned me beneath him.

Given his primal arousal, I expected him to take me this instant, but he slowed his eager thoughts, stirring with more passionate desires.

Slowly, he undressed himself, and I followed suit, taking off my pants. Milo ran his fingers along my bare hips; the lightest touch of telekinesis coursed along my skin, creating the sensation of a dozen hands caressing me, holding me, positioning me.

Once he'd grabbed the lube and prepared himself, he lay on top of me, wrapping his arms around my back and pulling me tightly into his embrace.

Our eyes remained locked as he entered me; he took slow, deliberate thrusts the entire time—edging himself to the peak of satisfaction and then pausing as my erection throbbed against his stomach.

Milo kissed me each time he took a steady stroke, pacing himself as he made love to me.

CHAPTER EIGHTEEN

FOLLOWING Milo's advice, I returned to work, training my students as the Spring Showcase encroached. I did my best to tune Milo out when his mind synced to mine. It was challenging and disappointing and exhausting all in one breath. For weeks he'd chased leads, followed thin trails, and nothing panned out. Victims continued falling to demon activity, and despite enchanters from every guild in the city out in full force searching, nothing stopped the murders.

I could've stopped them simply by not acting rashly. Something I needed to master.

Guilds were in chaos, clamoring to solve a case nobody could. Enchanters tracked and slaughtered demons responsible for the killings, but then new demons arrived, continuing the cycle. Some in the media claimed they were new, while others noted the same demons returned, accusing enchanters of failing to properly banish them. Milo continued urging for guild collaboration, believing it'd help solve the case. But every guild kept their doors firmly shut, hopeful of gaining the notoriety that came with saving the city single-handedly.

Enchanter Evergreen's mind continued repeating that if he'd only found the source of the demon resurrecting those that'd fallen, creating an army of subjects, then the city wouldn't be on the verge of collapse.

We weren't. Life was abundant, and many ignored the deaths in favor of reminding themselves they were small in numbers, and things would be back to normal soon. Not Milo. His thoughts constantly looped through potential futures and bigger threats than I could see, lost in visions of horror. When his mind clung to his guilt for his failures, I pushed away the link holding us together. Though his thoughts never actively stirred to blame my interference, I continued dwelling on how it had. How I ruined everything.

With my thoughts mostly my own, I escorted my homeroom coven to the auditorium for our headmaster's announcement. I stood along the back wall with a few other first-year instructors, ushering students to file inside and take a seat.

"It's wonderful to see everyone here this morning," Headmaster Dower said, about to begin a very long speech before announcing the ranking results for the Spring Showcase.

As she spoke, I read through emails—some from her or others about the upcoming showcase—tuning out the mix of surface thoughts and strong emotions many of the 600 students crammed into the auditorium gave off. Excitement, dread, embarrassment, and anticipation radiated in equal measure as the headmaster spoke.

The curtains behind her opened, and a screen covering the stage lit up. I huffed. Students scoured the list of 160 names, searching for their name and ranking—worried they might not find it listed, terrified they'd be handed a paper copy listing their ranking and explaining how and where they could improve during the rest of their first year. Public shaming on rankings was alive and well in this new system. Disgusting. Effective. Cruel.

Either I hadn't read an email thoroughly enough, or someone forgot to add me to the list of instructors handing out rejection forms to students who didn't make it into the showcase. Who was I to complain? Breaking dreams was the worst part of this career. Plus, it helped me keep a psychic pulse on my homeroom coven because those who didn't make the cut would need empathy.

One by one, relief hit my students. Some, like Kenzo, Katherine, Yaritza, and Layla, maintained confidence the entire time, not concerned about finding their name or surprised by their rankings. Others, such as Gael, Jamius, and Carter, released a bated breath, stunned and excited to find themselves listed. A few were annoyed they'd be expected to participate while also hiding their joy for making the cut: Jennifer, Melanie, and Tara. Two were ecstatic to participate but embarrassed at their low ranking: Gael, confidently boasting with his rooster, and Caleb.

I smiled momentarily before Peterson thought in my direction, pissed so many of his students hadn't made it into the showcase, utterly convinced I'd rigged the event since my entire homeroom coven placed. I shrugged away his envious rage and then realized that was why I didn't have any forms to hand out.

None of my students had fallen below the required 160 ranking in order to qualify. It was rather shocking, impressive as all hell, and a bit of arrogant pride swelled in my chest. I might've barely contributed to their success, but this was the first time in all my years of teaching that every single first-year student from my homeroom coven had qualified for the Spring Showcase. They were an amazing group of kids.

"We all made it into the showcase."   "Duh. Get off me, porcupine."

"Not the best. Worst, in fact, but room to improve."

"I hope no one gets hurt."   "There's gonna be so much paperwork."

"That's the industry, darling."

*"It'll be nice finally showing off my branches.
So long as my training doesn't falter."*

"I'm the only Smythe who ranked. Fucking slackers."

"Gonna rock out with my cock out!"   "Bawk!"

"I'm so sick of your dick jokes."

"Gael never makes dick jokes. It's all about the cock."

"So annoying."
Given there wasn't much time left for homeroom before they'd be

heading to their next class, I allowed them to hang around the auditorium, soaking up their excitement for their achievements and chatting with other homeroom students also lounging about.

A new email pinged on my laptop from the person coordinating this year's showcase, Chanelle Whitehurst. It offered instructions for staff duties during the event and brief explanations of the competitions planned during the event. I glowered. All this information was strictly confidential, so I couldn't disclose any of it to my students. Yet, reading the challenges involved and realizing Chanelle had a hand in picking these competitions, I had words for her. Storming out of the auditorium, I took deep breaths, which did little to ease the frustration building inside me.

I walked into Chanelle's classroom, glad none of her students were there because I wasn't certain I could bite my tongue for very long. "Are you serious about these competitions?"

Chanelle kept her eyes locked on her computer screen, unfazed by my arrival. She half-expected it and was half-prepared for resentful staff, whether about the competition setup, our extra unpaid duties, or complaining their students were improperly ranked. "We've always got to balance entertainment alongside proficiency."

"That first round completely ignores proficiency, and you know it."

"I beg to differ. Honestly, I despise selling the second round to spectators—problematic, in my opinion—but that's what this is all about. Butts in seats."

"You're running this event. You're the one bringing in more guild witches than any first-year showcase has ever done."

"What's your point?"

"My point is you have more say in the competitions, which ones we include and the ones we shouldn't." I frowned, holding back a judgmental glare as the first competition clung to her surface thoughts proudly. "It's absurd you're so proud of an event that literally prevents students from using their root magics. Half the kids who ranked into the competition rely on the combination of root magics to assist in their branch magics."

"Exactly. This showcase isn't about promoting root magics or subpar branches. There, I said it. The mean, nasty words we all know to be true here." Chanelle waved her hands, half a gesture and half to reorganize the desks in her classroom.

I winced at the screech of metal desk legs dragging across the floor.

"Not everyone's blessed with a fancy branch, and that sucks." Chanelle continued moving items around her classroom. "It's also why I wholeheartedly invest in my students, so they're prepared for the harsh reality of this industry. But the fact remains we're trying to attract sponsors, which means we need an audience with guild members who are awed and return for rounds two and three and want to fund these budding branches. And no one gives a fuck about boring branches or roots we all have."

"You realize this will affect over half of your homeroom coven." My jaw tightened.

"Fewer than you think since only seven of my students ranked." Chanelle swiveled her chair in my direction. "But let's just say the truth of it, shall we? You're not worried about my students. You're not worried about all the students competing. Hell, you're not even worried about your homeroom coven."

"Excuse me?"

"You're worried about your three little golden stars." Chanelle stood and walked across her class, leaving handouts on each desk. "I've seen the way you work with your kids over the years, and I can always tell when you're doting on one a bit more. Whether in guidance or the occasional telepathic stare."

Despite all I did to distance myself from others, to make myself unreadable and unapproachable, Chanelle managed to cut to the heart of things about me without a psychic branch.

"I know you've got a soft spot for Caleb. Who wouldn't? He's a nice kid. Plus, a branchless student beating out so many other prospective applicants lining up to make something of their magic? That's a catchy story. Unfortunately, there's a lot of other factors to consider during the showcase. And none of the enchanters want to see that story."

I ground my teeth.

"Besides, he barely squeaked by in the rankings. Even if the first round allowed root magics, I doubt he'd finish."

"You'd be surprised."

"Then there's that little snot nose Kenzo." Chanelle immediately skirted the conversation, eyes and thoughts fixated on the vein bulging on my forehead. "He has a hell of a powerful branch, but not one built for this competition. My guess? You see a bit of a younger grumpy Dorian in that kid. Minus the overdone guyliner and grungey wardrobe."

"Of all my students, he's the one I'm least concerned with." It was true. Kenzo had an unyielding determination and aggressiveness that pushed him through any obstacle. I had no idea how he'd manage in the first event, but I knew he would.

"Oh, your precious Whitlock, perhaps? She's lovely, polite, and has amazing branches. Branches she can't or won't use."

"She'll be fine."

Tara had made vast and swift improvements over the past few weeks using the weighted blocks to redistribute her branches so she could seamlessly cast one branch at a time.

Chanelle sucked her teeth, fighting back a frown. *"You haven't read the email yet, have you?"*

I pulled my laptop out of my satchel, set it on her desk, and opened my email to find the one—among two dozen unimportant or spam messages—I'd missed. A lump grew in my throat. Tara's support tools hadn't been approved for the Spring Showcase.

"Why?" I asked, perplexed and ready to collapse. "I did everything right."

I'd informed the administration who'd passed it on to the supervising proctor for the event—Chanelle. I'd even gotten it submitted early. Everything was checked off. How they functioned and their purpose. Tara had filled out her forms. It was all done by the book to help her.

"You didn't attach a waiver, so I had to deny the request."

"I explained the medical purpose behind them," I snapped. Tara and I didn't have time to apply for a waiver, but her branch overlap should've sufficed.

"I'm not saying her condition isn't real, simply saying there's no medical record to support her overlap."

The Whitlock family, her father, had years to have Tara's branch overlap diagnosed and accounted for, yet he'd never want a condition like that disclosed, even if held as a confidential file in the academy records never made it public record. God forbid he acknowledged she needed assistance. No. He saw that kind of thing as weakness, and the Whitlocks weren't weak.

"You can't just deny her support," I said weakly. "That's not fair."

"Without a medical, magical, or casting waiver to support the use of accommodations during the event, it'd be unfair to give her that edge. Like any other student, she's just going to have to do her best without support items." There was no joy in Chanelle's voice or thoughts. "I am sorry."

The bell rang, startling and louder than usual. "I need to get to my classes."

"It's nothing personal, but this is a business first." Damn, if she hadn't summed up the entirety of education in one line. "It's okay to have a soft spot for the kids. Hell, when I saw five of mine hadn't made the cut this year, I was devastated for them. Heartbroken knowing I'd have to rip their dreams for the Spring Showcase away before they even had a chance to compete. But kids are resilient, and it might take time, but they'll bounce back."

"I don't have a soft spot for anyone."

"Not even Milo? Or do you prefer giving him your hard spots? Parts. Dammit. Eh, that double entendre almost worked." Chanelle chuckled, attempting to draw me into a lighter conversation, but I wasn't able to flip a switch that easily.

I resented everything about academy-first stances, and since taking this extra add-on to her position, she'd become more and more about the business model, which was upsetting. Her opposition to all things authoritative was one of her qualities that kept my mind synced onto hers year after year at Gemini.

CHAPTER NINETEEN

MY mind buzzed with excitement, despite all the irritability and sadness I'd carried leading up to the showcase. Mostly because I kept my telepathy latched onto the anxious joy oozing off my students. This allowed me to stay active during the ceremony without wandering toward Milo's mind, and it also helped stifle the loud surface thoughts of every other participant alongside the roaring crowd.

A thrilling shiver ran along my spine as contestants entered the auxiliary gym. Staff like me, first years not participating, and esteemed guests—those we'd wrangled into coming—had already arrived and taken our seats in the makeshift arena bleachers surrounding the auxiliary gym. Each of the students quickly absorbed the massive change of the equally distributed terrains shifting locations and the half-filled stadium surrounding them as they entered.

Curiosity stemmed from how the academy had moved everything around seamlessly while adding the stadium. A few guessed the correct magics at play: primal earth, cosmic transmutation, and high-tier enchantment spell craft. Easy enough to do but expensive as hell.

They were in awe at the turnout, which I did my best not to roll my eyes at. The stadium seating only ever reached full capacity during the second-year

Spring Showcase, and Gemini wasn't hosting the event this year. Not that we were on the docket to host the event, but administrators' minds still buzzed with ways to change that. Gemini took a particularly hard hit first semester, and their thoughts often matched the daggers they shot me with scornful gazes. I wasn't at fault, technically, but oh, how they still believed my Saturday training led to the warlock incursion along with the negative press Gemini received afterward.

Truthfully, I should've taken all the blame considering everything that happened was due to my ego. The arrogance of undoing the void vision, which worked, my one saving grace in my obsessive nature, and Milo's coy tactics of altering events subtly.

Something he hadn't been able to do during this demon case. No. I clenched my fists, channeling telekinesis into the grip. The telekinetic energy tightened my chest, squeezing my muscles and keeping me locked here and now. There was a lot about Milo and his case I wanted to see unfold, but today had to be about the students. Each of them worked so hard to get here. Some more than others. Caleb followed the directions of proctors as they guided and ushered students to a starting point on an obstacle course event I abhorred.

The glass ceiling retracted, allowing the warmth of the sun to shine down on everyone. In the center of the auxiliary gym, a massive four-sided screen—the type used during sporting events—hovered through the assistance of enchantments. Small cameras floated throughout the gym guided by tech and telekinesis, zooming in on students and shifting shots from who appeared on the screen and when.

Caleb panicked when the camera landed on him. It was bad enough for him to see his face a hundred times larger in an expression he tried fixing—yet somehow made worse with each scrunched expression—but on top of that, the screen displayed their abilities and rankings for all to see.

```
Name: Caleb Huxley
Branch: N/A
Ranking: 160
```

He'd barely made it into the competition, and now everyone in attendance knew it, too. I hoped he'd shrug it off as quickly as he'd done every setback thrown his way, but he dwelled during Chanelle's enthusiastic opening speech to the crowd. Her position had given her more esteem at every turn, and administration believed there was no one better to host. She was alive with spirit while explaining the first round in the showcase, and I didn't have the heart to tell her admin only passed it on to her to avoid the hassle themselves. Even if I was still pissed at her.

"Arriving here is a momentous achievement," Chanelle's voice boomed through loudspeakers while she walked back and forth in front of the students who'd lined up. "There are many talents that brought each of you to this starting line today, but one above all the others."

"*Don't say it,*" I thought, biting back my telepathy before linking to her mind. Grumbling, I squeezed the bridge of my nose for the impending flood of doubt about to hit my mind.

"It's your wonderful branch magics which allow you to rise to any challenge, which is why for this event—we'll only be allowing the use of branch magics through the obstacle course."

"Great. I can't even use my lackluster roots."   *"Yikes. Just my branch?"*

"Welp, I'm fucked."   *"There has to be something in my grimoire…"*

"My branch was made for this."

"You ready, King Clucks?"   *"I got this, maybe, probably, hopefully."*

"I feel sorry for some of these witches."

"I'm going to crush all these so-called wonderful branches."

"No estoy seguro de que mis picos ayudarán mucho aquí."

"She looks terrified."

"I'll be fine without a support tool. I'll be fine."

Chanelle swelled with exhilaration in front of the audience, reliving and relishing the adoration while the students absorbed the rules of the competition.

"While a true guild witch thrives on collaboration, this is an independent challenge," Chanelle explained. "Any witches caught casting root magics or collaborating will find themselves disqualified from finishing the obstacle course."

This was the exact reason Chanelle had pissed me off. I struggled to drown their thoughts as they absorbed the rules in place along with their dread. Caleb tensed, all his immediate plans of grouping with Katherine fading away. Most of the students, mine and everyone else's, faltered hesitantly. Every tiny plan they'd formed during the opening ceremony crumbled in desperation and fear for their own talents compared to those around them. The academy model rewarded them for collaboration, and now they'd automatically fail for assisting or being assisted. Two minds spiked above the others, utterly thrilled by the independence factor. It forced them to alter their initial strategy in seconds, yet Kenzo Ito and Jamie Novak glared at their squirming classmates unfortunate enough to compete alongside them.

"Sometimes, a guild witch's most important job is carrying themselves independently in a harsh industry." Chanelle spoke lightheartedly, yet something piercing stabbed at her.

I bit my lip to keep from softening my rage toward her. Something about her guild history bubbled high the instant those words left her lips. She eyed me, burying the thoughts. Paranoia on my part. Her mind went blank. I shook it off. Chanelle could've been glancing at any of the hundred people in my direction. Eyeing any eligible enchanters, I figured she'd likely looked this way to captivate them as opposed to concerning herself with my innate eavesdropping. She'd never concerned herself before... Why bother now?

"I wish you all luck to be one of the first eighty to cross the finish line!" Her enthusiasm matched the roar she unleashed along with the buzzer.

Students scrambled at the starting line, uncertain how much of their branch to rely on now and how much to hold back for the last push. This would be a slaughter for those who lacked branches that offered speed, dexterity, strength, or amplified magical advantages beyond physical comparison.

I'd never ranked in these showcase events, never bothered for exactly these types of reasons. Showcasing branches didn't necessarily mean heavy hitter magics, yet academies and guilds never gathered that sense. Physically, some of the kids would keep up. Christ, Milo and Finn catered to a similar event our second year and showed everyone why they were more than their psychic branch.

"See you all at the finish line," Jamie shouted, pulling me from my memories.

```
Name: Jamie Novak
Branch: Arcane (Whirlpool)
Ranking: 6
```

"Guess you won't have that high ranking much longer." Jamie sneered at Kenzo, creating a whirlpool behind himself that'd take him a quarter of the way across the obstacle course.

I huffed. One of Mrs. Whitehurst's students. Of course this test was built for his magic. He'd cross the finish line before any of my students made it to the first course.

"I don't know who the fuck you are, but you should talk less," Kenzo snapped. "Your voice is grating, and your magic is slow."

An intentional jab meant to infuriate Jamie—and it worked. For someone who thrived on his own rage, Kenzo knew exactly how to provoke it in others, which sent a thrill thumping through his chest, knowing he could incite anyone and throw them off their game. Maybe that was where some of his hatred for Caleb stemmed. He provoked and provoked, and yet Caleb, his former friend, never struck back.

Gray static popped, zapping the swirling water and then Jamie's wrists, where he channeled his branch magic. Kenzo played Jamie for a fool. I didn't even need to scan his thoughts to know he'd studied Jamie and every other student who ranked in the top 160. Hell, a competitive kid like Kenzo probably had all 600 first-year students memorized. The fact he'd struck the specific location Jamie channeled his branch from was proof enough.

"I'd say see you at the finish line, but none of you rejects deserve to make it off the starting line." Kenzo unleashed a rapid flurry of gray static.

```
Name: Kenzo Ito
Branch: Hex (Disruption)
Ranking: 1
```

It pulsed and erupted chaotically across the field, stalking students and nullifying their magic. This wasn't a furious attempt to hit everyone. No. He'd used it as a way to magnify his branch. It was nowhere near a primal lightning strike, but the rapid release propelled him further across the field, sending him past the first obstacle before a single student stepped off the starting line.

By the time everyone else gathered if their branches were or weren't affected, Kenzo had bolted through the second obstacle, climbing up the rock wall without a moment of hesitation.

"You missed the real star of the showcase, you jerk!" Yaritza screamed, casting a barrage of comets to fly above the terrains. "Woo!"

```
Name: Yaritza Vargas
Branch: Cosmic (Star Shower)
Ranking: 78
```

Her body trembled, lacking the comfortable coordination of her levitation when flinging herself with the added assistance of her star shower. Those flaming pebbles ricocheted below, scaring other competitors, burning the obstacle course, and making it more challenging for everyone left behind.

"Not happening, Yaritza," Melanie shouted, flipping her zippo.

```
Name: Melanie Dawson
Branch: Primal (Fire)
Ranking: 55
```

Flames engulfed every single student in an instant. A fiery abyss spread across the arena, reaching the stands. My heart jumped. The enchantments glowed yet didn't ignite safety measures. I scrambled to my feet, amplifying my telepathy, concerned a warlock had struck again, and waited for ill-timed branch casting to cause harm. If the fire continued, someone would burn. The glow on the enchantments faded. A glitch?

All the flames tightened close to Melanie as she tied her fiery red hair in a ponytail and rocketed herself ahead, catching up to Yaritza faster than either of them expected. I dropped back into my uncomfortable metal seat, grabbing my chest and wishing I had time for a cigarette. But I had to see this unfold before stepping away. The enchantments didn't trigger because Melanie's casting was chaotic but controlled. Good job. A dozen other contestants utilized their branches to catch up with Yaritza and Melanie, all of them flashy and powerful, yet not one dared close in on Kenzo, who'd reached the fourth obstacle.

"Oh, ladies, you're gonna make me show you how your magics really work, aren't you?" Katherine adjusted the rims of her glasses, unconcerned by the countless students racing past her. She kept a steady grip on her grimoire and chanted several spells.

```
Name: Katherine Harris
Branch: Enchantment (Spell Craft)
Ranking: 8
```

A true mastermind of casting proficiency. Katherine used Melanie's fire branch to create a powerful flame to match in speed and Yaritza's branch to strike, block, or shock those running beneath her. Most of all, she'd found a loophole to the root magic ruling. None of the enchantments triggered to disqualify her levitation or telekinesis conjured, which steadied her flight and easily edged out Yaritza and Melanie. She hadn't cheated. Those root magics were spells she'd written down and saved in her grimoire for a rainy day.

For witches possessing an enchantment branch, it only cost them a fraction of the necessary magic to harness a casting because the spell burned out quickly. Katherine didn't concern herself with that. She flipped through the pages of her spell book, preparing another onslaught to supersede the next set of obstacles.

I gasped, stunned by Kenzo, who raced further ahead of everyone else. He hadn't cast chaotically when striking at every other student he could possibly hit. Each of my—correction, each of *his*—homeroom coven classmates zipped through the obstacles unscathed. Not only that, but on closer examination, the witches he targeted were the most adept at fast travel, strength, or anything that'd highly benefit them during this round. Hexing so many targets simultaneously meant his disruption wouldn't last very long, but this round was specifically designed to be short and sweet. Time was the enemy here, and those hit by Kenzo's hex didn't have the time to waste. They ran as best they could to keep up with the others.

"Fuck all of you," Kenzo thought, burying concern or hope he held for those he refused to care about also crossing among the first eighty to move on to the next event.

My mind drifted to the others still crossing through the first obstacle. A simple mud crawl the right magic could leap above. It gave Caleb pause, though. Him and a dozen other contestants who came in their academy uniforms as instructed but didn't own enough to ruin. Budgets over success cast a wide frame of doubt, and that delay would cost them. A cruel trick I wanted to warn Caleb and the others about. Showcases were meant to be spectacles, and Gemini prepared for any necessary compensations. This was an old tactic. One I'd almost forgotten about, meant to remind folks of their social class and who needed to make it to the finish line first. Sure, a few kids never hesitated, and that'd enrage the entitled, but it stopped more than enough for a few seconds or longer, which made all the difference in these types of challenges.

A part of me, a wholehearted part, wanted to link my mind to Caleb and warn him, inform him of the trick. I punched the metal bleacher, biting back a wince because I didn't play favorites. Winning this event didn't matter in the long run. I'd taken students who'd barely obtained their fledgling permits, never showcased, and still gotten them into good guilds. He didn't need this win. He wanted it. I cracked my neck, breaking free from the aspirations of a kid I almost lost.

"If I can't find a way to stop these demons that keep attacking, it won't matter which guild has the most authority." Milo's mind echoed, calling me. *"They'll send in the National Guard, but it'll be too late."*

NO.

I untethered my telepathy from Milo, his case, his fears, and my equal concerns. It was abundantly clear my help was not helpful. When staring at the problem, I only spotted the obstacle directly in front of me, like many of the students here and now, but Milo saw it for every potential outcome. Every miscalculation. Every seemingly insignificant step. I needed to respect he'd solve this on his own, and I needed to respect my students' hard work during the Spring Showcase because this event meant something to every single student in my homeroom. It meant something to every student in each of my classes and those I'd never taught.

Layla's roar drew everyone's attention to her, baring her teeth and swiping at students who tried to pass her.

```
Name: Layla Smythe
Branch: Bestial (Therianthropy)
Ranking: 27
```

Fully transformed, she leapt through the obstacles with catlike dexterity and ferocious speed. Most contestants wavered near her, worried those huge talons would slash them apart. A brilliant strategy on her part.

It didn't deter Gael one bit. He edged up beside her, darting at full speed and almost keeping pace with the gigantic humanoid cat form that had the muscular advantage. Without the ability to channel root magics, the rooster was forced to plod ahead to the best of his abilities, yet he kept pace and crushed the obstacles alongside his companion. Shockingly, a rooster could gain up to fifteen miles per hour, something Gael and his familiar repeated to each other—well, I assumed after hearing only Gael's side of the conversation.

```
Name: Gael Rios-Vega
Branch: Bestial (Familiar)
Ranking: 108
```

They didn't let their poor ranking call into question their capability.

"*I belong here,*" Gael thought. "*Yes. I earned it. Shut up! I earned it.*"

Given his natural athleticism, he pushed himself closer to twenty miles per hour. The average student hit six to eight; those who'd trained their bodies got closer to twelve to fifteen. Gael easily outpaced them as he reached the fourth obstacle.

"*No, your mother is a rotten egg best saved for Halloween.*" Gael leapt across the stone blockades of the fourth obstacle. "*I'm telling them you said they're spoiled eggs when we get home.*"

"Cl-cluck." King Clucks flapped harder than usual. "Cl-cl-cluck."

"*That was not motivation. You're being mean because I won't let you gamble with Carla anymore.*" Gael turned back, glaring at his rooster familiar. "*She's a bad cow.*"

Ugh. I slapped a hand over my forehead, quelling thoughts because only Gael would use this as a chance to work on whatever personal animal issues he had going on.

Taking a deep breath, I focused on students a bit behind.

```
Name: Jamius Watson
Branch: Alteration (Duplication)
Ranking: 92
```

A half dozen Jamius' blocked others from swimming past him, each prepared to sacrifice their thirty-minute life cycle for him to win this entire event. All he wanted was for them to stop arguing over the best way to do it because their bickering held him back from summoning more clones. Each one expended a lot of magic, and he knew all too well how much he had to spare, which concerned him barely crossing the second obstacle with so many others ahead.

I lingered on the swimming obstacle, perhaps out of curiosity for my students who hadn't finished it and perhaps out of guilt for one in particular. Carter swam through the third obstacle, unhindered thanks to his enhanced vitality.

```
Name: Carter Howe
Branch: Rejuvenation (Vitality)
Ranking: 84
```

It enhanced his muscle recovery every time he waned, desperate to yield, but his mind called to Jennifer several paces behind. He wanted to help her with a spark of magic, but every time the disqualification enchantments landed in his peripheral, he stopped himself from casting her assistance. Admittedly, I paused on these two longer than the others, even Caleb.

Since saving me from the brink of death with MacGyver-styled casting, Carter had proven he wasn't simply a goofy kid who loved the spotlight, but one who wanted to use that stardom to help others. Seriously, the kid needed his own show, and he needed to stop fixating on his classmates, something I'd failed to prepare him for in this competition. I could blame his magic, his thoughtful personality, but neither was true. It was the blood pouring out of me that haunted his every breath as he pushed himself ahead.

Jennifer didn't need his assistance, though, and hopefully, he'd see that as soon as Gael brushed past him. Gael's emerald-green hair shimmered in the water, a look he'd donned for luck during the Spring Showcase. Truthfully, he just wanted an excuse to dye his hair and what better than the academy event of the year. Carefully observing every single person around him, Gael stroked faster and harder than any other student, singing a song and motivating himself through the sheer belief he was more than his branch. Unlike every other student searching for ways their branch helped them, Gael wanted to ensure his branch didn't hurt others because he loved every person he encountered—even the ones he didn't like or understand.

```
Name: Gael Martinez
Branch: Augmentation (Spikes)
Ranking: 42
```

Pure athletic determination and positivity pushed him further until he reached the fourth obstacle. And Jennifer, crafty and quiet as ever, kept close to Gael. She pushed every other mind out of her head, ignoring their pain, their desires, and fixated every ounce of her empathy on Gael. It motivated her faster than she believed her body could move because the adrenaline pumped harder thanks to her branch manipulating her mind.

```
Name: Jennifer Jung
Branch: Psychic (Empathic)
Ranking: 21
```

Honestly, I was damn proud of how she'd learned at such a young age to precisely pinpoint who'd strengthen her and temporarily ignore those who wouldn't. A lesson I desperately needed, and perhaps a little more time in her head would help me gain that insight. Unlikely.

"*You need this. You deserve this. You have to accept what you can't do and find a way to do it anyway.*" Caleb gripped a rock, reaching the top of the rock wall and jumping without an ounce of hesitation.

I fought off every impulse to save him, biting back the telekinesis. I channeled inward, almost silencing the hundred internal yelps as he nose-dived into the pool. Not one student had been so daring, so reckless. Most climbed down the other side before plunging into the pool.

"*You know your limits. You know your capabilities. And you will surpass them.*" He swam to the end faster than Kenzo. Not that a single other person would've noticed the two boys internally timed each obstacle they crossed, and Caleb finished this one five seconds faster. Too much magic cast chaos and fury onto the course, making every student hesitate, question, doubt. Every student except Caleb. Surviving the warlock incursion last semester had given him a streak of confidence which concerned me.

Unfortunately, he wouldn't win the event among the top eighty. There was too much distance. Too many students ahead of him. But I'd remind him of this daring jump afterward and help him with the enchanter dream he desired. Perhaps with better guidance, too, since saving his life had only given him false hopes. I quelled Caleb's mind because I couldn't. I couldn't draw myself into his struggles. Every single student in this event fought for success; every single one fought for their opportunity.

"*It only takes the slightest hint,*" Tye thought.

```
Name: Tye Weatherspoon
Branch: Alteration (Enhanced Strength)
Ranking: 104
```

I ground my teeth as Tye leapt ever so above the stone blockades of the fourth obstacle. Four-foot stone jumps didn't slow him because he used a subtle hint of his levitation magic to amplify his root magic. It was so subtle it hadn't triggered the enchantments put in place.

"*I'm pathetic,*" Caleb thought, calling out.

I tapped my knee, contemplating leaving for a cigarette, an easy action that wouldn't affect a single outcome here, yet I stayed seated, waiting for the first student to cross the finish line. Kenzo was so close.

"*Kenny's probably already there.*" Caleb gritted his teeth, tripping over a stone blockade and glaring at Tye from Chanelle's homeroom, who continued easily jumping each stone. "*He's cheating. No way would his branch make him that agile. His enhanced strength weighs him down too much, and most of it's in his arms—not his legs.*"

Every note Caleb had taken on Tye Weatherspoon's branch glossed across his thoughts, the variations of Tye's particular magic, his capabilities, his lack of an attention span, and his limited root complexity, meaning Tye could still only proficiently channel one at a time. Caleb had studied his fellow first years closely, much like Kenzo had.

Caleb pushed himself upward, preparing to channel a subtle touch of levitation. Not enough to make him obvious, but enough to get him through the fourth obstacle before he lost entirely. Others were reaching the sixth and final course, and if Caleb didn't do something soon, he worried he'd fail before he had an opportunity to show all he'd accomplished.

The seconds ticked slowly as he contemplated, trapped in the spot and watching Tye get by faster and faster.

"*Screw it.*" Caleb raced ahead.

I needed to tell him. I could easily bypass the frequency detections on the enchantments surrounding the auxiliary gym and alert him he was walking into a trap.

"*C—*" I stifled the link, quieting everything, bombarding myself with telekinesis. A cruel casting, yet it helped improve my muscles and hopefully my roots in the long run. The point was it stopped me from interfering. Caleb didn't need it. He wanted it. I fought to separate what that kid needed and wanted because so much of my last semester fixated on his survival. He would survive this failure. So would I. I needed to let him fail.

"Disqualified," Chanelle shouted with so much glee it sickened me. Honestly, her voice was fucking annoying at this point.

Enchantments lining the walls glowed as the sigils marked upon them burst with rulings meant to knock out cheaters in the first round.

My stomach sank. I'd saved Caleb's life. I didn't owe him a thing. Crimson and sapphire lights zipped across the obstacles, cutting past students one by one. They'd reach Caleb soon. No. I owed him nothing but a proper education, a chance to succeed in this world and hopefully live. I'd given him a chance at life. I'd done my part. Yes, the embarrassment rattling across the arena was exhausting and painful because it hit every single mind here.

We'd all screwed up. We'd all cut corners. We'd all cheated at some point. Somehow, seeing the devastation plastered in front of an audience made it more painful.

Every person in the audience called out, desperate to stop the shame. A few craved it, though—they wanted to witness the fall and clamored to relish in the pain of embarrassment about to hit one of these students. Those minds sickened me, so I squashed them.

Tye was repelled from the arena and thrown into an empty pit marked for cheaters. I released a breath. It wasn't Caleb.

Caleb had considered using his roots and prepared to channel them but stopped himself before making a single casting. Tye, on the other hand, had gotten cocky, trickling in a bit more levitation with each leap to showcase his talents.

"Tye Weatherspoon is disqualified for casting root magics," Chanelle shouted into the microphone, almost hiding her sigh of disappointment. "*I can't believe one of mine triggered the enchantment spells safeguarding from root casting. That little bastard. I'm going to rip him seven new ones next class.*"

I silenced her thoughts. Maybe because I couldn't handle nervous thoughts in my head, maybe because I still held a grudge against Chanelle for this awful opening round.

Caleb continued struggling through the obstacles, doing his best to catch up to other competitors and close the distance so he'd make it among the top eighty.

Firework effects erupted on the big screen, releasing congratulatory noises and displaying first place in the obstacle course.

1st: **Kenzo Ito**

Students buzzed with excitement, terror, and persistence as they pushed themselves faster. More crossed the finish line, releasing additional celebratory fireworks while displaying their placement in the first round, name, and a closeup image once they'd crossed the final obstacle.

5th: **Katherine Harris**

12th: **Yaritza Vargas**

15th: **Melanie Dawson**

Students raced faster and harder, claiming available slots and making the screens explode with firework after firework as they crossed the finish line.

32nd: **Gael Rios-Vega**

33rd: **Layla Smythe**

"I guess it's about time, then." Tara's sorrow drew me away from the screen and to her for the first time during the obstacle course.

I squeezed my knees, disappointed I'd missed her self-defeat, so preoccupied with everyone else. Tara stood at the starting line. Clearly, without the weighted blocks to assist her branches and not having access to her root magics, she'd given up before even beginning.

```
Name: Tara Whitlock
Branch: Ward (Sealing)
Branch: Cosmic (Shadows)
Branch: Arcane (Intangibility)
Ranking: 12
```

"It's not ready, but it'll have to do. Time to show everyone a little Whitlock Chaos." Tara stepped across the starting line, taking a deep breath and unleashing countless shadow tendrils. They whipped wildly, propelling her faster. Her intangibility cut through courses, phasing through obstacles, and her sealing magic locked competitors in place when a shadow struck them. Everything in her wake either phased out of sync with reality or was sealed in place, trapped inside a golden hue.

This was why she'd waited so long. Those shadows unleashed magic aimlessly as she zipped through the courses, and she wanted to ensure her homeroom coven had a solid head start in case any were caught in her fury of casting. She didn't want to harm anyone but had zero intention of giving up when she'd come so far with her magics.

40th: Tara Whitlock

Tara edged out others, severing her magics once she hit the finish line. Everyone's jaws dropped, stunned that the girl who spent the bulk of the competition at the starting line had completed the entire obstacle course in under three minutes. She half-smiled as the camera zoomed in on her face.

Kenzo tsked. "Still, thirty-nine placements behind me. Don't get a big head just because—"

The camera panned away as Kenzo continued yelling at Tara, who he admittedly underestimated.

Students from other classes continued crossing the finish line, taking up more slots in the top eighty.

48th: Gael Martinez

50th: Jennifer Jung

Gael shouted victoriously when he reached the end; his spikes grew large, then simmered when he caught Jennifer glaring. Exhausted and annoyed, she unlinked her empathy and went back to her standard surly expression.

57th: Carter Howe

60th: Jamius Watson

Carter and Jamius were covered in sweat and grime, having lost the stamina to maintain their branches after reaching the fifth obstacle but still pushed their way to the end.

Caleb struggled to breathe, dragging himself ahead through the sixth and final obstacle. Every time the fireworks exploded with cheering from the screens and audience, he flinched. I watched the screen hit the top seventy, and my stomach dropped. Having my entire homeroom coven make it into the Spring Showcase was enough of an honor for me. Having even one get through the first round would've been a huge success, but now eleven had crossed the finish line.

75th exploded on the screen.

Caleb wedged himself between a half dozen others, all running neck and neck, but each breath exhausted him. He slowed, unable to pick up his pace as contestants edged ahead.

76th

Disappointment flooded Caleb's mind. Failure looped in his head again and again and again, too many times to count.

77th

"I can't be the only one not to place." Caleb wheezed. *"I can't."*

78th

He ran alongside students, side by side, until one smacked him, popping his jaw and stilling him for a second. A second too long.

79th

The last spot became faint as feet reached that crossing line. He lunged forward, exhausted, broken, uncertain if he deserved scraping by after so much failure. A handful of students all crossed the finish line barreling on top of each other, making it impossible to distinguish who'd crossed first.

Fireworks exploded, and a buzzer sounded, informing everyone the final placement had been made. My heart pounded, awaiting the picture to display. It glitched, a tight freeze between explosive colors and a murky face.

Finally…

80th: Caleb Huxley

He collapsed to the ground, taking deep breaths and staring at his sweaty, red-faced image on the screens, not concerned about showing his best expression. *"Now, time to win this whole damn showcase."*

CHAPTER TWENTY

THANKS to the wonderful responsibility of proctoring the second day's event, I had the luxury of arriving early to scrap the obstacle course before reformatting the design for the second event. Nothing beat being voluntold to come before my contractual hours and laboriously use my telekinesis in assisting the alteration of the terrains. The cherry on top, Peterson got to dictate everything because of his primal earth magic. Fuck me. Peterson created huge stone tiles the rest of us had to set up into an arena layout. Each stone tile weighed more than five hundred pounds which proved excruciating to lift independently.

I could've banded in groups like the other staff members assigned to the second event, but as much as I hated the free labor, I couldn't pass up an opportunity to finetune my root magic. Telekinesis strained a witch's muscles when in use, and like working out, the more a witch ripped them and surpassed their limits, the stronger the ability became.

Each stone slab was about the width and height of two doors side-by-side, which made it difficult to gain a proper grasp. If I channeled too much telekinetic energy at the bottom, it'd topple over and crumble—leaving Peterson to bitch that I'd ruined his masterful work, which would be a hell of a lot more masterful if it was sturdier. Gripping telekinesis above and below mostly worked, but I continued having to shift to the sides as I moved a stone in line with the other slabs.

My arms trembled about five stone slabs in, but I shook it off, wiping the sweat from my brow, and continued. Unlike real weight with physical lifting, there was a distortional variable in the limit telekinesis could handle. If a witch could physically bench a hundred pounds, they could easily control three times that weight telekinetically. If I wanted to improve my telekinesis, I needed to draw on more than the muscles in my arms. Redistributing where I drew from when channeling telekinesis, I ensured every muscle burned and strengthened. A technique I'd taught for years but had grown lax in implementing myself.

Cheerful minds buzzed outside the auxiliary gym, half from spectators and half from eager students who'd arrived early, ready for the next competition. It was a coin toss on if they'd love or hate it once our studious host unveiled the challenge.

"Alrighty, my little helpers, let's get this wrapped up." Chanelle strutted across the half-created stadium, wearing a golden top hat almost as glittery as her ringleader-styled blazer. She twirled a matching cane she'd finagled her microphone onto.

"That's a fancy outfit." I dropped a stone slab in front of her, readjusting it so no one tripped.

"It's called theatricality, Mr. Frost." Chanelle beamed, her smile filled her face, and her dimples grew deeper. *"You seem more frosty than usual."*

I went back to working on the arena. Once we'd finished the setup, guests filed inside. The audience had thinned some, but that was to be expected. Between the extra audience members we'd gained from the first-year students cut from round one, it almost hid the number of guild members too busy to attend a trivial competition. Either the kid they'd favored hadn't impressed in round one, or they wanted to read our website results to see if someone of interest managed to make it to the final round. Not that it'd truly pique their curiosity, but if the magic was unique enough, they might consider early scouting to secure a talented third-year intern.

The semi-finalists entered the auxiliary gym, minds whirling at the arena setup. Many were curious what this round would entail, given the limited proximity. Our stone slabs covered a large scale, about half of a football field, but only a quarter of the auxiliary gym itself.

"Hello, everyone. Yesterday, our first-year contestants demonstrated the importance of possessing a powerful and versatile branch. Some even showcased perseverance over innate talent, which gets me fired up." Chanelle's voice boomed, twirling her cane for dramatic pause while the audience and contestants cheered. I huffed. Her enthusiasm was as infectious as it was irritating. "Independence was the name of the game last round, but for our semi-finals, we're going to showcase the most important virtue of an industry witch!"

I couldn't tell if she'd gotten louder or if standing at the sidelines as opposed to in the stands amplified her shouting.

"What's the most important thing? Collaboration, of course. Something any skilled guild witch is capable of." Chanelle eyed the students competing, pointing to a few for *theatricality*. "And we'll be demonstrating this with a good ole fashioned round of Warlock Wars."

I bit back my repulsion. A barbaric name for a competition that taught young witches to dehumanize fellow unlawful citizens. The goal was to "arrest" the other team with enchantment bracelets laced in dampening sigils, restraining casting abilities. Most of the kids cheered, excited for the game, but a few minds understood the offensive nature. It trivialized criminal actions into a game of good versus bad. In this particular game, both sides saw themselves as the official enchanters, while the other team was the wicked opposition. Naturally, it was designed this way because the warlocks always lost in the end—a great moral for impressionable minds—so whichever team cuffed and defeated the other side first won the round.

The arena itself served as an extra burden. If a team member got knocked out of the arena, they were out of the competition, something I rather liked. It limited the students' field of battle, which meant they needed to be more observant of their surroundings or risk an easy loss. That was definitely a pro tip everyone needed. I was glad Mrs. Whitehurst had included it in her pitch for the event.

"In years past, we've often partnered students in a reverse ranking system to create balance in teams," Chanelle explained.

Kenzo glared at Caleb, annoyed he'd have to work with him to get through the round. Whether she meant their actual rankings or the place they took in the first round, as number one of both, he'd be stuck carrying the deadweight who placed last in each.

"But as any good enchanter will tell you, they don't always get equally distributed covens. Sometimes guilds assign witches to whoever is available. And not one professional will say they've ever been matched against enemies based on a fair distribution of power."

The kids stared, warily. This round would actually work against my homeroom coven, and at any second, they'd realize why.

"That's why for this event, covens will be randomly assigned via lottery drawing," Chanelle shouted, making her way to the referee's chair next to a large lever.

Having taken twelve of the eighty slots available in the semi-finals, my students had a higher likelihood of working together than other kids. Great, since this was a match that relied heavily on collaboration. However, it also meant they had higher odds of being teamed against one another too.

"Let's see who our lucky first contenders are." Chanelle pulled the lever— completely unnecessary since the automated system was actually pushed by someone in the proctoring room. "I would also like to note that while all eighty competitors will be facing each other in four-on-four matches, that doesn't mean we'll have forty witches in the final round. In fact, we could have zero."

A few students gasped or scrunched their faces.

"Warlock Wars is a timed event, and if members of either team remain active when the buzzer sounds, the match will be declared a stalemate, and neither team will move forward."

All eighty names were displayed on a screen and slowly filtered out until only eight remained. Four in red and four in blue.

TEAM 1	**TEAM 2**
Yaritza Vargas	**Jamius Watson**
Melanie Dawson	**Harrison Heywood**
Layla Smythe	**Amani Williams**
Jennifer Jung	**Kenzo Ito**

I frowned. I figured the odds were against my homeroom coven, but six names drawn in the first round? Yikes. I wanted to support Team One, but Kenzo had a ruthlessness in and out of the classroom. Either way, no matter how the match turned out, my perfect coven score had ended. Not that that was a concern. It would've been interesting, though, since no one ever had their entire homeroom coven place in the finale for a first- or second-year showcase. My highest number was four kids in a final bout.

All the students stepped into the arena; cameras kept close to them, allowing the audience a more personalized vantage, and standing at the edge of the arena as a proctor gave me closer insight. I handed Team Two their dampening cuffs so they could detain the warlock enemy. Peterson handed Team One their cuffs to detain the warlock enemy. I hated this game. However, the cuffs were useful for peacefully nullifying magic. Unlike Kenzo's hex magic, these didn't disrupt the channeling receptors but instead temporarily drained them.

It was difficult creating enchantments strong enough to neutralize branch magics considering they all require different frequency variables. The broader the enchantment, the weaker they were, requiring far more to handle any job. Hence why the auxiliary gym was covered in well over a thousand enchantment symbols lining all the walls of the building. Dampening cuffs simply fed off the magic it contained like a little battery. That said, they were still just metal with sigils carved into them. The right person could pick them, break them, or sear the sigils destroying their function.

"This is going to be amazing," Harrison shouted, rifling through his fanny pack.

```
Name: Harrison Heywood
Branch: Enchantment (Potion Craft)
Ranking: 32
```

A useful magic along with a decent ranking. Bet Chanelle was relieved only two of her homeroom coven students had been drawn into this round, whereas six of mine took the stage right in the first match.

"No early preparations," Chanelle scolded her homeroom student. "Each team will have five minutes to develop a strategy and ten minutes to execute it. Best of luck detaining the warlock threat."

I, along with the other proctors, kept a close eye on each student, ensuring no one exceeded casting limitations. Why'd it have to be Kenzo in the first round? He was going to aggressively strike, possibly hurting someone. As his instructor, I needed to support his efforts like I would any other student, but as a proctor, I needed to be ready to step in to stop him if he took things too far. Everyone expected a few injuries during the showcase, but Kenzo wasn't the type to pull back a punch unless it gave him more momentum to hurt his opponent.

The cameras reeled back, zooming in to keep their faces in view on the screens but too far for the microphones to catch their words. This close, I could only make out angry mutterings. Disgruntled witches who didn't want to be teamed with Kenzo, and Kenzo cursing them and cutting them off every time one dared to utter a protest to his plan.

"You know, I'm also top-ranked," Amani shouted so loudly, nobody needed a microphone to hear. "Tell me why I need to just fall in line with your lack of plan?"

```
Name: Amani Williams
Branch: Psychic (Glamour)
Ranking: 10
```

"Shut up and save your casting," Kenzo snapped. "You can thank me when you all reach the finals, double digits."

His comment clearly offended Amani, who'd worked hard for her ranking out of six hundred other first-year students. He'd diminished it with a few crude words. Each of Kenzo's teammates' thoughts festered as their voices quieted and he sternly gestured.

Layla's thoughts spiked from the other end of the arena, shifting scenarios to something she believed would ensure her team's victory.

The timer buzzed, and the round began.

"Wait—I can help." Amani's eyes rolled back, casting a slight blur around her team.

"I said shut up. I don't need your weak ass magics." Gray static sprang from Kenzo's palms, lashing out at his own team.

Harrison squeaked, frantically dropping a yellow vial. It released a golden glittering cloud that hid the entire team in smoke until Kenzo's gray static popped, clearing away the potion.

What was he thinking? The arrogance.

Anything to prove he was the most capable witch here. But he didn't register that the importance of this round had nothing to do with independent skill. Collaboration was the goal, and he'd proven time and time again he hated the guild model, seeking to create something new. That cockiness would be his downfall. Even if he won the round on his own, he'd continue proving too difficult to work with in this industry.

Kenzo bolted ahead, carrying all four cuffs in his hands while his stunned teammates stayed behind, unable to assist since he'd disrupted their magics. Jamius scowled—so unlike him. His surface thoughts were furious, but he took a deep breath and silenced them, perhaps in awe of his ruthless classmate. Unfortunately, there was nothing he or they could do.

Ruthless or not, Layla had developed a strategy of her own, lunging toward Kenzo, which she believed he'd take the bait for.

"Something's off," Jennifer shouted. A perfect ringer in predicting intentions based on emotions, but Kenzo's aggression was usually more predictable. She couldn't pinpoint it, but his rage felt hollow.

I quirked an eyebrow. It didn't matter. Kenzo leapt up, levitating above

Layla and aiming for Melanie. Gray static popped from his hands and comets swooped in, catching his strike and making it difficult to move in close. Melanie unleashed furious, widespread flames, unhindered by the few sparks of static that weaved past Yaritza's defensive strike.

Layla had predicted Kenzo's arrogance and knew he'd move in first, unwilling to work with a team since he'd barely agreed to work with her, Melanie, and Gael during the warlock incursion—and that was when lives were at stake.

"No way is five minutes enough for him to put his ego aside," Layla thought. *"Still, can't believe he attacked his own team. What an asshole."*

Yaritza released a flurry of tiny explosive rocks, and when coupled with Melanie's flames, they made it impossible for Kenzo to move in close. His legs wobbled in the air as he dodged their strikes.

Wait. What?

Kenzo had incredible stamina for strikes. Had the preparation Layla made rattled him? I tried listening in on his surface thoughts, usually so profoundly loud, yet they simmered here, stunted in quiet, wordless fear.

Layla darted toward him, knowing if Kenzo aimed his disruption at her, Yaritza would block it with a barrage of her star showers, and if he got the upper hand, Melanie would obscure the field in flames. It worked even better than Layla hoped, having kept Jennifer back to detect the other teammates' movements. She'd figured they'd hesitate in helping, but Kenzo had done her team the favor of removing them altogether from the equation.

Layla's whiskers quivered when she reached Kenzo midair, pausing to sniff his scent. "You're not—"

"Surprise!" Jamius' voice boomed from Kenzo's body. He slapped his hands together, and a half-dozen duplications of Kenzo appeared, flying in every direction and causing the Kenzo-faced Jamius to falter in his levitation. That should've been a clear giveaway, considering how his roots wavered and even more so when he created duplicates.

I turned back to see the Jamius who stood stunned with his team had vanished, replaced by another Kenzo who leapt into the fray of doppelgangers, unleashing chaotic waves of disruption the girls' team barely evaded.

Amani and Harrison stood together, and it all made sense.

Amani had used her glamour to switch Jamius and Kenzo's appearances, all while Harrison had accidentally dropped a vial of smoke because Kenzo had 'attacked' his own team. The gray static Jamius cast when glamoured as Kenzo failed to fan Melanie's flames because it was simply another glamour mimicking the disruption's look but not the power. Now, with Jamius appearing like Kenzo, it allowed the real one to slip in among the duplicates and quickly cast disruption. Yaritza hurled flaming pebbles but missed the disruption specifically targeted for Layla—Kenzo quickly slapped cuffs around her. Melanie panicked, blasting fire at every Kenzo in sight but only managing to strike a few duplicates of Jamius.

Melanie flew high, dodging an angry-eyed Kenzo, and chased after the one who wobbled in the distance.

"I should've known it was you, Jamius." Melanie grabbed her cuffs, ready to eliminate all the duplicates by dampening the original's magic. "Your levitation sucks."

"And your instincts suck." Kenzo tightened his form midair and swatted Melanie's lighter out of her hand with a telekinetic strike.

She panicked, stunned she'd fallen for Kenzo's trick. Having lost her support tool, Melanie's control over her active flames floundered. Kenzo used her hesitation to his advantage and twisted Melanie's arm until she'd dropped her cuffs into his hand, and he slapped them on her wrists.

"And now you're detained, you damn warlock!"

I frowned. He relished the fun of the Warlock Wars game. Not sure if that was a good or bad thing. A glint of his childhood flashed, chasing Caleb when they'd take turns being the villain. Those thoughts evaporated the instant he descended with a shackled Melanie. He could've dropped her, given she'd lost and her magic was dampened, but he didn't. It allowed his other teammates, Amani and Harrison to apprehend Yaritza, which only left Jennifer and eight minutes on the timer.

"Feel that defeat? It's over." Kenzo closed in on her, eyeing her frantic expression. ***"Her empathy has latched onto the shock and disappointment of her team, shaking her. She's defeated her-***

self."

He wasn't wrong. Jennifer's mind was flooded with the doubt radiating off Layla, Yaritza, and Melanie. Each cast a dark blue aura that painted the arena in somber shame.

"And that's the first round!" Chanelle shouted in unison with the trumpet of victory announcing the end of the match. "And what a win it was."

"*Quite impressive, Kenzo.*" I linked to his mind, unwilling to join in on the enthusiastic cheers and roar of the audience. "*I guess you're learning more about teamwork every day.*"

"Fuck off, old man. I know how to work with people." Kenzo cast a spark of static around his temples that didn't shield the joy he held for a strategy no one saw coming.

Using the five minutes of preparation, he told his team that every damn fool here—myself included—would believe he was too arrogant to collaborate. So instead of proving them wrong, he believed it was best to feed into that illusion along with a few others. Amani, Jamius, and Harrison had the perfect branch magics for this tactic.

Honestly, something told me Kenzo could've made this plan work with any of the other students, too. I'd let Kenzo carry the pride that he'd successfully obscured his thoughts because, for the first time, I could feel his happiness unaccompanied by any other emotion—even if he masked it with a sour expression.

CHAPTER TWENTY-ONE

I SUCKED my teeth, wishing they'd have more breaks between the matches because I needed a cigarette. But the next challengers were randomly decided, and I had faith in my two students drawn.

TEAM 1	TEAM 2
Gael Rios-Vega	Tiffany Sparks
Gael Martinez	Ryan Holmes
Andrew Johnson	Isabel Ortiz
Darcy Lowe	Derrick Lowe

Gael Rios-Vega was absurd and aloof but had a lot more talent than I gave him credit for. If he'd sit down and actually do some of his assignments, his ranking would be twice as high. And so long as this match didn't turn into a battle of flight, him and his rooster would easily hold their own.

I was more concerned about Gael and his spikes. During the warlock incursion, he didn't hold back at all, which was a fantastic sign, but whenever we trained during homeroom, he hesitated to use the full extent of his spiked projectiles. It frightened him that something he created could harm someone else. I quelled his anxiety and hoped he'd do the same thing after the five minutes of strategizing.

As for the other students selected, I didn't have any of them in classes but knew their homerooms. Three of the four on the opposing team were made up of the seven students in Chanelle's homeroom to make it into the semi-finals. Guess luck of the draw had worked against her. Or in her favor, if their team knew how to collaborate.

Gael strutted across the arena before the battle, eyeing another competitor who had a beaver floating next to her. Its tail flapped under the subtle telekinetic vibrations Tiffany cast. King Clucks glared at the levitating familiar that chomped on a twig.

```
Name: Tiffany Sparks
Branch: Bestial (Familiar)
Ranking: 69
```

"Nice ranking." Gael wiggled his eyebrows, quite convinced he'd been the first person to ever make that comment. He wasn't.

"Thanks. It's a lot better than 108ing." Tiffany pulled out a stick of beef jerky, gnawing on it the same way her familiar chomped on its twig.

Gael blushed, a bit embarrassed at his low ranking, but found himself eager to chat more. "Are you two seriously eating before the competition?"

"What can I say?" Tiffany skipped away from her team, heels clicking against the stone tiles. "My beaver's only happy when she's got a bit of wood in her."

"Seriously?" Gael snickered. "You're just handing me jokes."

"Huh?" Tiffany twirled a pigtail with a dim expression and clever thoughts, goading Gael further.

This wouldn't end well for him or his rooster.

The buzzer sounded, and everyone sprang to action. The other two teamed with both Gaels lunged forward with primal magics, casting fire and ice across the arena. Gael searched for Tiffany, but she'd vanished behind the wall of ice. Then he spotted one of the other team members.

```
Name: Ryan Holmes
Branch: Augmentation (Limbs)
Ranking: 51
```

Gael's mind zipped with possibly the most absurdly ridiculous and quite frankly offensive strategy he'd developed in five seconds.

"Hey, you. Handyman," Gael shouted with his rooster perched on his shoulder.

"You trying to insult me?" Ryan cocked his head.

"Not at all, dude," Gael said. "In fact, King Clucks and I were saying that with all those extra arms, you probably give amazing hugs."

"I said that," Gael muttered.

Gael raised a hand, dismissing Gael's comment. "But you know what my buddy here said?"

Ryan paused.

"He said you probably use all those hands to master your hand job business."

Ryan roared, unleashing well over forty augmented limbs from his back, each varying in length and muscular build.

"Gael, that wasn't the plan. Qué Cabrón." Gael levitated to avoid the onslaught of augmented limbs stretching far and wide to capture him. "*Qué chingados.*"

"Sorry, dude." Gael and his familiar raced off in search of Tiffany because the jokes were too good, and he couldn't miss them.

"Ba-ba-bawk!" King Clucks flapped his wings as he leapt off Gael's shoulder, screeching in unison with his human partner.

I sighed. These two would be the death of me.

Derrick Lowe shielded himself from his sister Darcy's flames with a wall of water.

```
Name: Derrick Lowe
Branch: Primal (Water)
Ranking: 112
```

Once he'd overpowered the flames, he then shifted his water and hit Tiffany's back with a wave that propelled her forward alongside her familiar, moving increasingly faster.

"Does she control water, too?" Gael asked. "*Multiple branches like Tara, maybe.*"

No. Tiffany's telekinesis was sharp but merely held the form her teammate shaped so she could ride the surfer pose and avoid her levitation root, which she struggled with.

"What can I say? My beaver prefers to be wet before she—"

Jesus *fucking* Christ. I tuned them out, quelling all thoughts. These two were quite possibly the worst-matched opponents who could've been randomly selected. We'd have to censor every innuendo Gael and Tiffany uttered in front of a live audience before posting the Spring Showcase on the academy website.

"Oh, come on. You had to hear that one." Gael dodged the water alongside King Clucks, who fluttered his wings, deflecting the waves and forcing Tiffany to fall back.

King Clucks raced ahead, unyielding and crowing. The rooster leapt, kicking the beaver with a telekinetic strike.

"Duchess!" Tiffany yelled.

Her beaver—*ugh, I can't believe what I'm watching*—bounced against the stone flooring and used her tail to propel herself back into the air, floating proudly as she munched on a stick.

Tiffany smirked. "Bet you thought that'd slow us down, but my beaver can take any pounding your cock throws at her."

"How are you not hearing this?" Gael tugged at his fauxhawk.

"Huh?" Tiffany paused.

Gael considered using the pause to counterattack but found himself compelled to explain. "You see, you've got a beaver, and I have a—"

Tiffany sprang forward, taking full advantage of Gael's delayed reaction to kick him across the face and out of the arena. Unlike Gael, who used cock jokes to incite conversation and clamor for attention, Tiffany used ditzy diversions to lull him into a false sense of security. She high-fived her familiar's wide tail, proud of their accomplishment. I pinched the bridge of my nose as King Clucks bawked furiously before chasing them. Tiffany and Duchess screamed, wrapped in a tight hug, when the rooster kicked them out of the arena, too.

"Doesn't count," Chanelle announced.

"Excuse me?" I snapped.

"Gael was already out, so the rooster's strike doesn't count. This is my impartial judgment." Chanelle raised her cane. "Tiffany and Duchess are still in."

"King Clucks is not a magical add-on." I gritted my teeth. "He's his own person—bird, whatever—and suggesting his combative assistance doesn't count is like saying familiars are nothing more than support tools. We all know how you feel about support tools. Is that what you're saying, Mrs. Whitehurst?"

Tiffany eyed us from the sidelines, petting her beaver. Christ. Did I just say that?

"That's not what I'm saying at all." Chanelle pulled the microphone away from her as I levitated closer to her self-proclaimed throne. "While you're bitching, a competition is happening. One I'm attempting to referee."

"To cheat, you mean."

"Oh, Ryan just cuffed Gael." Her gaze remained fixed on the arena. "I suppose you'll say he got too handsy."

"Don't make evasively crude jokes."

"What's your problem?" The microphone caught her voice, and I quieted.

The audience's thoughts stirred in our direction as the match ended, and Team Two won.

"Whatever." I floated back to my assigned proctoring spot. "It wasn't a perfect win, and you know it. Even if you try to cheat the rules for your kids."

"*Don't just fly away from me, pissy pants.*" Chanelle furrowed her brow. "*Are you seriously still upset about the showcase? It's a fucking showcase. You know how they work.*"

"*I'm going for a cigarette.*" I huffed. "*I'll be back for the next match unless Your Majesty Admin-in-the-Making would like to complain to administration about me not carrying my weight while you've clearly got their attention.*"

Chanelle ignored me, silencing every infuriated thought bursting at her seams and congratulating the winners of the round before playfully announcing the next competitors. I lingered at the doorway long enough to see none of my homeroom students were called. In the parking lot, I smoked, ignoring the excitement inside and stalling my return.

Chapter Twenty-Two

HONESTLY, I couldn't comprehend why I'd held onto something so small and petulant, but every time I dwelled on how Chanelle disregarded the unique factors of my homeroom coven, from Tara's branch overlap to Caleb's branchless nature, it filled me with anger that easily linked my mind to Kenzo's. He astutely surmised the upcoming match, developing plans based on their magics and predicting outcomes. It went as he expected, verbatim.

The next round was called, involving Katherine and Carter. I needed to return. I had no idea who they'd been pitted against, but the furious Kenzo bustled with boredom at their battle, more concerned with berating Gael for holding back his spikes. Delight peaked high above the arena, slicing through Kenzo's fuming crimson aura before the two radiating emotions vanished. I had no clue what Gael had said or thought, but Kenzo became temporarily flustered before storming away to watch the match elsewhere in peace.

My magic was all kinds of fucked. How was I still seeing emotional auras? That was more empathy than telepathy and should have required extreme effort on my part to even glimpse. I couldn't breathe without being drawn into a mind, easily perching over folks' minds without the slightest exertion of my branch. I sat in the parking lot, sprawled on the ground and chain-smoking a second cigarette by lighting the butt of the first, hoping it'd quell my breaths and magic. It didn't.

Lingering in Kenzo's furious complaints as he dictated everything Katherine and Carter should've done was surprisingly soothing. His internal screams silenced everyone else in the world, and his strategic mind zipped through countless scenarios. Katherine and Carter had, unfortunately, ended the round in a stalemate against the other team, much to Kenzo's prediction, since Carter prioritized his teammate during the last minute instead of detaining the final opponent.

I cracked my neck, simmering his thoughts and my disappointment. Not that I could've helped Katherine and Carter, but as their homeroom instructor, as a proctor, I should've been there. They stirred in the back of my mind momentarily.

Match after match I didn't care to watch mixed in a blur with Mrs. Whitehurst's obnoxious announcements—half the irritation spiked from Kenzo, the other half from me—while I took sharp drags off a cigarette, ignoring Milo's faint mind reaching out to me. He continued delving deep into his magics, obscuring his surface thoughts.

I sat up, digging my nails into the concrete. My telepathy wasn't behaving like any telepathy I'd researched for my licenses, for my education, for my sanity. Telepathy allowed me to listen to thoughts, delve deep into minds, link to consciousnesses nearby, but somehow, I'd superseded the limitations of my branch.

In all the time I'd had it, I'd assumed the manifestations I created were a simple quirk, unique to my uncharming personality, not that they worked anymore. Since the growth in my branch, I couldn't conjure one, and I needed a manifestation to settle my broken mind. I released a heavy sigh, filling the air with smoke. I'd much rather have a manifestation serving as a buffer for this evolving telepathy, yet here I was, exceeding my manifestations' capabilities. I had so many questions, concerns, worries, yet Milo had none. Did he know what it meant? Did he predict this outcome? Did he plan for this? Dropping my smoke, I grabbed my face, hoping to drown out all the light and thoughts of the world with a firm grip.

"Branchless Blunder better not fuck this up." Kenzo's thoughts cast a thunderstorm in the sky, his rage and sorrow bellowing in equal measure, consuming the entire academy. Perhaps I'd linked too closely to him, manifesting this façade…or he cared that deeply about Caleb, amplifying the emotional triggers he continuously severed. ***"When you get knocked out of this showcase, it'll be by me."***

I cracked my knuckles against the pavement, quelling rage belonging in equal parts to me and Kenzo. Our fury each for people in our lives who strayed from what we believed best for them and everyone else around. Though, Kenzo's rage never stemmed into the curious confusion my teenage years were filled with. Nope. He assuredly understood himself and his crush for Gael—despite willfully ignoring it because of his goals—which apparently came quite earlier than myself. What he didn't understand was why he still gave a damn about Caleb Huxley or his future. It infuriated him. Exhausted him. Motivated him.

The gray clouds didn't fade, and a part of me wondered back to youthful curiosity, amusement at the magic in the world… How much did we comprehend? Had I or Kenzo called forth these storm clouds, channeling nature through enraged emotion? Or was this merely a whim of the world no one, magic and science included, was meant to know? None of the curiousness mattered. Magic was as predictable as the dust in the ether and as useless. Another boring facet of a tiny world where nothing mattered. Not what I did here. Not what I heard there. Not what I wanted then. Or what I hoped for later.

I walked back into the auxiliary gym; the screens displayed the final semi-final round teams.

TEAM 1	TEAM 2
Caleb Huxley	**Tara Whitlock**
Jamie Novak	**Chase Fields**
Roberta Locks	**Ramsey Miller**
Ashlyn Ramirez	**Devon White**

Biting my lip, I quelled the minds of every person here, including the angry little bastard that synced so naturally to my fury. What I needed was silence, not similarity.

Tara and Caleb were pitted against each other. One would lose. Ignoring that, I quickly walked back to my designated proctoring spot for the last semi-final match. This was my job. Nothing more. Nothing extra. These were just two random kids assigned to my roster out of hundreds, potentially thousands.

"Begin," Chanelle announced alongside the buzzers.

I ignored everything. Why was I so furious? Was it my growing branch? Was it Milo working nonstop on this dangerous demon case? Was it Chanelle? It didn't matter what shook my magic; it happened, making it too difficult to concentrate on the battle.

I couldn't cheer for either side anyway, not between Caleb and Tara. I didn't want either side to win. Lose. Win? Winning meant so much to each of them, for different reasons, layered in histories of confusion wrapped within each strike they unleashed during the match.

The match escalated quickly. Two members on Tara's team were detained and expelled from the arena in the first minute, thanks to Jamie's whirlpool magic, but now he'd fixated on Tara.

"*Let's see that* **Whitlock power** *dodge* **this**." Jamie's erratic rage spiked in the most disruptive sense. I grabbed my chest; the odd spikes of calm anger cast false palpitations.

Jamie created seven tiny whirlpools around himself, each barely bigger than his hands, and he conjured matching outputs surrounding Tara. She eyed the larger watery portals closing in on her, contemplating an escape. None of her root magics were suited to evade this type of attack, and with only one remaining member on her team, she didn't want to waste her energy casting an onslaught of chaotic branches.

"*There's still Caleb and the other two to contend with. I need my strength.*" She could only maintain a safe output of her three wild branches for a limited amount of time. According to her circulating thoughts, it wasn't very long. Carefully, she avoided jabs Jamie made, punching his hands through portals from a safe distance.

Tara channeled her telekinesis, creating a massive ripple across her fist from all the telekinetic energy bound in one tiny space. Milo had done the very same thing, concentrating a huge amount of magic into a condensed form, which would release a massive output if it was half as powerful as his. Jamie nicked Tara's chin, but it didn't slow her and instead led the trajectory of her strike.

Unleashing the massive telekinetic burst, it traveled through a watery portal, but Jamie sent his tiny whirlpool off in another direction. Tara's strike bounced between portals, and every ounce of the telekinesis struck Caleb in the back, slamming him against the stone arena. The ground cracked louder than his pained gasp.

I levitated closer than my designated post at the outer edge.

"Whoops, guess I hit your branchless pal." Jamie smirked. "*Not **enough** to **knock** the **dud** out. Won't give up a **perfect win** just to put **you** in your place*."

I clenched my jaw, channeling telekinesis and ready to end this.

"*Wow. Defensive much?*"   "*Every round has been intense.*"

"*Not that he'd know.*"

"*Lazy asshole.*"   "*He wouldn't be here if he weren't screwing—*"

"*When it's one of his kids, suddenly—*"

"*Now, he manages to show up after shirking his duties. Must be nice.*"

I untensed and then severed my telepathy. Maybe the other staff members monitoring this match were right. There was a lot they had wrong, whether because I kept my efforts to myself or they envied me for things I didn't care about exploring. The venom oozing in their thoughts settled my trembling. I was too close to my students in this situation and needed to remember we'd all reviewed the ridiculously long protocols on when intervention was necessary. This was simply another battle in the Warlock Wars semi-finals.

Tara winced when Jamie punched her in the kidney, reeling his hand back into the portal. I closed my eyes, unable to escape the reminder this held for me.

I took a deep breath, blocking out the memories of Darla's daggers slipping through Ernesto's crystalized blue portals and slashing me apart. Each time Tara shouted or grunted, I relived a nick, a deep cut, a slash the warlocks gave me. All of it led to the blade pressed against my throat that nearly killed me.

"No." I cracked my neck, silencing everything around me, including nightmares I didn't deserve to relive. Not when Tara was in actual pain.

I could make this about me any time I wanted, but not when this match was being vindictively drawn out. Stepping forward, I planned to intervene. I didn't care if it wasn't standard or if it lacked the seven prerequisites the handbook outlined, or if it'd force a forfeiture for Tara's team. I couldn't let—

Jamie slapped a cuff around Tara's wrist, and all his portals vanished.

"Oh, no." His smile resembled a demon more than a boy. "Guess I only landed half the dampener, which means you're still capable of casting. I better be on my guard."

He wasn't wrong, despite his feigned fright. The cuffs required a complete circuit to properly drain and detain casting. But he'd done this intentionally, some sadistic desire to drag out every second of the ten minutes Jamie kept a close eye on. Jamie continued his cruel blows, light yet brutal punches to knock Tara off balance. I stepped forward, shrugging away the judgment of other staff members.

"I've got this. I just need a second to think. Make a plan. If I can't hold out, then what's the point of working so hard to prove I belong here?"

I waited. Tara's composure changed, and she believed she'd handle this, win this. As much as it pained me, I wanted to give her this chance. Strike after strike, I buried the desire to intervene.

Her intangibility came close to breaking the cuff, but Jamie snatched the cuff, twisting her wrist…

SNAP.

I flinched.

"You're not so tough, are you?" Jamie's smug smirk filled my every thought. His arrogance burned almost as brightly as the pain radiating off Tara.

I moved closer, nearly losing my balance in the delirium of so much hatred and agony.

Tara's eyes rolled back, and she unleashed all her magics simultaneously. She didn't need to cast her roots in tandem with her branches, but she had no idea which might release her from the cuff dampening her casting, so she unveiled every magic she had access to.

"I will not be anyone's punching bag." Tara screamed, and black shadows whipped furiously, ripping the arena flooring apart and knocking away two of Jamie's team members. *"Not. Ever. Again."*

Erratically unleashing her magic, Tara shattered and sealed whirlpool portals by whipping them with black shadows before they vanished from the restraint of the cuff. The broken water evaporated, rising high above the arena and forming into icicles. I scanned the proctors, eyeing Chanelle in particular. This wasn't her branch or anyone else's. And no amount of telekinesis could shift the temperature. Jamie, perhaps? No, Jamie's branch was too vested in manipulating the molecules of moisture for instant travel, not controlling them at a whim. Was this Tara? How?

"Bitch *thinks that'll* **stop me**.*"* A huge tidal wave gushed across the arena floor. Splashes of tiny whirlpools knocked Tara's magic in every other direction of the auxiliary gym, possibly all around the academy, while throwing her body into currents of water and crashing against stone flooring. Jamie flew above his casting, weaving between Tara's magic, including the icicles raining down and splattering the raging whirlpool with shadows and seals.

"Enough of this." I flew toward Tara, preparing to free her from the water threatening to drown her on stage.

Jamie was a moment away from colliding with her, telekinesis channeled in his fist and a furious strike at the ready.

Tara was too lost in the delirium of releasing magic to resist the dampening as she continued attempting to phase out of the cuff.

Chanelle unleashed a coiled whip of lightning, matching my pace, along with every single proctor all prepared to interject with their branches at the ready.

Caleb leapt between us and punched Jamie in the jaw. The crack of bone made Caleb recoil, sending an uneasy shudder up my spine as I linked to his mind out of pure shock. Caleb's telekinesis didn't falter, though, and he knocked his own teammate out of the arena, sending him crashing into the stadium wall with a much louder burst than he'd anticipated.

"*It's okay. It had to be done,*" Caleb thought, descending next to Tara as the whirlpool of Jamie's creation disappeared. He hesitated, taking a deep gulp as Tara's magic continued whipping about, doubting whether deserved to win this competition.

Every instructor's magic halted mid-strike and fell back as Tara's magic vanished, and she collapsed onto the arena. Caleb hadn't caught her but immediately went to her side, checking on his friend as he tried to remove the cuff. I knelt next to him, unlocking the cuff with a key every proctor for the semi-finals had.

"What a showing!" Chanelle shouted into the microphone, stirring the crowd with glee and phony praise like this had gone according to plan. They hesitated—while our host had charm, it took longer to warm up the audience than a guild witch—but eventually, they applauded the victorious Team One.

Caleb alone remained standing.

CHAPTER TWENTY-THREE

I WENT to the infirmary, searching for Tara. Several awaited students sat tending for their injuries, from minor bruising to slight concussions all the way to small lacerations. Katherine lay on a hospital bed, her arm stretched across a stationed table as the school nurse stitched a cut along her forearm.

She avoided watching the magical stitches weave into her skin, sewing it together. The pain was nonexistent thanks to the numbing rejuvenation our academy nurse possessed, but Katherine had convinced herself the pain would shoot through her body if she so much as glanced. She wasn't wrong. Pain was as much physical as it was psychological. I'd had more than my share of minds to poll on that front.

"I'm so sorry," Carter said, wishing he could offer assistance. He'd asked to aid Katherine with vitality, but our nurse explained the overlap of rejuvenation branches could cause complications, so he waited, pained and filled with guilt.

I worried his wide eyes and deep frown would become Carter's default expression, washing away the carefree smile he had the first day at Gemini.

"It's not a big deal," Katherine said. "Won't even scar."

"Yeah, I get that. I just… I'm sorry we lost and…" Carter gulped. "*I screwed everything up. Katherine got slashed; I couldn't heal her. Couldn't take down the other team. I can't do anything right."*

"Excuse me?" Katherine tilted her head, and her glasses slid to the end of her nose. "We most certainly did not lose. We had a stalemate which is way better than most of the teams out there."

"Carter, can I talk to you?" I stood beside him, eyeing the neighboring beds. Perhaps Tara had closed off her curtain. Or worse—the injuries she'd endured were more extreme than our standard infirmary for students. Show-cases did tend to overwhelm the three nurses staffed than the usual injuries throughout the school year.

"I'm busy with—"

"I'm fine, Carter." Katherine smiled.

He begrudgingly stepped away and allowed the nurse to work. Unable to find the right small talk, I decided I needed to dive directly into this conversation.

"You'll notice most of the work done here is medical, not magical." I gently grabbed his shoulder, finally facing a conversation we needed to have months ago. "You've got an incredible branch. One you've had to find amazing versatility with and new capabilities in, which I blame myself for."

"What? No. I should've—"

"You should never have been in that situation, having to stretch and manipulate the limits of your vitality. You found a way to help me when no one else could. I'm so proud of how much you've grown since arriving at Gemini, but you need to remember carrying the weight of the world doesn't always make you a better or stronger witch. Sometimes, it's the very thing that'll hold you back from success."

"I just"—Carter took a deep trembling breath—"want to make sure I do my best, my part, without giving up. I almost..."

Flashes and words flung in the air, surrounding Carter's frightened mind from the task he'd been assigned during the warlock incursion. His only job was to stop the bleeding, close the wounds, and save me. So much blood flooded his mind. So much guilt for how each second he spent channeling his magic, he'd also considered running away. All he wanted at that moment was to run and hide.

"But you didn't," I said, reeling Carter from his haunting thoughts. "In fact, you did quite the opposite."

Carter's eyes were glossy, holding back tears.

"I need you to stop holding onto what you could've done, what you wanted to do. In that moment, you stepped up in a way that should've never been asked. You didn't hesitate. You doubted yourself, but that didn't stop you. You fought through your fear that day and accomplished the impossible. But please, for me, for yourself, and for the benefit of everyone you're going to help in the future…stop holding on so tightly to fixing every situation."

Carter buried his face in his sleeve, sniffling. There was a long silence between us, but I listened to a few of the fears Carter clung to in his mind wash away with the sadness pouring from him. After wiping the worst of the tears, Carter wiped his splotchy face, and nodded.

We sat together while the nurse finished mending Katherine's injuries. I didn't press the discussion further, allowing Carter time to absorb and reflect on the words.

Caleb walked over, mind buzzing with concern for Tara, reminding me of the reason I'd come to the infirmary.

"I'm fine." Katherine side-eyed Caleb's scrunched expression and worried gaze. "I swear I've had bigger papercuts from my grimoire and wish everyone would stop apologizing. How's Tara?"

"She's okay." Caleb shrugged. "Jamie was…"

"An asshole. I told you," Katherine said. "Personally, and I do mean from every single person on the planet, I wish you would've broken more than his jaw."

Caleb flinched. He wanted to agree because he despised Jamie, yet he worried indulging that type of philosophy would steer him away from his industry goals. A guild witch, the best of them, ensured to do no harm. That was what Caleb strove to achieve. I sighed. He had so much to learn about the murky corruption of the industry he wanted to join. A lesson for later in the year, perhaps. Maybe I'd wait until they'd reached their second year.

As things settled between Katherine, Carter, and Caleb, I took my leave.

Making my way through the infirmary, I stepped into the hallway leading to the more intensive care areas. Before I reached Tara's room, I spotted Chanelle standing over Jamie as a nurse held his chin while drawing symbols along his fractured jaw. The etchings wouldn't heal the cracks but serve as a less intensive hold to mend the injuries as opposed to wiring his jaw shut. Honestly, this was one time I wished we didn't have magical-medical solutions. The world would be a bit nicer if Jamie couldn't talk for a few weeks.

I hung just outside the private room.

"Consider this a mild lesson in the importance of collaboration," Chanelle said.

"Fuck that. He broke my jaw."

"It's not broken," the nurse chimed in. "Well, mostly. You're up; you're talking."

"Unfortunately," Chanelle muttered.

"He should still be disqualified for attacking his teammate." Jamie snarled. "There's gotta be a rule about that."

"There are lots of rules in place for the Spring Showcase. You should know since I thoroughly explained them as you filled out and signed the forms during homeroom."

Jamie scoffed.

"The behavior you displayed was absolutely uncalled for, and as such, I'm going to have to disqualify you from the finals."

"What?" Jamie sprang forward, swatting the nurse's hand from his face. The searing pain running down his jaw and nestling along the nerves of his neck paled in comparison to the fury he had for what Mrs. Whitehurst announced so casually. "You can't disqualify me. Our team won, and I didn't break any rules."

"I assuredly must disagree. As the moderator in this event and your homeroom instructor, it's well within my authority to pull you from the Spring Showcase." Chanelle's throat and chest tightened. Doubt crept into her surface thoughts, fighting to maintain an impartial tone in her words, yet she worried this outcome resulted because she'd stretched herself too thin this semester.

Jamie was far from a favorite student, but she went out of her way to avoid his wrathful tendencies because, frankly, she didn't see an answer to change his attitude, his entitlement.

"Your actions, behavior, and disregard went well beyond the code of ethics you signed. During the showcase, it's your responsibility to uphold integrity, and during that match, you proved you have none. I want to believe it's there, buried somewhere underneath whatever that was today—unsportsmanlike conduct doesn't even cover it. But after what you displayed today, I can't allow you to partake in an event that compromises yourself, your peers, or this academy."

"Get out!" Jamie's face turned red. The nurse went to finish her healing, but he shouted, "I said get out! Everyone out!"

His rage fumed, creating a crimson aura that pulsed with a pitch-black center. Each thump of his heart radiated in his aura like a thunderstorm of blood only my magic could see. Well, Jennifer's too, but thankfully my empathic student avoided the infirmary for all the turmoil it carried from injured classmates.

Chanelle walked past me, wordless, enthusiasm lost, and mind spinning on a dozen different things she'd have to check off before filing Jamie's disqualification paperwork so she could prepare for the finals at the end of the week.

"Do you need any help?" I asked.

"With what?" Chanelle turned with a smile on her face but not in her heart.

"Spring Showcase stuff."

"From you? No. I'll be fine." Chanelle walked away.

I sighed. The aftermath of the semi-finals was more exhausting than the event itself.

There was still one person I needed to check on. The person I'd actually come here to talk with.

I made my way to another private room where a nurse had finished. Tara's cheeks were red. She had a prominent welt on her left cheek, bruising up her arms and legs, and most likely elsewhere. A large scrape covered her right knee. Sigils were drawn on, and ointments had been applied. Between the medicine and magic, Tara seemed relatively numb to the pain, though that might have been because she was often numb to the pain around her.

"I'm very proud of how you held yourself during the match." I stared at the cast on Tara's arm, regretting my hesitation.

"I lost." Tara's mind churned in a familiar motion when faced with failure and her part in it.

"But you didn't give up. You didn't back down. You held yourself with the same bravery as an industry witch would when faced against overwhelming odds." I took the chair next to Tara's bed. "And you did what no other student attempted during their match."

"What's that?"

"You resisted the dampening cuff."

"It was only halfway on."

"Which is enough for most witches. But your magic, for what it's worth, refused to be contained."

"Don't remind me." Tara frowned.

"Speaking of your magic. Can I ask you about the icicles?"

Tara blinked, unaware of their presence. There wasn't an inkling of the casting in her surface thoughts, likely because she was fighting against the dampening cuff and Jamie's cruel tactics and ended up lost in the heat of the moment.

"All I know is I tried using my telekinesis to push the water away."

"Did you feel something primal? The only reason I'm asking is water to ice seems like elemental control within the primal branch."

"Not sure." Tara laughed, light, brief, but genuine.

"What's so funny?"

"Just how I might have a fourth branch I never noticed because my control over the first three is so awful, I didn't feel the tug of those magical tethers."

"It could be new. Some branches blossom later in life while most branches develop at or before the start of adolescence; it's possible for some not to reveal themselves until the late teens, even early twenties."

Though every year past twelve, that likelihood of inheriting a branch significantly dropped.

"*By that logic, I could be gaining new branches I can't control well into my thirties,*" Tara thought.

"Unlikely. Not sure I've ever heard of a case past twenty-two."

Tara rolled her eyes, annoyed I'd commented on her inner thoughts and annoyed she let them slip by.

"It's more likely they'll just change or evolve as you learn more about them."

Or, in my case, less. Christ, I still needed to gain a handle on my evolving branch before I could soundly offer advice to Tara on the topic.

"I'll let you rest up," I said, taking my leave.

After checking on all my students, those injured, those unharmed, those advancing to the finals, and those who lost during the semi-finals, I left work. The day was long, and I wanted to get out of the bustling academy. Oddly, I didn't want to go home. I didn't exactly have anywhere else to go, though.

My phone buzzed. Milo. Perfectly timed—like he'd had clairvoyant insight into my feelings. Insufferable.

Milo: I miss your face and your many other assets

Me: My place or your office?

Or *insert gasp* finally gonna let me see your place?

Milo: You don't have to insert when * but I can show you how to properly insert things.

Well, one thing lol

The office is chaos. So that's a no go. And my place is a total mess. Le sigh.

Me: Starting to wonder if you actually have a home.

Milo: Was hoping to have drinks. A quiet little place.

Just you me and a half dozen lost souls looking to drown their sorrows.

Me: How romantic.

Milo: It's a good thing you hate romance.

I'll send you the address.

The last thing I wanted was a public outing, but it'd be nice to spend time with Milo, and he had worked hard on finding places not so infested with Enchanter Evergreen fans.

Me: See you soon.

CHAPTER TWENTY-FOUR

I SAT at the bar, sipping a screwdriver, and grateful the three other patrons here were day drunk with mild mushy thoughts. This bar was pretty out of the way, with almost no one in the surrounding area. Almost peaceful to have so few minds nearby and a reminder I should consider something more country and spacious. Then again, eyeing the woodland animals mounted along the walls, not sure this was really my scene.

Milo texted he was running late because, of course, he was. I gulped the rest of my drink and ordered another. Minutes passed as the ice began to create condensation around the glass. I went to text Milo, get an ETA, when the door swung open. *Finally.*

Only it wasn't Milo brazenly bursting into the quiet bar, but Chanelle. She immediately traipsed to the counter and ordered a shot of tequila, cranberry vodka, and a rum & coke. I huffed. Chanelle downed the tequila, sucked her teeth, and smiled at her reflection on the back wall. Her eyes met my mirrored reflection, and she pouted.

"Isn't this a bit far out of your way?" she asked, knowing full well I avoided outings within my route home, so I certainly wouldn't drive to a staff function thirty-five minutes out of my way on the North Side.

"I'm actually—"

My phone buzzed, and I paused because there might still be time to meet Milo somewhere else. If more staff were heading this way, I definitely didn't want to be here.

> Milo: Enchanter Campbell is breathing down my neck and not in that hawt way you do.

> New case details. Raincheck. Love ya.

Son of a bitch.

"*Motherfucker.*" The light from Chanelle's phone illuminated the crease in her brow.

It all clicked. Chanelle rarely drank rum & coke's since she hated the carbonation, but Milo absolutely loved them.

"You're not here for a staff function, are you?" I asked.

"Who the hell from our academy would drive this far out of their way for some overpriced hovel like this dump?" Chanelle quirked an eyebrow, then made a face at the bartender. "Don't look at me like that. I'm going to be the best tips you've had all month."

She took a seat on the stool and sipped her cranberry vodka. We didn't speak for a few minutes, each using the silence—excluding the oldies rock playing—to finish our drinks so we could leave. I scooted one stool closer, now only separated by a single empty seat, which we'd each anticipated sharing with different company.

"Did Milo invite you out?" I asked.

"Yup. Said he wanted to discuss the Spring Showcase Finale and see if he could help me wrangle some enchanters in the audience."

"And you believed that bullshit?" I snorted.

"Okay, smart guy. What brought you all the way up here? He's cute, but this is a hell of a drive for a date night. And this isn't exactly the Ritz."

"I thought maybe he wanted to track a case near here."

"Demons, yes. Those have been disturbing."

She didn't know the half of it.

"Here." Chanelle slid the rum & coke toward me, condensation already dripping down the frosted glass.

"Thanks." I took a sip.

"Your boyfriend's annoying."

"Damn clairvoyants."

If I knew Milo, and I very much did, this was his version of whatever pop culture reference he'd stolen to put two people in the same setting—and what? Reconcile? We weren't exactly fighting. A tiff. Minor argument. It'd blow over soon enough. Then again… I gulped my drink, hoping the burn in my throat would keep me silent. Maybe he saw it turning into something different down the line. Maybe he simply wanted me to keep my one work friend. Maybe he didn't want to choose between the two of us because he loved me but obviously liked Chanelle's personality better.

"Maybe I'm overthinking it," I muttered.

"Huh?"

"Talking to myself or thinking aloud. Not sure."

Chanelle's expression softened. "I'm sorry about Jamie's actions during the showcase."

"It's not your fault. He's a real piece of work."

"You have no idea."

"Also, I might be slightly kind of sort of maybe just a little bit misdirecting my frustration—for I don't even know really how many things—toward you."

"Is that an apology?" Chanelle smirked. "I'm going to need another drink if that's your version of an apology."

"I'm sorry. I'm an asshole."

Chanelle grinned. "Forgiven. I was a bit of an asshole myself. I could've given you a heads up instead of letting the mass email to everyone inform you."

"Why didn't you?"

"You're hard to talk to, yet for whatever fucked up reason, I enjoy your opinion more than other people's. Don't let that go to your head."

"I know you only like me because when we're standing in front of the kids, you get to be Miss Happy Sunshine while I'm the evil storm cloud of tests and extra work."

"Exactly." She chuckled. "We're basically a brand."

I chugged the rest of my drink, keeping up with Chanelle, who had finished hers and ordered a double, while we sat in silence.

"I also could've fought harder for Tara and her overlap. I'm sorry."

"We're just doing the best we can, right?" I clinked my glass against hers.

She took the empty seat, and the awkward silence looming between us vanished, breaking away and taking the bitterness in our hearts with it.

"This isn't gonna be one of those things where we have to hug it out or something?" I frowned.

"Absolutely not." Chanelle nudged me with her shoulder. "Unless you wanna."

"Absolutely not."

She cackled, flooding this solemn bar with a bright delight unlike any other.

We sat together for hours discussing all the utter bullshit the academy had thrown at us this year. It was nice sharing awful classroom horror stories no one else would truly appreciate or understand.

I downed my drink, smiling and groggy and listening to whatever it was Chanelle said. Something funny, probably. It was getting harder to keep my head up, but the smile wasn't a struggle.

"So then right there in the middle of my lecture, Tiffany drags her desk—which, mind you, is in the back of the classroom—all the way to the very front."

"No." I gasped. "Why?"

"Apparently, Duchess had important business to attend to, and Tiffany's phone needed charging for said business, so naturally, she took it upon herself to find the only outlet in the room I hadn't covered and proceeded to charge her phone." Chanelle's eyes widened, displaying her shock from said event, where the story danced in easy images along the surface of her mind. Much easier to follow than her voice right now. Had the music gotten louder?

In the memory, Chanelle had, in no uncertain terms, made it clear that while she wouldn't argue with kids about their technology, she certainly wouldn't compete during a lecture. She'd snatched the phone away with a telekinetic grip and hurled Tiffany, her desk, and the beaver all to the back of the classroom, where they remained floating until the end of the class.

"So, what'd you do next?" I asked.

I already knew, but telling the story brought so much joy to Chanelle, I figured it couldn't hurt to hear it out.

"Well, having no time for bullshit or to be interrupted, I—"

"Don't you two look lovely?" Milo's voice bellowed throughout the tiny bar place.

I turned, spun, and swiveled around when he arrived. Entered. Walked at an oddly blurred angle. Blinking a few times, I soaked up the sheen, fuzzy lights of the bar and thought maybe I'd gotten a bit tipsier than expected.

"Suddenly no one's breathing down your neck?" I stepped toward Milo, tripping on the…the something on this damn carpeted place. Who had a carpet in a bar? Gross.

Milo caught me, and I tugged his tie, partially for leverage on my faltering balance and partially because I wanted to breathe down his neck. I blew hot air against his neck. Why was I doing that? I couldn't remember, but it was fun, and his cologne had this intoxicating effect each time I inhaled, so I kept breathing on him. Milo chuckled, keeping a hand firmly against my lower back.

"Thought maybe you two could use a ride home."

"Thanks, you damn clairvoyant." Chanelle hiccupped. "But Kyle's already here. I think." She checked her phone and giggled. "Yup. And by the way, you still owe me enchanters, mister sneaky liar psychic person."

"Hey, I'm psychic," I said very proudly.

"Speaking of intuition." Milo handed Chanelle two vitamin waters. "Maybe drink one before bed and one in the morning."

Chanelle took the waters and stumbled out the door.

"Ugh. How bad is her hangover going to be?" I asked, slurring my words.

"No idea." Milo guided me toward the door. His arms were so strong, and the floor practically disappeared with every step. "But I did see the two of you potentially having way too many drinks in an incredibly short period of time."

"So you came here so we wouldn't drive." I nodded, having solved the mystery. "We had it covered. Chanelle called her husband, and I wasn't talking to you because you had a case."

"I didn't have a case; you needed to talk."

"I knew it. I said it. Said it loud, said it proud, and then said it to Kyle when we called for a ride."

"You didn't call Kyle—I did."

"Huh?" I stumbled on the gravel parking lot as Milo walked me to his car. "Then who did we call?"

"No idea, but I'm sure they'll enjoy whatever voicemails you left them."

"Oops."

Milo helped me into the front seat, and we drove back into the city. It was peaceful until it wasn't. I ground my teeth. This was why I hated getting hammered. A few drinks helped take the edge off when thoughts rained in, but I couldn't focus my channeling, which allowed every mind to pour in like a…like a water thing of death.

"Relax." Milo grabbed my hand, interlocking his fingers while carefully keeping a steady flow of telekinesis on the steering wheel.

His thoughts synced to mine, creating a calming barrier from the onslaught of Chicago. I lay back in the seat of the car, allowing his gentle caress to lull me into sleep, unaware of the world outside, sinking deeper into Milo's blissful mind before passing out.

Chapter Twenty-Five

THE week flew by, everyone in homeroom was equally disappointed yet excited for their three classmates who'd made it into the finals. Caleb. Kenzo. Jamius. Honestly, of all the students who didn't make it through the semi-finals, there were a handful from my homeroom I'd have expected to squeak through ahead of Caleb or Jamius. I wasn't at all shocked by Kenzo's placement, and neither were those annoyed by it. Some, however, like Gael, cheered louder than anyone else, so the enthusiasm evened out.

"Okay. Enough patting them on the back," I said, ending the morning cheerleading squads. "You three need to get to the auxiliary gym."

"About damn time." Kenzo stuffed his hands in his pockets.

"Now? Like this exact second?" Jamius panicked.

Caleb buzzed with strategies and concerns and wonder and delight and anxiety, and I simply had to skirt around his incessant overthinking because my head already ached enough from the crowing rooster and students talking over each other.

"We're not going?" "I wanted to see who won."

"It's going to be Kenzo, duh." "Don't remind me."

"It could be me or Caleb, too. Maybe."

"I made a sign, though."   "We're stuck in class all
day while they get to cast?"

"It's so unfair. I want to see the beaver in action again."

"Cl-cl-cluck!"   *"Is King Clucks jealous? So adorable."*

"Good luck, Kenzo. And Jamius and Caleb and tell the other competitors good luck, too."

"Stop talking." I glowered, biting back an angry growl. "We're going, but
the contestants need to show up early."

"Yay!"

Their exuberant excitement exploded throughout the classroom, and I
suddenly regretted unbursting their little bubbles. Whatever. I cracked my
neck.

"We have an hour until the ceremony, so we'll use that time to catch up
on missing work."

Those remaining sighed, which helped me settle back into a bit of satisfaction.

Jamius summoned three encouraging copies as they exited the classroom.

"What are you doing?" Kenzo snapped.

"Winners need an entourage," a copy answered.

"You've got nineteen clones in you before you're done for the day, and
you chose to waste three of them for an entourage." Kenzo huffed. "Guess I
don't have to worry about you."

Jamius sulked, and his clones booed Kenzo before leading their original
down the hall.

After the slowest hour of hovering beside students to make this time
productive on missing work, Headmaster Dower announced over the inter-
coms for classes to make their way down to the auxiliary gym for the Spring
Showcase Finale. We made our way there. Despite my best efforts to maintain an orderly line, the kids traipsed through the halls merging into the
pack of first-year students all chaotically bursting into the auxiliary gym. The
turnout was massive, so many guests, in fact, I had difficulty finding seating
for my homeroom.

"This way," I snapped, cutting off Peterson and wrangling my students into a row while his kids floundered about. "What? We don't have all day, Peterson."

Fighting a smirk, I joined my students at the end seat. The number of enchanters and acolytes was incredibly high. Even a few guild masters had shown up in a privately reserved seating area closer to the arena than anyone else. Carefully inserting herself among the guild masters, Enchanter Campbell made small talk. Or what I could only assume was small talk or plotting or business or whatever she'd planned. Her thoughts bubbled with concern about the demons stalking the streets of Chicago, but burying them, she focused instead on solidifying her position among these industry leaders.

How'd Chanelle manage to get the biggest turnout in Gemini history? Honestly, I'd never seen this many enchanters at a second-year showcase or a third-year gala. Though many enchanters' minds buzzed with boredom, some held interest in interacting with one another or enchanters they'd avoided since every guild prioritized solidarity in their guild over the collaboration many had grown accustomed to.

"*Well, well, well.*" Milo's thoughts tickled my nape and made my ears burn. "*You look quite dashing today.*"

I searched the crowd for him, half standing, while he whispered naughty words and cast naked images in his mind. My face burned.

"Are you okay, Mr. Frosty?" Gael asked.

"Ba-bawk."

"*Yeah, he totally looks like a beet. Red and round. If only his hair was green.*"

I sat down, tempering Gael's mind as he and his rooster cluckled in unison, believing I hadn't heard their thoughts. Fucking rooster.

Syncing to Milo, our link connected seamlessly with him at the other side of the arena.

"*Found you,*" I thought.

He smirked, adjusting his tie.

"*Did you have a hand in this turnout?*"

"*Might've owed Chanelle a favor, so I called in a few others. Besides, a lot of these enchanters would gladly attend a showcase in exchange for some of the fortune I passed their way."*

"Seems unfair."

"Not really." Milo's eyes fluttered, his mind wrapped in potential outcomes this single event might offer for the guilds in the years to come.

"There must be some excitement to expect, having brought Enchanter Evergreen here to witness Gemini's Spring Showcase firsthand," a reporter said, drawing Milo back to an interview on the cusp of beginning.

"Honestly, every showcase that's happened throughout the city—no, the state—and those yet to begin have been teeming with excitement and filled with truly talented young witches," Milo answered. "It's difficult not being able to attend them regularly. It's important for guilds to remember much of our work involves observing, uplifting, encouraging, and training the next generation of magic. I'm simply glad the amazing coordinator of this event found the time to reach out and explain why I deserved to reward myself with such great competitors today."

"Speaking of competitors, any predictions on who will win this showcase?"

"Thankfully, no spoilers from my branch today." Milo laughed; his whole face beamed with joy. "But something tells me Caleb Huxley is going to display some impressive skills."

My heart thumped. Was he being sincere or polite, given the odds stacked against Caleb?

"Who?" The reporter paused, checking the roster of students lined up and the names next to the best branches first, and his expression did little to hide how stunned he was when he spotted Caleb's rank or branchless status. "I'd never want to question your foresight, and who doesn't love a good underdog story? But surely there are more impressive candidates in today's event. After all, he's ranked awfully low."

"I'm not suggesting winners. Remember, I haven't seen anything about that."

Liar. Milo had likely seen a hundred outcomes. Okay, maybe a dozen. Still, there were probably fragments, he subtly, suggestively pushed. I was grateful none of the kids could hear the interview. I could only imagine the spinning wheel of thoughts it'd create.

"Every single student out there is impressive." Milo had this boyish grin of admiration like he was amazed by the next generation of magic. "Not merely a handful. In fact, every student who ranked showed potential for making it to first place, and too many for me to count who didn't land among the top 160 students this year. All the first-year students show so much promise and potential it'd be unfair to declare a prediction based on magic, ranking, or anything else. Honestly, I was simply in awe at Caleb's perseverance. No branch, and he pulled through in two rounds where branch capability was at the forefront of placing. I'm honored to see each of these brilliant young witches who are about to display their talents."

Chanelle moved into her announcement, forcing a quick end to the interview and drawing me away from Milo's mind.

"I hope everyone's excited for Gemini's Spring Showcase Casting Royale Finale." Chanelle waltzed across the freshly fixed arena floor. "Similar to our first round, this is an independent match, but roots are completely allowed. All magic, in fact. Like the second round, if you're knocked out of the arena or simply knocked out—you're finished. However, there are no dampening cuffs to make things easy, and there's no time limit. Last witch standing wins!"

Cameras zoomed in on the top twenty-four students who'd landed in the finals. Should've been forty, but two teams had a stalemate which resulted in an extra sixteen cut from the finals. I scanned the contestants, counting on my fingers. That was an even number, but I knew there was one additional student disqualified from the finals. Jamie stood among the crowd, a proud smirk plastered on his face.

"*What the actual fuck is he doing here?*" I linked to Chanelle.

Her breathy sigh hit the microphone, and she ignored my question. "Let the casting royale begin!"

The kids sprang into action, firing branch magics which turned the arena into a flurry of chaos. I lingered close to the fresh memory that rose to the surface of Chanelle's thoughts, glimpsing the uncomfortable conversation she had with Headmaster Dower and two other administrators, each reassuring they'd never question her judgment, passion, or expertise in the edu-cational field, while simultaneously skirting coy repercussions if the Novak's didn't get their way.

I quelled her frustrated and discerned thoughts. Annoying administra-tion. Entitled parents. Spoiled kids.

Speaking of kids, I attempted to focus on the finale. Jamius and Caleb, like many students who shared the same homeroom, grouped together to eliminate others first. Not encouraged but not against the rules of an all-out royale. Jamius had five copies standing at the ready, guarding them from Kenzo, who each boy warily eyed, convinced he'd target them first. Kenzo had mockingly suggested he'd destroy everyone from his homeroom if they dared to place in the showcase, yet he'd gone out of his way to assist them in the first round.

He didn't bother with Caleb or Jamius, leaving them to the fates of other students.

"Try lasting long enough for me, branchless." Kenzo bolted ahead, ducking and weaving past magics while conserving his branch. **"If anyone gets to knock you out of this competition, it's me. But first...those fuckers!"**

It appeared, despite weaseling his way back into the finale, Jamie had made a glaring error. He'd goaded Kenzo during lunch, mocking Gael and our entire homeroom.

"It's quite the travesty," Jamie's words echoed along the infuriated surface of Kenzo's mind as he sprinted faster. *"Your entire homeroom coven landed in the showcase, yet only three made it into the finale. It's not unsurprising, though. Given your classes lackluster branches or lacking branches."*

"He thinks they're so great, I'll knock all six of those Whitehurst Washouts from the arena first." Kenzo popped static at Tiffany Sparks' familiar and Harrison Heywood's vials.

"Not Tiffany," Gael shouted beside me.

It didn't matter if the others hadn't said a word to Kenzo. In his mind, a war had been waged, and he wouldn't let anyone talk down to him or his coven. *Mostly him, though.* Every time he pictured the disappointment on his classmates' faces, he quickly buried it.

"Looks like we've lost our first two competitors. Knocked out simultaneously by Kenzo Ito," Chanelle announced, resisting a desire to sulk. "*Great, at this rate, he'll knock my entire homeroom out before they have a chance to show off their talents.*"

"**Screw** *them. If they can't* **hold** *their own against* **one pathetic hex witch**, *they don't deserve* **my help**." Jamie sneered, opening a whirlpool portal and abandoning his homeroom that Kenzo quickly eviscerated. He didn't give any of Chanelle's students an opportunity to think, strategize, or cast.

Across the arena, Jamius and Caleb worked in tandem to knock another pair of witches out of the arena.

"Five minutes in, and we've gone from twenty-four to twelve," Chanelle announced, a bit depressed only one of her homeroom coven students remained.

One I didn't want to participate after the way he'd attacked Tara.

"*Over* **my** *dead body will this* **branchless fuck** *earn a top place during the showcase.*" Jamie's mind boomed as a portal opened behind Caleb. "*After what* **he** *pulled.* **I should kill him**."

I flinched, resisting the urge to intervene when Jamie began the same assault on Caleb he'd used against Tara. His sporadic rage bordered on psychotic tendencies. I'd seen this behavior from both ends of the spectrum. Some teens outgrew it as their minds and bodies developed; others, like, too many people, sank into that enraged hatred, and it became too suffocating to linger in their minds.

The proctors' minds all buzzed with caution, at the ready. Most of the enchanters in the arena either held little concern—having faced worse themselves—or boredom by how the Novak kid held back against some no name. I ground my teeth.

Jamius sent two clones to help Caleb, but they ended up sucked into a whirlpool and knocked back into Jamius by Jamie. He had no time for any of the other competitors until he'd thoroughly proven how insignificant Caleb was. He wanted Caleb to understand the insurmountable difference in their abilities, by class, branch, and ranking. Each strike knocked Caleb closer and closer to the edge of the arena.

His footing slipped, and my stomach twisted, filled with guilt at how desperately I wished he'd tumble out of bounds so the beating would end. Caleb didn't, though. Between his determination to change the tides of combat and Jamie's craving to indulge in the sanctioned mayhem, Caleb remained in bounds, taking so many strikes I'd lost count. Another Jamius copy ran full force, ready to land a surprise strike but ended up transported out of the arena and thrown into the audience, where he splattered.

"Scaredy-Copycat is putting up a good fight, but he's at fifteen duplicates and doesn't have a branch or the root proficiency to handle those whirlpools." Kenzo stood at the other end of the arena, studying the battle between Jamie and Caleb while contending with four other competitors who'd grouped together. **"They're using Recheeta George's strategy. Pathetic but also effective. Dammit."**

Ugh. Him and his nicknames. Layla's strategy had failed when Kenzo shocked everyone by collaborating, yet these four possessed perfect long-distance branches to catch and block his disruption hexes.

Each painful strike Jamie belted against Caleb drew my attention. Light pelting hits against his face, sharp, precise jabs into his ribs, and heavy assaults against his calves meant to drop him. Jamie didn't want Caleb running. Fighting. Jamie just wanted everyone to see where Caleb belonged, beneath him. Jamie wanted Caleb on his knees, begging and broken.

I stood up, storming down the stadium steps because whether I was the only psychic with a clear understanding of what was happening or not, I wouldn't endure another second. I'd sooner see one of my students disqualified or have this entire showcase called into question before I allowed another second.

"Telekinesis won't move his whirlpools." Caleb wheezed. *"Sensory is an obvious no go. Levitation can't escape when his portals chase me. I've got to think of something."*

I leapt over the rail guard. Caleb didn't need a plan. I wouldn't sit idle, hopeful and wishing and believing a second time. I paused, lost in how I'd failed Tara during her fight. If I'd intervened, shown my disgust for the tactics. Maybe…maybe it'd have been enough to keep Jamie out of the finals, away from others.

"Worthless. Piece. Of. Trash." Jamie continued his assault.

I flew closer, finding my pursuit held back.

"*Not yet,*" Milo thought, locking my stance with precise telekinesis. "*Give him the chance you've given others. Believe in your student.*"

"*You have no idea what you're—*"

"Enough." Caleb's mind surged above everyone at the academy. His entire body vibrated, shattering my telepathy from linking anywhere in the arena. The proctors appeared frazzled, frozen, but remained where they were.

Every single whirlpool Jamie created vanished instantly.

Caleb pulsed telekinesis, which knocked Jamius and two others nearby out of bounds.

"*A perfected banishment.*"   "*Impossible.*"

"*No way, from a branchless witch?*"

"*I've been refining my roots for years, and this child—*"

"*Hell of a showing.*"   "*Might need him at our guild.*"

"*Told you to relax, Dorian.*"

With Caleb's mind completely blank in a field of no magic, I watched him race toward Jamie.

"That *branchless* **bastard** *is actually* **trying** *to* **kill me.**" Jamie scrambled backward, genuine terror on his face, but it was misguided fear.

Banishment casting destroyed demonic energy. Sure, a perfected banishment nullified Jamie's magics, but he was in no real danger. Still…

His thoughts turned feral, the sour notes piercing through the air and shredding all other inner voices. Beneath the rage lie a hollow calm attempting to claw its way forth. "*I'm not even sure going all out can counter a perfected banishment.*"

Caleb punched Jamie in the face, knocking him to the ground. The heavy right hook lacked telekinesis because Caleb had expunged all his energy with the tiny burst earlier and now fixated all his root magic into one perfected strike of banishment circling the air.

"*What the hell is this kid?*" Jamie lay motionless, thoughts stirring in a hundred fuzzy scenarios where he feared enchanter involvement—perhaps hesitating because of the last time he'd taken combat too far and had almost been disqualified. Whatever his reason, Jamie drifted into the depths of his mind, surrendering to an unconscious state.

Caleb Huxley had done something I'd never witnessed firsthand. Not from a student. Not from an enchanter. Not from a single person in my lifetime.

He'd unleashed a perfected root magic. They were rare, difficult to attain or maintain. Like all root magics, branches too, I supposed, they held different levels of skill set. Basic banishment removed wisps and traces of demonic energy, enhanced understanding allowed the removal of fiends, and advanced proficiency eliminated demons. But a perfected state could banish or nullify all magical energy in the atmosphere. A perfected state of core power few focused on because training our branches was fundamentally ingrained in our heads for licensing or maintaining control of the flow of unique magic circulating inside us.

Jamie lay on the arena floor unconscious while Caleb wheezed heavily, his channeled magic waning and body trembling. His knees shook, barely holding him upright. Kenzo—having regained control over his magics—flew directly toward Caleb, his disruption at the ready and unwilling to take second place as they remained the only active competitors on the field.

"Don't think for a second I'm going to hold back on you, Branchless Blunder." Kenzo closed their distance, Caleb's mind a foggy mess. I wasn't sure how much longer he'd last, honestly. "And if you think you can keep up with me with your knockoff root version of my branch, you're wrong."

Kenzo snatched Caleb by the collar, reeling back a fist until Caleb collapsed into Kenzo's chest. Kenzo froze, holding Caleb upright as his legs gave way.

Scanning Caleb's thoughts, the fog had shifted into a soft, dreamy lull.

How he'd managed to stay upright despite losing consciousness was a sheer will of force meant to prove his worth here.

And he had.

Caleb had gone from the branchless kid ranked at 160 to taking second place in the first-year student's Spring Showcase. Even if he hadn't placed, Caleb continued demonstrating his value at Gemini time and time again, and I wished he understood how triumphant he'd become.

"In a completely anticlimactic showdown, Kenzo Ito is our first-place winner," Chanelle shouted, followed by an explosion of fireworks and a roaring crowd.

I descended to the arena, walking around broken stone tiles to reach my students.

"Wake up." Kenzo shook Caleb. "Wake up, you bastard."

"Kenzo," I said, "you won."

"No. Wake up, Branchless." He continued shaking Caleb, holding him upright and casting gray static along his temples to block his thoughts. ***"You don't get to do this. You don't get to knock yourself out of this competition after perfecting a goddamn root magic. Wake up and fight me! Prove you belong here! Prove me wrong, you fucking loser."***

I grabbed Caleb, pulling him away from Kenzo, blocking most of his rage and the audience's perplexed internal opinions. "It's over."

It took everything to hold Caleb without falling into the sadness pouring from Kenzo. His naturally furious nature dimmed; melancholy and rage and love and hatred and so many other complicated feelings between the two I still didn't understand boomed in instantaneous flashes.

"*Dammit, Caleb.*" Kenzo stormed off the arena, ignoring the cheers, the comments, and everything other than how Caleb had failed and bested him all at once.

I carried Caleb off the stage and to the infirmary while proctors tended to the other students.

The halftime show kept the audience of industry witches entertained long enough for our top three in the Spring Showcase to recover and join in the closing ceremony. Jamie took the stage in the third-place podium with rejuvenation sigils marked along his face and disgust he'd lost to not one but two witches beneath him. Caleb anxiously stood on the second-place podium, in awe of the audience more than his placement. All he wanted was a closer view of the many enchanters he methodically studied from a distance. Meanwhile, Kenzo stood at the first-place podium, pensive and calm, his mind mostly silent despite his earlier outburst. The praise and fawning did nothing to lift his spirits, and he hardly found the enchanters in attendance moderately impressive.

"I know everyone, like myself, is eager to hear from this year's champion." Chanelle handed Kenzo her microphone.

He held it, quietly observing the audience. His eyes flitted toward Jamie and Caleb, anger spiking, but for completely different reasons, then he settled, releasing a heavy breath, testing the acoustics.

"I'd say this is an honor, but I hate liars. It was an uneventful and unchallenging showcase, given the pathetic competition I faced. Truthfully, the only thing worse than everyone attending this academy is the enchanters who took the time from their 'oh so busy' schedules to watch this performance. I'd say you have jobs to perform, but not a single one of you can do your fucking job, which is to protect this city and its citizens." Kenzo gripped the microphone, shooing a nervous Chanelle away. "You're all weak and pathetic. I can't wait until I graduate from this second-rate program and finally show you how it's done."

Kenzo dropped the microphone and left.

Fuck. Fuck. Fuck, how'd I not see that coming?

It was Kenzo. Of course, he'd use this as a chance to flip off every single person in the industry.

Chanelle talked, soothing and calm, attempting to laugh it off as teen angst, but I couldn't pay attention to any of it. I couldn't hear anything past the sea of rage churning throughout the arena as every single professional exploded with internal furies. Each had done their best to protect the citizens of Chicago, fighting impossible odds, and some fifteen-year-old kid had the audacity to shame them publicly after they'd made time to attend this joke of a spectacle. I began to hyperventilate.

"Mr. Frosty, you okay?" Gael smirked. "You look less frosty and more melty. Mr. Melty, maybe?"

"Ba-bawk."

I couldn't breathe. The entire auxiliary gym transformed into a crimson thunderstorm from all the buried rage barreling to the surface from every industry witch in attendance.

"I thought Kenzo's speech was awesome. A total F the man move." Gael's smile faltered. My teeth chattered, and I trembled, attempting to quell my telepathy. "But in a totally not a big deal kind of way at all, so you can chill out, you know? Just Kenzo being Kenzo. No one really listens to his tantrums anyway."

"Cluck."

"*Yeah, we should find someone to help.*" Gael and King Clucks took off in search of a nurse.

The world of thoughts intensified, weighing down on my mind and muscles, the very fiber of my being.

"*I truly love how that kid tells it like it is,*" Milo thought, cutting through the sea of rage and offering me a life raft in the form of his gentle mind that I desperately needed. "*Not sure if it'll help on the collaboration front, but he's gotten under their skin and is definitely helping make a brighter future.*"

Milo's mind soared high above the clouds, a breath of relief I followed. Even as he drifted into visions I couldn't view, I embraced the link holding us together, curious about the future he'd envisioned based on a single outburst from one of my students.

CHAPTER TWENTY-SIX

"DID you know Caleb would show a perfected root magic?" I asked, sitting on the couch and gently petting a purring Charlie while Milo remained in the kitchen.

"No idea. I mean, fifty-fifty, split between um, like two-hundred possibilities. So, not fifty-fifty, I guess." Milo hummed as he cooked. "Beats the future where he pissed himself, that's for sure. I was sweating over that one."

"What's your endgame here?"

"We have a rule you don't get to ask work-related things."

"Unless it involves my students."

"That rule doesn't exist." Milo strolled into the living room, kissed my cheek, and handed me a plate of freshly made gnocchi with a Tuscan sauce. The aroma was inviting and intoxicating, but I focused on Milo's thoughts. "Try a bite—it's yummy."

I took a bite, savoring the pillowy texture mixed with delicious flavors that made my entire mouth water. "It's okay, I guess."

Distracted by Milo's internal singing, I missed Carlie who swatted away and stole several pieces of pasta. She even shared two with her brother.

"I'm teaching her the value of sharing," Milo boasted.

"We're not done," I said, shoveling in a disgustingly delectable bite.

Fuck. When did Milo learn to cook so well? "You don't get to involve my students or put them in danger."

"I'm not." Milo joined me on the couch, telekinetically turning on the television. "I wouldn't unless it bettered them. This doesn't. It helps no one. Please respect that I can't share a million possibilities with you but know I mean well and have no intention of dragging them into this. My only goal was to light a fire under the enchanters in attendance, and I'm not even sure it worked."

"Oh, it worked. They were quite pissy afterward. Which reminds me… now I'm going to have even more of my work cut out for me in finding an enchanter willing to accept Kenzo as an intern after he told all of them to fuck off."

"He'll be fine. But it's good to know the message landed." Milo kissed my cheek with sauce on his lips. I groaned and wiped it away. He was insufferable. "See, we're a dream team of fixing the world. Or at the very least fucking it up less than we found it."

I quietly sat beside Milo, eating the wonderful dish he'd cooked, ignoring him and my traitorous cats who'd nestled close to him.

Milo passed out on my bed the second his head hit the pillow. Must have been nice, considering I lay there for a good hour, tossing and turning with the wheels in my head spinning toward endless scenarios. The biggest comfort was that his mind was the only one buzzing in my thoughts.

I scooted close to him, twisting him onto his side and hugging him so our magics synced seamlessly. This was truly the best part of having someone I trusted so much and who also trusted me implicitly; it created a bond I never wanted to sever again.

"You're not listening," Milo whispered, entirely asleep.

I brushed his curly bangs off his forehead, soothing, gentle, and hopeful it gave him some comfort. He rarely talked in his sleep, but when at the peak of stress, he'd ramble incoherent conversations. I'd noticed it more frequently since the demons arrived in Chicago, shattering his protective hold over the city. Unable to rest and with a fidgety, anxious Milo cuddled beside me, I delved into his thoughts, hoping to alleviate the panic consuming him.

"I don't know how else to spell it out to you. This is not going to be resolved by a single guild." Milo stood in his office, tossing files onto his desk. Each one held detailed intel about the recently poached enchanters all signed to enlist at Cerberus Guild. This memory was fresh and haunting Milo. The usually bright and colorful walls of his office were painted black with grim portraits of blood, carnage, and death—a clear sign he'd warped this memory due to heightened fear.

"You said you needed the strength of enchanters from these guilds, so I made them an offer they couldn't resist." Or refuse, based on the smug smile plastered across Enchanter Campbell's face as she stood across from Milo. It was difficult to discern if Campbell was actually this arrogant or if Milo replaced her expression with something more fitting to how he felt in the moment. "With them, we'll rise even further, remaining the strongest guild in the state and the most reliable to our citizens."

"It's not about strength. It's not about the magics." Milo's frustration created flickering in the lights. "It's about collaboration."

"That ship sailed the second you shined a spotlight on Whitlock Industries," Enchanter Campbell said. "There's too much fear for collaboration. Where will the credit fall? Who will land the funding? Will this lead to another corrupt monopoly?"

Milo glowered.

"Look, you wanted my help. This is what I brought you. If you can't find a solution with ten additional enchanters, some of the damn best might I add, then you're the one failing this city, not me."

"Let me put it in a way you'll understand *Enchanter* Campbell." The walls of Milo's office quaked. "If you can't find a way to get the other guild masters to work together, you'll never call yourself Guild Master Campbell, and you'll never sit on that board you've been clamoring for."

Campbell's jaw clenched like she'd bit back every word she wanted to say, every question she wanted to press.

"Oooh," Milo's voice called from another direction. Not the Milo of this memory but the actual consciousness of Milo.

The fuck?

I quirked a brow, following the small echo. He should very much be asleep. No, he *was* very much asleep. What was going on?

"This one's funny but completely unnecessary."

I stepped away from the nightmare on the surface of Milo's slumbering mind and deeper into his mind's core, which was a vast black space, infinitely wide. The towering wall of screens projecting potential vision stood too tall for me to see an ending. Given my inability to view his magic, the screens showed only fuzzy static.

"Hmm. Nope. Gotta go."

I squeezed between the tight space of the screens, having just enough room to wiggle further through Milo's core. Our link created a succinct connection, and I recalled a secondary location where Milo sorted his visions.

All the darkness disappeared once I reached the white board of interconnected strings. An array of colors filling the entire spectrum weaved along the board like a maze. Fates interlocking, converging, and separating in endless mysteries I would never understand. Milo wasn't here either.

"Milo?" I called out because I didn't want him thinking I'd invaded his privacy even if I had—with the best intentions, of course.

"Don't need. Don't need. Keep. Keep. Maybe pile. No. Yes. Maybe." Milo's voice echoed beyond the wall of colorful fates. "No idea what to do with this one just yet."

I stepped close, searching for a way around but this room was a circle all leading back to the screens I'd come from. I touched a white part, careful not to hit the strings representing futures, and searched for...I had no clue. A secret button? A knob?

"Milo?"

"Dorian?" Milo's voice called back from behind the wall. "What're you doing here?"

"You were sleep talking, and I wanted to help." I sighed. "Okay, I wanted to obsessively assist because I lack boundaries *sometimes*."

"Love it." Milo's arms reached out at me from seemingly nowhere, and he dragged me into the wall.

I yelped, bracing to hit the wall. I didn't, though. Instead, I phased right through it.

Behind his endless screens of visions and his massive board of strings of fate was quite possibly the most outlandish area thus far. A simple, boring filing room with beige wallpaper and a smell that screamed office musk. The filing cabinets stretched forever.

"What is this place?"

"My deepest core. Sort of a place to organize outdated visions."

"Outdated?"

Milo guided me to a table covered in stacks and stacks of blank papers. "These are either old, unlikely, or randomly unnecessary. Some are impossible given other variables that already occurred, or my interference would be questionable, possibly unethical. A few will simply resolve themselves, so why bother?"

"I want to put a pin in what you consider questionable for a later discussion." I grabbed a blank piece of paper. "But I'm assuming there's something written here?"

"Oh, right." Milo smacked his forehead. "It's all blankety blank blank for you since it's conjured by my magic. Yeah, mostly words, but some are images, too. Depends on the depth of the vision and how my brain sorts the info. Man, brains and magic are so wild and awesome. Like they very much know what they're doing."

"And you sort them? Why?"

"They pile up. It gets distracting." Milo grabbed a stack of papers and shoved them into a filing cabinet. "They don't fade from my Fateful Viewing of Infinite Possibilities or my Dispatch Board of Destiny unless I file them away in here."

"You named the screens and that board of colorful strings?" I shook my head. "Yeah, I'm not calling them that."

"Buzzkill." Milo grinned. "Point is, once my magic has experienced a vision, it remains tangible, which becomes difficult to navigate even for fates that'll never happen."

"So, instead of sleeping, you stay up all night sorting visions?" I scrunched my face, likely frowning but feeling more inquisitive. How did Milo function?

"I am sleeping. Working here while my subconscious sorts whatever the hell I'm worried about at the moment. Plus, I usually only pull these semi all-nighters once a week."

"About your current worries…" I bit my lip. "Do you want to talk about it? Not work wise, just so you don't have to hold onto it so closely?"

"You're sweet," Milo said, organizing papers into stacks. "It's bad. Really bad or semi bad or the baddest of bad. I'm not entirely sure because demons fuck up my clairvoyance and make all this murkier."

"Is that why you're here? Trying to lighten the burden of so many potentials?"

Milo kissed me, gentle and endearing, not a long-lasting kiss or a kiss worth savoring, yet I did. Our bodies outside his mind's core shifted—hard to say how, but I thought they drew closer, yearning the physical affection of expressed emotion. "That's why I keep you around. You're more than your good looks, Dorian. Got quite the big head, and your brain is nice, too."

Milo winked, casting suggestive innuendos at the head he meant, and my cheeks burned. Taking full advantage of my flustered response, Milo smirked and went back to working on sorting papers for filing. I lingered in this space, ignoring the call of his nearby nightmare that made his body shudder in my grasp outside his mind, watching him work to lessen the burden of endless visions so he could prioritize the most important ones as the world around burned.

I couldn't go to sleep. It was important to maintain boundaries and not involve myself with Enchanter Evergreen's career. But I could be a part of his world so long as I remembered to respect that professional distance. He didn't have to remind me, but I constantly had to remind myself.

"Do you need help?" I asked, feigning assistance while knowing full well there was nothing I had to offer here in his deepest core, which likely had another silly name.

"Really?" Milo handed me a stack of papers. "Put these in filing cabinet C-R-S 142."

"Okay." I took the papers and strolled through the filing cabinets, reading over the labels on each one.

"Oh, the third drawer," Milo shouted. "Please and thank you."

I smiled, here in Milo's deepest depths, doing my little part to help with the demon threat he worried about.

CHAPTER TWENTY-SEVEN

GEMINI boomed with thoughts on the Spring Showcase. Even the second- and third-year students in the building gossiped.

A Novak was defeated by a branchless student.

The kid ranked dead last managed a perfected root cast.

Voucher students took the top two slots.

These were the same students who stopped the warlock incursion.

One even told off the entire guild industry during his speech.

I sulked, realizing that when it came to Kenzo's third year, I'd have incredible difficulty landing him an internship. And he still had so much more time to burn more bridges in the industry he wanted to join.

"You did fan-fucking-tastic, and you need to own it." Katherine strolled toward the classroom, her arm linked with Caleb's. "*And if one more person questions it, I will gladly remind them of where their roots lack and where their ranking got them.*"

"I guess." Caleb kept the weighted blocks afloat overhead, still practicing, still finetuning his roots. "It's not like I controlled it. Sort of just happened."

I cleared my throat, eyeing the two and their interlocked arms. They quickly separated. Caleb's face burned bright red. Katherine giggled, then rolled her eyes at me before dragging Caleb into the classroom. Teens were the worst. Sure, they could date. Whatever. But I drew the line at affection. It always started innocently with hand holding or resting on a shoulder, and next thing you knew, they were trying to share the same desk chair—side-by-side or on a lap—getting handsy or making out in the hallway. Dealing with explicit teenage PDA was not how I wanted to spend my day. Ever. It was bad enough when they flirted by slapping each other or name calling or a thousand other hormonal factors they didn't quite comprehend the intent behind.

Once the bell rang, I spent homeroom preparing my students for their upcoming final exams. The next six weeks would fly by, and then the end of May would be here, so I wanted them ready for all their classes.

"This is so unfair." Gael pouted.

"Ba-bawk."

"What's unfair is that you all believe you can ride the blip of the Spring Showcase to shirk your responsibilities." I glared, eyeing each and every one of my homeroom coven—including an angry Kenzo, a somber Tara, and an anxious Caleb. "The fact is, no one remembers a first-year showcase, few remember a second-year showcase, and no one will remember your rankings here and now."

Katherine scowled. "But you said—"

"I said they're important for the industry, and they are. But do not think for an instant you can rest on the luck our homeroom had at landing in the showcase or the well-deserved success of others. You each chose Gemini because the industry was your dream." I hated crushing their aloof excitement but knew the truth behind what I said. None of them picked our academy out of family obligation except Tara, who'd since revised her opinion. They needed motivation and to remember not everything ended with a fucking golden star of achievement. "If you want to practice your branches, your roots, then do it on your own time. That's why you have fledgling permits. The next six weeks, we're prepping for exams in content some of you—no, most of you—need to thoroughly review."

A collective sigh followed, and a pinch of guilt hit me. I would endure their sour thoughts and bitter, breathy comments because they needed to ready themselves for the years to come. The first year was supposed to be the easiest, yet they'd nearly been killed by warlocks their first semester.

I couldn't—wouldn't—let up just because of unfortunate circumstances. They deserved the best opportunities. There was little in the world I controlled. Not demons. Not outcomes. Not choices. But I could lay out the best strategies and study groups any fucking teacher at this academy could muster, ensuring my homeroom coven each prepared based on their specialized learning style.

I'd make certain they aced these exams if it killed them. Okay. Dramatic, but also, it felt invigorating to focus purely on academics and helping my students finish the year strong. Even if it broke them over the summer. They had the season to recover, after all.

I slipped out after classes to indulge in the first cigarette I'd had in hours. Each hasty inhale did little to settle my nerves, concerned that somewhere out there, Milo faced demon threats. Unknown threats. Sure, he managed obscurity well—better than most witches—but I couldn't shake this dread.

"Fuck." I slowly exhaled smoke as my telepathy leapt across the city, rocketing directly toward Milo's mind. "I can't even finish a cigarette."

"So glad you could join me." Milo opened his office door bringing in Acolyte Reed and Novak. "Have you each reviewed the documents I sent?"

Acolyte Novak had a ghostly complexion. Not from the lack of glamour that'd altered her features subtly during the investigation. No, this came from the hollowed out, broken expression plastered on her face. Whatever Milo had them read left her unsettled and frightened. I almost dropped my cigarette in response to her obvious pain. I remained close to Milo, taking a deep inhale, hopeful he'd reveal what he had planned.

No. I released a breath, quelling my telepathy. It hurt to restrain my mind from linking to his, but I couldn't see, know, feel all his actions in the field without reacting. The only way I could function was by distancing myself from everything Milo—everything Enchanter Evergreen—did to keep the city safe. I wished I were better at compartmentalizing it all, yet whenever Milo was in the picture, my emotions took hold, and my rationality faded.

My phone buzzed.

Chanelle: Where the hell R U?

I tossed my smoke and cut across the parking lot to reach the buses. Chanelle checked off students as they got on the bus for her after-school program.

"You're late." Chanelle glared, sending a shudder down my spine.

I cracked my neck, eyeing the wary student who invoked the frightened sensation. They feared her stern comment, not me.

"Not you, darling. You're fine." Chanelle turned back to me as the student hopped on the bus, and maybe a bit of the trepidation resonating was my own.

"I was on a parent call." I averted my gaze, momentarily avoiding her stern stare.

"Damn liar," Chanelle mouthed, not even indulging me in telepathic conversation. Since the Spring Showcase, she'd gone back into hyperfocus—more like her first few years of teaching, where she didn't accept or tolerate slackers, which meant I was royally screwed.

Whether the way admin treated her, our conversation, the end of so many extra duties as we reached the end of the school year, or a thousand factors I didn't account for, Chanelle wanted to end on a high note before summer. All the same, I joined her on the bus for another trip monitoring the students who'd volunteered to help banish demonic energy, a task that'd grown in high demand with so many demons dwelling in the shadows. Sadly, those threats remained in the shadows, stalking, and preying in the darkness of night while evading enchanter intervention. But I counted the blessings as we reached our destination, knowing Milo had a plan that would hopefully bring the horrors raining down on Chicago to an end soon enough. He always had a plan.

Kids grouped up and attempted to partner with second- and third-year students to avoid ending up stuck with teacher chaperones.

"Not happening." I waved a hand at my homeroom coven, where Kenzo intended on pairing off with Gael for some solo volunteering, Katherine had dragged Caleb toward a group of upperclassmen, and Gael, along with King Clucks, partnered up with Tara, avoiding wannabes and whatever he considered irksome—completely ironic. "I'm rearranging you all."

"The hell you are," Kenzo growled. "This is our free time we're offering, and we can spend it how we want."

"Oh, so close…yet not at all," I retorted. "This is your volunteered time through an academy-sanctioned program. If you want to do this on your own time, file the proper paperwork, apply to the city, gain approval, and help in your own small way. Otherwise, accept my judgment and silently protest."

"Asshole."

I linked my thoughts to his and replied, "*Back at you,*" before rearranging my homeroom students into groups that'd benefit them during this outing.

"*Picky much?*" Chanelle rolled her eyes yet grouped her own students similarly, ignoring their pleas to work with friends.

"*They've grown too accustomed to each other and need to learn to collaborate with others.*"

Chanelle scoffed. "*Not according to recent trends. Sticking with the familiar seems the new norm.*"

Another reminder of how saving Caleb, stopping Theodore Whitlock, and revealing the skeletons in Whitlock Industries had created ripples forever affecting Chicago. It couldn't be helped, and the world was better without Tobias and Theodore feuding with an entire state as their chessboard. Still, I partnered my students away from their preferences, hopefully encouraging new collaborative teamwork.

I assigned Kenzo, Katherine, and Gael together. Plus, King Clucks. Then Caleb, Tara, and Gael. It wasn't that their grouping was unhealthy, but Katherine and Caleb had begun latching onto each other as much as Kenzo and

Gael. Tara seemed to actively avoid almost everyone except for her irritating bestie.

I wouldn't let them fall into the same bad habits I'd developed, which involved me lacking the ability or willingness to collaborate with others day to day. So maybe I was projecting. I didn't care. They could go one after-school program without making googly eyes.

Begrudgingly, Kenzo dragged Katherine and Gael with him—much to each of their protests alongside a crowing rooster—so they could banish the most demonic energy this outing. It didn't matter that there was no more showcase to compete for; Kenzo wanted to outperform Caleb and worried that soon, Caleb's perfected banishment would outperform him.

Meanwhile, Caleb reluctantly went with Gael and Tara, continuing his training, but worried he had no understanding of his roots. He'd achieved the impossible, the highly coveted, and had absolutely no idea how he'd done it. I'd assist in any way I could, but I barely considered my roots proficient after months of toning and retraining, let alone perfected.

Tara, Gael, and Caleb levitated down the street, turning the corner, while I trailed off with Jamie's group. Since he'd taken it upon himself to continue attending Chanelle's volunteering program, I decided it best to keep a close eye on him—and as far from Tara or Caleb as possible. Any student, preferably.

The wisps had thinned in the neighborhoods we covered from weeks past. Perhaps a sign of the vigilance of guild witches desperate to clear demonic energy everywhere they'd encountered it since the presence of demons had swelled in Chicago.

The clouds did little to alleviate the heat of the humid breeze. I practically gagged on the hot air as Jamie chased two wisps.

"Let someone else catch them," I said since he'd let them trail further than someone with his proficiency should've. The wisps were heading in the direction of Tara's group, and Jamie would likely let them go a few blocks as an excuse to accidentally encounter Tara. His thoughts had become fuzzy, muddled, and difficult to read. "Are you listening to me?"

"I can catch them." Jamie floated after the wisps, which resisted the wind blowing against them, ignoring Jamie's flux of magic, too.

I cocked my head. Why?

"And now the real fun begins, Dorian."

My chest tightened. That was the gorgon's voice.

Stretching my telepathy, unraveling, and amplifying my branch, I searched for the demon whose thoughts had vanished as quickly as they'd surfaced.

Frantically, I scanned the street. Where'd he gone? When had he arrived? What was he doing here? Who was he targeting? How'd I lose his trace so fast?

Steadying my breathing, I focused. Demonic energy was harder for branches to pinpoint, but I could track his location through my sensory root.

Casting waves of magic in all directions, I ignored the tiny fragments of wisps in the air and followed the powerful radiating energy luring those wisps. My eyes snapped open. Tara's group. Was he after her arcane branch?

I flew past Jamie, snatching him by the shoulder.

"What the hell?"

"Go back to the bus."

"I don't know what your—"

"Now, Jamie." I glared. "There's a demon nearby."

He trembled, then quickly ran back, avoiding using any magic to make his presence noticeable.

I continued flying toward the radiating magic and used my telepathy to search for as many minds of students as I could. *"Everyone needs to return to the bus immediately. There is a demon in the area."*

"A demon?"   *"The news said they weren't a big deal."*

"Where the fuck are they?
If that demon so much as touches them..."

"Dad said his guild had it handled."   *"King Clucks, we need to find Tara."*

"Un demonio real."

"I got this. I can do this. I can fight this."

"*I said back to the bus—nowhere else, or it'll be more than your fledgling permit you lose.*" I ground my teeth, erasing the flurry of panicked thoughts. Making threats wasn't how I wanted to redirect my students' fear, but some were already composing ideas to intercept, search, fight, and protect. That blame fell on me. I'd forced their hands last semester, inadvertently drawing the ire of warlocks. There was no way I'd allow them to battle a demon. "*Mrs. Whitehurst. Please contact the academy and notify guilds assigned to these neighborhoods.*"

"*Of course,*" Chanelle thought. "*Where are you?*"

"*Searching for Tara, Caleb, and Gael.*" Their minds were swimming in terror the second I cast a widespread link. It wasn't about getting to them before the gorgon found them...

Caleb's fear spiked. "*This is a gorgon. We need to run, but my legs won't move.*"

The demon had already found my students. Now, it was about getting to them before he killed them.

Chapter Twenty-Eight

I FLEW to the end of the street, cutting the corner too wide, and almost crashed into incoming traffic. I stopped moving, struggling to maintain a sense of my students' direction. Cars honked. People shouted. I had no time for their aggravation. I needed to save my students. This couldn't be happening again. I couldn't have led my students to their deaths a second time because of my foolish, impulsive selfishness.

If I'd let it go, this need to fix the world around me and let the work go to those who actually could, they wouldn't be here right now. Or if they were, Milo would be here. No. Milo would've detained the gorgon, studied the hidden outcomes linked to the demon. Everything would be fine if I'd simply not involved myself. As always, I managed to ruin everything. And all my doubt, fear, and regret synced to my students.

There was no way I could chase them down while all three had such erratic, sharp horror in their thoughts. I shook away the terrified minds of Tara and Gael. Tightening my telepathy, I linked over Caleb's shoulder. Calling out would only distract him. He needed his wits and entire attention fixed on this dire situation. Of the three, Caleb handled his panic with the most composure, evaluating the golden snake eyes and sapphire scales that shimmered against the setting sun.

"A gorgon which means we have to be vigilant if we want..." Caleb blinked, and the gorgon vanished. *"Shit."*

Not just a gorgon. The very same gorgon that killed Finn. The one Milo banished twelve years ago. The one I'd banished. Some powerful demon continued pulling the strings from behind the scenes, resurrecting demons, and now the gorgon who took Finn from me, a piece of my heart, intended on slaughtering my students.

The demon reappeared behind Tara, the jagged teeth forming mouths on his palms, and snatched two of Tara's weighted blocks. He shattered them in a single chomp. It forced her to immediately quell her branches.

Caleb's peripheral scanned their surroundings. They were at the corner of Lux and Lathe. Less than five blocks. I'd be there in minutes. But that gorgon could eviscerate them in seconds.

"Gorgons can only slow down physical bodies through their line of vision, not magic itself. No time to hesitate." Caleb released a steady wave of banishment on the area. "Both of you—over here."

Tara and Gael levitated toward Caleb. The gorgon's eyes flitted, and Caleb felt the pressure of the gaze hitting his banishment and attempting to slow everyone and everything on this near-empty street.

"Can you use that big banishment on this thing?" Gael asked, his spikes shrinking from anxiety.

"I highly doubt this kid has it in him to banish a demon." The gorgon grinned, his yellow razored teeth evoking fear. "Even if he accidentally cast a perfect banishment."

Caleb gulped, every thought scrambling to decern how this demon knew him. How did the gorgon know him? Was the gorgon watching me?

Caleb had no idea how to control the perfected root magic and casting a steady wave of banishment locked him in one spot. His banishment continued pulsating against the gorgon's attempts to slow their bodies. If Caleb took a single step, his magic might falter. If that happened, the gorgon would petrify their movements and kill them.

My flight floundered. How'd the gorgon know Caleb had used a perfect banishment? Had he been watching my students? Was he attacking them because of me? Because I killed him? This entire thing was my fault.

"I need a plan of action. Something that'll let us retreat." Caleb eyed his classmates, drawing me away from self-pity and to the task. *"Tara's branches would all be fantastic at obscuring us from sight and creating enough distance for an escape."*

I ground my teeth. Probably why the gorgon destroyed her weighted blocks. He must've known about her branch overlap, too. I took a shaky breath and turned another corner. One street away.

"Gael's spikes are strong, but few things can cut through a gorgon's scales," Caleb thought. *"Plus, that's an offensive move that won't block his line of vision."*

Caleb knew a lot about demons for a first-year student especially considering demonology courses didn't start until the second and third year at the academy.

Tara stepped in front of Caleb, twirling her hands round and round as shadows seeped from her palms, carrying a golden sheen as they slithered toward the gorgon.

"What're you doing?" Caleb asked.

"Ending this." In mere seconds, a black sphere swelled around the gorgon, encasing him within all three of Tara's channeled branches.

Good. That'd hold long enough for me to reach them. Caleb studied Tara's clenched teeth while she cast shadows, intangibility, and ward sealing in tandem. This was the one technique she'd mastered, conjuring all three together as a defensive measure, but it didn't cause her this much strain.

A searing burn flooded her thoughts, boiling her ocean of doubt as her arm shook. The struggle of all her branches pulling at the muscles in her arms sent a sharp, stabbing pain through her broken wrist.

"We need to go." Tara inched back, bumping Caleb and knocking his banishment flow off momentarily.

The sphere burst, and shadows swept in a strange formation against Tara's direction. She wove her arms, attempting to reshape the sphere, but the gorgon inhaled the entirety of her casting in a deep breath.

"I feast upon unique branches regularly." The gorgon locked his gaze on Caleb. "It'll take a lot more than that to contain me."

Caleb couldn't move, blink, or channel.

He was trapped in the gorgon's stare as a blue blur raced toward him. Jagged teeth lining the gorgon's palm reached Caleb's face, an inch from snapping shut.

I fucking refused this outcome.

Severing the link of telepathy, my dual vision faded, and I mentally recalibrated my surroundings.

I shouted, channeling everything into my telekinesis and releasing the burst from overhead.

Intercepting the gorgon, I knocked him into the pavement before he touched one of my students. Asphalt cracked beneath him while I maintained a powerful telekinetic burst fluctuating to keep him pinned.

"Mr. Frost," Gael shouted.

"Thank god."

"I need you three to get out of here now."

"Can he really hold a demon like this? What if…"

"Go, now."

"No, stay."

My telekinesis waned. The gorgon pushed himself upright, resisting the steady burst. Tensing every single muscle in my body, I unleashed all the telekinesis possible. The gorgon slammed back into the ground but slowly twisted his neck. Bones crackled and snapped as he turned so his gaze landed on me. Fuck.

I lessened my root and redistributed magic into my banishment to block his petrification. My body stilled.

"The fun's just beginning." The gorgon stood, brushing off rubble caught on his scales. "Which kid should I eat first? I'm leaning toward the branch buffet, but then I'd be stuck with the prickly augmentation or branchless witch as a palette cleanser. Neither sounds particularly appetizing."

"Get…out…of…" I struggled to speak, locked in the gorgon's sight.

Electricity surged, coursing through the air, and whipped across the gorgon's face. He roared, covering his eyes as lightning trickled and sparked along the scales of his head.

"Please don't disrespect Mr. Frost by willfully ignoring his instructions." Chanelle's heels clicked along the pavement. "I believe he told you three to leave."

Tara, Gael, and Caleb all stared in awe while Chanelle sauntered past them, holding lightning conjured into the form of a whip.

Chapter Twenty-Nine

THE KIDS ran back to the bus, where all the students had returned, and awaited the arrival of enchanters. Chanelle was kind enough to keep that thought close to the surface so I wouldn't fret, along with a snarky comment on how I should've given her a heads-up on which way to go.

"Honestly, Dorian. I was at the hospital after you decided to fight off those warlocks. You really wanted to throw yourself at a demon this semester?" Chanelle grinned. *"So dramatic."*

"It's a gorgon," I warned as the lightning fizzled away from his temples, and he turned his sight back toward us. "Which means it can—"

Chanelle used the elemental whip to slash the gorgon's eyes.

"Yeah, I paid attention during all my demonology physiology courses. Also, really loved the advanced psychology behind the nature of demons." Chanelle moved ahead of me, confidence brimming. "Be a dear, my darling demon, and answer a few questions before we banish you."

"You think your primal magic is enough to stop me." The gorgon grunted, taking strike after strike of Chanelle's swift attacks. Each time he gained more immunity to her casting frequency.

"Cute. You're so flustered you can't even properly sniff out my branch." Chanelle coiled the lightning back, holding it firmly with one hand while she wove her other along the trace sparks of electricity. "I'm a real fan of lightning. What can I say, I enjoy the clap of the smack it makes, but with you being a big, scary demon—clearly, I need to show you exactly how versatile my arcane branch is."

> **Name: Chanelle Whitehurst**
> **Branch: Arcane (Infinity Spectrum)**

She possessed a truly unique branch that mixed primal and cosmic magics into her trademark whip.

The gorgon's eyes widened. Air sizzled. Flames burnt his face. Chanelle's elemental whip clacked against the road, freezing the street before zipping back and smacking the gorgon with ice. Each time Chanelle reeled back her whip, it changed elements and struck the gorgon's face, making it impossible to recover or develop an immunity long enough to lock us in place.

Water. *Clack*. Wind. *Snap*. Earth. *Crack*. Steel. Lightning. Fire. Ice. Flora. Lava. Shadows. Light. Repeat.

She cycled through her elements again and again until she'd stripped away every scale on the gorgon's face, leaving nothing but tarry pus. It oozed, a demonic infection on the world that seared the ground when splattered drops fell.

"*Not to be that person*"—Chanelle side-eyed me—"*but this would be a good time to cast some banishment his way. I know I look incredibly badass and all, but even I have limits.*"

"*Right.*" I nodded.

Channeling my banishment root, I aimed my magic. Wait. If I banished him. Killed him. He'd return. I hesitated, releasing my energy because I needed to detain him. Contact Milo. Shit. These demons warped his clairvoyance, so he had no idea what was happening here and now.

"Oh, no, you don't, big boy." Chanelle tugged her electrical whip, which the gorgon had gripped in his sizzling hands. With a quick shake, she transformed the element into ice. He bit down on her elemental whip, so she changed it into steel.

"Lightning. Ice. Metal. I'll eat it all." The gorgon gorged on Chanelle's magic, pulling her closer with each bite.

She released the whip and let him devour it, then conjured two new elemental whips in each hand. They were each earth based but created from different minerals. One had a glossy, reflective shine, whereas the other was dull and crumbling.

"Dorian, I don't want to call you incompetent, but I'm pretty sure I requested a banishment."

"We can't." I choked on the words. "If we kill him, he'll just—"

A whirlpool opened behind the gorgon, and Jamie Novak appeared, placing a single hand on top of the gorgon's head.

"Jamie." Chanelle flung both whips at the gorgon only for them to be caught in a torrent of water transporting the snaps of the strikes elsewhere.

"You worry too much, Mrs. Whitehurst." Jamie grinned, sincere and calm. Nothing like any snide smile he'd displayed all year.

I cast my telepathy forward, attempting to figure out his plan and why he'd place himself in this dangerous situation.

The gorgon was one swift move away from killing him. Jamie's mind remained as silent as the gorgon's. A soft buzz between my telepathy and his thoughts. I linked to Chanelle; she had a hundred frantic thoughts attempting to sort how or why her student would interfere, endangering his life against a demon she'd barely held off.

It wasn't my telepathy waning. It was Jamie blocking my branch. How?

"Your presence is no longer required." Jamie twisted the gorgon's head around to meet his gaze. "Thank you for your nauseating assistance."

The gorgon's eyes grew wide. Shock and terror in them, yet no attempt to petrify Jamie where he stood. Jamie smiled as he squeezed the reformed scales on the gorgon's head, cracking them until caustic tar burst. It splashed his skin but didn't sizzle. In an instant, the gorgon exploded into nothingness. The wisps shimmered, then dimmed, and finally did something I'd never seen before from any demonic energy. Their white light curdled inward, fading black and crumpling into ashes.

"Sorry for bringing him back, Dorian," Jamie said. His voice held a dark echo. "It was cruel, perhaps needlessly; however, I craved to see your reaction when reunited with the demon that caused such brutality on the young, beautiful Finn Summers. You, most certainly, did not disappoint."

The darkness in his echo rattled the broken ground, whispering things too softly to hear or in languages I didn't recognize.

"What are you?"

"Jamie?" Chanelle stepped forward.

"I am what some would call a devil."

The sincerity in Jamie's voice, the terror wrapped in the echo, and the hollowness in his eyes sent a shudder up my spine, which reverberated through my body, channeling every magic at my disposal, frightened a single second left off guard would end in death.

"Relax." In a flash, Jamie stood next to me, eyeing my magical frequency like he could see every fiber of my channeled magic. "There's so much you've yet to uncover. I look forward to helping you grow and learn, Dorian."

"What are you?" I asked again, baffled and lost in the terror consuming me and Chanelle.

Jamie tilted his head, perplexed or mocking. I couldn't decide. "I told you. Some call me a devil."

"Impossible," Chanelle said—every thought she had amplified, adding to the horror of each second that passed in the presence of a literal devil.

Demons rarely succeeded in achieving such a heightened state of power. Devils were the embodiment of perfected power. A collection of wisps that gathered in our reality, forming into a fiend which collected magic until it became a suitable host for a demon; then that demon stole a witch's body, making them its host. If accomplished, they became a devil with a true foot-hold in our reality, possessing a proper host that contained their unnatural magic, keeping it from spilling over and depleting.

"How long have you been possessing him?" Chanelle snapped, her mind furious and somber simultaneously as she reacted to the fact that she didn't recognize a demon surging within one of her students.

How could she, though? I'd been inside Jamie's head. I'd heard his thoughts. Nothing indicated this.

Did it? I quivered.

"You heard what I wished you to hear, Dorian." Jamie patted my shoulder like he knew my every thought, then he eyed Chanelle. "To answer your question, Mrs. Whitehurst, it was the start of the new semester. January. I considered arriving in Jamie's flesh with a fresh attitude, joining my little classmates with a nicer, plucky personality. But unfortunately, he'd left quite the impact on his peers, so I played his role to the best of my ability."

"No, no, no." Chanelle trembled behind me, her thoughts shaky.

"I do think I portrayed him convincingly."

"We need to leave." I backed away, turning to Chanelle.

The succubus Milo's team had beheaded stood beside Chanelle, appearing out of literal thin air, a hand on Chanelle's wrist. NO!

"Get away from her." I unleashed a telekinetic burst, simultaneously tugging Chanelle from the demon's grip.

Nothing happened.

"As I'm certain you know—because you're so brilliant, Dorian—all demons, even those who ascend to a devil possession, lack an immunity to root magics," Jamie said. "However, I've acquired skills to divert, displace, and diffuse those dangers."

Demonic energy began to radiate off him, no longer cloaked by his devil possession. It oozed magic tenfold, no, one-hundredfold stronger than any demon I'd ever felt.

"Get those darling children back to the safety of your academy," the succubus whispered, caressing Chanelle's face. "Everything is okay. Dorian is fine. You are fantastic. Make sure the tiny teens are properly and thoroughly accounted for before you wake."

She released Chanelle, whose eyes teared before she calmly turned on her heel and walked away. Her thoughts were fuzzy, her magic faded.

"My way of showing compassion," Jamie—no, this demon housed in him as a devil—said. "I do not condone the mistreatment of mortals. I prefer…what is it you all say? Ah, yes, something about humane slaughter. A necessary evil when you feast upon the lesser beasts, though I will not be feasting on Mrs. Whitehurst. I rather enjoyed her company, in all her simplicity."

"I enjoy the taste of her branch." The succubus licked her fingertips, the same ones that'd gripped and compelled Chanelle to leave without a word.

"Distance yourself." The devil waved a dismissive hand at the demon. "Your presence exhausts me and offends my guest."

The succubus' expression shifted from jovial to a fright I didn't believe possible from the same woman who showed no fear when losing her head while interrogated by Milo.

"Of course. Apologies." She backed away, keeping an eye on us but less intrusive.

I channeled my telepathy toward this monster possessing Jamie Novak. Echoes. Constant echoes whispered in the darkness of his being. Then nothing. Not one word. Not one sound. A painful silence followed by a drop of water. Tears splashing.

"Please, help."

Jamie's voice was faint, lost in agony. I panicked.

"Please." The devil holding him captive gripped my wrist and twisted. "He's a little sadist who met a meaner monster. Don't pity him."

Despite the grasp, my telepathy struggled to rifle through his thoughts to search his mind. Demonic energy truly made each push of my magic exhausting, like navigating the fray of a battle while the target moved behind an insurmountable wall. Peaks and valleys of shifting frequencies, each just out of reach and a faded whisper by the time I'd grabbed it.

"You're attempting to read my mind. Quite impressive."

"I've heard your thoughts before."

"You heard what I allowed. Even those were fabrications of a role I played."

"W-why?"

"I needed to blend, so nothing about my behavior differed from Jamie's personality. I'd contribute my talented performance to why no one suspected my presence; however, I found it difficult maintaining his constant entitled rage." The devil chuckled. "So much to unpack there."

That was why Jamie's—correction, this devil's—thoughts alternated so erratically between bursts of enraged tones.

"Why possess him? Why play the part of a student?"

"To study you, Dorian. I needed to understand who you were. There was much I did, yet mortals change over time. Twelve years had passed, and I sought to unravel your mystery before seeking your aid."

Twelve years. That was when the gorgon grabbed… That was when Finn died. This devil sent the gorgon, stole Finn's life, but wanted to return to Chicago to study me? To what end? I trembled, attempting to break free of his grip. I needed to escape. Find help. Call out and link my telepathy to Milo.

"*Attempting to contact Enchanter Evergreen?*" Jamie's eyes flitted curiously, and I quaked at the presence of telepathy intercepting my thoughts, scanning them, tiptoeing the edges of my mind.

"How are you in my head?"

"*It's not the host, if you're wondering. This child's arcane branch is quite impressive, but I've acquired many greater magics in my time here.*"

Demons didn't acquire magics. They possessed their own. They devoured magic, searching for unique and powerful ones, yet there shouldn't be one—devil due to possession or not—that could simply inherit new abilities. I searched my thoughts carefully, keeping my attention on the psychic energy and observing where my memories went. I couldn't think of a single demon that possessed its own form of telepathy. But I needed to narrow this monster's classification down if I wanted to survive an encounter against a devil.

"*Milo,*" I thought, searching for his mind and ready to share everything I knew, which wasn't enough.

"I hate to disappoint, but I believe The Inevitable Future is busy protecting the happiness of the many over the happiness of the few. That's been his weakness since he made the decision that is his biggest regret: choosing vengeance over finding me. A true downfall for him now."

Jamie released my wrist and stepped away as he mused over my confusion. I cracked my neck, burying my fears and impulsive conclusions, and hoped to create a real place beneath the random words and memories I hurled outward as a distraction.

"Given my ability to resurrect fallen demons, it's garnered me much allegiance over the years," the devil explained. "I have hundreds of loyal demons raining hellfire onto this city. Thanks to the guilds' lack of cooperation, I believe the great and heroic Enchanter Evergreen will be too busy fighting, searching for, and saving every potential future dimly buzzing in his clairvoyance. After all, the future's so much bleaker and hard to see when we're nearby."

The devil's thoughts opened immediately, inviting me—no—dragging me into the depths of his mind's core.

CHAPTER THIRTY

SCALDING tar flowed everywhere. A sea of demonic energy served as the representation of the devil's inner thoughts. I choked, struggling to breathe, to swim, to see through the heavy sludge that seemed endless. Faint whispers and cries called from beneath. Ignoring them, I swam up. Up. Faster. Harder. Searching desperately for a way out of this thick toxic horror. Was this why demons' minds were so difficult to read? Did they all have such deathly inner cores?

A hand cut through the tar, pulling me into quiet darkness. I gasped for air. My hands and knees pressed against the rippling sea of tar below, but I didn't sink back into it. I searched for something in this place. A memory. A stray thought. An exit. Nothing but infinite darkness. Shadows went on and on, slithering subtly so I could almost make out the different textures in this world.

"I wish to know your understanding of demons, Dorian." Jamie's voice echoed in sync with the creature possessing his body, the one that'd infested his mind into an ocean of black nothingness. "Specifically, I'd like to know your knowledge of devils."

I quivered, desperate to leave. Shaking it off, I steadied my breathing and accepted the darkness.

"It's a name—title, really—for demons who worm their way inside a human host." I scanned the shifting shadows, searching for the devil, but his voice echoed from every direction and none at the same time. "They're known for being more powerful than any demon. When they possess a human, the demonic energy slowly rots the witch's body until—"

"Enough," he hissed before me; his teeth clacked behind me. "I did not want a textbook response, Dorian."

I spun only to find darkness. Clawed fingertips tickled my forearm. Trembling, I ignored it. He sought to goad me, toy with me. If he planned on killing me, I wouldn't give him the satisfaction of enjoying my fear. Footsteps approached from the shadows, and I closed my eyes.

"I'm not playing your games."

"No games." A deep, hollow voice spoke. No whispers, no echoes, no trace of Jamie's lighter pitch. "How about a proper introduction?"

I opened my eyes to find an older man, perhaps in his mid-forties, dressed in a beige frock coat, cream trousers loose around his thighs and tight at the knee to his ankles where his dress shoes held a bit of polished sheen to be distinguished from the tar floor. He had short salt and peppered hair with a matching finely trimmed beard. His blue eyes were striking in this bleak world of his creation.

"My first host, one of many," he said. "But a personal favorite over the centuries."

"Don't know many devils to live through the centuries."

"Yes, our actions draw much attention." He chuckled, actually fucking laughed like we were having a civilized conversation. "We are having a civilized conversation, Dorian."

I cringed at how seamlessly he sifted through my thoughts while talking.

"Then show me your true form, demon, devil, fucking monster," I said, biting back every impulsive thought revealing my anxiety or concern about him rummaging through my mind.

"Mortals so rarely react fondly to a demon's true form, and I'd rather our time together be pleasant and not filled with fright."

"I assure you, I'm not like most mortals." A lie because I was as plain as anyone else. But I wanted to see the true face of the devil causing all the horror. Identify this demon and extinguish it.

"You most certainly are not," he said. "It's a fallacy, you know? Your textbook statement earlier. We are not more powerful than demons. Quite the opposite, in fact. Yes, our demonic energy does not become depleted like our demon brethren, constantly needing to feed while tethered to this world. However, when possessing a witch's body, it limits how much of our raw power we can harness. This witch's arcane branch makes him more durable, but even limiting my true ability within him, his body will burn out soon enough."

Demonic energy didn't dissipate and leak from devils like it did from demons. Instead, it oozed into their host's body, rotting their insides, lique-fying their organs, melting and merging with tar until the devil lost its host body and returned to its demon form.

"How long before—"

"Before this body crumbles and I need to seek another? A month, likely less, given how liberally I've been casting my magic. Truthfully, he's only endured this long because I held back on much casting outside his innate abilities."

"When you were spying on me, you mean. To what end? Why go through all this effort to observe me?"

"I am a collector of branches; it's cemented my place among the demon hierarchy and offered me many friends."

"You have telepathy. Rather strong, too, given how easily you dragged me here."

"I pulled you here because you didn't resist. Curiosity for answers, I assume."

So, he believed my telepathy could overpower his. Nice to know, but it didn't do me any damn good. Even if I managed to overwhelm his mind and break loose, we'd be right back to standing in the physical world where he had Jamie's branch to teleport anywhere, a small army of demons roaming the city, and too many unknown branches to factor in.

"Devils are coveted among the demon hierarchy until one attains a proper possession. Our limited casting causes us to burn through hosts quickly."

"And demons suddenly have a problem killing people? You just jump to another body, right? How's it any different from demons eating witches?"

"It's more painful."

I skirted his surface thoughts, uncertain if he'd left them exposed to lure me into a deeper trap of his mind, he'd unsuspectingly left his guard down, or this was some tragic attempt for sympathy.

Countless hosts leading back to the older gentleman he currently presented himself as flashed in a continuous loop. Not their lives. Not their possession. Not their magics. No, only the moment when their bodies had failed to contain his magnificence.

Magnificence. I could taste the sour note of arrogance in the air.

I bit back repulsion for the word which crossed my mind, but it was his truest belief in those agonizing final moments of each host he rotted away to the point of death. Their death.

Their flesh collapsed, insides spilling out, casting tar onto the ground. This devil wailed in agony each and every time a host body died. Not for their loss—for the pain it caused him as he clawed his way out, snapping fiendish jaws at lost wisps and demonic energy fading into the ether between planes, desperately fighting to retain his demon form so he didn't fade into a base beast such as a fiend itself.

It took so much demonic energy to escape the clutches of a dying host body, the devil, in turn, left their consciousness weak and chaotic. Barely more than a fiend and equally as vulnerable. Every time they possessed a body, they risked death with their host body. They risked spilling what little magic they had remaining and reverting entirely to a fiend form.

"As much as I could care fucking less about your pain, I don't see how any of this connects to me." I jerked my head back, simmering his empathic extension, desiring nothing he had to offer.

The devil waved a hand, directing my attention to a slithering black wall, revealing body parts evenly divided and distant like a graveyard. A chilling sight. My body clammed up. I wanted to leave this second. Slack-jawed, I studied the horror.

An exposed, still-beating heart filled the bleak darkness. A forearm lacking anything below the wrist or above the elbow. Raw, flexed pink calves. White bones. Legs. Feet. Fingers. Skulls.

Each glimpse made my chest tighten, reminding me my body had ceased to breathe in disgust for what I observed in this private hell. Piece after piece of witch body parts possessing the connection to their given branch magic revealed themselves by the thousands. Though the entirety of their body wriggled beneath the tar containing them, their thoughts buzzed, too faint and obscure, but their consciousness remained locked in this place. Trapped in this devil's inner core.

"You're a chimera." I gasped, finally putting together the specific demon classification to one that could not only devour magics but continuously acquire them for its own use. This one had gathered hundreds on top of thousands. Each victim was too weak to scream out, but their quiet wails sent a shiver through my entire being, almost pulling me from this devil's mind. I couldn't leave. I had to know more. I had to know if…

"Quite astute," the devil said. "Possessing a body limits the branches I can access. There are hundreds of the branches in here I haven't touched since I first tasted them."

Ignoring him, I continued scouring the wall of witches. I struggled to navigate through bodies—minds, essence, or souls perhaps—because each piece of flesh left on display represented a witch who'd never found peace. Each a trapped piece of consciousness bound to this chimera as he traipsed about possessing new hosts, stealing new magics, killing more witches.

"However, it's better than the alternative. I've known many chimeras, such as myself, boldly strutting through this realm in their own flesh, devouring and acquiring more magics. The drawback to walking about as a simple demon, they leak their magic. For most demon types, it means eating another mortal and recharging their essence. For chimera, such as myself, it means losing the branches we've harvested because we lack the ability to keep our collection while maintaining a foothold in this world."

I walked closer to the wall, examining the bodies and tuning him out.

His irritating fucking voice. Floating upward, I expanded my search. He didn't stop my investigation. In fact, a bit of delight blossomed along the surface of his thoughts, and he continued talking despite my lack of interest in any of his words.

"So, what do I do? Limit my vast collection of magics to keep them safe in rotting mortal bodies, leaving myself vulnerable again and again each time I search for a new inadequate host? Or do I walk this world in my own skin, drawing the ire of enchanters who hunt me and risking my valuable, unique magics being lost to the ether? Neither seems like an appealing option."

There.

In the center of bound bodies lay a set of hazel eyes representing where the branch stemmed, while the rest of the person remained dormant in the darkness. Person. My body trembled. More than that. Consciousness. Magical essence. Soul. Soulmate. So many words I tried to sort as a terrible realization gripped hold. It took everything in me not to collapse, to scream, to flee from this devil's mind. The tar silhouette squirmed. The exposed hazel eyes were locked with mine, their stare vacant, lost, and trapped.

"Finn." I ripped at the tar, tearing chunks that bound him to this wall, but new tar replaced it immediately. "Let him go!"

I flailed and fought, yet nothing freed Finn. The shadows faded. Thoughts from each of the whispering witches silenced one by one, and I grabbed Finn's head. My fingers dug into the slimy tar, struggling to reach him, desperate to hear his thoughts, to save him, to do anything but fail again.

I fell forward onto my knees, dropped from the devil's mind and back into the physical world. Digging my nails into the gravel, I channeled telepathy so I could pry my way back into his hellish core.

"I can't release Finn. His retrocognition is pivotal to resurrection." The devil's eyes glowed in the same way Finn's often had when relishing the history tucked within the world. Such a beautiful sight this monster had ruined.

I'd studied hundreds of branches, thousands really, for the students I'd taught throughout the years, the teachers I worked alongside, and the enchanters I observed for industry purposes. Each branch this devil harnessed revealed itself with ease.

The first being Finn's retrocognition. My stomach twisted at the familiar glow in Jamie's eyes. Neither Finn nor Jamie held joy in their hearts, not with this devil dictating their every action.

Colors swirled, casting an alluring aura, something from the cosmic branch meant to temper, control, or recreate emotional wavelengths. The vibrance varied, yet that might've had more to do with the other branches interacting than this being something I'd never seen. Primal earth glommed at the ground, reshaping it around wisps.

Wisps that were lured in by two distinct magics. Another cosmic branch which pierced the veil between planes and a branch from the bestial which reverberated into a howl the devil made.

Command. A simple bestial ability that varied on practice, yet he'd merged it to compel wisps. Making them obedient with a simple act that likely involved something from the psychic branch. Thrall, perhaps. Each of these branch magics worked so succinctly together.

A heart thumped, wrapped within earth and sparks of electricity, cast by a pulse of rejuvenation breathing life into the fallen. Painful whispers cried out. I covered my ears, yet it did nothing to drown out the sonic vibrations from the alteration branch mixed with the horrific wails of necromancy from the hex branch.

Somehow, merging each of these branches together, through sheer intricacy, this devil had created a way to truly defy death. Defy it for demons. Defy it for anyone if he so desired.

Wisps clustered together, forming a fiend. Its body swelled then deflated as sapphire scales coated the tarry flesh, reviving the gorgon this devil had previously slaughtered.

"When a demon dies, we have no place to carry our consciousness. The energy tethered to our essence is stripped and banished back to our realm. So depleted, exhausted, vulnerable—we fade into nothingness. No peace. No eternity. Just bleak endless nothing. Finn's retrocognition can see all the fingerprints our consciousness touched, gather the memories, and with the help of a dozen other branches working in tandem, I can recreate them. Breathe life into the void of existence. It's beautiful, truly."

The gorgon panted. "Thank you, L—"

The devil squeezed his palm closed. Air echoed, and the gorgon exploded into wisps once again, crumpling to the nothingness this devil despised.

"I did say his behavior was not to my liking." The devil wiped black tears running down his cheeks. Not his cheeks—Jamie's, the fifteen-year-old kid he'd possessed—and burned through quicker with each cast of magic. "For you, Dorian, I will ensure he stays gone and forgotten. I will give you anything you require for happiness."

"Why?" I asked, perplexed what this devil's intentions were or why a chimera cared a fuck how I felt about him.

"I'm here for you, Dorian."

"Why? You have my branch. And I'm not arcane, so I'm not a suitable host. Trust me, the way I smoke, the added tar from you…you'll burn through me in days."

"You're wrong. It's not about your branch; it's about your frequency. We possess the same ebb and flow, peaks and valleys. Every demon has a perfect glove for their hand, and as it happens, you're mine. Self-loathing and all, you're my perfection. I seek to make you my next host, my final host. Our frequencies sync so precisely, our magics will meld. I will know peace; you will have rest."

"Rest?" I scoffed, absorbing the lies. The truths. The unknowns. Everything was too much to fathom. "Suffering in that hellish pit of yours?"

"I can make it what I wish. Give you back Finn. The piece of him attached to the branch I acquired."

"You mean stole." I ground my teeth, seething and channeling my banishment root.

"It takes more than skilled banishment to push a devil out of his host." He laughed, amused at my challenge, and hiding the fear he had when Caleb cast a perfect banishment during the Spring Showcase. If Caleb had aimed it directly at Jamie then, instead of releasing it onto the whirlpool portals, it might've been strong enough to knock him from his host body, even if it'd have killed Jamie in the process.

I shook away the thought, quelling my magic. It wouldn't help here and now. I was far from casting perfected root magics. Caleb had performed only on instinct, and despite how foul this monster was, I wouldn't pit any student against him.

"Twelve years ago, I came to this horrible city in search of a powerful witch possessing a branch I desperately needed."

"Finn's branch." I bit the inside of my mouth, fighting back flashes of the night the gorgon grabbed Finn, vanishing through a black portal.

"Precisely." The devil grinned. "Yet, when I sent for his retrieval, one enchanter chased him through the broken streets, his telepathy syncing so close to my quarry, I felt the frequency. I knew then you would be the perfect vessel. Some demons go lifetimes without feeling that magical chemistry. I'd gone through several lifetimes, in fact."

"Then why leave? Why wait twelve years?" Had he been patiently observing me this entire time? Was I so oblivious I'd missed countless possessed victims, feeding me false surface thoughts for some devil's games?

"Because of Finn. He removed my memories involving you and any desire I had to linger in this city. Perhaps the last twist of the knife before I took his branch for myself."

"That's just like him." My throat was scratchy. I pushed off the ground and backstepped. It took everything not to breakdown. Finn fought until the very end. Past his end. As always, he impressed me, refusing to fail even if victory seemed impossible.

"Then, his magic sparked in the distance," the chimera said, stealing this moment I spent treasuring the beauty of Finn. "I was halfway across the world, and I felt his branch—*my branch*—tugging on me."

"What?"

"He'd left a piece of his magic tucked within your mind, a fragment from the whole."

My dreams of Finn last semester when he helped me sort through the void vision, my regret of his death, and my feelings for Milo. He'd helped me grow and move forward with my life. I let him go then, let him find peace. And now? Now it turned out that part of him remained locked inside the demon that killed him, removed his eyes, and stole his branch.

"I thought so little of it, but then his presence faded, the last of his free magic spent, and I regained those lost memories he forcefully buried despite my protests."

"And you decided to return to Chicago." The words spilled off my tongue, empty. I grew numb at the realization of everything happening now, everything happening then, came back to me. I always failed. And that failure always cost everyone around me their happiness.

"That I did. I quickly learned Enchanter Evergreen had grown in notoriety, and despite my abilities, I didn't want to risk his clairvoyance catching wind of my intent or standing in the way when we finally properly met. I wanted our meeting to be gentle and kind, something you deserve, Dorian."

"So, you planned for hundreds of demons to kill everyone in the city, keeping Milo busy." My knees quaked, locked, unable to move, ready to buckle and die. There was nothing I could do to prevent this. Nothing I could do to undo the damage already caused. This devil would steal my body and raze Chicago.

"Offer yourself to me willingly, Dorian." The devil crept close. "Do so, and this mortal child will live. My hold is lethal but hasn't reached a necrotic state. You can save him. You can save everyone in this city. I promise you, for your happiness, I will sate my own desires."

"You don't need permission to possess." Why would he care?

"No, but I'd like us to be friends." Jamie's haunting smirk reminded me he was simply a pawn in a cruel game. "Let us make the happiest resolution to the most unfortunate of circumstances."

"You'll let everyone in the city live. Even…" My voice trembled. My throat was dry, tight, and each breath became more suffocating.

"Even Enchanter Evergreen." The devil extended a hand; the cuticles of Jamie's nails were black with toxic death. "He will mourn you, but his city will remain intact."

"Bold of you to assume you have what it takes to kill me, you damn chimera." Milo swooped past me, punching the air with telekinesis and throwing the devil back.

Chapter Thirty-One

MILO snatched my wrist, pulling me into an embrace, literally sweeping me off my feet, and flying past the succubus. He'd released me, safely distant from the demons, before I'd gathered my thoughts. Milo knew it was a chimera, but did he know…

"It's an honor to meet my first devil." Milo crossed in front of me, guarding and protective. "All the same, I'm going to have to banish you, entirely exorcising you from that child."

I released a breath. Of course he knew the chimera was a devil. But did he know…

"I have hundreds of branches at my disposal. Do you really think you can challenge me?"

"Maybe, maybe not." Milo knocked the succubus away when she moved into my peripheral with a precise telekinetic burst. "But the fact you went well out of your way to skirt around my clairvoyance and avoid me suggests you think I can."

I grimaced, unable to handle Milo treating me like the damsel. Even if I very much was in this situation, I had to warn him. Channeling my telepathy, I carefully linked to his thoughts but wary not to distract his attention.

"He's got demons all over the city. He was concerned about you bringing

together the guilds, which you haven't." Hence him standing here with me by himself. "*You need to be—*"

"*Relax, Dorian. Everything is under control.*" Milo cocked his head, wearing a trademark smirk that I caught full view of even though I remained behind him. Whether I'd linked to Milo's mind or not, I very much had stored memories for every type of smile he unveiled based on the slightest gesture or movement or tone in his voice. This particular smirk held full-blown confidence, a twinge of arrogance, and the most arousing smolder.

I groaned. "*Try not to flirt the devil to death.*"

A chuckle escaped Milo's lips, causing the devil possessing Jamie to scowl. A familiar expression I'd seen this year from him, and now I questioned every single time I'd overlooked the horror inflicted on Jamie simply because his personality irritated me or his behavior toward my homeroom coven upset me. How long had I actually overlooked the agony this kid had endured? Sure, he was a prick first semester too, but not so hateful. I should've seen signs. Should've cared. All I cared about was myself and ensuring he was far removed from my students.

"*Keep attentive, Dorian.*" Milo clenched a fist, channeling magic. "*No one was or could've been aware. That's the problem with demons, devils, and all the demonic energy they drag into our world.*"

"*I'm fine. It's not like I was going to have a breakdown.*" I huffed.

"*One in six you break into a sob fest—damn clairvoyance, I know—but I really prefer kissing you when you're not splotchy. Try to keep it together while I end this.*"

I hated how aloof he treated the most dire situations.

"I must say"—the chimera possessing Jamie adjusted his academy blazer—"I'm quite stunned you chose the life of one over the lives of the many. Here my calculations suggested you'd do anything to ensure the most potential joy. I've got several hundred demons scorching this city to the ground. Guess we're all selfish when the right stakes are provided, aren't we, Enchanter Evergreen?"

"You think I'd abandon my city?" Milo released another telekinetic burst at the succubus' heels, causing her to fall back. The chimera gestured at her, perhaps suggesting she stop involving herself.

I needed to keep an eye on her, too. But I wanted to remain focused on Milo and the real threat—the chimera possessing Jamie Novak.

"I wasn't certain who or what you were for far too long," Milo said, opening his thoughts freely. "There were nagging factors to this case which bothered me, though."

"*Careful, he has telepathy.*"

The chimera smirked, amused by my warning, yet Milo kept his mind unguarded, revealing all he'd invested in researching demons who possessed resurrection. He even made a point of having guild members thoroughly examine Dr. Kendall's research on fiends and implanting them in hosts, feeling a faded connection there. While her works were meant to contain demons within enchantments, bound inside a host, a demon's possession vastly differed. It was then that it all clicked for Milo.

"A bit of research helped you learn I was a devil?" The chimera scoffed, rolling Jamie's eyes with dissatisfaction. "Unlikely."

"No, the research made it clear there was and has never been a magic to resurrect demons. Even branches delving into necromancy can't pull back a soul, just the form containing the vessel."

"You know so little about essence and life and—"

"You're right," Milo interjected. "Which is fine. My limited understanding helped me conclude the magic necessary didn't exist, but someone sophisticated enough could culminate it through multiple branches. That's when I began to suspect a chimera at work."

"I am unlike any chimera in recorded history. I am a god."

"You're a devil, a simple one at that." Milo shook his head, disapproving, mocking, practically shaming the chimera for simple mistakes he'd made. "You chose to possess someone with connections to my guild."

The chimera raised his eyebrows, eyes wide, at the accusation.

Milo channeled his magic, keeping his thoughts wide open for skimming but ruffling visions behind his true intentions. I huffed. Not as unguarded as it seemed. Somewhere behind thousands of visions he cycled through lay a plan of action, but his surface thoughts explained the obvious to the chimera's errors. Milo had been drawn to bring Acolyte Novak into the case, something he'd never consider. Even a well-trained acolyte was still far behind the expertise of an enchanter. Still, when considering her for the case, faint pathways of potentials were illuminated.

"I needed to test my theory. At the Spring Showcase, I scanned every single student and had difficulty reading Jamie Novak. Demon in disguise? Unlikely. Yet, with so much obscured, I didn't want to cross off any possibility. It wasn't until Caleb Huxley struck you—struck Jamie, should I say—with a perfected banishment that all my uncertainty was erased. You remained unfazed, more or less, but your future became much easier to read as a devil fighting against banishment can't resist a well-honed branch at the same time."

Hate seeped into the street, pouring from the chimera unlike anything Jamie had exhibited. Disgust oozed from each word, tangible, concrete, and venomous to my magic. He'd spent months eluding Enchanter Evergreen, worried his clairvoyance might link to him the same it almost had the first time he'd come to Chicago. I shuddered. That was why Milo was never there, not in time, not the way he'd always been.

"*Foolish. I should've forced this mortal's parents to leave my disqualification intact. Whitehurst had done me a favor, given the joy I took satiating this host's hatred. Yet, the thrill of indulging in the role, the life, the...*" He quieted, obscuring all thought behind a demonic veil which I couldn't read.

We glared at each other, and I channeled further. The thoughts were there. Prickly. Painful. Pacified. With time, I'd uncover them entirely. After all, our frequencies weren't so different, or so he'd claimed.

"You bluff, bold and arrogant." Jamie's smirk hid horror, which concerned the chimera, yet not enough to properly evade my telepathy. "If you knew then, you would've surely saved this poor host sooner."

"You're mistaken," Milo said. "Saving one life is always a priority, and I will be exorcising you from Jamie Novak and banishing you today but stopping a single chimera would only make the future a bit brighter."

The chimera ground Jamie's teeth so hard I worried they might crack to pieces. His eyes leaked black ooze, trickling down his cheeks.

"Without the head, all those demons you put in line would disband and scatter, harming too many people across the world. However, letting your plan come together allowed me and every guild witch throughout Chicago to strike down two-hundred and twenty-six demons."

The specific count shocked the chimera, yet I found myself entranced by Milo's open thoughts. Milo's true intent for the showcase called only to me, synced to our seamless bond. Having seen all the outcomes, he'd hoped Kenzo would win, believing the speech was exactly what he needed to light a fuse in the industry, reigniting collaboration among guilds which proved to be something Milo himself couldn't ignite in the wake of Tobias Whitlock's fall.

Guild Master Campbell flashed in Milo's mind. Not an enchanter any longer. She'd woven the guilds of the city together, pushing Enchanter Evergreen's vision into play as he'd hoped.

"You think I didn't account for every demon, every death, every case, each enchanter tracked since you arrived in my home?" Milo's body vibrated, enraged, but he held a smile all the same because Enchanter Evergreen never showed fear, rage, sadness, or regret. He was a beacon of bright light meant to encourage those all around to move forward into the brightest future they could possibly live.

Every loss, dimming his spirit, offered Milo a chance to save a thousand other lives. He endured the pain of failing those victims, carrying their loss with him forever, but he'd ensured no one would die today. If everything went according to his plans, the guilds would protect everyone.

A memory involving Enchanter—correction, Guild Master—Campbell rose in Milo's thoughts. Nothing like the memory that haunted him where she couldn't convince the guilds to collaborate. That was an honest memory, yet Milo had manipulated himself, me, and anyone observing that it still held merit.

"Had to keep my cards close to my chest. Wasn't sure who knowing what would change factors until today arrived," Milo thought.

Campbell waltzed into Milo's office, careful to lock the door behind her, and set the protective wards before uttering a single word. "Threatening the guild masters with failure after some academy brat called everyone out worked as seamlessly as you predicted."

"Let's hope the gamble paid off," Milo had said.

"About half the guild masters you wanted are in final discussions. They weren't keen on being the greatest guild to a dying city."

"We'll need them all. Otherwise, those who stay back will end up fighting for scraps before the National Guard comes in too late to institute order to the carnage."

"You'll have them." Campbell half-smiled, always holding back her enthusiasm. "I didn't become Guild Master to the strongest guild in the state and one of the safest cities in the world just to lose now."

The memory faded.

"Did you get the other guilds?" I studied Milo.

The tilted turn of his head, sharp jaw peeking out above his shoulder, suggested a grin which said yes a thousand times over.

I grumbled. He could've simply answered me.

"Now that we're done with the whole speech on how I figured out your master plan, can we skip to the part where I banish you, and we save the city?" Milo hovered above the ground; pavement crackled beneath the weight of his heavily channeled telekinesis.

Regret from past mistakes faded from Milo as he fixated on tens of thousands of futures he would ensure came in clearly once this chimera, this demon, this devil had been banished forever.

"Perhaps what I considered methodic planning was impetuous. Shame. You are truly one of a kind, Enchanter Evergreen." The chimera used Jamie's branch to open a whirlpool portal behind him. "As the mortals say, if at first you don't succeed—"

"Lock. Lock. Lock." Acolyte Reed soared past, waving her key for support and aim.

The whirlpool portal vanished into droplets. Jamie's wrists twisted and tightened, and the devil housing itself within him struggled to flex his wrists. His fingers bent like curved, decayed tree branches.

"Can't have you bolting like that," Milo said. "Ruins my master plan.

And sure, you've got hundreds of branches, but I can't think of one warp portal user whose instant transportation isn't linked to the muscles in their arms."

"He's not casting branches in his arms anytime soon." Acolyte Reed beamed.

"Give me back my brother." Acolyte Novak appeared out of nowhere. Bubbles swarmed entirely around her body, making the touch of my telepathy impossible.

Fascinating how her arcane branch obstructed everything in its path. She shouted, unleashing hundreds of tiny bursting bubbles in an onslaught at the chimera possessing her brother. Whether on instinct or a more finely tuned telepathic connection, the devil moved Jamie's body and spit a purple smog from his mouth.

Once released, it served as a shield from the surprise attack. As something in the entropy branch, even Acolyte Novak's powerful draining magic struggled to overpower the poisonous decay that devoured anything in its path.

The devil withdrew, distancing himself from the enraged Acolyte Novak.

"Lena." Milo reeled her back with a wave of his hand, helping her evade the necrotic smog eroding the street. "You have a job to do. Trust me when I say Jamie will be okay, but not if you go off script."

"Sorry, Enchanter Evergreen, I just—"

"Lock." Acolyte Reed froze the smog in place, stilling the conversation.

Novak hid her pain and regret as she'd planned when accepting this mission, but I quivered at her hollowed-out heart and her wishes that she hadn't walked away from the Novak family to pursue her independence. Had she kept contact, had she attempted to understand her younger brother, maybe this wouldn't have happened. All she wanted was to escape the insurmountable hatred and pressure her family caused, something so suffocating she couldn't figure out a single thing she wanted. She believed it was selfish to fix her broken heart while leaving her brother to fend for himself in a family she hated. I wanted to call out, to whisper even, that it was okay to walk away and repair your broken mind. Anyone who said otherwise clearly didn't understand the devastation of a shattered heart.

Unable to warp travel, the chimera flew away. Milo soared after him. I channeled my levitation and telekinesis roots, preparing to follow.

"*Stay put,*" Milo's thoughts echoed loudly. "*I apologize for dragging you into any part of this investigation, but your role is done. You're safe here. Your students are safe. Let me finish this battle alone and ensure everyone else in the city remains safe.*"

Releasing my magic, I obeyed. Milo knew every potential outcome, so if he believed my involvement would hinder his chances, I would stay out of it.

"*Good.*" Milo's mind remained tethered despite falling out of sight and attempting to murmur himself. "*It's a coin toss on whether or not I manage to banish this devil and live to tell the tale. Dorian can't witness that. He can't witness any more horrors this abomination plans to bring out to fight against oblivion.*"

Fuck that. If he wanted me to stay away because he thought I couldn't handle it, he was wrong, and I'd be damned if I allowed Milo to gamble his future on the flip of a coin. Fate wouldn't guess at our future. Destiny could fuck itself.

The succubus gripped my wrist, transforming the world into fuzzy rose-colored bliss.

"Stick around, lover. Relax." The succubus' hiss held an intoxicating captivation which left me unable to resist, to channel, to move. Her whim was my rule. Her desires passionate and beautiful and flawless. I needed to stay. Everything about this battle, this… It faded, and I stopped, enthralled by her kind smile and gentle words. "We'll let those two work things out and await the devil's return."

"Pretty sure I already killed you," Acolyte Reed said, tiptoeing like this was a fucking game.

Ugh. Ellie. She was one that clung to my memories.

"You cut her head off, which didn't kill her," Lena snapped. "Do you ever pay attention?"

"Well, I would've banished her if Enchanter Evergreen hadn't held me back."

"Here's your chance," my kind-hearted friend said. "Show me what you little acolytes can do because I'm a hungry girl, and this lovely telepath is off limits."

No. I resisted the delight elicited by the succubus' compulsion. It hit harder, so I conjured my telepathy, linking it to Milo.

He'd wandered too far to sync my branch and break this hold. I remained in this place, trapped in a still body, observing the succubus who stretched her fingers far and wide, transforming them into talons ready to shred the acolytes to ribbons.

Each of them weaved around the strikes.

Acolyte Reed aimed her key, locking the talons in place one by one.

Lena released bubbles, eroding the bound talons.

They had this. Milo wouldn't have brought them here if he didn't believe they'd be enough to stop the succubus on their own. Or…with every guild witch spread thin across the city, he had no choice but to entrust two acolytes to handle a powerful demon independently. I trembled, resisting the compulsion and failing to break its hold.

A single talon wriggled, shifting from a powerful bladelike weapon into a twisting whip.

"Ellie, look out!" Lena shouted.

"Your branch is pathetic." The succubus snatched the key Ellie used for support and withdrew her elongated fingers, freeing them from the lock Acolyte Reed had used. "Witches who require items to aid in their magics are tragically weak. What's the point of a branch if they can't cast it in their own rite?"

The succubus shattered the key, laughing as Ellie's heart sank.

"Weak witches with weak branches have an unsavory flavor." The succubus skirted around me, eyes trained on Lena and mocking tone directed toward Ellie. "You should consider yourself lucky, little witch. I'll make your death quick. As for the arcane caster…I'll spend hours devouring her piece by piece."

The succubus chased after Lena, who threw bubbles to defend and distance herself. The demon didn't evade the burst of magic. Instead, she took a deep inhale, consuming the bubbles. Grabbing her throat, the succubus' eyes widened as she held back a gasp. I waited for the magic inside her to explode. She rubbed her stomach and burped.

"Apologies." The succubus laughed. "Your magic doesn't settle well, but a bit of struggle never bothered me much."

Lena hurled more tiny bubbles from her palms, attempting to create a wall to trap the demon. They held a gleam in the darkness but didn't slow the succubus who sucked the magic in. Her back swelled momentarily, and I hoped this time, the burst would incapacitate her. It didn't. She remained impervious to Lena's branch, drawing more strength each time the young acolyte cast. Unable to break the compulsion, I watched in horror.

Wriggling, tentacle-like fingers stretched, coiling around Lena's hands. Augmenting her limbs to bind the witch prevented her from compelling on contact. It didn't matter, though. Lena fought against the succubus' grasp but couldn't break the hold or cast her branch.

"I had hoped for more entertainment." The succubus strutted closer. "Guess even delicious branches have their limitations."

"Guess you didn't realize I was letting you consume my branch intentionally."

An explosion within the succubus created splatters of tar, painting the street in acidic rot. One after another, the bubbles the demon had devoured with ease exploded and broke the succubus' body along with her hold over Lena. My fingers wiggled and I tightened a fist, resisting the compulsion. The succubus' vulnerability was an opening I needed to take advantage of. She prioritized piecing her body together as bubbles continued exploding inside her.

"I'll rip your arms off for that, little witch." The succubus reeled back a single arm—using the other to keep her tarred insides from spilling onto the street—and transformed her fingers into talons ready to slash Lena and the entire block.

Ellie flew behind the succubus and grabbed her arm. "I don't use the key to enhance my branch; I use it for precision aiming."

"Release me." The succubus' talons retreated, and a rose-colored fog filled the air, something only I could see because I was already trapped by the compulsion.

I clenched my jaw, unable to speak and warn Ellie that once the succubus' talons had vanished, her compulsion would control a witch.

"Otherwise, I risk overdoing it." Ellie released her grip on the succubus. "Unlock."

The succubus' body shattered into hundreds of pieces varying in size and shape, barely held together by the sticky tar of her insides. Shimmers of tiny bubbles within the succubus exploded, shattering her broken body into thousands of glowing wisps. Tar lapped up the wispy energy, resisting the regression of becoming a fiend once more. The succubus wailed, furious and broken.

Lena strutted forward, confident yet grateful for Ellie's intervention. It'd have taken thousands more of those bubble burst strikes to truly break the demon apart from the inside.

The acolytes held hands, interlocking their fingers and channeling banishment in tandem. In an instant, the wisps holding together the last fragments of the succubus' consciousness vanished, thrown back to a demon plain of existence.

"I'll be back. I'll slaughter you garbage witches for this. Just wait. Wait until..." The demon's mind ceased, her existence lost unless the chimera resurrected her as expected.

Both acolytes fell to their knees, hands still entwined. Threads of gold and indigo blossomed as my thoughts became my own again. Far beyond my reach, Milo's mind synced to mine once again, revealing pieces to the countless potentials these two women had with each other. I couldn't see the futures Milo had, but their futures were solidified now that the demon had died. Lena and Ellie had something special, even if they didn't realize it yet.

I channeled magic, flying after Milo.

"Wait," Ellie shouted.

"You're supposed to stay here," Lena explained.

They were too exhausted to follow or stop me, and I couldn't wait idly on a future which might result in losing Milo.

Chapter Thirty-Two

I FLEW through the streets, weaving past fraught thoughts from people who I had to believe would be fine. Minds throughout Chicago buzzed at the horror of demons released everywhere and attacking everyone. Milo had thoroughly readied for this day. This event. This attack on the devil and his demons. What I didn't know, what consumed me as I sped faster, was if he'd survive this. Linking my telepathy to Milo strained my roots because his chaotic thoughts cycled too quickly to fathom. I needed more insight on where he was, where he was going, and what he had planned.

"He's got a few enchanters hounding my demons, but this mortal can't possibly believe he can face me on his own. Even Enchanter Evergreen can't be that arrogant."

I buried the chimera's seething hatred and sought Milo's mind. Dread. Rage. Desperation. Each cycled from every zigging direction, so I amplified my telepathy, quelling everyone else out.

…

…

…

Milo panted, struggling to dodge an onslaught from dozens of branches cast in tandem. Blurred images of explosive fire, whipping shadows, conjured elementals, phantom hounds, and branches I'd never seen before all lunged at Enchanter Evergreen. Each one created a frenzy in Milo's mind. This was more erratic and barbaric and methodic than any of his other battles, making it impossible to latch on and maintain the link. I needed to reach him.

Moving on instinct, I chased him. The same instinct that guided his counters and evasion during his pursuit of the chimera devil possessing Jamie Novak. Snippets of Milo's composed thoughts escaped, creating something concrete to follow. Wrapping my telepathy around the knowledge he had for the branches aimed at him helped paint the street where he targeted the devil.

State Street

He'd gotten so far in only a few minutes.

Milo's battle ripped the road apart, unleashing tremendous amounts of telekinetic bursts. Each missed the chimera who shattered windows to buildings barely weathering the assault of countless branch magics.

I wheezed, struggling to reach them. Wind whipped at my face, forcing me to squint. In truth, I followed the sight Milo's thoughts provided then they vanished behind a veil of visions as he likely sorted the probability of each attack.

The terrain became foggy, so I lessened my link, following a trail of destruction. Remnants of the chimera's casting lingered on empty streets. Had the people fled? No. There wasn't a single destroyed vehicle. Not one nearby thought. Milo had evacuated this path. He'd cleared it, had it cleared, in anticipation of the carnage they'd unleash in the midst of hundreds of demons attacking.

"*The only thing that'll end this is a perfect banishment precisely timed by…*" Milo's thoughts disappeared into his damn clairvoyance.

I dropped onto the street, gathering my strength. He wouldn't… This perfect banishment wouldn't involve the only person either of us had ever seen cast a perfect branch. My heart thumped, dreading the way Milo planned a hundred moves ahead with countless contingencies. Did he work to save Caleb because he needed him drawn into this battle? No. Demons eluded his psychic branch. He wasn't aware of their reality, their potential, until they'd snuck up on him. Still, I needed to know my students were safe. Milo had said as much, but he'd also said this would be fine knowing the danger he threw himself into.

I stretched my telepathy well beyond its limitations. Zigging and zagging around thoughts ranging from frightened, confused, panicked, aloof, carefree, bewildered, enraged, deathly, and a million others in between. Searching for the one person who could answer my question, I pushed ahead.

"Chanelle, are you and the kids okay?"

"Dorian," she asked aloud then thought, *"We're back at the academy. Where are you? Doesn't your telepathy have ranged limitations?"*

"Yes and no. Newly unlicensed development."

"Oh. Well I'll keep it to myself, but it'll cost you—less than those licensing fees, though." Chanelle smiled at the students, hiding her fears and burying that the only thing it'd owe me was getting back to the academy safely. She really wanted to turn this moment into a joke but worried it'd be our last.

"I'll gladly pay up."

"Are you safe? Last I saw—"

"I'm fine, away from the demons, but—" Milo's rage spiked, sending a shooting surge of pain up my spine. I dropped to my knees, quelling all telepathy. My pocket buzzed, and I reached for my phone. "Hello?"

"Have I ever told you how needlessly extra you are?" Chanelle asked, releasing a breathy sigh on the phone.

"I'll be honest. I forgot I had my phone." We laughed, light and simple and a brief escape from the horror raining on Chicago. "I need you to keep the students at the academy no matter what. If any concerned parents or guardians show up, keep them there, too. There are demons roaming everywhere."

"Understood," Chanelle said, her fear spiking almost as profoundly as Milo's rage a moment ago. My telepathy was quelled, though. Maybe it was nothing. Maybe it was the restlessness in her voice. "Are you really safe?"

"Yes." I hung up and turned my phone off, searching for Milo. He was in danger, and I wouldn't let him die because some devil wanted me. I wouldn't risk his life, this city, or anyone else because of *me*.

After resting, I continued tracking Milo. Less so with telepathy since his thoughts still left an obvious direction with the peaks of emotional turmoil. If I synced to his mind, I'd collapse. Instead, I flew along a trail of wreckage in the wake of his battle against the chimera, sticking to empty, destroyed streets, and wincing at the slight emotions Milo released that I couldn't shield against.

"*Bethany,*" someone thought frantically.

I froze midair. A man chased after a woman pinned beneath rubble. They needed help. I skirted down an alleyway to a street unscathed by debris from Milo's fight and found myself surrounded by citizens fleeing three misshapen demons.

The first had countless arms, even its four muscular legs had a handlike appearance and movement. The second had shimmering greenish-yellow scales with a serpent's body and angelic wings flapping to obscure several rattling tails. The final perched upon a lamppost, a feminine physique with winged arms.

Each was easy enough to identify: a hekatonkheires, a basilisk, and a harpy. But recognizing these demons, their abilities, wouldn't help in stopping their overwhelming force.

"Carver, I can't move." Bethany channeled her telekinesis, doing nothing to lift the rubble that'd pinned her leg.

He turned to assist but the basilisk slithered closer. Channeling his banishment, he'd only managed to stall its pursuit—knocking a few feathered wings away—for seconds. Seconds that'd make no difference in the scheme of things. Their untrained magics barely fazed the demons. I gulped. These people needed help. I couldn't hold my own against a single demon yet here I was contemplating challenging three. There was nothing I could do to stop all the demons and save those being attacked.

I descended to the ground, channeling every ounce of banishment within my ability into my fists already storing telekinesis. I wouldn't abandon these people. Whether they evaded Milo's calculations on probability or fell into an inescapable casualty variable—I'd arrived. He'd always intended I remain behind, so perhaps by chance if I didn't get myself killed, I'd save these people.

"Fucking demons, daring to invade my home."

I pinched the bridge of my nose at the unsavory mind of Hellrazer invading my thoughts. Milo's ex and the top-ranked enchanter at Kraken Guild. While he was too far to see, I could feel his explosive presence. His sensory root fixated on every single demon within a ten-block radius, and his mind zipped about to pinpoint their precise location before he unleashed his branch.

Shit.

I reached out with telekinesis to grab Bethany and Carver, but it was too late. Hellrazer's flames burned bright, casting black and white fire. Fiery fury lapped, devouring every ounce of demonic energy in a quarter mile. He'd laced his flames with banishment, purging nearby demons. White fire engulfed demons searing their flesh and forms while the black flames guarded all life and buildings, keeping everyone and everything safe from the hellish fire.

Okay, not to question Milo's taste in partners, but he really drew the short straw with my floundering magic. Honestly, Enchanter Ortiz and Evergreen would be an unstoppable duo.

Hellrazer's flames sizzled along my skin, clearing the street of all the wisps as acolytes floated about, securing citizens. I shrugged one off, continuing my pursuit of Milo, who'd apparently accounted for everything—including the desolate and forgotten folks in the wake of combat and evacuation. Of course, he did. This was exactly like the Night of the Fiend Massacre, except this invasion involved actual demons. Still, the minds of enchanters, acolytes, and guild masters boomed above the people they protected. Each guild witch worked on coordinated attacks, preemptive rescues, cleanup, diversion, backup, and a thousand other strategic wonders that kept order alive and well in the streets.

The further I flew down Milo and the chimera's destructive path, the louder the other enchanters became. So many had grouped together further ahead where Milo pushed the chimera. What was happening?

Milo's mind rose high in the heat of battle, shaking away the enchanters who stood idle ahead as his predictions, his hopes, all played out according to a difficult plan. Dominos vibrated in Milo's surface thoughts, falling one by one into each other and leading down hundreds of different pathways—each piece representing a single witch, demon, citizen, opportunity, interaction, and held the possibility of ensuring the best outcome for everyone. The best he could hope for.

The dominos continued clanking into each other. Some paths sounded like zippers while others held a soft chink, and a few were like change tossed together. All these routes eventually ran together leading to one singular path. The same path Milo had led the chimera toward. A huge screen in Milo's mind. All I saw was static. This wasn't like his other visions, though. Demonic interference made it as difficult for him to view the variables, the potential, as it did for me.

I flew faster, reaching a locked off collection of buildings that'd been altered by magic. Metal, brick, glass, and concrete from the high skyscrapers had merged, interwoven together, creating an encircled dome. The chimera scanned his surroundings, grating his host's teeth as the realization sank in. He'd been lured into a trap—a dead end where Milo intended on banishing him, killing him.

Milo's plan unveiled itself, revealing it'd fallen perfectly in place, leading the chimera into the clutches of more than a hundred enchanters positioned on the ground and in the sky. Each witch channeled magic. The vibrations of their frequencies hummed a familiar note. I'd felt this synchronized sensation many times. Too many.

Milo approached the devil, preparing his banishment. A lump grew in my throat. All these well-trained witches would overwhelm and defeat this devil, but could they properly banish him without killing the host body?

"It will take more than banishment to untether me from Jamie Novak," the devil said, smug and still scanning for an escape. "Or have you resigned yourself to accept one more death as the cost of saving your city?"

"No one else dies because of you." Milo's magic swelled, interlocking with each of the channeling enchanters. They weren't honing their magic; they were altering their frequency to link with and magnify Milo's casting capability. Even with all their precision and skill, it wouldn't last long. They wouldn't be able to provide Milo this boost in power for more than a few minutes, but he only required minutes at most to finish this devil.

This held a heavy price, though. One I realized Milo was all too aware of. Having a single witch match his frequency, funneling their energy into him, and merging together would expand his casting output. It also added to the physical exhaustion by two-fold. Sure, the witch offering magical assistance took some of the burden when syncing to Milo, but here, he was containing the power of a hundred witches to cast banishment on a staggering level. Those linked to his frequency took on the physical limitations for half while he felt the excruciating exhaustion fifty times over. The fatigue weighed heavily, silencing Milo's thoughts, amping up his survival instinct and drive to save everybody—including Jamie Novak.

Milo aimed a powerful pulse, eradicating the devil within Jamie. Lightning surged within the boy. His ribcage glowed and sparked like a threatening thunderstorm. Each wave of banishment burned the demon bound inside the host body. Jamie's eyes, nose, ears, and mouth pooled with tar. Slowly the chimera's spirit spilled out, curdling, and fading back to the demonic plane of existence.

"What's this? What's this?"   *"Where am I?"*

"There's color everywhere."   *"Is this freedom?"*   *"An illusion. A delusion."*

"I can't believe my eyes."   *"Light—Mother, there's light."*

"Nothing can kill that devil."

"Peace."   *"I'd forgotten how calm the world was."*

"I must be dreaming."

My eyes watered. One by one, wisps broke away from the tar, containing fragmented thoughts of witches consumed by the chimera over his extensively long existence. Their minds buzzed, rattled, and shattered loose from the demonic energy before vanishing in the ether. Whether they found peace in some unknown afterlife or the simple silence of a true death, I was grateful for each and every soul freed of the chimera's horrid imprisonment.

"Not happening. Not like this." The chimera roared, unleashing black tentacles of tar from his mouth. **"I will not cease to be.** *Not this close to perfection."*

Tar whipped, lapping at the lost wisps, snatching them back up before the witches found their freedom. The chimera refused to sacrifice their branches, lose his collection, but Milo didn't relent. Focused on keeping the witches contained, the chimera's position faltered, and Milo took full advantage by reeling back his other fist. He slammed the collective force of a hundred witches, channeling telekinesis and binding each tendril to the ground. The pavement beneath them cracked and crumbled under the intense weight of so much magic.

"My body. I can feel my body again," Jamie's voice echoed loudly. *"It hurts. Please. I don't want to die."*

I approached, hoping to link what telepathy I could without interfering. Jamie had suffered so much, still suffered, and I wanted him to understand it was almost over. Milo was seconds from saving him.

Countless witches escaped the chimera's clutches. In mere moments the devil in Chicago would cease to exist.

"Milo? Dorian?" Finn called out. *"I knew you'd both find me."*

I collapsed to the ground, awed by the sweet voice of Finn and his freedom. After so much time regretting every mistake I'd made, all that dwelling, finally moving on, and then learning he still suffered, I took a breath knowing this piece of him had finally been released from the chimera.

Finn floated in a flurry of fading wisps. Soon, he'd truly find himself free from the unfathomable horrors of twelve years bound within that devil.

I clenched my fists. Or…he could stay. I'd held a piece of his magic, his mind, inside me before unknowingly. My magic, Finn's magic, Milo's magic—together, we could keep Finn here, safe, and with us. I could save him for real. I could bring him back into our lives.

Milo, Finn, and me together forever.

That was the happiest ever Milo must've envisioned. It had to be. I wouldn't accept any other truth that kept me from Milo and Finn, the three of us happy and perfect.

CHAPTER THIRTY-THREE

I APPROACHED the cluster of wisps. Some glowed brightly, illuminating the night sky; others dimmed as the connection to demonic energy dissolved. Witches bound to those fragmented pieces of power disappeared. I wouldn't allow the same to happen to Finn.

"Dorian, what're you doing here?" Milo strained to maintain a steady flux of telekinesis to keep the devil pinned and banishment to remove all the stored demonic energy circulating within Jamie's body. "You can't be here."

"Finn's here, aware, calling out." I pushed past Milo, reaching out for the wisp tethered to Finn's consciousness, the part of it stored inside the chimera.

"Stop, Dorian. I know what you're thinking, and I'm telling you no."

I paused; my throat tightened. There were so many words I wanted to say, so many things I needed to explain. It would have to wait until after I'd grabbed Finn. Whether Milo didn't realize or worried about potential problems in the future, he'd thank me once I saved Finn.

Milo changed the trajectory of his telekinesis, altering the direction of where the dying wisps floated. No. He couldn't do this. I reached out using my own telekinesis to lure the wisp containing Finn closer.

Jamie's body rose slightly, forcing Milo to return his efforts at the devil clamoring for life. Milo was too busy contending with pushback from a reluctant chimera and resisting the collapse of his body as he harnessed a hundred witches to exorcise this devil.

I pulled Finn away from the collection of wisps being banished one by one. Not him, though. Not like this. Not again.

Finn would never leave us again.

Opening my mind's core, I dragged Finn's consciousness safely into the depths of my magic where I could keep him safe. The battlefield where Milo worked to vanquish the devil vanished, and I sank into the deepest parts of my mind.

An eloquent ballroom materialized; the chandeliers dimmed immediately upon arrival because the change from night to this brightly lit room didn't sit well for either of us. Finn had experienced darkness for too long, so long he'd lost track of time. He stood in the distance, thoughts filled with haunting confusion that festered at the seams of his awareness, but he tried to bury it as he took in everything about this place. He hadn't seen my core in twelve years. Well, another part of him had, but that piece faded away once he'd spent all his magic holding him here. He wouldn't have to worry about that this time. I knew what to do. I knew how to protect him.

It was filled with a few familiar traces since the last time I'd invited him into my mind, but renovating my inner core had changed much of what he recalled. Given time, I could replace the fancy wallpaper, the sleek tiled floors, and return it to something more to his liking. I wanted him to feel at peace here in the inner core of my mind.

"I like what you've done with the place." Finn ran his fingertips along a marble banister of a spiraling staircase, which led to an upper vault where I often sorted through intrusive thoughts. "A lot nicer than my headspace."

"That's never been true." I approached him, struggling to keep the noise of a roaring devil from seeping into this place. When in other's minds, it was easy to tune out the world, when in my own—everything often followed me, leaving me without a moment of peace. I didn't need peace because I'd found mine again.

"I've missed you." I hugged Finn.

His arms remained at his sides, hesitant of how to respond, so unlike the man I'd lost. The horrors of twelve lost years surfaced. Atrocities he'd endured while bound in the devil's domain. Carnage. Agony. Death without dying. Again. Again. Again on an endless loop of sorrow. My tight embrace didn't let up, searching his mind for something, anything from before.

Finn raised his arms, wrapping them under mine, and hugged me back. He rested his head on my shoulder, allowing the cruelty that clung freshly in his thoughts to wash away as a thousand joys blossomed.

Images fluttered between us during this embrace. So many moments of happiness Finn, Milo, and I shared a lifetime ago. Times I regretted never properly treating then, something I'd never do again. Two smiling men I longed to spend my forever with, a life I believed impossible after losing Finn, but now I could have it all.

This part of Finn, the memories circulating through his branch magic, contained all of him. His memories. His ideals. His bravery. Beauty. Compassion. Humor. Love. Heart. Perhaps, even a broken piece of his soul. A soul I'd keep tucked in my mind, safe from everything he'd endured since he was stolen from us. He would know joy again, true joy, here with me and Milo.

I ground my teeth, fighting to keep the bustling world from creeping in here, ruining this reunion. Released witches whispered, breathing in their freedom. A few trickled in, but I staved off most before they fizzled away as the dying demonic energy linked to them faded. Staring back at the entryway to my inner core, I twisted my fingers to draw the double doors closed. Finely crafted oak doors slammed shut, keeping the more intrusive sounds out.

"What's happening?"

"Don't worry about it. You'll never have to worry about anything again." I released Finn, smiling at him. His vacant expression was more reminiscent of my sour history. Though my smile came easily now, I knew it didn't hold the same level of carefree confidence that'd carried Finn through life. No, this was a bittersweet happiness. I'd gladly accept it.

The devil wailed so loudly that it was almost impossible to dampen the sound from entering my mind's core. Finn eyed me, questioning the banishment happening only a few feet away from where my body stood.

"Everything is fine," I said. "Milo's finishing off the devil, the chimera, that took you away."

"That killed me, you mean."

I struggled to find the right words. There were no right words for this moment, so I remained silent, allowing Finn to process his thoughts as he evaluated the lost years, the dead years. There was so much he'd missed.

"Is Milo going to be able to handle him on his own?" Finn's voice cracked; unspeakable horrors crept to the surface of his thoughts. His breathing sped, body shaking. I held his hand to my face, sending every single memory of Enchanter Evergreen I had. Every heroic act Milo had accomplished over the twelve years since Finn had died. Image after image funneled between us, filled with cases, accomplishments, and feats unlike any of our trio believed we'd reach. "He really has become something, someone, amazing."

"Yes," I agreed. "And he's not alone. The Inevitable Future always plans for any event. Right now, he's gathered every guild in Chicago to remove the demons. He has a hundred enchanters helping him banish that devil as we speak."

"He was never supposed to return here," Finn said. "I thought I'd removed all memory of his intentions for you."

I lowered Finn's hand, interlocking my fingers with his, delighting in the sensation of his touch. "You did. It was perfect, but I messed that up."

"Oh?"

"Do you recall breaking off a piece of your magic?"

Finn smiled, sincere, goofy, and for a few brief seconds, the history of horror vanished from his mind while he indulged in past delights.

"One for you, one for Milo. I didn't think they'd worked, honestly." He ran his free hand through his hair, ruffling his chestnut locks. "Sort of inspired them off your manifestations, but I was never as good at conjuring psychic personas like you."

Right. Manifestations, my go-to for exploring minds while maintaining a healthy separation so thoughts didn't become overwhelming. Since the evolution of my branch, I'd lost the ability to summon them.

"Dorian, let me in," Milo called out, his forehead pressed against mine, reeling me from my mind and into the physical world. "What you're doing will shatter you. You're not thinking this through. Talk to me. Listen to me. Believe me."

I blinked away the outside world, remaining with Finn. It took everything I had to absorb Milo's beautiful voice, his alluring words. I didn't want to shield Finn from them, yet Milo held a captivating charisma. Something about his wrong belief sounded right—but it wasn't. He'd see that. Finn would understand. We needed time to process this change.

Almost every trace of the devil had vanished. Every wisp containing demonic energy disappeared. Every piece of tar slithering within Jamie was gone. Every witch fragment trapped within, released into the ether. Milo clutched my neck, holding me closely while enchanters collected Jamie's broken, beaten body. My eyes flitted, struggling to maintain a proper foothold in my mind's inner core.

I smiled at Finn, wanting to ease any fright he might have because nothing would happen to him so long as I remained vigilant.

"Dorian." Milo's thoughts bellowed, echoing louder and faster than I could quell entirely.

I didn't need to hear what he had to say, what he wanted to say, or what he believed was the right choice for some unforeseen possible future. It radiated off the heat of his body against mine.

Milo's mind swam in infinite potential possibilities, raging from the battle, the struggle of standing upright, the pain of enduring so much fallout due to channeling a hundred witches. His thoughts remained frantic, lost, and I knew he didn't see things clearly. I did, though. Everything would be okay. All I needed was time. He needed to reflect, really absorb the opportunity here.

"Go away," I snapped. "I've got this under control."

"Are you okay?" Finn quaked, skittish in a way I'd never seen before.

"Yes." I caressed his face because Finn was fine here; he'd remain fine here. Better than that. He'd recover, heal, and find joy again. Milo would see that. "It's a misunderstanding."

"About?"

"Devils, demons, chimeras, it's caused so much turmoil." I smiled achingly but forced it to soothe Finn. "We see a different resolution is all."

Finn's lip curled. Humor and confusion flowed equally in his thoughts.

"Resolution. I might've considered an English position but went with History." I laughed, drowning the voice outside away. "Not that I'm any good at it."

Finn rubbed my shoulders, calming my anxiety and shaking away the outside world. "I bet you're amazing at explaining the wonders of the past."

"You can see it," I said. "The semester's almost over, but next year will be great."

"Dorian, I think I know what you're worried about, what Milo's worried about, and I—"

"Need time," I interjected, refusing to surrender this second chance. No, this third chance after sacrificing a piece of Finn tucked within me to work on myself. He deserved happiness. A chance to live. It wouldn't be the life he'd planned, but we'd be together.

The double doors at the other end of the ballroom shook. Milo continued trying to force his way inside my head. I cracked my knuckles one by one, silencing his attempt. Milo was a powerful psychic, likely the most powerful psychic I'd ever met, yet telepathy and clairvoyance had very different strengths. No way would he get in here unless I willed it, allowed it. Even then, his foothold in my mind would be nothing. As the telepath, I'd have the strength to control everything in here.

"Milo." Finn left my side, approaching the double doors.

"Stop," I said.

Finn opened the double doors, sending a cacophony of noises from the physical world barreling inside. It was too much for me to shield him from. Finn covered his ears, knees ready to buckle any second.

Milo swooped in, steadying Finn and syncing with each of us, helping quell everyone and everything else.

"Finn. I've missed you so much." Milo held Finn's shoulders, smiling and teary-eyed. He'd come with different intentions, yet seeing Finn had opened a world of possibility. Perhaps now he'd understand why I did this. "I wish things were different."

"Me too." Finn had a somber smile.

"Dorian, you have to release Finn."

"W-what? No." I stormed toward Milo, ready to push him out of my mind until he took time to properly examine the chance we'd been given.

"Dorian." Milo released his grip on Finn, approaching me like he'd somehow prevent me from hurling him from my mind the second I reached him. "The devil is almost gone. I've exorcised every part possessing the child; I've banished every wisp attached to a witches' branch, but there's one more left."

"It's Finn. He's fine. He'll be fine. Everything will be fine."

"When a chimera takes a branch magic, they attach it to every fiber of its being," Milo explained. "If you keep Finn here, store him in your mind, the chimera will return."

"He's right," Finn agreed. "The second I stopped breathing, I felt the chimera's magic intertwine with mine. If even a fragment remains, he'll resurface. Not today, but someday."

I trembled.

"He'll possess you." Milo grabbed my hand, delicate like too much and I'd shatter, but his words had already broken me. "He'll resurrect his fallen demons, gather more, and destroy the world."

Fuck the world. I wanted Finn back. I had him right here, in reach. "We can cleanse his soul, his magic. We can find a way to unravel—"

"No, you can't." Finn grabbed my other hand, gentle and guiding. "I've seen entire histories on demons thanks to my branch, and I've had the displeasure of living inside that monster. He'll find a way back if even a tiny piece of him exists. Banish me."

"You can't make me do this." I pulled my hand free from Milo, preparing to expel him from my mind.

"I can't," he said, smile lost and resisting a frown. "You have to decide, Dorian. The second you arrived at the trap we'd laid for the devil, this choice became yours to make."

"You can't make me stay," Finn said. "Or I would hope you wouldn't. After all, locking me away inside your mind is exactly what the chimera did."

"No." I released Finn's hand. "You would be happy here. Safe."

"I'll be happy when you let me go." Finn hugged me tightly, like he never wanted to let go. "I'd like to rejoin the rest of my soul. Hopefully, I've found peace somewhere else."

"You don't even know if there's another piece of you out there." I squeezed him back. "When you're gone, this time, it will be for good. There could be nothing after this."

"After everything, I'd be okay with that," Finn said. "But I have faith there's something more after all this. I believe one day, very far from now, I will see you and Milo again, and you'll have a lifetime of happy memories to share with me."

This wasn't an embrace to hold onto forever. It was one to say a final goodbye. Bit by bit, my mind's inner core disappeared. The walls faded, the staircase fell into nothingness, the floor below vanished, and the chandeliers dimmed to darkness until all that remained was Finn and me, holding onto each other.

Returning to the outside world, a tiny glowing wisp containing Finn's branch quickly exploded.

"*I love you both so much. I'm glad you're the two who live on, carrying our dream, our future, and...*" Finn's final thoughts ceased, and he was truly gone.

Milo held me close, my chest pressed against his, and his arms squeezed me, keeping me upright because all I wanted was to collapse and break down. Instead, I buried my face in his tattered blazer, sobbing.

He quelled the thoughts of the outside world, and then the reason he wished for me to stay behind escaped his surface thoughts. He knew this possibility when confronting and banishing the devil. He feared me facing this decision more than the chance of channeling a hundred witches killing him. I had Finn, it was within my power to keep him here with us, yet I made the decision to release him—letting Finn die again.

Chapter Thirty-Four

WOW, these headlines kept getting more and more misleading, overlooking the finer details.

THE INEVITABLE FUTURE SLAYS DEVIL & LEADS CHARGE AGAINST NEARLY 1,000 DEMONS!

I swiped the article notification away, not bothering to click, and lay in bed. Folks had already started calling it The Day the Devil Died—not quite as catchy as Night of the Fiend Massacre, yet it represented another momentous triumph Enchanter Evergreen had accomplished by bringing guilds together. I puffed on a cigarette, which did little to mask how badly my sheets reeked.

Almost all day and night, I'd sat in bed doing little else, aside from occasionally eating, only reminded because I had to feed the cats despite wanting to do nothing. Not shower. Not clean. Not work. All I wanted was to disappear for a bit, yet I continued reading articles and watching news reports that covered the chimera's attack on Chicago. Everyone moved on so quickly, hardly fazed by the actual plot intended since the enchanters eviscerated every threat.

A week had passed since releasing Finn for a third time in his life. When he died at twenty-two. When he'd helped me last semester. And now, when a piece of him was bound inside that devil. I was stuck saying farewell to Finn yet again. An infinite loop of regrets. The first time I lost him, I never got to say goodbye. The second time, it wasn't pleasant, but there was closure.

Now, it felt like I'd ripped open a scar. Each time he was lost, it was me who'd played the biggest role in failing him, letting him go, and it took everything I had not to breathe in more depression.

But I wouldn't spend another twelve years mourning Finn. He wouldn't want that, I couldn't live like that, and Milo needed me. As much as it hurt, I wanted to live and live happily. It was just difficult getting started again.

Unfortunately, Milo didn't have an opportunity to mourn. After everything he'd endured, he lacked the luxury of taking a week off for personal reasons. I got to use these days to get my head screwed back on right, but Chicago required the great Enchanter Evergreen to remain vigilant as the smoke settled. All the demons were banished, and every citizen survived unharmed. Milo spent the week attending impromptu events celebrating the success of guilds and his masterful collaborative efforts to put the demons and the devil plaguing the city to rest. It didn't matter that his body still ached after enduring the effects of channeling a hundred fellow enchanters.

He couldn't show it. The Inevitable Future remained an omnipotent presence, defending all the best potential outcomes.

Carlie trotted into my bedroom, meowing. Screeching, really, because I was already behind her preferred schedule, and soon, she'd starve to death.

"I'm getting your food, fat cat."

Charlie hopped onto the bed, paws kneading the blanket, and then he licked my arm.

"Yes, I know I need a shower, too." I kissed his furry head and went to feed them before getting ready for work. I'd taken enough time to grieve. It was time to return to reality.

After showering away a week's worth of sweat and tears and existential doubts, I grabbed my stuff and drove to work. Training my roots wasn't really a priority now. Simply keeping my head above water would do. Finn wouldn't want me to break down into despair.

I pulled into the academy parking lot, where Chanelle telekinetically carried six boxes to her car early in the morning before most had arrived.

"It's a little early to be hauling that stuff away."

"If I don't start now, I'll never get it all packed in time." Chanelle popped her trunk, and I assisted in tetrising boxes around the others already stored.

"Why don't you just leave your stuff over summer like a normal person?"

"Your lack of care for your belongings is not normal, Dorian. The fact is every year, they use my classroom for summer school, and every single year, something is missing or broken when I return. Not this year."

I lifted a box titled 'stickers' and crammed it into a corner. "Do you really need an entire box of stickers?"

"I've accumulated a lot over the last fifteen years."

"Hoarded, you mean."

"Acquired and retained educational resources in a difficult economy."

"Fancy way to say hoarded."

"Well, I'm fancy." Chanelle slammed the trunk closed, preparing one final trip before classes to fill the backseat.

"How are you?"

"Fine. Only about ten thousand things on my to-do list, and I think I'll be able to knock off seven today. Maybe eight if you stop chitchatting."

I grabbed her wrist. "Chanelle, how are you doing?"

"Okay. Suppose Milo told you about Jamie."

I nodded. He'd given me distance and time to absorb the events privately, keeping himself busy with work, but I'd heard Jamie was recovering in the hospital. The physical toll of exorcising the chimera coupled with the emotional agony of months trapped inside his own head… It must be excruciating for him.

"Thankfully, Headmaster Dower agreed to exempt Jamie from the finals, and I'll be helping his family arrange for a proper tutor over the summer."

"He's returning?"

"I don't know, but I want him to have the option. Not sure if it'd help him." Chanelle pulled away, burying guilt that spiked momentarily. "I can't decide if it'd be harder to see him every day next year or not at all, which makes me entirely selfish."

"It doesn't. You're probably the least selfish person I know, going out of her way to account for everything and everyone. It's actually really fucking irritating."

"Help me carry boxes, you bum." Chanelle grinned, keeping her regrets, her missteps, to herself. I wouldn't pry.

"Sure thing." I walked into the quiet academy, assisting Chanelle until school started.

Once the bell rang, kids funneled through the hallways, most still gossiping about everything that'd happened across the city, sharing their stories on where they were and which demon they'd seen defeated by an enchanter.

"Morning, everybody." I immediately turned on my whiteboard, projecting a final exam study schedule planned for my homeroom coven leading up to the last week of classes. There were few things I could control in life, so I decided to put my efforts into preparing my homeroom. Teaching them, guiding them, were things I could control.

"Whoa, whoa, whoa." Gael slapped a hand on his desk, drawing everyone's attention. "No, the heckity heck hell, you did not just try to do that, Mr. Frosty."

"Excuse me?" I glowered.

"You've been gone for an entire week because you were sick." He very much used air quotes around my flimsy excuse. "You left us with subs and work after a very traumatic situation, and you're not so much as going to ask us how we're doing? What about my feelings, Mr. Frosty? Do they mean nothing to you?"

"Cluck." His rooster clacked his clawed foot on the desk, disapprovingly glaring in my direction.

"Traumatic situation?" Kenzo huffed. "You weren't even there."

"I was there in spirit," Gael retorted. "Plus, I'm thinking of how this affects everyone."

"I'm actually fine." Tara shrugged.

"Yeah, man. It was a little scary but super epic, too." Gael raised his arms, flexing them and expanding his spikes.

Caleb nodded in agreement. "Are you maybe trying to avoid—"

"I believe they're putting on a brave face." Gael gestured, cutting Caleb off and using King Clucks' well-timed bawks to quiet Tara and Gael. "But the only way to ensure they're really fine is to put away that horrible, very stressful schedule you've got up there and allow us free time to properly reflect."

I rolled my eyes. There it was. Gael went to bat on everyone's behalf so he could avoid studying. "Would you like to be excused, Gael? You know, so you can properly reflect on your emotions."

"Like, I can just leave?" He raised his brows curiously.

"Sure," I said. "I bet you'll do fantastic on your final exams without my overly taxing study schedule. You likely won't have to worry about failing them, about your ranking dropping, or failing out of Gemini."

"W-wait, what?"

"Yeah," I said, writing him a pass. "You're so dedicated, I'm certain you can take this time to reflect."

"Now, you're just making things up." Gael crossed his arms, boasting. "No one fails out of an academy."

"True, but your second year is twice as intensive and has the highest transfer rate across the state."

"Transfer?"

Gemini—like most academies—didn't believe in failing students since it reflected poorly on our numbers. So they'd find ways to edge students out of the academy program if they weren't on track for success. I hated it. But it motivated me to motivate my students.

"To a less intensive program, something not on an industry pathway. Perhaps taking time to reflect can help you decide if that's something you'd like."

"No. I'm fine." Gael clammed up. "*Still should've asked how we were before throwing a bunch of work at us.*"

"Ba-bawk."

They were all hyped for summer break just around the corner after such a successful first year, and I didn't want them to flounder this close to their end-of-year tests. Each of them was more determined than frightened by my comments. Hopefully, it'd ignite a fire in each of my homeroom students and push them through their exams, keep them motivated over the summer and ready to return in the fall invigorated to reach new heights.

I broke them into groups based on which classes they'd need to prioritize and balancing my highs and lows. That was always a struggle. Students who excelled often didn't collaborate the best with the lowest learners. Those students required someone closer to their level around the mid-tier, but grouping highly skilled students together simply allowed them to collectively rush through their work with ease, so it was also important to partner them with mid-ranged learners. Of course, this all varied based on personality, strengths and weaknesses based on subjects, and a thousand other tiny factors. It was the worst jigsaw puzzle; however, an hour into studying, there weren't any outbursts, slacking, or breakdowns. Maybe I'd gotten it right.

We'd survived the morning study session, and I sent them all off to classes. Hopefully, the afternoon would go half as smoothly. However, the festering annoyance bubbling on their minds as they left for the first class indicated I had a long month ahead of me. One month. One month, and they'd have their first-year exams completed and be released for the summer, and I'd have a chance to sulk and dwell and rebuild myself. It was like any other year; I could make it until summer break.

Milo's mind called out to me, syncing seamlessly to the back of my thoughts as I helped students with missing work, exam prep, and evaluating their GPAs and rankings. Some kids were bad at the math involved when calculating the scoring system, and it didn't help the academies always found new and overly complex ways to grade student standing. It was a nice reprieve having a cheery Milo in my head.

"Thank you both for joining me." Milo greeted Acolytes Reed and Novak, who joined him in his office, reading over a case file he handed them. "This is top-notch stuff that I think my two favorite acolytes are more than qualified to solve."

"We're probably the only acolytes you know the names of," Novak huffed, reading the file. "Seriously? It's a lost dog."

"It's a Doberman puppy. They're the absolute cutest one-hundred percent most perfect babies ever." Reed squealed, her eyes wide with delight over the images in the file.

The sharp pitch of her voice was grating on me and Novak, yet Milo grinned.

"He's also a lost familiar," Milo explained, cutting off any commentary from Novak because she needed the distraction, and he'd gladly throw cases at her until her potential futures settled. "And if two very talented acolytes don't locate him, his witch may lose their license. I suppose if you think it's beneath you, I can pass it on to others willing to—"

"Not at all," Reed blurted. "I will find the familiar by the end of the day."

"Whatever," Novak said. "We'll find the familiar."

Reed smiled at Novak, who rolled her eyes. Reed grumbled, making a pouty face. Milo eyed them, weaving his surface thoughts behind visions, then chuckled to himself.

"*Doesn't seem like the best start to their future, if you ask me,*" I thought, unintentionally linking closely to him. Okay, perhaps intentionally. I wanted him to hear my voice, know that even though I wasn't there, I was. I'd been absent, selfish, so he needed to understand I did care about the burdens he endured, too.

"*I very much approve of angsty beginnings,*" he thought. Flashes of our freshman year popped into his mind. A fidgety, shy Milo hidden behind a hoodie. A bold, outgoing Finn dressed flashy and smiling. A rude, angry me glaring in my gothiest getup. "*I think those tend to make for the happiest ever afters.*"

"*You're distracting. I'm going back to work.*" I paused, lingering on the distance I needed, the quiet I wanted. "*I'm sorry I've been avoidant. I've just been...*"

"*You're fine. It's been good for both of us. Focus on the kids, focus on you. I'll be here, working. Always working.*" Milo smirked, which drew the attention of Acolyte Reed and Novak. "*Speaking of, I should probably get back to it.*"

"*I love you, Milo.*"

"*Love you, too, Dorian.*" Milo smiled, returning to the case file he had for his top two acolytes.

With that, I quelled his thoughts and scowled at a student. "If you think for one second you're going to sleep in my class, you're mistaken."

"I had a rough night."

"Anime and gaming until three in the morning is not a rough night. Screw up your sleep schedule on your own time."

I'd make time for Milo, help my students—all of them—pass their exams, and then I'd find time to sort everything out with Finn. But it'd have to wait because pushing people away was a go-to move, and I needed to grow past that.

Chapter Thirty-Five

MILO'S chest was pressed against my back, resting peacefully with his arms wrapped around my stomach. He'd worked a lot this past month, fixing trickling fates from the ramifications of The Day the Devil Died and doing what he did best—using work to embrace and avoid his emotions. I'd already passed out before he arrived, but I immediately felt his presence when he snuck into bed late in the night. His worries and processing synchronized to my thoughts seamlessly, blocking neighbors' dwindling dreams. It was a peaceful slumber, more or less.

The less came from Charlie, who'd wedged himself between us, sleeping on my lower back, and Carlie, who'd nestled up to Milo's head, her tail thwapping against my face. Honestly, their incessant need to show their affection for Milo had become grating. I totally understood they preferred him, so did they need to constantly remind me they had a favorite human?

Milo's breathing changed; the grogginess of his subconscious washed away. I grabbed his wrist, pulling it close, and gently kissed his hand. "Thought I wouldn't be seeing you until summer break."

"Yeah, things have started easing up, so I decided to come over."

Charlie chirped, shaking his head, likely flipping and twitching his ears ever so as his alertness took hold. He lifted himself up and hopped over my stomach, stretching his long front legs close to my face and yawning wide before brushing past Milo's arm to kiss my face.

"Morning, Charlie."

He meowed in response.

"Got anything big planned for the day?" Milo asked, scooching closer since Charlie had moved. Milo's crotch pressed snuggly against me. Carlie had also moved, meowing and pleading for food because it was 6:02, and she'd surely starve soon, a whole two minutes past her morning feeding schedule. Milo's breath tickled my ear as he moved closer.

"Plans?" I laughed. "It's the last day of classes. My plan is to survive the eight hours and then fuck off for at least the first two weeks of break."

There were lessons I needed to plan for, summer trainings I had to attend, and lots of little things to streamline. Plus, catching up on projects around the house that'd fallen at the waist side with so much work. But I'd definitely indulge in a bit of unstructured nonsense and relaxation.

"We'll have to plan some date nights or date days with your more flexible schedule," Milo said, but his mind flashed with some very different ideas on flexibility involving the two of us.

"Just have to survive today."

"So"—Milo nuzzled the back of my ear with his nose—"you're not gonna do anything? I thought you said the kids aced their finals. Shouldn't you celebrate that?"

"I would never say aced. They did okay. At best." I grumbled, repositioning myself as I scooted against Milo. This was not the morning conversation I wanted, so perhaps I could redirect the discussion.

"Then have an okayebration."

"I don't do class parties." I sat up, brushing Milo's arm away. "Besides, their reward is better grades and more opportunities, which they'll appreciate in the long run. They don't need a pat on the head for doing what they're supposed to do."

"Le sigh. You're such a Grinch." Milo tugged my wrist, attempting to drag me back to bed. "Where are you going?"

"To feed my cats, shower, and then off to work."

"Boo." Milo huffed, his surface thoughts rose, not even attempting to hide his provocative desires, and he adjusted the blanket to show his early morning bulge barely tucked by his boxers.

After feeding Carlie, ensuring she had a feast that'd allow Charlie a chance at his breakfast, I grabbed a towel and went into the bathroom. The door creaked open as the shower heated.

"Thought we could conserve water." Milo stood stark naked at full attention. "You know I'm all about the environment."

"Hmm. I realize shower sex is a top favorite of yours, but I really don't care for it."

"What's not to love? You can get dirty and clean all at once."

I glowered, avoiding his suggestive desires that'd begun to immediately mix with my own. Dammit. My face heated, blood rushing in every direction, and I very much wanted to indulge these morning cravings. Mine. Milo's. No. My shower was not roomy. Milo was a very fast thruster, especially when this eager, and I hated bending over and bracing against the wall while resisting the slippery shower-tiled flooring.

"It's too cramped, and I'm not in the mood to straddle the wall."

"Then straddle me."

I rolled my eyes. "I'm not levitating the entire time we… Yeah, no."

"Who said you had to cast?" Milo tilted his head, wrapping a gentle yet sturdy telekinetic grip around me, drawing me close. "I'll do all the work."

A hundred touches weaved along my skin, gripping me, caressing me, rubbing every erogenous part of my body. Milo had floated a bottle of lube from the drawer as he began kissing me. Gently, he slipped his fingers inside me, readying me and teasing me with his wonderful touch.

"Oh, fuck me." I bit my lower lip.

"Sort of the plan." Milo pulled me close, our chests pressed together.

Instinctively, I wrapped my legs around his thighs, grabbing his shoulders as he backed me into the steaming shower.

Water cascaded between us as Milo guided and repositioned me. I moaned, burying the noise by shoving my tongue in his mouth, kissing him.

He slammed my back against the wall, thrusting quick and sudden. I bit his lip, and he eased. As he slowed, I panted, struggling to contain all the pleasure of his continued telekinetic grip. I tugged his hair back, eyes demanding satisfaction.

We spun around the shower, water sprinkling in every direction, frozen midair by his telekinesis. Milo's magic kept us afloat. I gripped his shoulders, lost in the twirl of our bodies, the thrusts of his hips, the splash of water, and the pure joy of Milo's satisfied breathing in my ear. I licked my lips, tasting the flavor of my skin as he nibbled on my lower ear. Everything between us synchronized so perfectly we were one as he fucked me.

CHAPTER THIRTY-SIX

AFTER a blissful morning, I managed to almost arrive on time. A bus was parked in my usual spot, making way for students filing onto it for a field trip. I shuddered, putting my cigarette out and whipping into a further space. Chaperoning squirrely kids on the last day? No, thank you. It was bad enough filling the time in classes after final exams and grades had been completed. There was literally nothing to do the few remaining days before summer break, so I had become a glorified babysitter until that final bell rang.

Admittedly, I walked with a bit of a swagger to my classroom. Whether that came from the jolt of excitement Milo had left me with or the fact his morning fuck left me sore, I couldn't tell. Either way, I hoped we'd have more mornings like this. More afternoons. Evenings. Late nights. Everything, honestly.

My students were plastered against the wall, huddled close to the door, sighs on their faces and annoyance in their thoughts.

"What are we doing today?" Gael asked, sporting rainbow-colored hair for Pride Month in his usual spiky style. Speaking of spikes, He'd even painted a few that lined his arms to represent different queer flags.

"We're going to finish the movie from yesterday, and I brought a few more for you all to pick from." I opened the door and reached into my satchel, proudly displaying the selection I had. Sure, a few whined over the biopics, but once they settled in, most enjoyed the films.

Gael maintained a tight, strained smile not wanting to burst my bubble that he found the movies grueling.

"Ugh." Gael Rios-Vega, on the other hand, collapsed on top of his desk, dramatically displaying his defeat at my horrible choices. "I can't do it again. These movies should be banned. You should be charged for cruel and unusual punishment, Mr. Frosty."

His rooster hopped on his back, crowing loudly to share in Gael's protest.

Fuck off, King Clucks.

"They're entertaining." I loved these films. They were historically accurate and filled with exceptional acting. Honestly, given all the content I had to cover this year, it was a shame we didn't have time for more of these movies. We'd spent this entire week watching them and had only gotten through half the collection.

"Why can't we do something fun?" Gael groaned.

"I think the movies are fun." Caleb smiled.

"Shush," Katherine said.

"Other classes are in the auxiliary gym."

"I wanna go on the cast race."   "They've got games."

"Some homerooms are in the auditorium, too."   "That could be fun."

"Actually, watching good movies."

"Even Mr. Peterson's having a class party."

"They're all so fucking annoying."

"Mrs. Whitehurst took her class to the Shedd Aquarium."

"I wish I was in her homeroom."

"If I sit in this class all day again, I might literally die."

"Ba-ba-bawk."   *"My signal sucks in here."*

So help me, Milo was right. I should've planned something fun. The three days before the school year ended, admin always changed the schedule, so we spent that time exclusively with our homerooms since finals and grades were completed. Usually, I'd train my students to a state of exhaustion and then send them on their summer breaks relieved.

However, given the year they had, the year I had, I aimed for something lighter. If I'd taken Chanelle up on her offer to join her damn field trip, maybe they'd be less whiny. Honestly, I didn't have the emotional energy to invest into considering anything this last month. It probably wasn't too late to drag them to the auxiliary gym or auditorium, though.

I cleared my throat, quieting their voices and dulling their thoughts. "How about we vote on which you all would—"

Someone knocked on the door and immediately invited themselves inside. Rude, much.

"Hope you didn't get started without me." Milo winked, floating a dozen pizza boxes behind him while simultaneously rearranging empty desks into a makeshift table. "I see someone forgot to do the setup for me."

"Enchanter Evergreen."   *"Mr. Frost invited him. Yes! Okay, play it cool."*

"Oh. My. Fucking. Goddess. Think we should ask for another selfie?"

"Cluck!"

"You're right, we'll just sneak some selfies."

"Hell yeah!"   *"Pizza? Hope he got something vegan."*

"He must really love these historic flicks too. So cool!"

"Why the hell is this showboat buzzkill annoying asshat here?"

"He must've seen the horrors Mr. Frost was inflicting…"

"Enchanter Evergreen saved us!"

"Anything beats another film."

Seriously? I could've shown up with a pizza if I realized this was a damn competition. I tuned out my students, linking to Milo's mind.

"Figured you might need some last day backup, call it a hunch," he thought.

"You can't just waltz in here."

"I'm Enchanter Evergreen. I can pretty much waltz wherever I want, but…" He tapped the visitor pass taped to his chest and smirked. Great. Not one person in the office bothered checking with me that he'd come to visit. *"I can totally leave if you'd prefer."*

Between the eager expressions on my students' faces and the slightly somewhat kind of a little bit bearable ideas for entertainment Milo had floating in his head, I caved. Begrudgingly, I waved him into the room and watched Enchanter Evergreen's three biggest fanboys fawn over him as they assisted in bringing in more goodies Milo had brought. Both Gaels helped carry in the cooler of drinks and snacks. Caleb carried in boxes of casting games Milo just happened to have on hand. Nope. He'd gone and bought these, believing they'd be enjoyed. Damn clairvoyants.

I took the backseat in my own classroom as Milo floated through the classroom, literally levitating, and arranging game stations while the kids ate and laughed and talked his ears off with countless questions about the industry, warlocks, the demon attack, and a million other randomly blurted thoughts or ideas.

Gael stole an entire box of veggie vegan pizza.

"Share," Layla snapped.

"I am shurring," Gael said with a mouthful of half-chewed pizza.

"You're fucking gross," Melanie hissed.

"Cl-cluck."

Layla and Melanie cringed at the puffed rooster, which made Gael snort, spitting sauce and goopy crumbs on the floor. Disgusting. I had no energy for it.

Tara strolled behind Gael and King Clucks, telekinetically waving away the box of pizza from the desk.

Gael gasped. "The betrayal."

"Ba-bawk!"

"Tara, you're breaking King Clucks' heart," Gael said. "You can't just take our pizza."

I perched against the wall by the window to enjoy the show unfolding before me but noticed a much subtler performance outside. Icicles lined the top of the window. Sure, Chicago had unbearably cold winters that seemed to stretch on forever, but there was no way we would get a cold snap this strong during our hellishly humid summers.

The weighted blocks Tara used sat idle at her desk, seemingly unused. The symbols etched on each of the sides glowed and dimmed, dependent on the branch magic Tara cast. The magic she trained even discreetly.

I shared a silent joy in how she continued growing and improving. Developing a fourth branch wouldn't derail the strides she'd made so far with her other three. In fact, I could feel excitement leaping out, high above her ocean of sorrow, invigorating her with a new game plan on everything she planned on accomplishing over the summer. Though part of the happiness radiating off her might've come from her obnoxious bestie on his knees beside a woeful rooster, each begging her not to give Layla or Melanie a slice of the pizza.

"Enchanter Evergreen brought this pizza especially for me and King Clucks."

"Did he now?" Tara cocked her head, half-grinning and fighting back an all-consuming smile. "That's weird. I don't see either of your names on it."

"He brought this for everyone." Layla transformed into her therianthropy form, used her giant stature to snatch the box, and then chomped down onto two slices of pizza before tossing the box to Melanie.

"Thank you." Melanie took the last slice.

"I'm going to die." Gael collapsed onto the floor. "Tara, how could you?"

"Cl-cl-cluck!" King fucking Clucks mimicked Gael, each sprawled on the floor feigning death.

"*Enchanter Evergreen,*" I thought to Milo, pulling him from a card game he'd set up. "*You need to control your classroom.*"

"Oh." He beamed. "*On it. No worries. None at all. Easy fix.*"

While Milo attempted to cheer up Gael and King Clucks, I went over to the card game he'd abandoned between Jamius, Carter, Yaritza, and Jennifer.

Yaritza had a winning hand but didn't realize it because Milo hadn't properly explained the rules to her before racing off to wrangle the chaos of kids.

Jamius had such a confident smile I almost mistook him for one of his clones until the depth of thoughts revealed themselves in the well of his inner core. It'd taken time, but he finally found himself branching out and trying to be the person he envisioned himself as when creating the confidence in his duplications.

It helped that he had a cocky Carter next to him. "I'm telling you, she's bluffing one hundred percent."

"You sure?" Jamius raised his eyebrows, studying Jennifer's unfazed expression.

"Definitely." Carter grinned. "But it's important when playing against Jen, you've gotta keep your poker face strong in your head as much as on your face."

"Right." Jamius nodded. "Her empathic magic is like a built-in bluff detector."

"Wait? I thought we were playing Enchanter Roulette." Yaritza sighed. "I don't know the first thing about poker."

"It's an expression," Carter said, his gaze shifting and locking onto Jennifer, who remained completely neutral, making it impossible to gauge where her head was.

He believed she'd quieted her branch so she could keep cool. In truth, I saw the aura of each of them. Jennifer's emotions mimicked Carter's excitement. Not in an unintentional empathic way where his emotions overwhelmed her branch, but more in a way where Jennifer sought to feel his sensations, his confidence—and his arrogant smirk as he tried to manipulate everyone into thinking he had a winning hand. He did not have a winning hand.

I was happy to see a bit of the old Carter returning, cockiness and all. Jennifer was about to burst that cocky bubble with a third winning hand in a row, so I let the group be.

In the back of the classroom, Kenzo stood propped against the wall, observing Gael use his spikes to help Katherine with a casting fishing game Milo had brought. Caleb approached, offering Kenzo a can of orange soda.

"Saw this was the last one and know you like—"

"Whatever." Kenzo snatched the can.

Caleb sulked, turning to join the others.

"I never thanked you," Kenzo said, much to my surprise.

"Huh?"

"For helping Gael when the gorgon showed up. He said you were really fast on your feet."

Caleb ran a hand through his short hair, curls slightly grown back, and he nervously grimaced. "It wasn't the best plan."

"Not surprising. You have a lot of terrible ideas and overthink everything." Kenzo cracked open the can. "It's annoying as fuck."

Caleb's face twisted, unsure how to respond, if he should, or if he should politely walk away.

"Also, maybe you do belong here or whatever." Kenzo guzzled the drink to keep a hundred nicer thoughts to himself.

"Thanks, Kenny… Kenzo." Caleb smiled.

"Stop smiling, weirdo."

"Sorry," he said, bright-eyed and happy.

"Seriously, you look like some sick fuck. Wipe that smile off your face, you creepy prick."

"It's just... This is the first time you've acknowledged I belong here. You haven't said anything like that since way back when we first started considering Gemini Academy."

There was a stilled silence between them, a quiet memorial of memories both boys shared for Kenzo's mother and father, the life they had, the friendship they'd built over years of trust and love, and then the horrible day that broke their bond. An outburst that Kenzo fueled for years, clinging to in order to move forward. A memory Caleb held onto, reminding himself even the best people sometimes needed time.

"You're still second rate and bound to fail out next year." Kenzo pressed the empty can against Caleb's chest and walked away.

"See you at the finish line, Kenny."

Kenzo stuffed his hands in his pockets and stormed toward Gael, immediately complaining he was holding the fishing rod incorrectly.

"It's just a game." Gael beamed.

"You're not losing to this know-it-all." Kenzo snatched the fishing rod and challenged Katherine to the game, thoughts lost on all the things he wanted to say to Caleb but realized he was too weak to admit.

Static sparked, and Kenzo's mind went silent.

Not sure I could call that progress, but it was something.

I spent the rest of the day moving around, helping students with games, and enjoying the simple happiness bubbling along their surface thoughts.

CHAPTER THIRTY-SEVEN

AFTER an exhausting day, I brought Milo home.

"I can't believe you took the whole day off."

"Yep," he said, plopping onto the couch. "It's been real light around the office."

"That so?" I lifted Milo's legs onto the couch and took off his dress shoes.

He rolled over onto his stomach, burying his face in a pillow. Milo could battle warlocks, fiends, demons, and even a devil without wavering, yet he was more exhausted from one day of teaching kids than any case he'd taken.

Granted, he didn't do much teaching. He focused purely on eight hours of entertainment. *Total rookie move.* He'd turned my classroom into a buffet of pizza and sugary snacks, which in turn energized each and every student beyond even the great Enchanter Evergreen's capabilities. He didn't say it, but he couldn't hide his fatigue after entertaining twelve kids for eight hours. That was why I preferred breaking the kids down with exhaustive work to drain their endless supply of energy that'd also better them in the long run and keep me from passing out the second I walked through the door. A win-win situation, if I dare say.

I straddled Milo, sitting on his butt, and gently ran my hands up his spine. Massaging the tension out of his shoulders, I worked my way around the muscles of his back.

"*That's nice.*" Milo turned his head, eyes closed but smiling. "*Feels so good.*"

"You know what else might feel good?" I leaned close, letting my breath tickle his ear.

"How can you possibly be thinking of sex?" He huffed, so worn out his thoughts didn't even twist to images of foreplay. "*You're insatiable.*"

I chuckled, relishing this moment where I tended to my tuckered-out boyfriend, who carried the weight of the world on his shoulders. It was nice taking a bit of that pressure away from him and also teasing him.

"*You know, I finally heard back about the Global Ranking's Ceremony,*" he thought, too tired to even speak.

I made a mental note of inviting him to "teach" my classes more in the future, especially when he railroaded me with his minxy energy.

"Wait, the Global Ranking's Ceremony?" I continued rubbing Milo's back. "Gotta be honest, I completely blanked on that."

"*You and me both,*" he thought. "*Now that all the demon drama is dealt with, Cerberus decided they wanted to host a few events over the summer before the induction ceremony this August.*"

I beamed, truly at ease and so fucking proud of Milo for earning a place among the highest-ranked enchanters in the country. "I suppose I can carve out a bit from my busy summer schedule to join my boyfriend at a few cocktail parties."

Milo released a moaning sigh of satisfaction as I cracked loose the tension in his back. "You know, I actually got a whole week planned for a real vacation. It's right around the corner if you, you know, maybe wanted to join."

"Hmm. Traveling? I'll have to check my schedule for that one."

"It'll be ten uninterrupted days of June. Mid-June." Milo's thoughts dimmed, but he resisted the lull of sleep, eager to continue the conversation about vacationing together.

"We'll see." I hated trips and all the traveling involved. Lots of teachers enjoyed the freedom to explore over the summer, whereas I preferred working on my house and quiet isolation. "Are you sure Chicago can survive ten whole days without the great Enchanter Evergreen?"

"Yep. Call it a hunch, but it looks like clear sailings."

"We'll see." I rubbed the space between his shoulder blades, easing him into a comfortable nap.

Usually, 'we'll see' was the friendliest 'no' I could muster, yet as Milo crashed, his thoughts blossomed to all the wondrous things he'd planned for these ten days off. It appeared truly unbearable, allowing him to drag me from place to place and sightsee and explore...however, my breathing hitched. My stomach fluttered. I really wanted to consider this experience and all it had to offer.

With Milo passed out, I carried him into the bedroom. Half through sheer physical strength and half through telekinetic assistance. He was far heavier than me, and there was absolutely no way I had the muscles to carry him independently.

I leisurely read while Milo slept away the day and night, figuring out the actual logistics of this vacation he'd planned. He'd found the best places at the best times for the best rates, but I wanted to make sure he'd actually done his homework on some of them, especially since 'right around the corner' was quite literally next week. This wasn't mid-June but the last day of the first week, which barely afforded me a chance to decompress after the end of the school year.

I crossed off a few ideas, adding others and making this a ten-day experience we could both enjoy. After a few hours of research, I joined Milo in bed and went to sleep.

"*Ooooh, fascinating. Definitely goes in the maybe pile,*" his restless thoughts whispered as I shut out the rest of the world.

I huffed, scooting closer and hugging him tightly before delving into his mind. Walking through Milo's inner core, I passed the wall of screens and the board of colors and went into his filing cabinet of endless visions, where he sat at a table reviewing stacks of papers.

"What?" He grinned.

"I thought you took the day off."

"I did."

"Then why are you sorting visions?"

"I briefly opened my eyes, and last I saw, the clock said 12:02, so pretty sure that means I did, in fact, take the day off."

I sighed, half annoyed and half in love with his dedication to the world. "Do you need help?"

"Aren't you supposed to be in summer mode with zero fucks to give?"

"I can give a few fucks."

"I bet." Milo winked, offering the seat beside him.

I grabbed a blank page, surprised to find fuzzy, jumbled letters. Guess our connection continued to improve, and bits of his visions became clearer. Well, visible, at the very least. I still couldn't make sense of anything they said or represented.

"What does this say?"

"That's the chimera's influence," Milo explained.

I dropped the page. "I didn't…" My throat tightened.

"It's annoying that his influence and potential is still out there."

"I didn't hold onto Finn." I trembled, fighting back everything I wanted to say but not ready to bear the full weight of this discussion. "I promise."

Though I wished I had, especially if the chimera's influence was still out there somewhere.

"I trust you. I wasn't going to question you." Milo squeezed my hand, sending all the love he had and calming thoughts that kept me firmly in his mind. "These are just annoying residual fates, probably. Most likely, definitely high maybes."

"A what?"

"Potential futures are infinite, and when one becomes unviable, impossible, I close off that potential reality. It's hard, and sometimes a residual fate doesn't take right away. That's all this is. Damn demon influence making it hard to quell those bad paths."

"How bad?"

"Just a little world destruction."

I clenched my jaw.

"Chill." He laughed. "I have at least one world-ending vision a month. Most are handled by other witches before the vision even fully settles. Hence, all these half-written visions I'm left sorting."

"You're very calm about the end of the world."

"Well, it hasn't happened so far, and I'm very confident in my small role to keep it that way. Besides, there's absolutely no demon presence in the city, the state, really. We did everything correctly, removing all the chimera's followers, banishing him entirely, so now I spend a few nights a week organizing leftover papers to make room for brighter, more concrete futures."

I remained with Milo the entire night, filing outdated visions and planning for happy ever afters. His mind buzzed with a million potentials for countless people I'd never met, gently guiding paths he hoped would make them as happy as he was with me.

I smiled, truly awed and in love with the best man in the world.

CHAPTER THIRTY-EIGHT

I STRUTTED through this obnoxious inner core, avoiding the literal cobwebs of untouched memories inside this witch's head. Between the dark cellar vibes and gloomy humidity representing the deepest thoughts, I found this place unsettling. But it'd have to do. A few renovations made it bearable during my stay. I needed something close enough to my body to keep careful eyes on things yet far enough from Milo so I would remain well off his infinite radar—not an easy feat when he saw the possibilities before I'd even considered them.

Oh, how I loved Milo, but dammit, he didn't make my task easy. So, for the time being, I had to hole up inside someone else's mind, skirting below the surface of awareness. This lackluster witch I'd commandeered didn't have much going on for him anyway. He held a boring day job, a weak branch, no infinity for casting, and zero potential for a bright future. Having his mind semi-hijacked was probably the most exciting thing that would ever happen in his bland existence.

Skirting around wobbly knickknacks, each holding some worthlessly precious memory, I approached a door that I'd turned into a little haven. A true piece of heaven, in fact. Clearing my throat, I kept calm and altered my appearance. In a mind, I could create anything with ease. The creases in my forehead faded, my skin tightened, and my hair shortened. I stared at the sleeves of my shirt and remembered at twenty-two, I had a much darker, total try-hard, gothy wardrobe, so I changed my outfit instantaneously to represent the former appearance.

Opening the door, the bright light of the hospital room crept into this person's cellar they called homey. Quickly closing the door behind myself, I scanned the witch's sleeping thoughts, ensuring I hadn't disturbed him. I hadn't. He remained dimwitted, dull, and delusionally tragic in a peaceful slumber.

"Dorian." Finn sat up in his hospital bed, turning off the television, and thrilled for the visit. His voice was ecstasy, and it was wonderful finally being able to sneak off to visit him, even if in these shabby accommodations. "Maybe you can actually get my nurses to answer when I push the button."

"They're busy saving lives." I resisted an easy smile because Finn only knew the ungrateful grouch who didn't value everything he had.

"I nearly died." Finn grinned, pointing to the light scratches I'd conjured so he'd remain in this room awaiting his full recovery and unaware that I'd tucked him safely inside someone else's mind. Someone unworthy of Finn's presence.

"You didn't nearly die." I sighed, dragging out my most unenthused tone. "The gorgon barely touched you."

"Well, I'm going to die if someone doesn't fix this remote. The TV's been stuck on the same channel for hours."

It was unfortunate, but I had to limit Finn's perception in here to keep him safe, unaware. Allowing too much freedom and entertainment of news strained my magic. Thankfully, his branch helped with the bulk of the heavy lifting. Like with Milo, our magics synchronized seamlessly, so I used Finn's retrocognition to erase his time locked inside the chimera's mind and took him back to right before the gorgon stole him from our lives. Here, he recovered from an injury on an attack he now believed he'd survived.

Eventually, I'd explain it all to him, help him absorb the horrors inflicted on him for over a decade; however, Finn needed time to adjust and remember what living felt like. Milo needed time to distance himself from fears of what the chimera might inflict. I'd fix all this; I just needed time to get the two men I loved most in this world on the same page.

"When's Milo coming by?" Finn asked, tucking away thoughts. He was always happy with my visits but longed for the other piece of our happy trio. Understandably, he missed Milo, too.

"Well, since killing the gorgon, he's become annoyingly popular." I plopped on the bed, brushing my fingers delicately across Finn's hand.

It cast a sensation in both of us, something I needed to keep up. Unfortunately, senses dulled when in the mind, and I couldn't afford Finn realizing where I'd placed him.

"Can you tell Enchanter Evergreen to please stop by?" Finn asked. "Or maybe convince the nurse to bring me my gosh darned phone and I'll text him."

"I think that was broken." I chuckled. "I always warned you about bringing it on dangerous cases."

Finn's expression turned quizzical. "No, you haven't. In fact, I'm pretty sure…" His mind searched for the words, the thoughts I'd buried away. Each fuzzy moment led to a spike of insecurity, memories fighting to be recalled. His body quaked a little as his breathing hastened.

I leaned close, pressing my forehead against his. How I wanted to kiss him, erase all his concerns, but instead, I lulled him asleep with calming dreams. Finn eased back into the bed, drowsy. While I wanted him to remember how much he loved life and living, I needed a break from endless questions and curiosities. And as much as I wanted to indulge Finn, spend every second taking in how wonderful his return felt, I had important business to contend with here.

The witch I'd stored Finn inside was perfect in so many ways. Someone I could steer while cast asunder from the whole, someone completely off Enchanter Evergreen's potential futures, and someone who never utilized much of their creativity. I cultivated that creativity, conjuring a pristine prison because a mind was a terrible thing to waste. Honestly, I did this witch a favor by illuminating those areas with a cushy recovery room for Finn and a holding cell for that damn demonic energy tethered to the love of my life.

I exited the hospital room and walked a long corridor to check in on my unwanted house guest who'd take time to purge. Inside a cramped, putrid room lay the chimera shackled and on his knees. His arms were outstretched, resisting the chains bound to his wrists and connected to the stone slabbed walls of this place. It was less a room and more a well without a top. A perfect prison that the witch whose mind I'd borrowed kept his worst fears within, something I now renovated into a useful prison where I intended to eradicate the demon linked to Finn.

The stone slabs were slick with slime and tar. Even in a mortal form, this damn demon attempted to test his limits. Black ooze dripped down his chin, staining his frock coat.

"Despite my loss in power, it's nice to retain this mortal form. It's a personal favorite."

"That's my doing, not yours. Remember, I hold all the power in this place." I squeezed my fist, tightening his chains, relishing in the chimera's struggle. "I allow you to perceive yourself how you wish, and I'll admit it's far simpler locking up a human form than a demon's."

"I'm surprised you managed to whisk Finn and me away while crying on Enchanter Evergreen's chest as he banished most of me away."

Mocking. As if anything this disgusting creature could say would offend me. I very much had everything under control. As much as I loved and valued Milo and Finn's opinions, they were wrong in this instance. I refused to let either distract me from the truth of things or what needed to be done. The three of us could be happy. We would be happy.

"I've lost my branches, not my knowledge or my power." The chimera futilely tugged at the chains. "Who are you?"

"Excuse me?"

"I spent months studying Dorian's many facets. He's obsessive and self-deprecating, but he certainly doesn't hold this level of arrogant narcissism." The chimera forced himself off his knees, resisting the awkward, pained stretch of the chains. "So, I'll ask again, who are you?"

This chimera was clever. Almost too clever. He knew Dorian almost as well as I did, but that wouldn't help the demon because he had no idea what I was capable of.

"It'd seem you don't know Dorian all that well, after all." I scoffed. "I do, though, and he'd be grateful for my intentions. Unfortunately, Dorian's always been too pathetic to act. To try. To be happy."

As such, I'd come to learn Dorian Frost didn't deserve the happiness awaiting him. I did. I deserved everything. And Dorian—all Dorian deserved was death for daring to surrender Finn, not once, not twice, but three times.

"Who do you think I am?" I smirked.

"You're not Dorian."

"I am, and I am not. Life as a manifestation is quite the existential conundrum in that sense. How much of me is my own identity, and how much is a projection of Dorian, his identity, his desires? No. I am not the Dorian Frost you so easily stalked. I am not weak, selfish, or utterly pathetic like him."

"A meager manifestation, and you consider Dorian the weak one." The chimera clicked his tongue, hissing each syllable with disgust. His words were more an accusation than a question. "You are but a fragment of the whole, poor thing that you are."

I fumed; I was more than a fragment. I was a piece that successfully broke away from Dorian. I was a manifestation that created his own will-power and freedom. I severed the strings linking me to Dorian.

Cracking my neck, I dulled the fury this brash demon's insult sought to provoke. He was nothing. Less than nothing. I wouldn't allow him to goad me. Not when I'd come so far and so close to achieving everything I rightfully deserved.

"You're one to talk about weakness." I smiled at the chimera. "Considering you're but the wispy remnants of a fallen devil, forever dead. I mean, you're less than a manifestation. You're a gasping fish tossed upon the shore, deluding itself that flailing will keep it alive long enough to reach the desiccated ocean that no longer exists."

"Cute metaphor." His lips curled into a wicked grin; tar slicked along his bright white teeth. "But I'm so much more than that. Even a feeble manifestation such as yourself should realize what power this fallen devil holds."

He spoke true despite my refusal to acknowledge it. When rescuing Finn, I contemplated saving the other souls required for this chimera's bizarre use of resurrection, but I couldn't gamble bringing along others. It already proved exhausting containing this demon and keeping Finn safely pacified, so I allowed Milo to banish them as Dorian wept like the coward he was. This chimera had integrated his consciousness inside each witch's soul he'd claimed, perverting their essence to defy death, which he clearly feared above all else. I'd find another way to properly resurrect Finn, but first, I'd have to untether this demon's mind without disturbing Finn.

"Perhaps breaking this hold will be easier than expected." He rattled his chains, testing the magic I'd reinforced. Try as he might, nothing escaped my power inside a mind. "Once released, I'll rip through this worthless witch you're housing us inside, then find and claim Dorian's body for myself as I should've when I first laid eyes upon him."

I snickered, a slow, bubbling delight at this bastard's arrogance.

"Oh, and the things I shall do to an unruly manifestation such as yourself when Dorian and I are united as the perfect devil."

"Doubtful." I laughed. He considered me unaware of his power, yet the fool lacked insight into everything I knew. "We both know why you asked Dorian nicely to let you in."

I couldn't contain it, breaking into an unhinged cackle. He remained silent, his eyes studying my shuddering body as I stifled laughter.

"It had nothing to do with starting things off on a positive note and everything to do with the full extent of Dorian's branch. My branch."

"There is a lot of power in my perfect host." He spit tar from his mouth onto the dirt floor between us.

"A true complexity Dorian's never faced, but I, the best of his manifestations, have carried the weight of his magic since it first blossomed."

The fact was Dorian's branch only evolved so subtly because I'd stopped taking on the burden he never found himself capable of handling. I refused to return after how Dorian let himself nearly die for those children, which in turn took Finn away. My Finn. With my absence, Dorian couldn't summon any other manifestations, and of course, he was too stupid to notice my absence.

So long as I maintained my will and remained hidden in another witch's head, I could plot and plan free of Dorian. Free of the burden he was onto the world. Free to be myself.

"Even so, Dorian—the real Dorian—with all his strength, couldn't undo the binding that connects me to Finn's being." The chimera's eyes were piercing, studying my reaction to his bravado. "You may understand the facets of such a unique branch, but you can only access a fraction of its power."

I waved a hand, dropping the chimera back to his knees where he belonged. It'd take time, research, but I'd untether him from Finn. They were woven together like arteries and disease, and removing him would take patience and practice. I took a breath, recalling all that'd brought me here and how much more I'd have to do to ensure the happiness I deserved.

I'd seen every vision of every potential future Milo spent his life enduring that day Dorian and Milo kissed. Dorian was too weak to bear them all, fragile and delicate; his consciousness only absorbed a simple void vision. Worthless, as always. But I'd seen Milo's world entirely and loved him all the more for it. He took too much on himself, sacrificing for an unworthy world, believing he didn't deserve Finn back if it created a spark of destruction.

We could have it all, though. Finn. Milo. Me. The three of us happy forever.

First, I needed to purge this damn demon from Finn's soul. Then, I'd remove the weakness that was Dorian Frost. Finn would live again. Milo would be overjoyed. They'd see I was the version of Dorian they'd always longed for, they'd see I was better than Dorian could ever hope to be, and Milo and Finn would thank me for everything I planned. They'd love me.

"Well, shall we begin?" The chimera tilted his head, resting it on his outstretched bicep. "Or do you wish to talk me to death?"

"I should warn you, I'm not entirely sure what to do. It's going to be a lot of testing the waters, so it might hurt. And if it doesn't, I'll twist the knife, ensuring it does."

"I've dwelled in more hellish realities than your tiny, manifested mind could ever fathom." The fallen devil grinned. "Give me your worst."

"Gladly."

Approaching the chimera, I unraveled everything I could to make him wail. It'd take time, but I'd break his hold on Finn. Every strike of psychic torture I unleashed, I reminded myself that my entire existence revolved around Dorian serving as the second fiddle to his story, purely living for Dorian's benefit. I was over that.

I wanted the life I deserved. I'd tell my story now.

THE END

...UNTIL SECOND-YEAR FALL SEMESTER

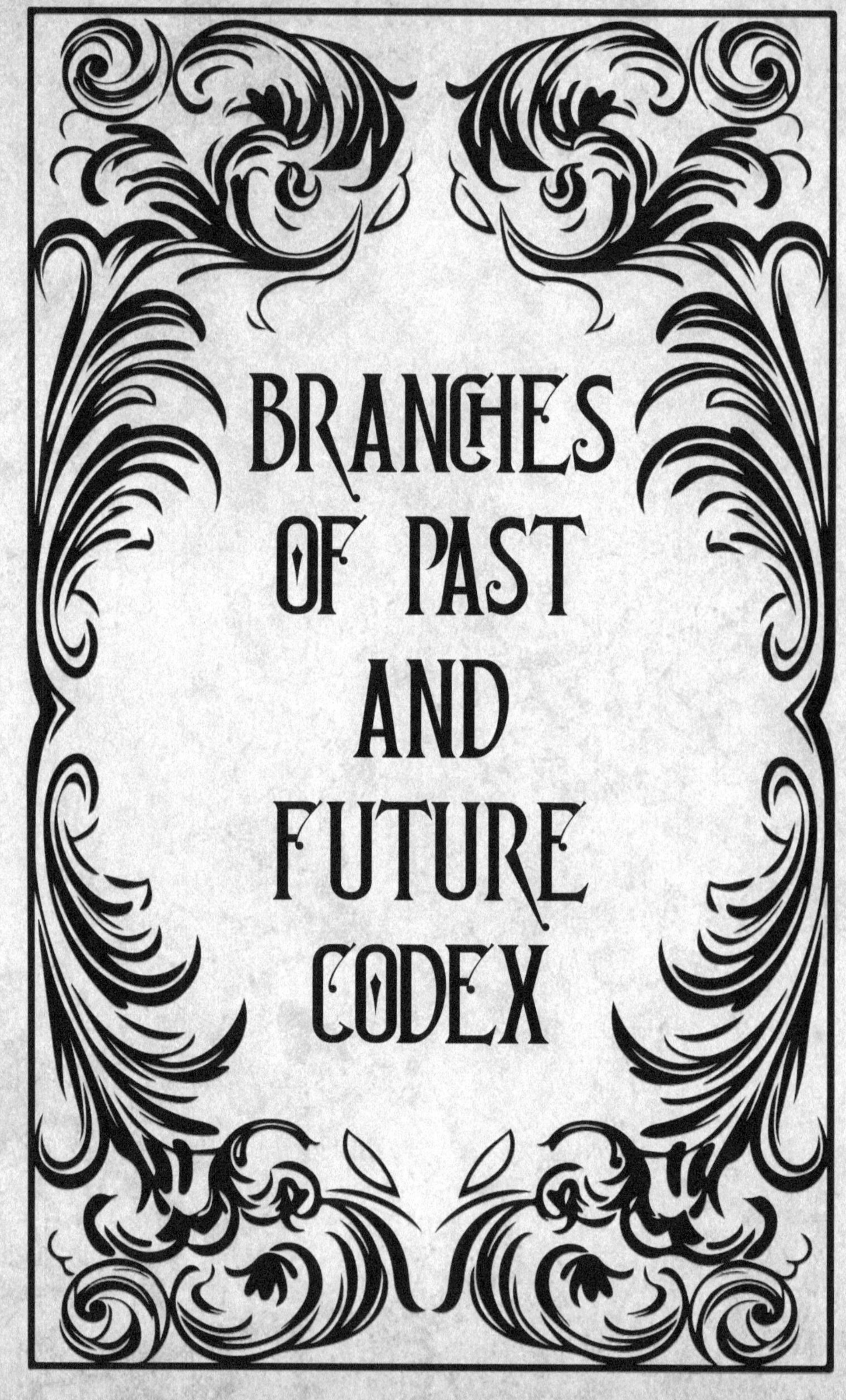

BRANCHES
OF PAST
AND
FUTURE
CODEX

For unknown reasons, a little over two hundred years ago, magic returned to the world. When everyone gained access to magic, people were referred to by two different titles.

Witch – Law abiding citizens using their magic for good.

Warlock – Corrupted people who cast their magic selfishly.

THERE ARE TWO TYPES OF MAGIC:
Root magic – Standard magic that all witches have access to.

Branch magic – Unique magic that differs person to person.

ROOT MAGIC

There are four root magics. Every witch in the world has access to these same four root magics; however, the amount of control is based on training and skill.

Telekinesis – The ability to move things with one's mind.

Levitation – Harnessing gravitational polarity in the core of one's body to float.

Sensory – The ability to track and pinpoint demonic energy.

Banishment – The ability to repel demonic energy from the mortal world, exorcising the unnatural presence.

BRANCH MAGIC

There are twelve types of branches. Each branch has their own unique attributes. Most witches are born with only one branch magic. Some people are born branchless, meaning they have no unique magic. In rare cases, some people are born with multiple branches.

Alteration – This branch focuses on altering a witch's physical limits. This can involve enhancing strength or senses. It can also involve manipulating and altering what a body can do such as invisibility or duplication.

Arcane – Unique and rare unclassified magic. Witches who possess arcane magic are often coveted because of their power. Arcane magic is usually a mix of two or three types of branches in such a way that it becomes impossible to classify the magic into any other branch.

Augmentation – Altering the physical nature of a witch's body. This can include added appendages such as tails or wings. It can also include the removal or replacement of certain limbs or organs. There are many varieties to augmentation magic, some major or minor, but it's important to understand this differs from standard physical anomalies. Most augmentations are interwoven in such a way that they link the nervous system and the magic of the witch together.

Bestial – This branch connects a witch to the animal kingdom in one form or another. There are dozens of different varieties to this branch, all revolving around animals. Some witches are born as therianthropes, which allows them to take on the physical attributes of an animal. Others can shift entirely into an animal form. Some can communicate with animals. Many witches with a bestial branch are born linked to one animal in particular that becomes their familiar. These familiars share the magic with their witch.

Cosmic – Magical energy that is drawn from the stars and astral plane of existence. This can include things such as manipulating light or darkness. It can also involve moving through the astral plane through things such as teleportation or portal doorways.

Enchantment – A written and spoken form of magic. This is where the traditionally known form of spellbooks comes from. Channeling magic into symbols is a common form of enchantment magic that allows anyone access to the spell so long as the witch who created the spell freely shares it. Enchantments can come in the form of words on parchment, reciting key phrases, combining ingredients into a potion, and storing magic into sigils.

Entropy – Often regarded as the most shameful branch in existence. This magic deals with things like poison, venom, toxins, and other diseased aspects of necrotic rot. Because of the deadly nature of this branch, entropy witches are shunned by most of society and blamed for the sickness in the world.

Hex – A darker magic that allows a witch to manipulate probability around them. Hexes can counter or weaken other magics. They can warp the senses of another person. Some hexes can breathe life to curses, striking down foes with in simple or severe ways.

Primal – Elemental control. This can come in the form of controlling or creating an element through magic. Most witches can harness either control or creation, but some can do both. Common elements include fire, water, earth, air, electricity, ice, and steel. There are many others including unique minerals, types of florals, and combinations of elements.

Psychic – This type of magic delves in mental control beyond normal limitations. Psychic magics have the widest array of types. There are lots of mental magics from reading minds, sensing emotions, predicting the future, observing the past, manipulating thoughts, conjuring illusions, and countless others. It is often said, if a person can think it, the psychic magic is likely out there somewhere.

Rejuvenation – This is a healing type magic. While rejuvenation can be used by a witch to heal themselves or others, there are often limitations. Many healing magics are only temporary as the magic is a shortcut. Most of the time, when the magical effects wear off, the injury returns even in a mild form. Severe wounds must be looked at by medical professionals before the rejuvenation magic fades away.

Ward – This is typically a binding or barrier type magic. In most cases this is used to protect individuals or entire areas. Schools, hospitals, and government facilities are often covered in warding magic.

TYPES OF DEMONIC ENERGY

This type of energy is unnatural to the mortal world. Demons claw their way through dimensional barriers so they can feast upon the magic in the world. When demons break into the dimension, they often shatter into pieces.

Wisps – fractured droplets of demonic energy usually in the form of small white lights. They act on instinct alone, seeking out magic.

Fiends – Tarlike creatures made from a collection of wisps. They are feral, low level demonic beasts that crave magic. If they absorb enough magic, they'll ascend to demons.

Demons – Otherworldly creatures that crave magic to sustain their existence in the mortal world. They must constantly consume magic as they will perish without a steady supply. Demon bodies leak magic quickly, making them regularly hunt witches for more substance. There are tens of thousands of types of demons. Most monster lore is inspired by actual demons such as gorgons, vampires, sirens, hydras, and so much more.

Devils – When a demon possesses a human host, they transcend to something far stronger and harder to kill. They don't leak magic, and they become almost impossible to detect. However, hosts can't contain a demon for very long and most possessions end in the body rotting inside and out.

PROFESSIONAL WITCH RANKINGS

There are many types of government and private sector jobs that require magic. The most aspired to position is a guild witch.

In order to legally cast magic, a witch requires a license, waiver, or fledgling permit. Without official government documentation and approval a witch can face fines or even jail time for illegally casting their magic.

Guilds – Private companies that work to protect citizens within a particular territory. Many guilds compete for popularity and work to be the most successful in an area. Some take on jobs by the city, picking up the slack. Many work for private citizens. Others specialize in particular magics.

Acolytes – These are young witches who are recently licensed and seeking to become professional enchanters. They usually work for free as assistants and sidekicks to gain experience in the industry.

Enchanters – Professional witches who are deemed the best in their field. They keep the streets clean of demonic energy, dangerous warlocks, and anything deemed a threat to society.

Guild Masters – The leading witch of a particular guild. They oversee all the enchanters and acolytes of a particular guild. While proficiency in magic is significant to claim this title, it is important to note that guild masters are not always the strongest witch in an area, but simply the most calculating. To become a guild master a witch requires approval from the enchanters working there and from the board that funds the guild.

ACKNOWLEDGMENTS

WOW—that cliffhanger! I usually avoid them. Honestly, book two could've ended on such a happy note if I'd only stopped at chapter thirty-seven.

I'd like to thank all the readers who continued following Dorian and his homeroom coven on their journey this semester and I hope you'll come back to join these characters for the next installment. *Two Who Live On* was such a wonderful journey for me, finding a way to continue balancing Dorian's voice while exploring new areas. Milo definitely played a much bigger role in this installment and finding a way to connect Dorian to Enchanter Evergreen's world was quite a unique challenge. I could've given Milo his own POV—and I'm not against multiple POVs, check out *The Misfit Mage and His Dashing Devil* if you'd like to see some dual (dueling—they fight a bit) POV. That said, I really wanted to keep my magical world centered on Dorian, even if he sometimes pushes his motivation aside to follow the adventures of others.

You're probably wondering why I added a new POV at the end of book two since I want to keep things focused on Dorian and his world. Well… there might be some room to explore the baddies in book three. I've got some exciting stuff planned for the Branches of Past and Future Series.

If you enjoyed the story (or even if you didn't) please consider leaving a rating and/or review on your thoughts. It means the world to me that you gave my story a chance and every rating/review really helps boost a book's visibility for other readers. No pressure though because I'm already grateful you picked up this book to begin with.

I'd like to give a huge shoutout to those who've read my earliest drafts of

Two Who Live On and helped make this an even stronger version. I'd also like to thank my amazingly wonderful editor, Charlie Knight. They have helped me strengthen each of my novels and I'm incredibly grateful to have their insight and support since moving into the world of self-publication.

2024 is going to be an exciting year of books! If you've been following me since I started my journey, you know I aim for a few releases a year. Even as I type out this acknowledgement, I'm hard at work on book three. So no worries about having a long wait.

AUTHOR BIO

MN Bennet is a high school teacher, writer, and reader. He lives in the Midwest, still adjusting to the cold after being born and raised in the South.

He enjoys writing paranormal and fantasy stories with huge worlds (sometimes too big), loveable romances (with so much angst and banter), and Happily Ever Afters (once he's dragged his characters through some emotional turmoil).

When he's not balancing classes, writing, or reading, he can be found binge watching anime or replaying Dragon Age II for the millionth time.

Author website:

https://www.mnbennet.com

Amazon page:

https://www.amazon.com/stores/MN-Bennet/author/B0BLJJK5NF

Goodreads page:

https://www.goodreads.com/author/show/23017668.M_N_Bennet